This
belong
to:

Teressa
White

THONG
ON FIRE

THONG ON FIRE

AN URBAN EROTIC TALE

NOIRE

ATRIA BOOKS

New York London Sydney Toronto

ATRIA BOOKS
1230 Avenue of the Americas
New York, NY 10020

Song lyrics written by Reem Raw, Robb Hawk, and Queena Marie.
Used with Permission.

ISBN: 978-0-7394-8077-9

ATRIA BOOKS is a trademark of Simon & Schuster, Inc.

Manufactured in the United States of America

This book is dedicated to all the Juicys, Candys,
Carmieshas and Saucys in my hood.
Lift yourself up and fly with the strength of
your own beautiful wings.

You are capable and lovable
Competent and delectable
Gifted and gorgeous
Fly and formidable

So keep doin the damn thang!

Acknowledgments

Father, thank you.

Missy, Nisaa, Jay, Man. Tyrone the terrible tyke.
Y'all got my whole heart

Reem, Hawk, Spoons, Queena, Speedy, and Gita. We next!

Angie, Aretha, Melissa, and everyone who grinds hard at
NOIREMagazine.com, I have nothing but luv for ya.

STAY BLACK

NOIRE

Hottt Saucy!

This here ain't no romance
It's an urban erotic tale
Hottt Saucy's on a mission
And she ain't about to fail

Body of a goddess
But a devil in disguise
Chinky eyes full of dollar signs, slick tongue full of lies

From chips to bling and finer things, Miss Saucy's out for self
She'll play you like a herb then put yo ass back on the shelf

Sexing is her weapon, she'll go grimy to exploit it
She schemed a dope plan and hooked the top man
But her demons just wouldn't stay dormant

A hustler's dream, the best of cream,
her booty made her sublime
She worked her game and stole some fame and
slicked herself a goldmine

Top of the world wasn't good enough and
greed got Saucy dippin
But gangstas see out both their eyes and
the big one caught her slippin

So this here ain't no romance
It's a straight-up shiesty game
Slide too close to Saucy and get burnt up in her flame

In the Beginning . . .

HAVE YOU EVER scratched and schemed your way into somebody's heart? Laid some ill na-na on a gangsta and then hustled him straight outta the game? Traded your goodies for even more goodies? Have you ever schemed on your best friend? Plotted on some real gutta shit that you knew was gonna devastate her, but you went ahead and did it anyway? Did you use what you got to grab what you wanted? Committed acts so grimy that even God looked down on you and cried? Oh? That ain't how you living? Well there's a stunna up in this party tonight, so you betta get on your game and clock ya' man. Goodnight, hater! Don't knock my hustle. Didn't nobody slump my boogeyman in the middle of the night. I was just a lost little girl forced to make it in a grown woman's world. A child turned out by the rulers of the game. Shit, when you get thrown into a snakepit you better learn how to wiggle! It's all about survival, baby. And not only did I learn the code of the streets, I made my own damn rules and got paid in the process. So listen close, but watch your pockets. I'm a Harlem girl. A scandalous bitch. A ruthless mama. Me and this city are just alike. Grimy. And we never, *ever* sleep. So take some notes and get up on a few things. My name is Saucy Sarita Robinson. When life gave me lemons I did *not* make lemonade. I slipped those lemons in the next bitch's purse, because this is how I'm living.

Seung Cee

*S*HE OPENED HER EYES *the moment the doorknob turned. Lying in the darkness, the little girl smelled cigarettes and oranges and hated them both. The air was still. Footsteps crossed the wooden floorboards, slow but deliberate. She closed her eyes quickly, knowing what was coming but powerless to stop it.*

Deep, excited breathing. Directly above her. Suddenly the Harlem night seemed hotter than usual. The child began to sweat. A weight settled down beside her on the bed. She held her breath and waited.

The first few caresses were random and innocent. A finger traced the Asian curve of her closed eyes, then twirled a sleek lock of her curly black hair. The outline of her nut-brown lips was drawn. And then the fingers began to creep. Over her chin, past her barely budding breasts, and down below her tight stomach.

The sheet she lay sweating under was slid back, and her dirty night-shirt hiked up. The hiss of excited breathing was the only sound in the room. Urgent fingers were inside her panties. Pulling on the waistband until they were down past her knees. Sweaty hands parted her thighs and spread her legs wide. A nose pressed into her flesh and she heard a deep inhalation of breath. And then warmth and wetness enveloped her down there and slurping sounds rose in the air.

The girl lay rigid in the darkness as the soft tongue probed and licked at her private spot. She didn't cry out or move. She'd get her ass beat if she did that. Besides, the action going on between her legs that used to feel stank and nasty didn't bother her so much anymore. If she held still and didn't fight it, it wasn't no worse than sitting in Mister Jack's lap while his thang jumped outta its box.

Already she was a survivor. She could get through almost anything and forget most of it when she needed to. But there was no way she could forget the gifts. She lived for those. The wrinkled dollar bills that she'd find on her dresser in the morning. The cheap rings and bracelets and dollar-store necklaces that glittered and shined, but eventually made her skin turn green. Or sometimes the small bag of candy. Every now and then there might be fruit. A lopsided apple. A banana going brown. Or maybe a nasty orange. It really didn't matter what she got. As long as she was getting something out of it, she could survive it.

A moan flew from the girl's mouth, surprising her. She arched her back. She was shocked by the spark of heat that was trying to catch fire between her long, shapely legs. The tongue darting between her lower lips picked up its pace, licking the soft young mound that hadn't even started sprouting hair yet. Grown hands cupped her curved ass cheeks as she was gulped from like a fountain.

And then the body nestled between her legs began to tremble. The nibbles and licks became longer and harder. Fingers dug into her ass and penetrated her hole. Whomp! Whomp! Whomp! A thrusting pelvis smacked into the mattress, humping hard, fucking like a dog.

And then it was over.

The girl lay still, her eyes squeezed closed. The bed creaked as the weight rose, then slow footsteps crossed the floor once more. She held her breath until she heard her door open, and only then did she dare open her eyes again.

And when she did, she saw her mother standing in the hall. Tall, Asian, and beautiful. Creamy skin, dark silky hair hanging down to her waist. Smoking a cigarette and staring into her room from the doorway.

The orange-smelling figure walked over to her mother and they embraced. Lips parted and tongues tangled as they kissed hotly, sharing her young juices between them. The girl stared in silence as the same fingers that had just penetrated her ass slid up her mother's long, toned thigh, and disappeared under her short kimono, digging in her pussy.

Her mother smiled then lowered her head, nuzzling the slender neck and kissing the firm brown breasts of her dyke lover.

"Come me now, King," Kimichi said in her halting Asian English. She turned away from her daughter and held out her hand. She led the woman toward her bedroom, from which the sounds of wild sex would soon be heard. "Seung Cee very nice, yes? But now it my turn."

Chapter 1

THIS WAS GONNA be my last damn time riding somebody's nasty Prison Gap bus. Babies were crying, music was blasting, and every ghetto trick in New York City was trying to get upstate for a trailer visit. I elbowed the hefty sistah who was sitting on my right. A licked-down watermelon stick was clutched in her fat fist, and she was snoring like a truck driver when we hadn't even hit the highway yet. I pushed her ass even harder. She had the whole damn window to lean up against, but she insisted on pouring that chocolate Jell-O all over me.

I crossed my legs and tried not to let too much of my Fendi jacket touch the stained cloth seats. There wasn't no telling how many skeezers had sat their stank asses here before me, and I wasn't anxious to pick nothing up on my last trip.

New York was hot as hell for September, and right outside, Columbus Circle was live and jumping. Brothas was hoopin' under lights and slamming killers on the handball courts in Central Park. White boys skateboarded off half-pipe ramps about to bust they asses. A Sabrett cart sat on the corner where tourists lined up to buy dirty franks with onions and sauerkraut.

The bus I was on had a big number 4 taped to both sides. Fifty dollars and an eight-hour ride would get me upstate to Sullivan County's Woodburne Correctional Facility where my gangsta boo, Sincere, was finishing up his last two months of a one-year bid.

Sincere was originally from L.A., but had come to Harlem to run product with some Haitians that he was down with in a major way. But you know how it goes. Niggas got shiesty, shit got shady, and Sincere ended up getting knocked for associating with known felons and violating his parole.

For the past ten months I'd been climbing my ass on the bus right along with all the rest of the jailhouse wifeys, and enduring that long-behind ride upstate, not only to see my sugar daddy, but to keep his game alive. Shit, couldn't no prison bars keep a gangsta like Sincere on lock. My boo was getting his hustle on from deep inside the joint. He controlled the money game by keeping his buyers and his suppliers isolated and totally dependent on him for all contact, and my job was to be the information broker who helped him keep the two ends from meeting.

Life with Sincere was sweet, even if he was locked down. He did his bid, while I held down his three-bedroom apartment that he had let me decorate with the finest shit money could buy. I shopped my ass off, tricking his chips to keep myself looking and feeling grand. And best of all, I didn't have to worry about shit except helping him keep his empire thriving while he chilled lovely in the belly of the beast.

So twice a month I made a product run. I picked up a sample package from a designated location, and carried it behind the walls of the medium-security prison where I tongue-slipped it to my boo. And in return he slipped me two addresses. One to the spot where the remaining product could be found, and the other that told me where the money would be waiting to change hands.

Even though I was traveling on some fake ID I had bought from some white businessmen in Midtown, shit could go wrong at any time. It was risky as hell transporting drugs into a state prison, but today's trip had a dual purpose. Nothing coulda stopped me from getting next to Sincere's black ass on this goddamn visit. The game had changed, but that nigga just didn't know it. A little birdie had dropped some real gutta shit in my ear, and if I played my cards right, I would walk outta that prison with some chips and some payback all at the same time.

Tossing my curls, I checked out some of the stunts who were straggling onto the bus. According to my Rolex we should have been moving by now, but there were so many baby mamas dragging their whining kids and shopping bags full of food and toys, that we were running behind.

I elbowed the snoring Fat and Fruity sitting there leaning left and flopping all over me until she opened her eyes and straightened her ass up. That watermelon stick wasn't doing shit to cover up all that Henny coming outta her pores. She gave me a shitty look and sucked her teeth, then pressed her face against the booger-crusted window and went right back to sleep.

Unlike a lot of these chicks, I never slept on the bus. I didn't care how tired I was or how long I had to ride. I never closed my eyes anywhere unless the atmosphere was right, and them gangsta bitches riding the Prison Gap bus didn't make me feel exactly cozy.

Twenty minutes later the bus was full and I was watching the streets of Manhattan slip past outside. Big girl was still knocked out on my right, and some bugged-out chick with three stair-step kids was fussing on my left.

"These goddamn kids!" she complained, slapping the bottom of her toddler's sneaker to get it back on his foot. "Ain't nobody *tell* you," she said, twisting and turning his foot and trying to force it back inside the expensive little sneaker, "to take off your goddamn shoe!"

The baby hollered like she was breaking his ankle.

"Shut the fuck *up!*" I muttered, turning away from them. I hoped like hell he wasn't gonna be crying and fussing all the way upstate. At least not sitting next to me. I knew his mama had heard me because she sucked her teeth real loud.

"'Scuse me?" This ho was actually tapping on my arm.

I looked down at her grimy-ass hand with the raggedy, bit-back nails, then straight into her face with much heat in my eyes.

"Don't fuckin' touch me," I snapped, shaking her off.

She quit messing with the baby's shoe and gave me the bitch-hell-no-you-didn't look.

"Well fuck you too! I was just gonna ask you what time it was, but now I see! Ya Chinese-looking trick!"

"Well stop smoking crack and buy a fuckin' watch!"

"You better leave her crazy ass alone," a girl who was sitting in front of her turned around and laughed. "Bitch prob'ly know karate."

I knew where this chick was going, but like most people she had totally missed the mark. Don't let the chinky eyes fool you. At five feet nine, with a hundred and twenty pounds of titties, ass, light brown skin and slanted eyes, I'd been hearing that "Chinese" shit all my life. The real scoop was, I was half black and half Asian. My father had been a heroin fiend from Harlem, and my mother was a Korean prostitute who had turned him out while he was stationed in her country with the marines. Daddy had married Kimichi and brought her back home to New York with him, and when he got popped in an armed robbery a few years later, me and my moms were left stranded on 128th Street with nowhere else to go.

I kept my eyes forward and ignored the chick in my ear. What she needed to do was take care of all them nasty-nosed kids and keep her dirty hands up off of me. A lot of bitches assumed I was soft because of the way I looked. And yes, I was a dime from head to toe. I'd gotten the best of both worlds. Long, curly hair, soft brown skin, chinky eyes and a dazzling smile. And the body. Yeah, the body was from Bally's and every inch of it was tight. A nigga could eat a whole meal off the hump in my ass. In fact, if you put me in a butt-out contest with hoes like Buffie, or Nutmeg, or Ki Toy, I'd shut all of them down. My lady lumps were just that humped.

We made our first stop about an hour later, somewhere outside of the city.

"Okay, people!" the bus coordinator yelled as we pulled into a gas station that had a convenience store attached. "This is a ten-minute stop! You can go in the store and get something to eat, use the bathroom or do whatever. Just be back on this bus in ten minutes, or be left!"

Big girl next to me was still snoring up against that nasty window and I left her ass right there. The wheels had barely stopped turning when I grabbed my Dior purse and matching overnight bag. I jumped out my seat and beat most of the mamas and their babies down the aisle, then hopped off the bus.

A second bus going to Woodburne had just pulled up behind us, so I hurried up inside the store and found the bathroom. A few people had gotten in there before me, but I cut the line and pushed my way in front of two little girls, then found an empty stall and locked the door behind me.

I checked my bag and made sure my doe and my sample product was straight, then I flushed the toilet with the tip of my shoe and walked back out. At the sink, I washed my hands and pretended to mess with my hair. I arranged my jet-black natural curls around my shoulders while I looked in the mirror and checked out everybody who stepped through the door behind me.

And they were checking me out too.

I had on a pair of Baby Phat jeans that showed off my small waist and bubble ass and a satin corset under my jacket. I laughed inside as chicks walked in the bathroom and glanced around, then zoomed in on that full phatty package in my trunk before looking away, like what I was holding could possibly be ignored. My attention shifted when a tired-looking broad walked over to the sink and smiled at me through the mirror.

"Hey," she said shyly. She had red freckles on her yellow pie face and a big rotten grin. "You going to Sullivan?"

I shook my head as I calculated her situation at a glance: She was young, broke, trifling, and going upstate to visit a criminal nigga who was depending on her to keep his gear fresh and his commissary fat.

"Nah. I'm going to Woodburne. They right next to each other though."

She pumped soap from the dispenser and rubbed it all over her hands.

"This my first time riding. My baby's father just got sent up for something he didn't even do! But I'ma keep it real, regardless. He got five years, and me and my son gone do all five of them years right along with him."

Stupid ass. She was looking at me like I was supposed to agree with that nonsense. Her picture came through real clear. Home-permed hair that had broken off all around the edges, dirty sneakers, nice body, but no style. I gave her a phony smile, then strutted out the bathroom without another word.

The little convenience store was hopping. I grabbed a pack of Doublemint gum, some Red Hots, and a pineapple soda, and found the end of the line. I tapped my foot as more people came in and went out. I wanted to hurry up and get back on the bus and try to find another seat. Sitting up under Big Girl's funky ass for the next few hours just wasn't gonna do.

Five minutes later I was going out the door holding my goodies in a brown paper bag, when some ghetto drama popped off right in front of me.

"Uh-uh, bitch!" yelled a girl who had been walking out the door right ahead of me. She must have come off the second bus because I didn't recognize her from mine. She was skinny and had big titties, and was holding the hand of a little boy who was about two. He looked like a typical jailhouse baby who'd probably been making bus trips upstate his whole life. He had on baggy jeans, a Rocawear shirt, and a tiny pair of fresh blue Timbs. Mad gold chains dangled from his neck and both of his wrists, and two diamond studs were in his little ears.

"I don't know who you on your way to visit," she beefed to a thick sistah with long braids who had been just about to come in the store, "but it better not be *my* goddamn man!"

"Bitch, please!" the other girl said. "Talk that shit to *him*! If Naequon say he wanna see me, then ain't you or nobody else gonna stop me from making a visit!"

"Naequon ain't say shit! You not even on his list! Your ass is 'bout to be riding eight hours for nothing 'cause only one of us is getting up in that jail, and that's *me*!"

Hands went up and somebody got smushed.

Blows got thrown and the baby got knocked to the ground.

"No fighting in here!" yelled the old white man behind the counter.

Your ass is about to get vict'd.

It was the perfect diversion and city slickstas took full advantage.

I glanced behind me and saw people on line sticking shit all in their pockets and up under their clothes.

Homegirls was tussling. Scratching faces and busting lips.

"I'm calling the police!" the white man yelled, running out from behind the counter.

Both girls were cursing and screaming. The baby was still stretched out on the floor with his legs in the air, scared and hollering at the top of his lungs. His little hat had fallen off, and one of his gold bangles was on the floor.

I didn't even think twice. I rushed over to where that baby was laying, scooped up that little bangle, then stepped over those two fighting bitches and got my ass right back on the bus.

Unfortunately for me, I had to sit right back down next to Big Girl again. Everybody had either left something in their seats, or had left somebody watching their seats, and as usual the bus was packed to capacity.

We stopped a couple more times, but I waited until we hit Sullivan County before getting off the bus again. This time when I went into the gas station bathroom I took care of business for real. I took a baggy from a zipper compartment of my overnight bag and pulled out three wrapped condoms, then went through what had become my twice-monthly routine.

I opened the first condom and wiped off some of the goo, then blew into it and stretched it out. Then I took a small blue balloon from the other plastic bag I had stashed in my purse.

I slipped it into the condom and slid it all the way down into the tip. Tying off the thin, slippery material as close to the balloon as possible, I bit off the remainder and spit it in the toilet, then parted my pussy lips and pushed the package as deeply inside me as I could get it. I did this three more times, until my coochie was nice and stuffed. I contracted my fuck-muscles over and over until I felt comfortable, then left the stall and washed my hands.

I knew the drill, and when we got to the penitentiary I breezed past the prison paperwork and the guards like a champ. I sat in the waiting room chatting and blending in with the hundred million other wifeys as we waited for our men. This was one time when I wasn't trying to draw attention, so I kept myself in the middle of the crowd.

As always, I found me a dumb-ass who had too damn many kids for her own good, so I latched on to her and "helped" her out.

"Here, girl." I grinned at a chick I'd seen practically falling off the bus with all her shit. "Let me help you, ma." I snatched her diaper bag, then scooped up her barely walking little brat as she dragged a big bag of food and three other whining kids behind her.

I stuck with the little family until I saw them bringing Sincere out, then I pushed that soggy-tailed baby off my lap and ran over to an empty table to see my boo.

"What it be like, sexy?" Sincere greeted me with a warm hug and a kiss. I grinned up at him and returned the love.

"Hey baby," I said, checking out his six-foot-five-inch, muscled body in his Enyce shirt and starched prison pants. "I missed you, baby. Is everything okay?"

He nodded, and winked at me with a grin.

"It's all good, baby girl. Now that you here."

We sat down at a table and held hands, catching each other up on the details of the last two weeks. As we chatted I looked around, busting bitches tryna eye my man. I laughed inside because Sincere was too fine. With caramel skin and thick, curly hair, his dark eyes and dimpled chin was enough to turn any bitch out. Which, along with his long dick and even longer cheddar, was how he had gotten me.

I'd met Sincere through my best friend Tai. Me and her had grown up in the same building on the Upper West Side of Manhattan, and gone to school together since the third grade. Tai and me were opposites in looks, but we was tight as hell and she always had my back.

I was working at a gentlemen's club called the G-Spot when Tai decided she wanted to hook me up.

"I know this gorgeous guy who wants to meet you," Tai had told me while wolfing down her second slice of pizza with extra cheese, jalapeños and pepperoni. She was treating me to lunch on 125th Street, and trying to convince me to meet her friend.

"You know how I do, Tai." I picked at my crust. "I ain't looking for no relationship or no Big Daddy who wanna fall in love and have a house full of screaming kids and all that shit. I do what I do, and that's how I roll. Damn, girl. Get up on a napkin. You got grease dripping all off your chin."

Tai had wiped her mouth and waved her hand. "Yeah, yeah. You hook up with paid niggas and live large off their asses. That's why you don't want no relationship, Saucy. 'Cause even if a dude *is* clean and decent, if he can't trick his cash out on you, then you don't wanna be bothered with his ass."

I nodded. "And what's your point?"

She stopped chewing and laughed. "I guess I don't have one. Unless you consider the fact that your money train is about to jump off the damn tracks. Ain't that guy from the navy getting ready to head out to sea? Don't you usually find your next victim before you let the one you scamming dry up? And just how many damn bank loans did you get that stupid-ass guy to take out for you anyway?"

Tai was right. I had been milking the shit outta this old-head in the navy. He had rented me an apartment in Manhattan and only wanted to see me once a week. His military pay was good, but he had a wife and some kids down in Brooklyn, so he had taken out a navy loan and paid my rent up for six months in advance. He was rotating back out to sea in a few weeks, and while my rent was paid up for two more months and I had some real fly jewelry, I didn't have nothing stable lined up after that.

"So who is this guy who wants to meet me? And if he's one of them paid niggas that I like to roll with, then how the hell do you know him?"

Tai rolled her eyes. More grease dripped down her chin as she pushed another slice of pizza into her mouth. "His brother comes in the studio where I work. He had a party a couple of nights ago and invited me. He saw that picture of us on my key chain and started hounding me to introduce you."

I went along to meet him reluctantly, but for once Tai was on target when it came down to men. She knew I wouldn't even entertain no broke-ass herb, and I found out in a hurry that Sincere was far from that. He had high-powered connections and long bank, and we clicked right off the bat. Sincere was real raw and spontaneous with his dick, and I liked that shit. He liked to sneak up on me anywhere and everywhere and get him some na-na, and that turned me straight out.

"Open them damn legs," he demanded one morning when I was standing over the stove trying to fry him some potatoes. We had been up fucking all night and my gushy was good and sore, but Sincere still had much juice left in him.

"Ouch!" I squealed as he bent me over. My titties barely missed the damn frying pan full of bubbling grease, and I braced myself with my palms against the stove as he started biting my neck and fingering my clit through my mint-green thong. He bit me hard on the back of my neck, then slung me down to the floor and got on top of me. I liked that rough shit, but I wasn't gonna let him see it.

I raised my knees and fought him off, pushing against his chest and slapping at his hands. He balled his fingers up in my hair and wrapped a long piece around his fist. I wasn't about getting my damn hair yanked by *no* motherfucka, and when I opened my mouth to scream on him, he bit my bottom lip then dragged his scratchy chin down my chest and caught my nipple in his teeth, biting it too.

I arched my back and he almost sucked my whole titty into his mouth, like he was gonna swallow it. That shit hurt and felt good at the same time, and my scream came out sounding real close to a moan. He was grinding his hard dick on my mound and I opened my legs as he gripped my hips and pulled me up to meet his deep strokes.

Pussy sore? Not no more!

Sincere got me naked on that floor, and with the potatoes frying to a crisp in the pan above us, my sexual hunger went into overdrive. Sincere pulled out his pretty dick and stroked it a few times. A big drop of semen wet the head up, and I massaged his thighs as I looked at it, my mouth watering. He got even more aggressive with me and slammed that dick straight up in my tunnel and then pulled it out real quick. I gasped and he plunged in again, then snatched that meat away as my pussy muscles clenched and tried to lock it down.

We played that game for a few while Sincere stared in my face with his thumbs brushing my hard nipples. He was rocking me up to the edge, then letting me slip back as my nipples got even harder and the slow burn of a gigantic nut started working its way from my asshole all the way up to my aching clit.

I couldn't take it no more. The next time that nigga slid that perfect meat up in my wetness I locked my legs behind his back and held on. I bucked my ass off the floor, screaming as tiny splatters of grease exploded out the pan and rained down on us.

Sincere snatched his dick outta me again and grabbed it in his hand. He pressed the tip to my glistening pussy and slid it up and down over my clit, back and forth, until I came like that. Then he moved down lower, sliding his lips down my stomach as his teeth clinked on my belly ring. He dug into my skin as he gripped my thighs, his fingers separating my folds, splitting them apart as he lapped at my curly brown mound, then covered my clit with his hot lips.

Sincere handled my body like he knew all my secrets, and when he finally slammed that big dick up in me again we was both shrieking out loud, me from the orgasm that had my pussy quaking like one big gigantic nerve, and him from that hot grease jumping out the pan and starbursting down onto his back.

And sitting across from him in prison right now and laughing at something he said, I realized just how good our thing had been while it lasted. Even knowing what I knew, it was hard for me to just give my good thing up, but this nigga had a debt to pay. He had shit all over my life, forcing me to do all kinds of craziness just to survive, and he was about to know it.

We spent the first hour of our visit in the reception room playing by the rules under the guards' watchful eye.

"Yo, is the baby still sick? Did you take him to the doctor?" he finally asked.

"Of course," I said, smiling sweetly at his code words. Our baby stayed sick 'cause we played this game twice a month. "But he's better now. Fat and happy and in the best of health."

Sincere reached out and ran his fingers through my hair, and seconds later I stood up.

"Excuse me, boo," I said, playing the game out. "I gotta go to the bathroom."

I slipped off my jacket and stood up, knowing I had every male eye in the room stuck to my high, bouncy ass.

"You bakin' that cake, baby." Sincere laughed with appreciation. I was eye candy and both of us loved flaunting that shit. Sincere had once told me that every inmate on a visit probably went back to his cell and tore his meat off to the memory of what I looked like from behind.

Inside the visitors' bathroom I worked quickly. I pulled down my jeans and stuck one finger up my pussy, feeling for the condoms that were full of a mixture of heroin and cocaine. I pushed down like I was taking a shit, then extracted them one by one. I tore the condoms open and dropped them in the toilet, then took off one of my earrings and poked about twenty tiny holes in each balloon.

When that was done, I took a small alcohol pad from my purse and cleaned off the tip of my earring and stuck it back into my ear, then placed the balloons snugly in my mouth, two on each side between my teeth and my cheek, making sure none of them got close to the silver barbell stud in my tongue. As soon as I was satisfied, I flushed the toilet and booked.

This is where shit had to speed up, and I made sure it did. Back at the table I sat down across from Sincere and forced myself to keep up with his easy conversation. He leaned back in his chair, relaxed and unstressed, and two minutes later when the guard announced that everybody was free to go outside to the picnic area, he came around the table and took my hand.

We walked outside with everybody else. But there was one difference. Sincere was doing all the talking, while I just nodded my head and moved my lips a little bit. In the open air of the fenced yard, we headed over to an empty picnic table, and that's where Sincere went for the switch.

Before sitting down he scooped me up in his strong arms and gave me a long, deep kiss. We made the transfer expertly, just like we'd done countless times before, and when I felt him swallow for the last time I knew it spelled success.

"You been brushing your teeth?" Sincere joked after he sat back down. "Your mouth tastes funny."

I laughed and kicked him under the table. "That's pussy, baby," I teased him. "You ain't had none in so long you done forgot what it tastes like."

I giggled, shaking my long hair and letting it flow, because I knew how much he liked it when I did that. The next hour or so dragged by. I was nervous inside, but I damn sure didn't show it. I played it off like this was just an ordinary visit. We went back inside and both of us got tuna sandwiches and a bottle of Pepsi for lunch. It was right about this time that Sincere usually told me the address for the money pickup. I always played dumb like shit didn't stick in my head, so he told me early enough to give me enough time to memorize his directions way before the visit ended.

"I think I'm gonna start taking the baby to see a new doctor," I prompted him when he finished eating his sandwich.

"Do you know where I can find any good ones?" I rubbed his fingers, flashing dimples at him from all directions.

"Yeah," he said. "I know of a few."

He wiped his arm across his forehead. "There's a real good pediatrician at thirty-two . . . damn!" Sweat started popping up all over his skin and he ran his hands down his face. "It's hotter than shit up in here."

I took a small bite of my sandwich and shrugged like the temperature felt just fine to me.

"Drink some soda," I told him, sliding him his can. "Thirty-two what? Gimme the rest of the address so I can take the baby."

Sincere stood up and stretched his arms over his head, then shook his head back and forth a few times like he needed to clear it.

"The baby, boo," I urged him. "You know how hard it is on me when he gets sick. Just tell me where you want me to take him."

By now sweat was dripping off his chin and his shirt was soaking through.

"Sit down, dammit!" I whispered, glancing at the COs to see if they noticed. "And tell me where to take the fuckin' baby!"

Sincere started taking big deep breaths and walking around in circles.

"What the hell is wrong?" I asked, getting nervous. That shit was getting to him faster than I had expected. I didn't know how long it would take for his stomach acids to go to work and the drugs to seep from the balloons, but I'd wanted to be long gone by the time he got to this point. "Gimme the fuckin' address, dammit!"

"S-s-something ain't clickin'," he muttered. He started moving his mouth all funny. Gulping real big like he was trying to swallow a whole fuckin' desert. "What is this? W-what? What you . . . what the fuck . . . Saucy?"

"Yeah," I laughed, coming straight up outta my game. "That's me, baby. You got my name right. Let's see who else name you know. You ever heard of—" I cupped my hand around my mouth and whispered what had been the most precious name in my whole world to him, then grinned. Sincere looked shocked and shook, and that's when I knew for sure that my boy Akbar had been speaking the truth.

"Oh yeah. That shit sounds familiar don't it? Well it just oughta 'cause it's payback time, motherfuckah!"

"Bitch . . . you set me . . ." Sincere fell to his knees and leaned on one arm to brace himself.

"Boo!" I screamed. "Oh my God! Baby you okay?" I jumped up and ran over to him. The second I put my hand on him he collapsed to the ground. His eyes rolled around a few times then got stuck up in the back of his head as his body stiffened and twitched, and thick white bubbles started foaming up out of his mouth.

Every bitch at the table next to us started screaming, and the guards came running.

"He's epileptic!" I yelled. "I think he's having a seizure!"

The guards pushed me to the side and tried to hold Sincere down as they radioed for help, but who the hell could help him now? Growing up with my daddy I'd seen enough OD'ing junkies to know exactly what was up.

Inmates and their visitors were crowding around being nosy. Babies were crying, kids were still running back and forth all over the place, and shit was just totally erratic.

"Call a fuckin' ambulance!" I screamed and jumped up and down hoping to create even more chaos. I blended into the crowd as the prisoners were herded back to the holding area and all visitors were ushered back outside to the reception area. A guard came in behind us and announced that today's visits were being terminated for security reasons, and told us to go back outside and board our buses.

Wifeys and girlfriends started going off. Cursing the guards out like crazy, dragging their kids behind them, mad as fuck that their visit had been cut short.

Me? I was mad too. Yeah, I'd gotten the revenge I had come for, but not only did that stupid fuck Sincere have a real weak system, he had checked out before giving me the address I needed so I could pick up the connect money.

That meant I needed another hustle to get me through the coming winter. The rent on Sincere's apartment was paid up until the end of the next month, but now that he was history and the Haitians' drugs were gone, I'd have to find me a new nest to keep my ass off the ground. As I rode that nasty bus back home, I put on my thinking cap and tried to figure out who would be the next victim in my never-ending quest to stay laced.

Chapter 2

I WAS ONE of the youngest chicks in Harlem to kick a heroin habit.

My father had met my mother in a whorehouse while he was stationed in Korea, and when he came home to Harlem he brought back more than just a pregnant Asian ho. Kimichi was a straight-up duji fiend, and by the time they settled into a cold tenement apartment on 109th Street, Daddy had joined her in playing games with the needle too.

I'd been told all about the day I was born. Some crazy street madness had been waiting to welcome me into this world. My parents were stretched out on a pissy mattress in a dilapidated dope house, drinking wine and sharing some works. Kimichi had slapped her arm red until she finally found a vein. The needle hit the spot, she plunged and pushed, but in the middle of the hit her water had broken. She was soaking wet and Daddy begged her to leave, but Kimichi kept right on getting high, just like I wasn't barreling down through her uterus and trying to squeeze my way outta her worn-out coochie.

By the time the drugs were gone and Daddy had talked her into going to the hospital, it was almost too late. I slid into this world mad as hell, sucking oxygen and screaming for my next fix.

Kimichi's nodding ass got arrested, and when the nursing staff whisked me off to the intensive care unit, she screamed out to my father in her thick Korean accent, "Seung Cee! Name she Seung Cee!"

But Daddy was just as buzzed as she was. Seung Cee didn't mean shit to him. Sun-she? So-see? He turned it over in his mouth a couple of times, and when they asked him what he wanted to name his new daughter he wrote down Saucy for my first name, and then Sarita, after his new girlfriend.

I stayed in the hospital until I kicked that heroin habit, and then they put me in a foster home waiting for family placement. My Uncle Swag came to get me as soon as he could. His wife had recently had a baby girl too, and she wasn't trying to hear no noise about taking in an ex-addicted infant with special needs who cried all the time. But Uncle Swag wasn't pressed about my fragile condition. He rescued me from foster care and took me home with him. He took care of me all by himself. Changing my Pampers, fixing me bottles, dealing with my constant crying, wife or no wife.

My daddy couldn't have known it back then when I was going through all them changes because of that monkey him and Kimichi had put on my back, but the name Saucy would come to fit me from head to toe. Hot, spicy, sassy. Yeah, all that. Saucy. Hottt Saucy. That's me.

Like a lot of kids who had drug addicts for parents, television raised me. Daddy and Kimichi had gotten me back from Uncle Swag's custody a few weeks after my second birthday. Both of them had cleaned up and kicked heroin long enough to satisfy the courts. But it wasn't long before they sidestepped over to cocaine, so I sat in front of the television just to stay out the way. I grew up loving music videos, rappers, and anything else that showcased young black girls looking glamorous, getting the bling, and commanding the spotlight.

We lived in a tiny apartment over a record shop. It was owned by a guy named Al, who was raising his two sons, Taleb and Tareek. Taleb was a few years older than me, and real quiet and serious, but Tareek was my age and we loved all the same things.

Whenever Tareek came upstairs to my house, we would sneak into my room so he could try on all my raggedy clothes, even my panties. He would cup his hands up in front of his bony chest and pretend like he had titties.

"They gonna be real big one day!" he told me, his arms outstretched and his fingers wide like he was holding two watermelons. "Big like this!"

Tareek's father used to beat his ass every day. By the time we was old enough to start school there were extension cord marks up and down his legs and all over his back, chest, and neck. He stayed upstairs at my house as much as he could, but one day my daddy got drunk and laid on the couch with a cigarette burning in his hand. Our sofa caught on fire and smoke was everywhere.

After that, Tareek wasn't allowed upstairs no more, so we played downstairs in his father's shop where we would listen to music all day. We'd watch endless videos on BET, and make up our own stylish moves in the mirror. I'd shake my little ass and Tareek would shake his little ass too.

"I'ma be Harlem's top video girl when I grow up," he bragged one day, jumping in front of me in the mirror and swaying his narrow hips from side to side.

That shit pissed me off because Tareek was skinny and buck-toothed with peasy hair. Everybody knew I was the pretty one. People liked to put their fingers in my curly hair, and strangers stopped me on the street and told me I had beautiful eyes and a gorgeous smile. Who the hell did Tareek think he was? I elbowed him in his stomach and then grabbed the back of his shirt and slung him down to the ground.

Tareek had his info twisted and I was determined to make sure he got it right.

There wasn't but one top bitch gonna come outta Harlem, and that was *me*.

• • •

Uncle Swag used to have a daughter named Paris. She died the spring we both turned eight. Paris was one of them spoiled-ass rich kids who made you wanna beat the hell outta them. She lived downtown in what seemed like a mansion to me. Compared to the freezing-in-the-winter, boiling-in-the-summer rat-trap I lived in, it probably was.

Me and Paris were the same age but we were nothing alike. I lived with Kimichi and her pimp lover, King. Paris had a mother and a father and a baby brother, and I didn't have nobody. I was poor and dirty, and Paris walked around looking like a sparkling black princess. I lived in a dilapidated Harlem apartment upstairs from a record shop, and Paris lived in a high-rise suite downtown. My daddy had gotten shot dead trying to rob a check-cashing place, and Paris's daddy was a big willie who worked for the state, a shot caller who rolled with important playas and carried big bank. My mother was a street junkie and Paris's mom was a sanctified housewife. I crawled into a grimy bed every night, catching feelings when my panties got snatched off and my legs was yanked open. Paris rested peacefully in a platform bed with stars painted on the ceiling and frilly lace curtains hanging over her head.

"Turn that shoe around the other way," Paris tried to boss me. It was the Friday before Easter and the only reason she'd asked Uncle Swag to bring me to her house was so she could show off all the new gear her mother had bought her.

"Don't tell me what to do," I snapped, bending up her white patent-leather shoe and shoving it back in the box damn near sideways. Her new clothes were thrown all over the place. The bed, the dress, the floor . . . most of them sporting price tags so high they boggled my mind. She had name-brand everything. Sailor dresses, party dresses. Panties. Socks. New denim short shorts and back-out tops to match. Skirts with flowing peasant tops. Three pairs of Nikes, some Timbs, and two pairs of shiny shoes with low heels. Cute little summer outfits that would have looked too fly on me. She even had one of those dressy knit ponchos and a real Gucci purse in the same shade.

"These shits is ugly anyway," I said, tossing the shoe box to the floor with a smirk. "You shoulda got something with a high heel on it. Don't nobody like flat shoes with buckles on them no way." I mighta been talking mad shit out loud, but deep inside I woulda died for them patent-leather shoes, and was wishing I had Paris's whole life.

Uncle Swag was my father's little brother and I coulda ate me a mouthful of his ass. He worked some kinda high-post government job and people all over Harlem swarmed around him trying to shake his hand and get his attention. Like Daddy, Uncle Swag was tall with sexy bowlegs and had pretty choco-late skin, but that's where the resemblance ended. Daddy had been a grimy, peasy-head, ball-scratching, stank-breathed needle fiend, and Uncle Swag was paid and shiny, holding swole pockets and pushing a jet-black Maserati. He was down with people on the streets and looked and smelled good, and when-ever he came around I told myself it was just to see me. I had even convinced myself that he liked me better than he liked his nappy-headed daughter Paris.

"Sweet Saucy!" He would laugh real loud and grab a hand-ful of my long curly hair before twirling me around and picking me up. "Girl you getting taller and prettier every time I see you. You been a good girl? Tell Uncle what you want for your birthday."

I lived to see my Uncle Swag rolling up to my block in that big black whip with the deep cream interior. I would sit in the window for hours fantasizing about how much doe I'd have if I was his daughter, all the shoes I'd sport, all the designer clothes and jewelry I'd possess, and all the smart shit I'd talk, if only I had been born Uncle Swag's baby girl instead of Daddy's!

Whenever he pulled up to the curb with those spinners moving, niggas would scatter from their apartments like roaches, rushing over to admire his g-ride. The young boys on the block would be fighting each other trying to get appointed to stand guard over Uncle Swag's whip.

I knew Uncle Swag felt real sorry for me and Kimichi 'cause my daddy had gotten himself smoked. Sometimes he came by with money for Kimichi, and he was always packing a bag full of food for me. Cereal and milk, Pop-Tarts and franks, and always a little bit of fresh fruit too. I knew Uncle Swag worried about me and I played that shit up to the max.

"Saucy," he would put his big strong hands on my shoulders and say. "You ain't nothing but a little pork chop bone. I brought you some pretty red apples, baby, and don't you give nobody none of them either! You eat every last one of 'em by yourself, you hear?"

But Uncle Swag could keep his Pop-Tarts and his little red apples 'cause right now I had my eye on his daughter's orange Gucci purse. It was calling me and I wanted it bad. I didn't own nothing that even came close to looking good with it, but that didn't stop me from feening for it anyway.

"Hey! Lemme hold that orange Gucci," I told Paris, making my voice sound real sweet even though I hated her. "You wearing that cute yellow and blue dress to church, right? Lemme get your orange Gucci until next weekend when I come back over."

Paris was sitting there rubbing the back of her neck. She looked up at me with an evil face and said, "Why you so worried about what I'ma be styling for Easter Sunday? You going to church too?" She covered her mouth and giggled. "Oh, that's right. I forgot. You ain't got nothing to wear."

I stood there and took that shit while Paris laughed her head off. As much as I hated myself for it, I continued to beg. I wanted that damn purse!

"Come on, Paris. You got all them cute bags hanging up in your closet—"

"And they gone stay hanging up in my closet too."

"Damn! I don't wanna keep the bag forever! My birthday is coming up soon. I know you gone let me hold it for my birthday."

"Then you know wrong."

I muttered, "Ugly bitch." Then I snatched one of her new skirts off the bed and flung that shit across the room.

Paris just shrugged, rubbed her neck again, and gave me one of her bitch-I-got-ten-times-more-gear-than-your-ass-will-ever-have looks.

"You real ugly, you know. Baldheaded, too."

Paris just shrugged. "Chill, Saucy," she said. "With your dirty mouth. You know how my daddy rolls. I might be ugly, but at least we ain't broke. But don't worry. I'ma let you play all this stuff. *After* I show it off a few times."

No thanks, bitch, I thought to myself, staring at her as she got down on the floor and started polishing her toenails some ugly blue color. Something grimy flashed inside of me and I got real hot. I swung my foot and kicked that bottle of nail polish so hard it flew across the room, hit the mirrored closet door and cracked wide open. Blue goo spilled all over Paris's white carpet. It splashed the toe of her new Timbs, got all over the flap of that bright orange Gucci purse I'd been begging for, and dotted the hem of the pretty peasant skirt I'd thrown on the floor too.

I stared at the mess I made and felt a little better inside. But Paris wasn't fazed at all. She never said a word. She just got up and walked over to her dresser and got another bottle of nail polish in the same color. She clamped the long end between her back teeth and twisted it open, then calmly went back to polishing her toenails again.

"Bitch."

"Whatever, Saucy." She squinted as she dabbed polish on her little toe. "But too bad you messed up that Gucci bag. If you had begged just a little bit longer I woulda let you have it."

Fuck Paris and all her fancy shit! I thought, stomping toward the door. When I grew up I was gonna get mine in this world. I was gonna take every damn thing I wanted, and I wouldn't have to beg nobody for nothing! I turned around at her doorway, then marched right back over to where my cousin sat. I

swung my foot again and sent that second bottle of polish flying through the air too.

I was still mad with Paris when Aunt Ruthie called us into the
kitchen to eat dinner. I walked in there dragging my feet 'cause
I hated everything she cooked. All them damn vegetables and
lettuce and baked meat that didn't taste like nothing. I wasn't
big on stuffing my stomach anyway, but if I had to eat, then
gimme some hot chicken wings from the Chinese man on the
corner, or maybe some barbeque ribs and fries, or some Ramen
noodles with a frank sliced up in it.

Aunt Ruthie didn't really like me and I knew it. Whenever
I came to her house she made me strip naked outta my Harlem
clothes at the door and then get straight in the bathtub so I
could be scrubbed clean.

"Girl, you got to be washed," she would say, hustling me
into the bathroom, " 'cause ain't no way in hell you climbing in
Paris's bed smelling like that!"

Yeah, Aunt Ruthie fed me and ironed my clothes and she
didn't feel me up or beat my ass. She treated me all right when
Uncle Swag was around, but when he wasn't there just her
whole attitude made me feel dirty and low, like a nasty little
beggar. The only time she ever really touched me was when
she was scrubbing me hard enough to make my skin scrape
off. She *never* hugged me or told me I was cute. She never let
Paris come over to my crib neither, and I knew it was because
of Kimichi.

I'd heard Aunt Ruthie telling one of her ugly church friends
that my daddy must've been a real fool for dragging that Chinese hooker outta some back alley in Seoul when there were
plenty of two-cent whores up for sale right on the streets of
Harlem.

I might have been just eight, but already I understood that
women like Aunt Ruthie looked down on people like Kimichi and me. My mother stuck out in Harlem because Asian
junkies with half-black children weren't an everyday sight on

our streets. But I had Aunt Ruthie figured out, though. Paris mighta had the finest stuff money could buy, but she was still ugly, short, knock-kneed, and had her mama's big forehead. Whenever we were out together I was the one people ooohed and ahhhed over. They played in my curly hair and rubbed my smooth light-brown skin. They told me I had the cutest little bowlegs and the prettiest slanted eyes, just like a black Chinese. Nobody said much of nothing about Paris, except when they was complimenting her on her clothes. She was just regular looking. There was nothing cute about her at all, especially with that rock-head of hers, and I didn't care how pressed she dressed, or how many top beauty salons permed her hair and hot-curled her bangs. There was no hiding that big shiny dome Paris was packing, and even Aunt Ruthie knew I looked way better than her daughter did.

I kissed Uncle Swag's cheek as I walked past his chair at the head of the dinner table. He grinned and nodded at me as I took the seat across from Paris. I could feel Aunt Ruthie staring at me, looking for something to be disgusted about. I always tried to act real sweet and innocent around her, but she knew what it was. She took up for Paris all the damn time, but if she hurt my feelings too bad, I'd just get Paris alone in her room and kick her ass until I felt better.

Aunt Ruthie mighta been richer than me and Kimichi, but when it came to being up on her shit I had her blinded. She might have been black, but she wasn't half as slick as my Korean mother was. She left her stuff laying around everywhere, and I hit her purse for five or ten dollars almost every time I visited because she carried so much bank that she didn't even miss it.

I played with my food a little bit and laughed when the baby, Kaz, threw broccoli chunks all around the room. Uncle Swag laughed too, rubbing his little boy's head and reaching over to push some dry-ass turkey in his mouth. Aunt Ruthie acted like she was mad about all that food getting all over the floor, but I could tell she was fronting and felt real good about her little family.

I couldn't really blame her, neither. It was real warm and cozy up in their crib. Nothing like the life I lived with Kimichi and King.

We were still laughing at the baby when Paris started rubbing her neck again and acting up just to get some attention. She grabbed her stomach, then made this funny noise and threw up all over the table.

"Paris!" Aunt Ruthie hollered. Her and Uncle Swag jumped up at the same time. Aunt Ruthie got to Paris first and pressed a bunch of napkins to her mouth.

"What's wrong, baby? Is something you ate bad?"

All this shit is bad, I wanted to say, but instead I pushed my plate away and kept my mouth closed.

"I don't feel good," Paris whined. "My head hurts, Mama. It hurts so *bad*!"

Aunt Ruthie felt Paris's forehead. "Swag, this child is burning up with fever!"

Paris started crying. She kept saying her neck felt twisted and her head felt like it was busting open. She covered her face and complained that the dining room lights was hurting her eyes.

Aunt Ruthie started crying too, and all the cool seemed to drain outta Uncle Swag. He looked worried in a way that I'd never seen before.

"You think we should call the doctor?" he asked, heading toward the phone.

Aunt Ruthie shook her head as she got Paris up from the table and they rushed together toward the bathroom.

"No. I'ma catch a taxi on over to the emergency room. You run Saucy home real quick, then meet me there. Don't waste no time standing around talking to that momma of hers, neither. Just drop Saucy off at the door and come straight over to the emergency room. I mean that shit too, Swag. My baby is sick."

Three nights later the door to my bedroom popped open again. I held my breath as the sound of King's footsteps crossed the room. Pulling my sheet back, she kneeled on the bed and spread my legs. She slid my panties down to my ankles, then took them completely off, and then her warm lips were on me. Licking. Sucking. Probing my hole and making it hot and wet. I squirmed, my booty rubbing against the linty sheets. Little sparks of heaven shot through me and I couldn't help it as my legs slid open wider, my back arching as my hips rose to meet her tongue.

King reached under me and cupped my butt. She stroked my cheeks and licked me faster. I squeezed my eyes tight as she fucked the bed, her body hammering as she humped down into the mattress. *Whomp! Whomp! Whomp!*

"Ahhhh!" I cried out, my body shivering. For the first time ever, delicious tremors rocked me from head to toe. My fingers pulled at her short hair. I pushed her face deeper inside me, shocking both of us with my greed. Consumed, I grabbed at my sheets and wrapped my legs around her head, clamping my feet, locking my ankles together, and grinding myself all over her face.

She tried to pull away but I was busy searching. Reaching for something that I needed more than air. I yelled out loud as I tried to get it. Rubbing myself everywhere trying to put that fire out. I was closer, just about to fall off the unknown edge when King wrenched open my legs and snatched her face away.

She glared at me in the darkness.

"You's a nasty little bitch," she snarled, wiping her mouth and rocking back on her knees, leaving cold air where her warm tongue had just been. "Little kids ain't supposed to like that shit. You been getting off the whole time, ain't you?"

I opened my mouth to deny it, but before I could say anything the bedroom door was opened once again.

"Please," my mother whispered urgently, speaking directly to me and ignoring King. "Come to me."

I was dazed. The three of us had played this game for a long time but it had never gone down like this before.

"Your daughter's a fuckin' freak," King complained as I

walked toward the door, the throbbing between my legs slowly fading.

I stopped in front of Kimichi. She smoothed her straight hair, then put her hands on my shoulders. Her large slanted eyes looked sad.

"Is bad news, Seung Cee," she said, using the name she had tried to give me at birth. "It is Pawris. She pass away, yes? You cousin is dead."

I didn't sleep for the rest of the night.

Kimichi had cried a little bit but my eyes were dry as sand. All I could think about was Paris being dead, and all the nice shit she had left behind. That big old bed. The endless clothes. Those patent-leather shoes. That orange Gucci purse. Shoot, Paris didn't need none of that stuff no more!

By the time the sun came up I was already dressed and ready for school. Kimichi was sleeping naked on the dirty floor in the living room, and King had passed out on the sofa. Her legs were wide open showing her big hairy pussy, and an empty vodka bottle was on the end table beside her.

I walked the few blocks to school with my mind whirling. Tightening up my scheme, making sure I had plenty of tears ready. Inside my classroom I went straight to my desk and sat down. I didn't even bogart any of the play areas the way I usually did. I didn't hold my hand out demanding nobody's lunch money neither. I had fought to be the attendance monitor for the week, but I let a boy named Chester take my place and I didn't make him pay me a dime for the privilege of doing it.

The moment my third-grade teacher, Mrs. Gladman, walked in the classroom I started spazzing out.

"Saucy!" she said, sticking her purse into her desk drawer then coming over to see about me as I wailed as hard and loud as I could. I was such a troublemaker in her class that she'd had to put my desk dead smack in front of hers, and this was the first time I was actually happy that her eyes were directly on me.

"Don't cry, honey!" she begged, looking shocked and really concerned. "What's the matter? Do you feel sick or something?"

I shook my head no, wailing louder.

"Did somebody hit you? Hurt you? Is everything all right at home?"

Oh I was performing my ass off now. Shaking in terror, rubbing my fists all in my eyes. Clapping my knees together under the desk.

Mrs. Gladman bent down next to me and put her arm around me. As much as I had cursed her out and terrorized the other students, she probably couldn't imagine what could have my bad ass so scared and hysterical.

"What's going on, Saucy?" she asked quietly, stroking my hair. "Whatever it is, you can tell me and I promise I'll help you. I *promise*."

That was exactly what I wanted to hear. In fact, I was counting on her to say just that! I kept up my act as Mrs. Gladman led me out of the classroom and down the hall to the nurse's office. I cried the whole way, lips trembling, working them tears to death.

I sat in front of the nurse whimpering and shaking. She was a nice fat lady with a wide face and real red lipstick.

"We're both here to help you, sweetie," the school nurse said, leaning over me and taking my hand. Her perfume was sweet and thick. "Please, Saucy. If something bad has happened to you, we really, really need to know about it."

She sure didn't have to ask me twice. I pictured Paris's big old comfortable bed and that orange Gucci purse, and then I opened my mouth and let all the beans spill out.

"Mister King—my mommy's girlfriend. She kissed me on my pussy last night!"

A social worker from the Department of Family Services picked me up from school and took me for a physical exam at Harlem Hospital. When we left the hospital I was taken straight to a foster home. I gave them Uncle Swag's number, then sat listening to the social worker's side of the conversation as she made arrangements for him to come pick me up.

"Oh, Saucy," he said, hugging me to his chest the next morning when he came to get me. Uncle Swag was still fine, but his eyes were red like he hadn't slept in a long time. He glanced around the crummy foster home that was almost as raggedy as my Harlem apartment. "Paris is gone and we'll have to bury her, baby. But we sure ain't gonna lose you too."

Uncle Swag told me that Paris had been killed by a virus called meningitis, and while I knew that was too bad for her, it was high time for me. In a matter of days I went from a dirty Harlem girl to a downtown diva. It was hard for me to hold myself together when Uncle Swag led me into Paris's old bedroom and told me to make good use of everything in it. I wanted to jump up and down and scream and kiss him and do a booty dance to celebrate my good luck, but instead I nodded slowly and forced myself to drag my feet over to her room, then pause at the door and look over my shoulder at him with big sad eyes.

"You sure, Uncle?"

"Yeah, darling. I'm sure. You were her best friend. It's what Paris would have wanted."

For a minute I wondered about what Aunt Ruthie might say when she saw me styling all of Paris's stuff, but she was too broke down to even help with the funeral arrangements and she mostly stayed in their bedroom crying in the dark. Her sister Roz had come from upstate to help her out. She stayed in Kaz's room and took care of him, and that left Uncle Swag to take care of me.

On the morning of Paris's funeral I hid in her room with the door closed until it was time to leave. I was excited. The apartment was full of people and I could hear them out there talking and crying and comforting Uncle Swag and Aunt Ruthie. The moment I stepped into the living room it seemed like everybody shut up all at once. I stood in the middle of the room smiling and profiling because I knew I looked just that good.

Paris's yellow and white sailor dress was a little short, but otherwise it fit me perfectly. I had on her white church gloves and my feet were balled up in her white patent-leather shoes with the shiny buckles. Her lacy tights were too short for me and wouldn't come all the way up to my crotch, but I figured couldn't nobody see all that so what the hell. Hanging from my shoulder was that fly orange Gucci bag. Yeah, I knew it didn't match the outfit, but so what? The flap with the blue nail polish on it was out of sight, pressed against my side, and my thick, pretty hair was curly and shiny and hanging down my back in black waves.

"My lawd . . ." Aunt Ruthie sobbed out loud, breaking the silence and stealing some of the attention away from me. I sucked my teeth under my breath thinking that's where Paris had gotten that shit from. They just couldn't let me shine the way I was supposed to without trying to get all in the spotlight too.

Aunt Ruthie fell against her sister, tears running from her eyes. "Lawd, that's my baby's Easter dress," she said, crying into a black handkerchief.

"Saucy," Aunt Roz said, dressed all in black and giving me an evil look. "Why don't you go change into something else, dear. Something more . . . appropriate. You do have something of your own that you can wear, don't you? I bet you'd feel a lot more comfortable in some of your own clothes."

All eyes were on me again but this time I didn't like the way it felt. We *were* going to a damn funeral, right? That meant Paris was *gone*. Saucy was *here*. Why should all them cute clothes go to waste?

"Leave her." Uncle Swag spoke up. He looked at his watch and started waving folks toward the door. "The limos are already waiting downstairs. Besides. It don't matter what the child has on. Life don't have a damn thing to do with fancy clothes."

At the church I barely glanced at Paris laying up there looking stiff and funny in that big white box while everybody sang and cried around her. I was too hyped after taking my very first limousine ride and couldn't wait to ride that bad boy back home again. There were five of them. Stretched out. Long, black, and sparkling. Cars that screamed money. I just knew every other driver on the road was looking at us with envy because my uncle had big doe.

The next few weeks woulda been the bomb if everybody around me wasn't so damn sad all the time. Hell, I was happier than I'd ever been in my life, and when Kimichi called and told Uncle Swag that King's nasty ass had gotten sent upstate and asked if he would bring me to our old apartment to see her, I told Uncle Swag I didn't wanna go.

Why should I? For the first time in my life I had everything I needed and almost all of what I wanted. They'd put me in a new school where nobody knew the old dirty, raggedy Saucy. Every morning I gave Uncle Swag a kiss and jumped outta his Maserati in front of that big old school a happy child. I felt like a shiny little model on a runway as I walked into that school like my feet were touching a red carpet. My hair was always pretty and decked with Paris's cute bows and barrettes, and I never wore the same outfit twice in a month.

I had enough smarts to hide some of my glee around Uncle Swag though. I made sure to catch an occasional sad face and teary eyes like I was thinking about Paris every now and then for Uncle Swag's sake. But for real though, I didn't miss nothing about her ass. Every chance I got I closed the door to Paris's old room and rolled all over that big-ass bed. I yanked all her gear out the closets and tried every stitch of it on, even the ugly stuff. I crammed my feet into her too-small shoes and gave not a damn when my toes caught a cramp.

In no time at all I had taken over Paris's space and was working on making the life she used to have all mine. Aunt Ruthie tried to fuss when she found out Uncle Swag had asked the courts for permanent custody of me, but he shut that down real quick.

"Woman, I done lost my only brother and my only daughter. You think I'ma lose my only niece too? Saucy's a sweet little girl and she needs us. Who knows what that dyke bitch was doing to her up in that filthy apartment. You can say what you want, but Saucy Robinson ain't going nowhere. I love her, and she loves me right back. Life is too short for bullshit, Ruthie. Losing Paris shoulda taught you that."

Yeah! I wanted to scream out loud as I stood with my ear pressed to their bedroom door. Aunt Ruthie could just chill with all that "when is she going home" shit. I *was* home. And she could just believe that.

Chapter 3

BY THE TIME I was fourteen Uncle Swag couldn't do a damn thing with me. He treated me like a princess and had spoiled me to death, giving me everything I even thought about asking for. And believe me, even though I loved my uncle more than I loved air, I asked for a whole lot.

My cousin Kaz was about seven then, and had been so smothered by Aunt Ruthie that he couldn't even wipe his ass by himself. After Paris died she had totally babyfied Kaz, even coming between him and Uncle Swag to the point where my uncle couldn't have no kind of real relationship with his son. But Aunt Ruthie never could tell me shit, so after a minute she didn't even bother to try. She gave me my space and I gave her hers. She stayed stuck up in her room and I stayed running the streets. Her dealings with me were kept to a bare minimum, and that was more than enough for me.

I was a hot, wild, and crazy young girl and enjoying life to the fullest. I got respect and admiration from all the young come-ups on the street because my uncle Swag was a nigga in the know. He was power in the flesh. Our Upper West Side Columbus Avenue apartment was always live and filled with music and important people coming and going. Uncle Swag worked for the state government, but the G's he hung out with were club owners, record producers, and black businessmen who kept Harlem running smooth.

Me and Uncle Swag both loved us some music, and one of his tightest dawgs, Tollie Jones, was a record producer who was always giving me mixtapes and telling me about the hip-hop celebrities who were constantly after him to hook them up with some gully beats.

"I wanna go to L.A. and meet me some rappers," I told Tollie one day. "You know Nellie, right? How about Puffy and Nas? Yo! Introduce me to Jigga!"

Tollie just laughed. "You ain't gotta go way to Los Angeles to meet no stars, Saucy. Rappers hang out in New York and Atlanta too. But them some ocean dwellers, little girl. You still swimming in a freshwater pond. You ain't ready for none of that."

"Yeah, right," I said, dancing all up in his face and showing him some of my new moves. "You just scared Jay-Z might see all a' this and wanna get with me. He'll stack all them other girls on some ice real quick once he gets a taste of the Sauce."

I was out there. Just begging for trouble and drama. Uncle Swag did his best to keep me in his sights, but all I had to do was give him a sad look and hang my head down a little and he would give in and basically let me do my thing—as long as I did the do in school. Of course, school was the last damn thing on my mind. I was smart and passed all my exams with no problem whenever I bothered to show up, but even when I was in the school socializing, I wasn't trying to actually sit up in no boring-ass classroom.

My days were all about flossing in front of cute boys and showing off my designer clothes, fierce ass, and bomb titties. My nights were spent drinking Hypnotic, smoking trees I'd copped from 116th Street, and hanging out with my girl Tai when I was supposed to be at the library.

"Let's go see what's shaking in Harlem," I told Tai one Friday night. Tai lived downstairs from me on the fourteenth floor, and we were in her bedroom with the door closed smoking a blueberry blunt and listening to some Ying Yang twins.

"For what?" Tai asked. She was dipping Spanish olives into a big cup of ranch dressing and sucking on two fingers after every bite.

"To get us some beer and find us some niggas!" I said. "And stop eating that shit. It looks so nasty."

"You the one nasty, Saucy. I don't even know why you be fuckin' with all them dudes like that. Clowning with them niggas and letting them get all up under your clothes just so they can get you high and buy you shit." Tai frowned, twisting her lips. "I bet you don't even remember half of they names."

I laughed. "See. That's why you ain't got nobody chasing after you," I told her. "It ain't even about they names. It's all about the dope, the dick, and the doe."

Tai sucked her teeth. "You need to stop tripping. Your uncle gives you almost everything you ask for. You ain't gotta grind with no corner boys unless you want to."

"Well, maybe I want to then! So what? Guys like to fuck and they wanna fuck me. What's wrong with that?"

"Look, Saucy," she said while trying to hold her breath. She pulled on the blunt again then blew the smoke out toward the window. "I'm just saying, okay? You ain't gotta fuck everybody just because they wanna fuck you. I know you been through a lot girl. You told me about that dyke King and what she used to do to you. But that one horrible thing ain't gotta rule your whole life girl! You don't have to sell your body short just because one person took advantage of it."

I stared at her like she was mental. I knew what the real problem was. Tai was jealous. She had a flat ass and knocked-knees, and didn't no real playa wanna be seen with her. We had been best friends since I moved downtown, and over the years my slim package had gotten phatter while Tai's apple frame had just gotten fatter. She wore dope clothes for a big girl, and kept her hair and nails done, but she coulda actually been cute if she stopped eating so damn much. Tai was my girl but she had zero self-confidence, and what cool hustler wanted to fuck somebody who had corn chips stuck in their teeth and a stomach that was four times bigger than their ass?

"I don't fuck with everybody, Tai. And that bitch King wasn't the only one who got with me, either. Girl, I been fuckin' since I was six years old! Kimichi used to put me in bed between her and Mr. Warren, and when he got up to leave we'd have enough cash to eat for a month. Plus I used to ride that little dick popping outta Mister Jack's box just like it was a pony. How you think we kept our lights turned on in Harlem? Ain't nothing wrong with fuckin' as long as you getting something out of it, Tai. Rememer that. You oughtta stop letting that nigga Geoffrey bust all them free nuts up in you without giving you nothing but hickeys to show for it."

"Shut up! I get stuff from Geoff. Just because I don't throw all his goods in your face don't mean he ain't dishing it out."

I looked at Tai, and then at the platinum tennis bracelet I was sporting on my left wrist. She had no clue that it was her man Geoff who had paid for this shit. I had his stupid behind wide open just like all the other guys in our school, and when he showed me the bracelet he'd been planning to give to Tai, I gave him a real good reason to change his mind and slide it to me instead.

After Tai sprayed some air freshener around the room and I checked my shit out in the mirror, we booked, creeping out as quietly as we could. Tai's mother hated the sight of me. Back when I was twelve she had hallucinated up some crazy shit, and for years I had sworn to her and Tai that it wasn't true. I had been standing next to Tai's father one day, just looking out their living room window, when Tai's moms came in and started wildin'. She was screaming and swinging on Mr. Watkins like a maniac. She told Tai she'd caught me grinding my ass around while Mr. Watkins had his hand stuck down inside the back of my shorts. It took me two whole years to convince Tai that her mother had been seeing things and that shit wasn't true.

We left our building and ran toward the train station, and pretty soon we were uptown in Harlem and I was feeling grand. As much as I had hated Harlem as a little kid, I couldn't stay away from it now. The aura of this neighborhood was right and relaxing to me. I'd been born here and it was good to be home.

All the action was up here, and I was definitely a girl after some action. If I felt like cruising these streets and Tai didn't wanna hang, I didn't even sweat it. I would hop my ass in a cab in a minute and ride up to Harlem to see how many corner niggas I could pick up.

Me and Tai could always get our young asses up inside one of Harlem's clubs, but sometimes they got extra and refused to sell us any liquor. We wasn't taking no chances tonight, so we stopped at a corner liquor store to get some mini Bacardis before going inside.

"You got 'em turning heads," the dude at the counter said when I tried to show him my cute hips and round ass instead of a photo ID. I had on a thin mint-green shirt with a slit all the way up the middle and no bra, and his eyes were zooming in on my nipples. "You might be old enough to fuck, but you sure ain't old enough to drink."

Well, I was already doing a whole lot of both, and of course my little ass was heading for trouble in a major way. Inside the club we partied as hard as we could. I was on the dance floor screaming out all the hot rap lyrics I'd studied and memorized, hooks, verses, bridges, the whole shit. The DJ threw on a slow stripper song called "Envy" by Reem Raw and Robb Hawk, and the guy I was dancing with pulled me into a deep nasty grind and started whispering it all in my ear.

Look what I found,
Pretty brown,
Yeah I gotta have!
Her bottom half'll have you digging out ya pocket stash!
She got a latch on my soul,
The way her body wrap 'round a pole
With her ass out on roll,
Her passionate stroll got my shit on brick,
Them glossy lips will make a nigga trick off chips!
Her eyes telling me she wanna come sit on this,
Everybody in the spot tryna hit on Miss!
So I gotta strategize,

Feel the vibe when she passing by,
No lie, she can send me home satisfied,
Her frame's mean . . . everything that I fantasized . . .
Gotta step to her, let her know that I can handle mine!

Yeah I can see why they envy ya baby!
Now pull ya benjies out, start tippin my baby! My baby!
   My baby! My baby!

He whispered that shit so hot and freaky in my ear that I
didn't even protest when he pulled me into a booth and started
tonguing me down. He smelled like a real man and his lips were
so soft! He reached under my shirt and rubbed my titties until
my nipples started aching, and when his hand trailed down to
my lap and he slipped his fingers under my skirt, my pussy
was nice and wet. I let him slide two of them up in me, and as
he massaged my clit with his thumb, I arched my back, then
reached under the table, found his lap, and squeezed his rock
until I came.

"Saucy!" I pulled away from ol' boy as Tai slapped me so
hard on my shoulder that she damn near broke a bone. Her
face was sweaty and all her curls had fell. "What y'all doing
hemmed up in this corner? I thought you came to dance, girl!"

Dude slid his fingers outta my pussy and I laughed and
kissed his lips again. Tai dragged me back out on the dance
floor and I got back in my club groove. Near the end of the
night so many niggas had passed me dutches that my head
started hurting. I switched up and starting drinking Alizé
when one of the dudes who was clocking me started buying me
double shots, and I made sure he spent some real money too.

By the time the club started emptying out I was blasted.
All I wanted to do was get me some hot wings or something,
then go home and black the hell out. I hadn't meant to stay out
all night, but the sun was already coming up when we stepped
outside. But when I staggered into the crib at six in the morning Aunt Ruthie was up waiting for me. She called herself fed
up enough to open her mouth and get in my business. She con-

vinced Uncle Swag that I needed some boundaries laid down and he went for it. She said I was shopping too much, and as smart as I was, my grades were slipping in school. She accused me of being spoiled, selfish, and ungrateful. She told him no teenager needed as much jewelry, shoes, CDs, and money as I had.

Uncle Swag put his foot down and declared that my ass was now on a curfew and a strict budget. Fifty dollars a week. What the hell was I supposed to do with that?

"Saucy, baby girl you gotta slow down just a little, okay? I know you like going out and having fun with your friends and that's cool. It really is. Just slow down a little, okay? You know you the only baby girl your uncle got left."

I got pissed off with Uncle Swag but I couldn't stay mad with him because he acted like slapping rules on me was hurting him more than it hurt me. See, my uncle was the only person in the world who understood how fucked up my life had been before Paris died and I moved downtown. I'd gone through some shit no little girl should have to go through. Because of that trifling ass Kimichi, all kinds of fingers had been in my young pussy. Dicks too. Grown tongues had licked all over my clit. The hardest part about all of that had been the feelings it turned on in me, even when I was too young to understand what those feelings were all about.

But young or not, I knew what felt good to me, and right after I entered the eleventh grade I hooked up with a guy named Plat from 112th Street and got my first real good fuck that made me lose my mind.

I had already been tricking all the wannabe's I went to school with, but that was just for fun. I took their money and talked them into buying me gifts and stuff, but them young sons couldn't handle the kind of nookie I was putting on them and I was always scared my uncle would find out. These fake cats played like they was hood, but they had housekeepers and whatnot at home, and jumped in limos when school was over and headed home to apartment buildings that had doormen waiting outside. Just like Uncle Swag and Aunt Ruthie, their folks had gotten some ends together and fled the hard life of Harlem, and they felt safe and protected in their Upper West Side world.

But I was looking for a real thug nigga. Street-hard is what turned me on. And Harlem was full of that. I started sneaking uptown to get a glimpse of Plat every chance I got. He was tall and had a goatee and thick, muscled-up arms like Suge Knight. I got a thrill outta watching him do his thing on his corner grind. I knew he wasn't no big-time hustler and he didn't sit too far up the ladder of importance, but there was something real hot about that low-level action he was involved in, and I decided that Plat, with his smooth dark skin and piercing eyes, was gonna get him some of my goodies.

Plat was the type of nigga who was into 69ing all night long, which was cool with me. His dick was kinda short, but it was real fat and I liked it. He would sit back and play with my hair while I wet that thing up and mopped it with my tongue, licking it from top to bottom. Plat liked his brain real juicy, so I would spit on his dick just a little bit so he could hear that slippery slurping sound that he loved so much. He was thicker than most men, and I could hardly put my whole hand around his meat, but I jerked it to that funky hot Saucy rhythm and Plat's dick would just get harder and harder. As soon as I felt him getting ready to shoot, I would cup his big, heavy balls and suck on that dick like it was a sweet fat cucumber.

When it was my turn, I would get on my hands and knees and back my big ass up to his face. Plat loved the feel of my ass. He'd smack it and watch it jiggle, massage it, tooting it up so he could look straight up my pussy and into my uterus, and y'all know he stuck them fingers up in there too. He'd start out with one, and by the time he got to drilling and tickling my G-spot, my stuff would be sopping wet, my juice dripping down his hand.

He'd lay on his back and ease me down on his dick, then hold one of my ass cheeks in each of his big old hands while he lifted me up and glided me back down on his short dick, stretching my pussy wide with its thickness.

"Saucy," he would pant, reaching up to grab my bouncing titties as I pressed my palm against my pubic bone and played with my swollen clit, rubbing my warm juices all over it. "Put that pussy on me, girl! Yeah. Lay down, baby. Put them titties on me too."

Me and Plat fucked like little devils. Lapping, rubbing, digging. Biting and squeezing sticky flesh, body parts pulsating with mad sensations. He couldn't get enough of me, and even though I preferred my pipers long, Plat was fat on the real, and I couldn't get enough of him either!

Ya know I had Plat feeling like a big willie. Whenever I came on the block he started acting all swole, slapping me all on my bouncy ass to let his boys know how hard he was knocking this out. All of those niggas was sprung on my looks, so of course my head got big. Plat was putting in work in all areas with his nice dick stroke and all the shit he bought me, but I was young and hot and it wasn't long before my eye started shifting.

I learned some street lessons when a cute guy from Lenox Avenue named Akbar caught my eye. He was a straight thief to the bone. Akbar taught me how to put on a girdle and boost from department stores, and how to slide a square's wallet from his back pocket when his guard was down. Akbar told me that men took one look at a hottie like me and lost all their common sense.

"Saucy, you got everything any man would want. You got the right face, the right body, and the right type of heat in your eyes too. You ain't gone find a nigga, a chink, or a honkie out here on these streets who don't wanna fuck you. You just gotta use that to your advantage and catch 'em with their dicks hard."

Akbar spent hours teaching me how to get next to a lame sucker and hustle him for his doe or yay without having to give up nothing but a fake smile and one or two little feels. He musta known what he was talking about because it worked damn near every time.

Well, almost every time. Right after my seventeenth birthday I was scheming at a jewelry counter in Macy's on Thirty-fourth Street, dazzling the young white clerk just like Akbar had taught me.

"Gee," he stammered as I tried on chain after gold chain. "They all look great on you."

I laughed inside. Damn right they did. I had on a real tight shirt that was cut so low my titties were bulging out like two round grapefruits. Like Akbar had said, the hand was quicker than the eye! This guy couldn't take his eyes off my cleavage and I had already unhooked one chain and let it slip down inside my shirt and was working on getting another one.

"Let me see that one over there." I pointed. "No." I shook my head as soon as he had it out the case. "I like that one over there better. No! Gimme that one too."

I had his head going and I knew it. He couldn't keep his eyes off my hard nipples and I could almost see the drool sliding out the corner of his mouth.

But whoever was in the back working the security cameras must have been on the job for real. After I smiled at the dumb white guy and told him thanks but no thanks, I started walking toward the door. Something told me to look back, and when I did I saw a wrinkle-faced white woman coming after me with a badge in her hand.

Shit had gone wrong, but Akbar had schooled me well. I ducked into a row filled with old lady dresses and without slowing my stride, pulled my shirt away from my body, letting the chains slip down the inside of my shirt and fall out on the carpet. I strolled quickly through the store crisscrossing through several departments before heading toward the exit again, and I wasn't surprised when I was stopped by two store detectives before I could make it outside.

"Excuse me, miss. Can you come with me, please?"

I wasn't above nutting up and causing a whole big scene in public, but I decided to chill. After all, I knew the rules. I didn't have a damn thing on me and no matter what they *thought* they saw, the bottom line was, they didn't have a damn thing on me either.

After that I decided to leave the boosting for the real

thieves. Akbar's game was small-time, and picking pockets and lifting shit from department stores wasn't no honorable profession for a bad bitch like me.

I was out one night popping my ass in an over-twenty-one club when I met Big Dip, and that's when I really started understanding what the street game was all about. Dip was a drug man who was down with connects in Philly, Baltimore, and Virginia, and that nigga took one look at me and decided we were gonna make each other large.

Dip taught me a whole lot about hustling. Working side by side, we started moving product and out-slicking some of the baddest niggas in New York. Beating them at their own gangsta game and walking away paid in full. Yeah, I was still a young thing, but hell. A city like this one never sleeps. New York, New York. You know what they say. If you can make it here, you can make it anywhere. But you gotta have a cutthroat mentality to come out on top on these ruthless streets. And the night Dip got popped I proved without a doubt that I was a cutthroat Harlem baby to the max.

There was no place I would rather be heading to on a Saturday night than deep into the night life of Harlem. Uncle Swag was working late and Aunt Ruthie was already sleeping. I'd snuck out of the apartment and past the doorman wearing my absolute best shit, and I knew I looked like a whole damn bankroll of dimes. I had on a short emerald-green low-rider DK skirt with a matching halter that dipped low in the front and had two horizontal straps in the back. My satin thong in the same color rested right below the two deep dimples above my ass, and had a row of diamonds running across the top. White gold with real diamonds hung from my ears and around my neck. Some eyeliner and just a little glossy lipstick passed for makeup 'cause my face was already hot. I had washed my hair and let it air dry into a cloud of curly ringlets, then rubbed some Pink Oil Moisturizer on my hands and tossed it around until it shined. Julie at the nail shop had tightened up my tips in emerald polish with diamond-chip swirls. My toenails had the same awesome design, and my long, sexy bowlegs was killing them.

Bouncing out the lobby with my hips on high sway, I waved at Frank, the night doorman, and he tipped his hat my way. I wasn't worried about him telling Uncle Swag a damn thing because me and Frank had an understanding. He understood not to open his fuckin' mouth about all my coming and going, and I understood not to open my mouth about all his coming. In the building's administration office. Late one night. All over my sixteen-year-old titties.

Dip was parked at the corner and waiting for me in his midnight-black Expedition with the chrome spinners.

"Get your fine Chinese ass up in here," he said, showing his pretty pearly teeth.

I laughed. "How many damn times I gotta tell you I'm not Chinese, stupid." I climbed up in the whip and crossed my legs, appreciating the way his eyes praised my curves.

"Yeah, baby. Whatever. Your eyes is chinky and your shit is tight every time I see you, girl. Chinese or Japanese, you a stunna for real."

Traffic was heavy as Dip drove up the West Side Highway with the windows open and the music blasting. We passed a flask of rum back and forth between us, and when we got into Harlem the streets were live like it was the middle of the afternoon. Dip parked outside a corner candy store and took me around the back and upstairs to a large loft where there was a party going in full swing.

"Go get me a drink," I told Dip, even though I was already high and half-drunk too. The air was thick with sticky green, blueberry, and Nestle smokes, all the smells mingling together as people chilled and got lifted.

"Yak," I yelled at Dip's back as he moved toward the bar. "Get me some Yak!"

The DJ was cutting up, playing a N.J.S. jam and the dance floor was rocking. I peeped all kinds of big-money rollers in the house, most of them chilling in booths and balling hard.

Dip took forever to get back with my drink and I smoked a vanilla honey dutchy while I was waiting for him. I had a feeling he was conducting some business, and when he came back the look in his eyes confirmed that he was holding some weight. I gulped down my drink and then Dip kissed me and took my hand and pushed his way out onto the packed dance area. My favorite club banger from the mixtape *Gag Order* was playing and I worked my hips and ass like I was starring in a video.

We next!
So line 'em up, nigga put ya titles up!
Can't do it quite like this, we get it in then
We wreck!
N.J. N.J. N.J.S.!
Slow it down for these niggas let 'em catch they breath!
Yes! It's R.A.W. still ducking them double U's, still puffin
    that wonderful,
Chill in the hood comfortable
Yep!
Next up to bat,
Give 'em the Gag Order 'cause you niggas never know
    who's next up to rat!
Runnin back homey, put it on rewind,
I know they mad 'cause they swag on decline
Pick a date, you get smashed on my free time,
Other than that, I'm in the lab on a deep grind
I'm a star, you been on the bench warming the wood up,
And when you slacked off and sat down, we stood up!
Yeah we up next so respect it nigga, we sending mixtapes
    back with rejection stickers!
Homey I'm bout to do my number, his shit whack, you
    wood, you move lumber,
I do this shit in my slumber!
We next!
So line 'em up, nigga put ya titles up!
Can't do it quite like this, we get it in then

We wreck!
N.J. N.J. N.J.S.!
Slow it down for these niggas let 'em catch they breath!

All my hard practice in front of the mirror musta been paying off 'cause I had niggas shook, ignoring their dance partners
and focusing totally on the way I worked my goods.

"You killing 'em, baby," Dip laughed as those other cats
stood around wishing they was him. "You straight killing 'em."

A few minutes later I damn near killed myself trying to get
off that dance floor, ducking behind Dip as I almost broke my
ankle trying to hide.

"My fuckin' uncle!" I yelled, grabbing the back of Dip's
jacket and hiding behind him. "My fuckin' uncle is up in
here!"

Dip laughed. "For real? Girl you high and trippin'."

Oh, I was high as fuck. But I wasn't trippin'. Uncle Swag
was working, but it wasn't up in no office like Aunt Ruthie
probably thought. He was chilling in the house dressed in
some fine rags himself. His tall frame, handsome face and big
smile was unmistakable, and so were the high-level drug dealers he was rolling with. They were sitting in a booth about
five-deep, and I recognized them from other Harlem clubs as
being some real dangerous big willies.

"You gotta get me outta here," I told Dip. "He thinks I'm
home in my damn bed sleeping."

Dip shrugged. "Then he's the one sleeping. You ain't no
little baby, girl. That nigga got some big ol' eyes, he should see
that."

"Just get me out of here, Dip. Let's find us another party.
For real. I'm serious."

He shrugged again and put his hands on my shoulders as he
walked behind me, blocking me from Uncle Swag's view. "Then
we out, baby. I'll take you to this other spot I know about. But I
gotta make a quick run first. You down for a little dirty ridin'?"

As soon as we got in the whip, Big Dip broke out some more
rum, a bag of chronic, and a little coke he had in a gold case.

"You ain't taking me nowhere to get knocked, are you?" I asked as we sped across the bridge getting blasted. I was high, excited, and nervous all at the same time. I wanted to know every damn thing. Who he was gonna meet, how much product he was carrying, how much cheese he was gonna break me off at the end of the night.

"What you so worried about? You don't trust a nigga? I ain't new to this action, baby. I grind these streets for mine eh'day. Just chill. I'ma hook you up real nice so you can get a couple pairs of them Giuseppes you said you wanted. Cool?"

That got my nose open even wider than the powder! I'd seen a pair of cherry-red Giuseppe shoes that would kill the Marc Jacobs dress I'd boosted, and if Dip was willing to buy me two pairs, then I was definitely down for this dirty ride. The only reason I was even a little bit worried was 'cause it was my first time actually making a run with product right in the whip with me. I had heard all kinds of stories about DEA agents jumping out of bushes and crawling from under tables with their guns cocked during a buy. I didn't want none of that. But I did want those damn cherry Giuseppe heels.

We came off the highway and drove down some regular streets with houses on them. We stopped at a traffic light and I saw Dip was steering the whip with one hand, and rubbing his dick up with the other one.

Caine always got him rock hard. The shit he had was high-quality and it had me feeling good too, so I didn't say shit when he pulled into a parking spot across from a deserted playground and told me to lean my seat back.

"I need a lil favor before we make this run," he said, reaching for my breasts. He flicked his fingers over my nipples, then leaned his whole head over until he was mouthing my tittie through my shirt. "I need you to open up them legs, baby."

I laughed and lifted my ass and slid my skirt up until my naked booty cheeks was touching the leather seats. Dip stuffed his hands all in my pussy before I even had a chance to get moist.

"Wait!" I told him, pulling on his digging fingers. "You

gotta work on this shit before you just run up in me with them dry-ass logs, boy."

He grinned, then licked his middle finger and worked it around my hole until I started getting hot. "Yeah," I moaned, squeezing his wrist so I could control his finger and keep it right where I wanted it. "Yeah . . ."

I was like a wet sponge inside. All he had to do was press the right spot and pussy liquor ran all outta me and onto the seat. Dip pulled his fingers out and sucked them almost dry.

"Yum . . . Know what your pussy tastes like?"

"What?" I laughed.

"Like some Big Blo bubble gum. Creamy, sweet, and delicious."

I told him he was crazy as he helped me climb in the back seat, then got out on his side and met me back there. We stretched out in the back with me leaning up against the far side door on my elbows and Dip getting him a comfortable spot on his knees. He pulled my thong to the side, then grabbed my left ankle and lifted my leg up, letting it hang over the seat. I braced my other foot against the console between the two front seats, and Dip went to work kissing my smooth thighs, making hot swirlies behind my knees and sucking my upper legs until I was moaning and gripping his ears.

He pushed his nose against my pussy and started sniffing real deep. Inhaling my insides hard enough to know what my breath smelled like. He ran his tongue all through my soft pussy hairs, pulling on them with his wet lips.

My breathing got deeper as he slid his hands under my ass, smacking his lips and inching his fingers closer and closer to my asshole. My foot jerked against the console and I reached down and pressed my mound real hard, then flicked my clit as he tongued it down.

"Move ya damn hand," Dip said, brushing my fingers aside with his chin. "I 'on't need no damn help with this pussy."

By now my stuff was so wet I coulda slid a whole truck up in there. Dip sniffed it real deep a few more times, getting off on my scent, then started licking my slit like it was a warm honey bun. I shivered as he flattened his tongue, licking my whole pussy, and letting it slip between my lips and partly into my hole before swirling it all over my throbbing clit.

My ass was quivering as I arched my back and Dip dug into my booty and moved me around. I was pushing his head down deeper into me, trying to slow myself down, but wanting to come so bad I was panting out loud. He was running his hands everywhere on me. Up to my breasts, squeezing my thighs, dipping in my navel, digging in my ass.

I hooked my left leg around Dip's head and fucked his face, shivering and moaning out loud as he slid his tongue deep up in me. It felt extra long and he was vibrating that shit, making cum run outta me as I ached for his hard dick.

And he gave it to me too. Dip came up off my pussy and grabbed hold of my ankles, sliding me roughly down the seat and making me bump my head on the door's armrest. When I was laying flat he fell on top of me and guided his dick inside my wetness, shuddering 'cause he wanted me so bad.

"I need it hard," I whispered into his neck. "Deep, baby. Don't play no games, nigga. Fuck me right."

He loved that shit. He got real guttural with his moans, growling all in the back of his throat as he pounded my pussy hard the way I liked it. I gripped his dick with my inside muscles and rode that shit out, digging my nails into the skin on his ass as he clenched his cheeks. Dip pulled my legs wider so he could get deeper in the pussy. My knees was spread wide and pushed up near my neck as he leaned forward on his thick arms and pounded me, then withdrew, pounded then withdrew. He rubbed the head of his dick all around my wet opening and I got hotter than I could stand. I grabbed his ass and pulled him back down into me, then screamed into his shoulder as I felt his dick spasm when he lost his nut. As soon as I felt that hot cum filling me up I came too, rotating my hips real hard and sucking his dick as deeply into me as it could go.

We was both stank and sweaty, so as soon as we were back in the front seat Dip turned on the air conditioner and passed me a pack of wet wipes outta his little console box. The moist little towels felt good and smelled good too, and I wiped my face, neck, titties, and coochie for days, using about ten of them.

"Next time you gotta wear a fuckin' hood," I told him as his warm cum flowed from me. I wiped myself again, then balled up the wipes and threw them out the window.

"Yeah," Dip said, pulling out into traffic again. "Next time, baby."

We passed the flask back and forth some more, and thirty minutes later we were parked outside an all-night diner in Queens. There was a lot of activity in the lot and Dip had pulled his ride into the last free space right up front. He looked all around, checking out the status in all his mirrors and stuff.

"What?" I asked.

"What?"

"No, what to you. What you looking all around for? Everything is cool, right?"

Dip frowned and kept his attention on a group of thug niggas standing around a fly Escalade on our left.

"Yeah," he finally said. "It's cool. Let's stroll."

Dip was a big nigga, and when I climbed outta that g-ride with him I loved the way all kinds of heads started turning. I was killing my tight green skirt so I knew the attention we was getting was more about me than it was about him. Dip put his hand in the small of my back and guided me up the few steps to get inside.

"Order whatever you want, Shawty," Dip said. "Just keep your mouth closed and when you see me fin'ta bounce, be ready to move with me."

The diner was about halfway full and it felt like a damn meat freezer inside. The air-conditioning was turned up so high I was hugging myself and rubbing my arms even before the waitress showed us to a booth right across from the main counter.

"How ya'll doing tonight," she said, smiling at Dip and nodding toward me. She was skinny and pretty and not too much older than me.

Dip looked real serious, but not nervous. I watched the way his eyes swept the whole place in a matter of seconds. I held my breath until he nodded at the waitress, then I slid into the booth, cursing under my breath when the cold plastic seat touched the back of my thighs.

"I'll be right back," Dip said, getting up almost as soon as he sat down.

I watched him walk down toward the end of the long counter, then go behind it and dap out one of the cooks before disappearing in the back.

Dip wasn't gone two seconds before one of the guys sitting in the next booth stepped to me.

"Whassup, baby. You hungry?"

He was cute as hell. Short, with pretty brown skin and nice braids in his hair. Pressed out in urban gear. Thugged down. *Real* cute. My head was nice and buzzed, but I didn't know nothing about Queens so I wasn't about to cross Dip.

"Nah," I said, smiling. "I'm with somebody. I'm waiting for him to come back."

He nodded but said, "Aiight then. But lemme know if whatever that nigga feed you don't get you full, you hear?"

I grinned real big and started to say something hot and freaky, but then the waitress was all up in my face, pushing a menu at me wanting to take my order.

"Um, I'ma just wait for my man to come back and see what he wants," I told her, pushing the menu away.

"No," she said, sliding it right back at me. "You gone order right now. He's having whatever you're having. Dig?"

Hell no, I didn't dig, but I ordered a cheeseburger deluxe and a Sprite anyway.

"Good," she said, smiling. "Your order will be right up."

I looked toward the kitchen for Dip, but he was nowhere in sight. My cell phone chimed with a Jeezy cut, and when I reached in my purse I saw Tai's number on the caller ID. I ignored it, waiting for Dip as I kept my eyes on the counter trying to see where he had gone.

All that rum and Yak I'd drunk made me have to pee. But I

was scared to move. What if I went to the bathroom and Dip came out and thought I was gone? That nigga might roll out and leave my ass way out in Queens and then how would I get back home?

I was still sitting there looking for Dip and rubbing my freezing arms and squeezing my legs together when the waitress came back with our food.

"Here you go," she said, setting the platters on the table. "You need some ketchup?"

I nodded, and as soon as she walked away Dip came back and slid across from me with a grin.

"Where was you?" I whispered, looking around. "You scared the shit outta me! I thought you left me!"

He looked calm and relaxed. "Leave you? Baby, please. A nigga would have to be outta his mind to do some crazy shit like that."

The waitress was back again, this time with the ketchup. She put it down in front of me, but as soon as I picked it up Dip slid her his whole plate.

"Yo lemme get a doggie bag," he said, picking up a fry and biting it. "She'll take hers to go too."

Minutes later I followed him out the door and down the steps to the row of cars parked out front. He was carrying a brown take-out bag in each hand and I was about to pee on myself for real.

"Wait," I said, shivering as he clicked open the SUV door. "I gotta pee, Dip. Real bad, and I can't hold it neither."

He glanced around, then got in and stuck the bags up under the middle console. Them niggas was still loitering a few cars down. My man Tommy Danger was blasting from their stereo and mad traffic was shooting past up and down the avenue.

"Just get in, Saucy. I'll take you up the block to McDonald's."

I shook my head and shuddered. Already I could feel the hot sting of pee trying to force its way from between my legs. "I ain't gonna make it," I said, then jetted back up the diner steps trying to keep my legs pressed together.

And I almost didn't. I got in that bathroom and barely got

my thong aside as I squatted and let go and pee splashed all over the toilet seat. I couldn't have been in there more than five minutes or so, and when I got back outside the parking lot was quiet, them niggas with the Escalade were gone, and Dip was still sitting in the driver's seat where I'd left him.

"Goddamn!" I said, opening the door to climb in. "I almost didn't ma—" My words froze in my mouth. Dip was looking at me and breathing real hard. His eyes were wide and desperate and both his hands were pressed against his throat.

Bright red blood was soaking his shirt and running down into his lap. Little red drops were on his lips, and some was even coming out his nose.

"Oh my God." I reached for him, then caught myself. I heard a siren in the distance and the street survival skills Dip himself had drilled into me kicked in hard. Dope. Cheese. Bullets. Cops. *Outtie.*

"I'll be right back, baby," I told him. I reached under the center console, my hand sweeping from side to side. Dip's eyes was begging me the whole time I was trying to find those take-out bags full of doe. When my hands came up empty, I cursed and backed away from the whip. Whoever had popped Dip had gotten what they came for. Damn. There went my riding bonus and those cherry-red Giuseppe shoes too.

"Just hold on, Dip," I lied dead in his face. "I'm coming right back, baby. I'm 'bout to go get you some help."

With one last look over my shoulder, I slammed the door shut and bounced.

Chapter 4

"Y<small>OU NEED TO</small> chill on all that drinking and getting high," Tai told me the next morning. "You ain't scared of doing all them crazy drugs? I mean, you got liquor fumes coming all out your pores, out your hair . . ."

I was laying in her bed exhausted and with sore feet. I stuck my head under a pillow and gave her the finger as she opened the curtains, sending sunlight streaking into the room.

"If your uncle coulda seen how fucked up and raggedy you was last night . . . your shit was wide open girl."

"I know," I mumbled, digging deeper into her bed. "That's why I called you instead of him, remember?"

I heard her sigh.

"I ain't gonna be stealing my momma's car in the middle of the night to come get you off the streets no more, Saucy. If my momma finds out you told me to steal her keys and take her ride, both of our asses gone be dead."

While I had to sneak out all the time, Tai's mother never checked up on her. She actually trusted her, and that really tickled me.

"She ain't gonna find out, Tai. Not unless you keep running your mouth all loud like you doing."

"You was lucky I finally decided to answer my phone. You didn't answer yours when I called you."

I rolled over and squinted at her. I'd walked what felt like thirty thousand blocks last night and my toes were killing me. "I already told you, Tai. We was in the diner when you called. Dip had disappeared in the back on me and I was busy looking out for him."

She got real quiet for a second, then said, "Did you see who shot him?"

I shook my head. "Nah. I told you I went to the bathroom because I had to pee real bad. He was already popped when I got back."

"But you said you caught a ride into Manhattan on a water truck. What did you do about Dip?"

I sat up and looked at Tai like she had a dick on her forehead.

"I left his ass right there!"

Her eyes got big. "Oh my God, Saucy. He probably died!"

I shrugged. He probably did. But what the hell was I supposed to do about that? Dip was the one who had turned me on to this game. He knew the runnings and the risks ten times better than I did. I was just glad I had to pee when I did. Otherwise, there might have been two dead bodies propped up in that Expedition last night.

Besides, I was the one who got stranded and left out there to find my own way home. No sooner than I'd slammed the door on Dip, that cute little man who had tried to holla at me in the diner came strolling down the steps.

"What's wrong, baby girl. What you do? Eat and run? I told you to get wit' me if ya man's bank was too short to get up in ya belly."

Him and his boy was climbing into a fresh cream-colored Caddy parked two cars over. I saw my opportunity and jumped on it.

"Yeah," I said sexily, strutting over to his car. "That nigga came up a little short. But his loss might be your gain."

He started his engine and grinned at me.

"That right?" He dismissed his boy with a hand gesture without taking his eyes off me. "Yo, Jamal. Climb in the back, man."

And then to me: "Yeah, baby. Toss that herb who brought a dime like you to some raggedy-ass diner. You wanna party with a winner tonight? I'm Wakim. Jump your fine ass on over in here with me."

Tai stood up and opened the window. The breeze coming in felt good and all I wanted to do was roll over and go back to sleep.

"But wait a damn minute," she said, turning toward me, her eyes suspicious. "You ain't tell me about no cream Caddy, Saucy. You mean you made me come get your ass when you was rolling around town in a Caddy? I thought you said the damn water man had kicked you outta his raggedy truck?"

"He did. But that was after I ditched Wakim at the house party."

Tai looked at me with her eyebrows up. She slid off her bathrobe and I closed my eyes when I saw all that meat hanging out the side of her Miss Piggy pajamas. There's some shit big girls like her just shouldn't wear, ya feel me?

"You bailed on Dip to go party with some niggas you didn't even know? Damn. You should have at least called an ambulance for him, Saucy. Called the cops. Called some damn body."

"Nah!" I sat up. "Who I shoulda called the cops on was that skinny Puerto Rican bastard who made me suck his dick for a ride across the bridge!"

Tai looked all shocked, but I was mad as hell.

I didn't know shit about Queens, and Wakim and Jamal had taken me deeper into I-don't-know-where-the-hell-I'm-at territory to this house party he said his man was throwing. The two-story house was rocking when we rolled up. People were hanging out all over the second-floor balcony and the music was loud as hell. Wakim took me inside and up to the second floor. He offered me some X, but I said no and smoked a blunt with his man instead.

The house was full of wall-to-wall niggas, and everybody was getting they heads buzzed. I drank and danced with Wakim, and even though I was a lot taller than him, I let him rub up on my ass as we leaned wit it and popped wit it too.

Wakim was really trying to put it on me when I felt my cellie vibrating on my waist and unclipped it. The caller ID said PRIVATE, but the music was so loud I couldn't hear a damn thing.

"Hold on!" I screamed into the phone. "I'm going outside! Don't hang up!"

I left Wakim dancing by himself and started toward the balcony. The door leading out there was packed with bodies so I ran down the stairs yelling, "Hello! Hello! Hello!" into my cell phone the whole time.

With my finger stuck in one ear and the phone pressed to the other, I walked out the house as about five niggas was walking in. I bumped dead into one of them and his body was so damn hard I yelled, "Ouch!" He stared down at me looking all mental, and I gave him the same look and then rolled my eyes as I walked off the porch and down to the curb.

"Hello?" I said into my phone. "Who this? Don't be playing no damn games on my phone. Who this?"

I heard static but I could see that the call was still connected, so I walked down a few cars and was just about to yell into the phone again when I heard the screams.

Niggas was wildin' on the balcony and chicks were screaming like crazy. I looked up and saw a couple of homeys climbing over the banister. About five of them jumped down and hit the grass running fast, and I knew what time it was.

That hard nigga I had just bumped into was now out on the balcony waving a gat, demanding dollars and jewelry, and threatening to pop the next fool who jumped over the railing. My heart damn near stopped. I dropped down and duck-walked my ass around the car I was leaning on. I stayed crouched down, breathing hard, until common sense told me to waddle my ass toward the next furthest car, and then the next one, and then the next one, until I was safely down the block.

When I finally stood up my knees were aching, my leg

muscles were burning and my heart was trying to come through my chest. I had to pee again, but I ignored that shit and started walking real fast. For what felt like miles. I passed a whole lot of houses that were shut down for the night. A few dogs barked, but otherwise the streets were quiet and the only sound I heard was my four-inch heels clacking on the concrete pavement.

I had just crossed a street when I saw the brake lights of a truck glowing from a driveway. I ran past three houses and flagged the driver down just as he was backing into the street. He rolled down his window and I flashed him a sad smile.

"Hey, mister. I need a favor. My girlfriend just dumped me to hang out with some guy she met, and now I don't have a ride home. Can you take me into Manhattan?"

He had looked at my legs and hips, then up into my face.

"Ain't you kinda young to be out by yourself this late, mami?"

I smiled. "Yeah. That's why I gotta get home. My daddy's gonna kick my ass if I miss my curfew."

He smiled back at me. "I understand. I got a daughter about your age myself. Get in. I'll give you a ride."

"Saucy!" Tai closed her mouth, then opened it again as she listened to my story. "You sucked the truck driver's dick? You told me the guy just offered you a ride!"

"Well, yeah, he told me to get in, but as soon as I did he tried to play me."

And it wasn't the dick-sucking part that had made me mad, neither. It was the fact that I didn't get all that was due to me out of it.

"Gas costs money," he'd said, putting his truck in park and opening his pants before I could even get my seat belt on.

I stared at him. He looked fatherly. Probably even older than Uncle Swag. I was young, but I wasn't dumb, and it had been a long, crazy night. Old men liked their dicks sucked too.

"How bad you wanna get back to Manhattan?"

I didn't give it another thought. I slid across the seat and put my head in his lap and went to work. *What the fuck.* I'd sucked plenty of dicks, and like he said, nothing in life came free.

But his ass had tried to yank me. I'd swallowed his muscle so good he'd started singing real loud in Spanish. But as soon as we left Queens and got over the bridge and into Manhattan, he pulled over and told me to get out.

"Okay, we're in Manhattan, baby. I'm about to make this U-turn. Out you go."

Of course I'd screamed on his ass and all that, but it didn't matter. He was behind the wheel, and that truck full of big water jugs wasn't moving an inch without his say-so.

If it wasn't for Tai I woulda had to walk home all the way from the Queensboro Bridge. I'd called her and she'd done me a favor by picking me up, so I guess she had the right to bitch and chastise me now. It was the price I had to pay for asking her to steal her mama's car. I sighed and put my head back under the pillow while she screamed on me about how crazy I was to be getting in trucks with strange men and giving them head just for transportation.

As far as I was concerned, listening to Tai talk her shit was no different than sucking that old man's dick. It showed me that life would always be a bitch, and there was no such thing as a free ride.

A few months later my whole world caved in.

Uncle Swag got knocked.

The feds came gunning for him while he was in a meeting at work, and pictures of him with his hands cuffed behind his back and being led out of his office were being flashed all over ABC, NBC, CBS, and CNN too.

Tai and I were cutting school when I found out. I was sitting with my head back in a sink at the Locks of Love hair and nail salon, and Tai had gone next door to buy her second platter of fried fish and chips. A nice Robb Hawk cut was playing over the speakers and I was loving the way my girl Carmiesha's fingers were working my scalp.

"Raise up," she said, gathering my wet curls up in a towel. I sat up and wiped my face with the facecloth she was handing me, and when I opened my eyes, the first thing I saw on the television hanging from the wall was Uncle Swag.

"Oh shit!" I jumped up from the chair. "Yo!" I waved my hand back and forth real quick. "Turn that music down for a second! Yo turn that fuckin' music down!"

By the time they turned down the music and found the remote for the television, I'd missed most of what the reporters had said. But the little bit I did catch scared the shit outta me. Uncle Swag was being arrested for signing off on illegal liquor licenses to unqualified bars and clubs. They were hitting him with tax evasion charges and accusing him of taking kickbacks too. My whole body was shaking when Tai walked back in the shop chewing a mouthful of fish and dropping gobs of tartar sauce all over her titties.

"What's wrong?" she said, noticing the panic in my face. I felt like I had just swallowed a huge rock and it was sitting on top of my bowels.

"I gotta get home," I said, drying my face and snatching up my purse and book bag. Tears forced themselves from my eyes and I had no way to hold them back. My uncle was my world and I loved him hard. "Something bad happened to Uncle Swag," I sniffed. "I gotta go home and see how to get him some help."

"Hey where you going with wet hair?" the blow-dry girl called as I ran past her and toward the door. I threw my hand in the air.

"Not now!" I hollered. I almost broke the damn door down getting out of there, and if Tai hadn't been light on her feet and right on my heels, that door would have swung back and knocked her ass out.

"I think she wanted you to pay her," she huffed, trying to keep up with me as I jetted down the block toward the subway.

I never even slowed my roll. Pay that trick no damn attention! The only thing I was focusing on right now was Uncle

Swag, and finding out what I had to do to help him get out this mess.

When I got inside the apartment I could barely see Aunt Ruthie sitting in a chair in the dark living room rocking Kaz's long-legged butt on her lap.

"Turn on the television!" I hollered, throwing my bag on the floor. "Uncle Swag got arrested. He's locked up!" The second I clicked on the light, I knew shit was much worse than I'd thought.

The crib had been tossed. Shit was all fucked up. I walked through the apartment with my mouth open, unable to believe my eyes. Every dresser drawer in the house had been emptied out. The mattresses were torn off the beds and the stuffing was falling out. Books from Uncle Swag's den were tossed all over the floor in the hallway, papers scattered everywhere. They had even dragged shit out of Aunt Ruthie's closet and swept her dresser clean, breaking bottles of expensive perfume and leaving glass all over the damn floor.

I almost broke down when I went into my room. That big old bed had been sliced down the middle and then all the way across, gutted like a deer. My satin sheets and blankets were all cut the hell up. My shoes and clothes were ripped and torn and in one big pile in the middle of the floor. My jewelry box was empty, and every diamond, pearl, and precious metal I'd owned was gone.

It looked like a tornado had gone through the apartment, tearing shit up from one end to the other. Debris crunched under my feet as I walked slowly back to the living room where Aunt Ruthie was still rocking her oversized baby.

"They had a warrant," she said, and shifted Kaz on her lap, and the way he looked at me I knew he wanted to get down. She let out a short, bitter laugh. "But Swag left a dirty trail leading straight to his own front door."

I bit my lip. "Well what do we do now? Are they gonna pay for all the shit they tore up? I know they don't think we gone live up in here like this! Did you hear from Uncle Swag? Do you have the number to his lawyer?"

Aunt Ruthie yawned and started patting her foot.

"I told Swag a long time ago to stop fooling around with them Haitians and signing all them fake documents. This is what you get when you climb in bed with drug dealers and low-down criminals. He knows I wouldn't go down to no jail-house even to see about my own mama, and if he has a lawyer I don't know nothing about it."

I stood in the middle of the demolished room staring at her. The chair she was sitting on was almost the only piece of furniture that wasn't broke up.

This chick didn't have no fight in her. I hated the way she had tucked her damn tail between her legs and given up. Uncle Swag was in jail, his picture all on the damn news, and all she could do was sit there rocking a fifty-pound pony and patting her damn foot. I could have yanked her off that chair and stomped her into the floor.

"Aunt Ruthie, we gotta do something. We can't just be sitting here looking stupid and waiting for something to happen. The first thing we gotta do is get Uncle Swag out."

She gave me a funky look, and opened her mouth, but then the doorbell rang and we both jumped. I threw Aunt Ruthie a funky look of my own before answering it. I looked through the peephole and when I saw Tollie standing out there I snatched the door open and almost fell into his arms with relief.

"Tollie! Damn I'm glad to see you. Uncle Swag got—"

Tollie pushed into the apartment and covered my mouth with his big ol' hand. He shook his head quickly, then let me go and put his finger to his lips. I caught on real fast, understanding his signal. I had never stopped to consider that the house might be wired, but if the feds had Uncle Swag boxed in then there was no telling how they had gotten their info.

We spent the next fifteen minutes passing notes. Tollie would write on a piece of paper and let me and Aunt Ruthie read it, and then we would write down whatever we wanted to say back and let him read it. Tollie knew a whole lot more than what the news had reported. Not only was they saying Uncle Swag had been playing both ends against the middle and hooking up Haitian felons and illegal immigrants with fake liquor licenses for their clubs, they also thought he was involved with the murder of a Bureau of Alcoholic Beverages employee who found out what Uncle Swag was up to and ended up floating dead in the East River. They'd waited a long time before making a move, laying in the cut until they got enough of what they needed to shut him down.

Aunt Ruthie wrote that four men in street clothes had come barging in like they wanted to knock the door down. They'd handed her a warrant and even gave her a chance to read it, then went to work tearing shit up. She said they confiscated every computer in the house, even the one Kaz used to play his video games on. They told her all of Uncle Swag's bank accounts had been seized so not to bother trying to use her debit or credit cards. They'd even found the safe Uncle Swag had had built into the wall in their private shower.

"Damn," I said out loud, shaking my head after reading all that.

Tollie just shrugged, like, "Hey, this is what these cats do."

By the time we finished "talking" I felt even worse. In my head I kept seeing that picture of Uncle Swag being rushed down the sidewalk on Park Place in handcuffs. I was proud of his ass though. He was a G for real. Wasn't no trying to hide under no jacket, or holding his head down in shame for my Uncle Swag. He walked outta that building and got into that car like those cats holding his arms was on his payroll and the detective driving the unmarked car was his damn chauffeur.

Tollie said they probably wasn't gonna give Uncle Swag no bail because of the murder charge. He told me and Aunt Ruthie to grab whatever clothes we had left and come with him. He was putting us in a hotel for the night.

"What about tomorrow?" I asked him after he checked us into a five-star hotel on the East Side. Any other time I would have been wildin' about staying in such a fly, high-class joint and ordering shit from room service that I couldn't even pronounce. But right now my whole life felt shaky. Without Uncle

Swag I was lost and ass out. All I wanted to do was go back to living the way I was used to.

"Don't worry," Tollie said. "I'll try to get in to see Swag tomorrow and we'll get this shit figured out." He reached into his pocket and pulled ten one-hundred-dollar bills off the top of his money clip. My eyes followed that green as he passed it to Aunt Ruthie.

"Call downstairs and get something for the kids to eat, Ruthie. Order them a movie too. I'll be back to check on y'all tomorrow."

Tollie kissed us both goodbye and left. Aunt Ruthie went over to the sofa where Kaz was coloring in a book they'd given him at the front desk. She sat down and pulled him into her lap. I took my shoes off and plopped down on the bed, then sat there with my eyes glued to the zipper on Aunt Ruthie's Manilio Argucci purse where she had just stuck all that doe.

Chapter 5

I DIDN'T EVEN act like I was going to school the next day.

I heard Aunt Ruthie getting Kaz up and dressed for school in the other room, and I laid in the bed thinking and staring at the ceiling until the door slammed and they were gone.

I wanted to call Tollie and see if he'd left to go see Uncle Swag already, but even if he had, it was still too early for him to have any news. I got up and took a shower, then got dressed and went in the outer room and chewed the two chicken nuggets Kaz had ordered then left on his plate the night before.

Aunt Ruthie had the grand that Tollie had given her last night, but I was almost broke. With only sixty-seven dollars, my platinum tennis bracelet, a diamond choker and a pair of diamond studs, and almost no clothes at all, I felt damn near naked.

I hung around the hotel room for hours waiting for Aunt Ruthie to get back. It shouldn't have taken her more than an hour and a half to get Kaz to his school across town and come back, but at noon I was still by myself and I started thinking the worst.

That bitch had left me.

I gave myself a hard mental kick. I knew I should have slid some of that money outta her damn purse, but her sanctified ass had practically slept with it between her skinny legs. She was probably glad Uncle Swag got knocked. A baller like him had to have some emergency chips stashed somewhere, and Aunt Ruthie probably planned on sticking him and getting rid of me at the same time.

I thought about my options and came up with a real short list. Aside from Dip and Plat, all the other niggas I'd fucked with were basically small-time hustlers. Kimichi was still living in Harlem, but she'd gotten kicked out of our old apartment, not that I wanted to be with her ass anyway. Every now and then I would run into her on the streets when I was hanging out. She was skinny as hell and looked a hot-ass mess.

"That's your mother?" Tai had asked me one night after we left the club and Kimichi ran across an avenue full of traffic and caught me going into a twenty-four-hour McDonald's.

I was too embarrassed to answer. Kimichi had on a pair of high-water men's plaid pants and a dirty muscle shirt. Her long legs looked ridiculous in those short-man pants, and she had black socks and platform sandals on her feet.

"Seung Cee!" she screamed over and over. She was so high she was weaving on her feet. "Oh!" She tried to wrap her bony arms around me. "I look for you, Seung Cee!"

She smiled and showed a mouth full of rotten teeth. She tried to hug me again and I jumped back and hid behind Tai.

"Girl!" Tai said, pushing me toward her, refusing to be the blocker. "Go 'head and talk to your moms, Saucy." She held her hand out to Kimichi. "How you doing? I'm Tai, Saucy's best friend."

I had looked over my shoulder for a month straight after that. Hoping Kimichi's scary-looking ass didn't roll up on me again. My moms was straight out there, but at least Tai was still high on my options list. I dialed her digits and her phone rang for a long time. Just when I thought it was gonna roll over to her voice mail, she picked up.

"Saucy! I'm in *class!*"

"Well dip your ass outta there then," I told her.

"Is your uncle still on lock?"

"Yeah. But I'm chillin' hard in a phat hotel, girl. Why don't you cut out and meet me over here? We can take a cab uptown and pick up some sticky, then come back and drink up all these little bottles of liquor they got in the bar."

"I have exams coming up, Saucy. So do you. I'm sorry about your uncle but you need to bring your ass to school. Shit. They gone take my damn phone. I gotta go." Click.

Fuckin' Tai! I was down and almost out, but I was a fighter and there was no surrender in me. I tossed my cell phone on the bed and was sitting there trying to figure out my next move when Tollie showed up.

"Hey," he said, kissing my cheek as I let him in. "Where's Ruthie?"

I shrugged and strode across the floor in my cutoff shorts that barely covered my ass. "I don't know. I think she cut out on me. She went to take Kaz to school this morning and never came back. Shit, it's almost checkout time so she probably dipped."

"Calm down, Saucy," he said, but I noticed that the "it's all good" look he'd had on his face yesterday was gone.

"Look," he said, leaning his elbow on a small table. "I saw Swag this morning and shit is bad. It's worse than any of us thought."

"What?" I said, my fear getting me hyped. "Whatever go down you and his boys is gone look out for him though, right? Y'all gone get the bail money together and get him out, ain't you?"

Tollie reached into his jacket pocket and pulled out a blue rectangular bag. It was one of those soft plastic things you put bank deposits in.

"There ain't no bail, Saucy. Ain't no money either. Not even to pay his lawyers. Everything he had was in that fuckin' safe they busted into, even though them dirty fuckers only officially reported about a third of what Swag told me was in there."

He dropped the blue bag on the counter.

"Hold on to this. Give it to your aunt when she gets back. It's enough in there for her to take y'all back to Harlem and find an apartment until some of them niggas who owe your uncle money start paying their debts."

Oh I knew better than that!

"And who the fuck is gonna make them pay, Tollie? What are we supposed to do? Go to the police if they decide they wanna stiff him? Stiff us?"

Tollie shook his head. "It's fucked up, Saucy. But that was your uncle's downfall, baby. He was overconfident. Sloppy. He didn't stack his shit properly for the rainy days. That emergency stash shoulda never been kept in his house. But he thought he was flying under the radar. Thought he was too smooth to get caught. He's gonna try to cut some kinda deal soon, he said. Let's hope it works."

He shrugged, then pushed the blue bag toward me.

"Take this, Saucy. Tell Ruthie to make it last as long as she can. I gotta roll down to Atlanta, but I'll be checking on y'all and I'll make sure you get a little bit more bank soon."

When Tollie left he took my hope with him. Uncle Swag was being held in a federal prison and you had to be eighteen to visit him. I opened the bag Tollie had left then sat at the table and counted the thick stack of bills inside. Ten thousand dollars wasn't a whole lot of money but it was a good start. It took me about five minutes to decide what to do with it. Harlem was a moving town. Shit changed hands every few minutes and if I could hook up with Plat and move some weight, I could flip that ten and make it forty or fifty in just a couple of days.

I stuck the money down in the bottom of my Dooney & Bourke purse and grabbed my cell. Downstairs I asked the doorman to hail me a taxi. I had just climbed into the back of the yellow cab and was giving him an address in Harlem when I saw Aunt Ruthie walking up to the front of the hotel. I didn't understand what Uncle Swag had ever seen in that run-down bitch. She didn't have half the fight in her whole body that I had in one strand of my damn hair. I was a survivor and she was already sunk. Her whole fuckin' life was over and you could tell just by looking at her.

I shifted my purse on my lap, feeling the weight of the money inside.

Fuck Aunt Ruthie, I thought as the cab pulled away from the curb and into the Midtown traffic. Let that bitch call her sister or go out and fend for herself. Kaz was cute. She'd find somebody to feel sorry for him and give them somewhere to stay. As for me? I was still wearing clothes that had played out two days ago. Harlem was calling me loud and clear, but first I was taking my black ass shopping.

In three days I was back down to nothing.

Well, almost nothing. I went to Michael Kors on Madison Avenue and caught a dope sale. They had a red Indian-collared, crocheted shirtdress in there that fit me like a mutha! It was sleeveless with just a thin satin lining, and it stopped right under the hump of my ass. I saw the perfect Vachetta Mazatlan shoes to match it too, and walked out of there with several get-ups that set me back more than a G.

I took a taxi over to Nordstrom in New Jersey and found the cutest ruby earrings ever, and ya know the bracelet to match it ended up in my purchases too. I bought some jeans at Burberry, two cute bags at Gucci, and some new boots at Neiman Marcus that I planned to save for the wintertime, when it got cold. You know I had to get me a powder-blue leather jacket and some powder-blue Timbs to match, and a bunch of other stuff to replace all the fly gear them feds had ripped to shreds when they tossed our apartment.

I wasn't just focused on self, though. Back in New York I went in Macy's to get some thongs, and saw a diamond choker in a markdown case that just screamed Tai's name. It wasn't my style, but it was perfect for her. I shopped my ass off and didn't feel bad for spending almost half of Tollie's money neither. Shit, I'd been traumatized as fuck by Uncle Swag getting knocked, and shopping helped relax me and make me feel better about myself.

But then I got down on a flip deal with Plat and that nigga

did me wrong. He claimed he got beat by a connect and the whole thing went bad. I felt stupid as hell. Instead of turning Tollie's money over, Plat had turned me over. And fucked me in the ass while he had me in the right position.

"Damn, Saucy," Tai said. It was almost eleven at night and I was sitting in her kitchen watching her fry some bacon and make blueberry pancakes. "How's he just gonna do you like that? That shit is messed up. I thought that nigga Plat was cool?"

I groaned and pushed my hair back, then twisted it up into a roll. "I thought he was cool too. But that nigga was jerking me from the gate, girl. He's still swole because I crossed him out for Akbar. That's what's real."

"Yeah," Tai agreed. She opened the refrigerator and looked inside. "I'ma scramble me some eggs. Want some?"

I shook my head. Tai's mother had been walking back and forth. In the kitchen, out the kitchen, past the kitchen. I knew her nosy ass was probably sucking up every word we said.

"So did you ever catch up with him to try and get your money back? What's he saying about that?" Tai asked.

I sighed. "He ain't saying shit because I can't call him. He must be hiding underground somewhere because I can never find him when I'm in Harlem. His number is in my cell phone, but that shit got cut off. Either Aunt Ruthie stopped my service, or maybe nobody paid the bill."

Tai scrambled her eggs and spread a slice of American cheese on top and let it melt. Then she squirted a gob of ketchup on top of the cheese and poured almost half a bottle of syrup over her pancakes.

"So where you stayin'?" she asked and chewed hard on a piece of slab bacon. Her mother walked past the kitchen again and I waited until I heard her house shoes going down the hall.

"I was gonna ask you to see if your moms'll let me chill here for a minute."

I saw the look on Tai's face. I hadn't stayed more than two nights in a row at her house ever since that night she had poked a hole in her uterus tryna give herself an abortion when we was fourteen. Somehow Mrs. Watkins got it in her head that the baby and the hysterectomy Tai ended up getting was my damn fault. How?!? I didn't get Tai pregnant and tell her to wait so long to get rid of it! I didn't unbend the coat hanger and shove it up her pussy! All I did was sneak her the gin so she could get drunk first!

"Just for a minute, Tai. Maybe a week or two until I can get on my feet."

Tai stuffed some pancakes in her mouth. "I already know what she's gone say. But I'll ask her."

My stomach felt shaky as I watched Tai grease her plate. I felt like a beggar again. Like that dirty raggedy Saucy nobody gave a damn about. Like that nasty little girl who was so grimy you had to scrub her down before she could come in your house because she might fuck up your child's sheets.

When Tai finished eating she stood up and put her plate in the sink. "C'mon, Sauce. Lemme ask her before she goes to bed."

But her moms was standing right there as soon as we stepped out of the kitchen. Before Tai could say a word, her mother beat her to it.

"It's late, Tai. It's time for your company to leave. Goodnight, Saucy. Tai, lock the door behind Saucy and make sure you put the chain on it."

"Ma," Tai said as her mother turned to walk away. "Ma, I was gone ask you—"

"I *said*, lock my damn door, Tairene. And chain it too. *Goodnight*, Saucy."

Tai gave me a helpless look and walked me to the door with my bags. As I stepped out of the apartment I heard her get smart with her mother. "Ma! You know her uncle got in trouble. She can't go back home!"

Her mother answered her just as the door was closing.

"Oh, she ain't gotta go home, baby. She just gotta get the hell up outta here!"

Chapter 6

I**T TOOK A** lot for me to keep myself together as I waited for the elevator to come. Any other time I would have been riding upstairs to my own damn apartment and crawling into my big-ass bed to crash. Instead, I pressed the down button and when I got to the lobby I looked around for Frank. He was standing outside the building dressed in his navy blue uniform with the shiny gold buttons. His stomach was triplet-sized, and the toes of his pointy shoes was curled up in the air. I left my bags by the door and stepped outside and got ready for what I was about to do.

"Whassup, Frank?"

He turned and looked at me and a smile spread across his face that reminded me of that syrup running over Tai's pancakes.

"Little Miss Saucy! How's everything, darling? You doing well in school? You're such a smart girl. I bet you're making all A's, aren't you?"

He made me sick with that "friendly doorman" shit he pulled with all the tenants. I hated the way he pretended to kiss everybody's ass and grin all over himself like a happy-ass slave. And he could cut all that how I'm doing in school bullshit. This motherfucker had rubbed his little tiny balls all over my nipples and shot his load on my neck. What did he care about how I was doing in school?

But I needed him.

"I'm doing good, Frank. Look, you working all night to-night, right?"

"Surely, surely! Why? Are you going out for awhile? I'll be right here waiting to open the door for you when you get back."

I shook my head real quick.

"Nah, I'm not hanging tonight." I gave him the sad face. "My uncle is in some trouble, you know. My aunt got sick and went upstate to stay with her sister. I'm locked out. I was gone ask you if I could, uhm, stay at your place for a minute. You know. Since you don't be there at night anyway."

His fat little tongue slid across his lips.

"Er—I don't know, Saucy, I mean, I'm sorry your people are having troubles and you don't have anywhere to stay, but you're kind of young. I could get in a lot of trouble, you know. Maybe even lose my job if anybody found out I let a tenant's child stay in my apartment."

I wasn't too young when he was titty-fucking the hell outta me, but he had forgotten that small point. "Look, Frank. No-body has to know. Just give me your address and your key, and I'll catch a cab. I'll be waiting there when you get off work in the morning and I'll give you the best damn breakfast you've ever had."

I could read his nasty thoughts in his eyes. I knew damn well his little dick was sticking straight up underneath all that stomach too.

He looked around nervously, then peered into the building to make sure nobody was coming out.

"Okay," he said, digging into his pants pocket. "Get your bags. Breakfast sounds real good. You can skip the eggs and the toast, though. I'm a meat man. I like mine soft, brown, and warm."

I stayed with Frank for a few weeks. I stayed high outta my mind for a few weeks too. He paid my cell phone bill and kept a roof over my head. We actually got us a little routine going. I gave him "breakfast" every morning, and he put some money in my pocket every night. He lived in East Harlem and every night when he left to go to work, I was out the door right behind him.

"You be a good girl while daddy's gone," he would call out before he left. Just hearing that shit made me mad. Frank was a sick motherfucker and I had to get my head tore down before I could even let him touch me.

"You have beautiful breasts," he told me one morning as I held on to both of his man-titties to keep myself from being thrown off of him. My head was spinning. I was on top of his great big stomach, riding his little tiny dick. That was the only way I could really fuck him because his dick barely reached the gushy when he tried to get on top.

"Just hurry up," I muttered as he gripped my ass and moved me back and forth on him. He was laying on the living room floor enjoying his "breakfast." I had just killed a case of beer before he came in, and I was dizzy as fuck. His stomach felt like a waterbed. It was covered in stretch marks, and it was jiggling and sloshing all over the place. I honest to God did not know if his dick was inside me or not. I couldn't feel a thing down there. The only thing I felt was sick, and even though I tried, I couldn't help it when that beer came rushing up outta me and splashing all over him.

"Saucy!" he yelled as I gagged some more, then rolled off him and hit the floor. "What's wrong?" He sniffed the air. "Have you been drinking, young lady?"

I almost laughed at the sternness in his voice and the concerned look on his face. He musta thought he was my father for real. One of those fathers who have no problem fucking their own daughters.

Three nights later I was partying with this down-south baller. I'd met him in Saks Fifth Avenue and he whipped out his green and paid for the Prada dress I had been thinking about boosting. His name was Dante and he was a newly signed artist who had come to New York to shoot his first music video.

I told him my name was Saucy, and his silly tail sang to me all the way to the cash register.

> Some mistake me for a pimp cuz I walk with a limp, so good yeah!
> And some mistake me for a gangsta and they be saying I'm too damn hood, man . . .
> But I'm just your average hustler, yep from up around the way
> With that dirty-dirty down south flavah like Cajun steak!
>
> I like Prada . . . On my fine, sexy women . . .
> I like Cristal, gold bottles let's keep it poppin till we get finished!

By the time old boy was finished paying for my Prada dress and told me I could go back and pick out a bag and some shoes to match, I was singing right along with him.

"Yeah you like Prada . . . on ya fine, sexy women!"

He started laughing. "They call you Saucy, huh? Well let's do us a down-south remix, then! *I like hot sauce . . . on my fried fish and chicken!*"

He was funny as hell and sexy too! I told Dante my dream was to break into the video scene and asked him if he had any connections to help me get in the door.

"Girl, you so damn fine niggas would pay good money to have you in they production. If I hadn't already paid for all my video hoes you woulda definitely had the top spot. Next time I hear about something opening up, I'll put you on."

Dante wanted to party, so we hit a few clubs and we drank and smoked until we was both sweating and feeling good.

"Yo, Shawty. Why'ont we go to your crib and hit some skin?" he suggested. He told me he was staying at his boy's crib and he said the cat's wife was real religious. After dealing with Frank's soft fat ass, I was all over old boy. He was young, fine, and best of all, hard as hell. I'd already put my hand in his lap and felt what he was carrying, and his country-ass was a true piper.

We got to the crib and hit some lines, then I danced for

him while he took off my clothes. We were tearing Frank's
sheets up when I heard the door slam and some keys hit the
table.

"Sweetie, I'm home!!!" Frank yelled from the living room
and I panicked like a mother.

"Get up!" I tried to push Dante off me. "Get the fuck up!
Frank is here!"

Dante held my waist and thrust deeply down into me as
hard as hell. He had the cum face on, and his dick was jerking
when I pushed him off me. He collapsed on the bed next to me
just as Frank walked in the room.

All three of us was breathing hard.

I jumped up and grabbed the sheet and put it over me,
ready to fight Frank's ass if I had to. I figured he would go for
me first since I was the one who had brought some stray nigga
home to his bed, and I was hoping Dante would be able to pull
his big ass off me before he killed me.

But Frank surprised the hell out of me. Instead of jumping bad or trying to kill us both, he stood there in the doorway . . . and cried. The perverted motherfucker cried! Fucked
my head up!

Big, fat tears rolled down his jiggly cheeks. His eyes were
full of pain and disappointment, like my betrayal had cut him
in his heart.

"Saucy. You have to leave my house, Saucy. Please. Leave."

My mouth was wide open as he turned and walked out the
room. I had expected some kind of fight. A knife. Some fists
swinging. Shit flying through the air. But the tears? Never! I
heard the front door open and slam, then I looked at Dante.

He reached between his legs and squeezed his wet dick then
grinned. "Your daddy's a good-ass man, girl. If you was my
daughter I'da fucked your fine ass up."

I slapped him on his hard stomach. "Shut the hell up. That
is *not* my father. Where the hell am I gonna go now?"

Dante rolled over and stood up. He peeled the soggy condom off his long black dick and dropped it on the floor. "Well,
ya can't come home with me. Maybe you can find a hotel room

or something. But first lemme introduce you to my man. His name is Greco. He pulls a hellacious grind down at a club called the G-Spot."

I was seventeen and a half and I had just landed my first job.

I'd heard a lot of good things about the G-Spot, but the cover charge was high and I'd never been inside. The minute I got in there I loved it. Everything about it was live and exciting and I knew I could make enough bank to get me an apartment and get on my feet.

I was never one to click with a lot of females anyway, but I figured out real quick that I needed to keep my distance from some of the crazy-ass chicks up in the Spot.

"I don't have no dance gigs open right now," Greco told me. "Give it a couple of weeks, though. These bitches in here be illing so much that somebody'll be getting tossed in a minute."

Two days later I had a prime spot. One of their top dancers, Money-Making Monique, was cool enough to give me a hookup, and I worked that stage with her and her girl Honey Dew like I was born for it. I had a prime body and it turned me on to show it off. I liked the way I moved on the stage, and got a thrill out of what I could do to the men in the audience. It didn't matter what kind of man it was. Old, young. Married, single. If he was in the Spot when I got on the stage, I left him with a rock in his pants.

It was wild! And I was having a ball. The hours were good, the cash was great. I got to sleep all day and party until the sun came up. I started working the back rooms regularly too, and it wasn't long before they started calling me Brainiac due to all that good neck action I was laying down. I can't tell you how many cats told me that hands down, out of every other bitch they'd ever been with in life, they'd never had their top done the way I put it on them.

One of my most famous clients, and the one who had the biggest, sweetest dick, was the NBA rapper Thug-A-Licious. For real! I was actually with him the night before he got took down, and if I had known it was his last night on earth I woulda put that neck pussy on him ten times harder!

But it was right about this time that the worst damn thing in the world happened too. It caught me by surprise and rocked my world so hard I didn't know if I would ever get back up.

I was coming outta my cheap little hotel room when I stopped dead in my shoes. Aunt Ruthie was standing in the lobby talking to the desk clerk. Didn't nobody but winos and hoes live up in here, and she looked so outta place in her long frilly grandma dress that for a second I was struck dumb. What the fuck was she doing here?

I was just about to turn around and run back up the stairs when she looked up and saw me. We stared at each other for a moment, and all the old shit between us was in both of our eyes.

I took my time walking toward her, bouncing my steps like everything in my world was grand. Her hair was longer but she still looked old, tired, and drug out, like somebody had wiped the damn sidewalk up with her.

"Whassup, Aunt Ruthie? Did Uncle Swag get his deal?"

She looked at my skimpy clothes, ass and titties busting out everywhere, and shook her head. "No. He got dead, Saucy. Dead. The streets caught up with him and choked his ass dead."

Dead? My knees wobbled and I fell against the wall. Dead?

"Don't lie like that," I moaned, tears falling from my eyes. "Bitch you ain't never liked me! But you ain't gotta lie like that!"

"He's gone," Aunt Ruthie said quietly. She reached for me and held on to me as I howled. "They got him in the shower, Tollie said. Came up behind him and strangled him with a towel. He's gone, Saucy."

I cried from the bottom of my soul. All I could see was my Uncle Swag. My hero, my *spirit* daddy, the only man who had ever loved me from the heart and not the body.

Dead.

I broke loose from Aunt Ruthie and slid down the wall. I

fell on my knees trying to catch my breath, then stretched out on that nasty floor and wailed like somebody was ripping my heart outta my chest.

"I know you loved him," Aunt Ruthie kept saying over and over again, and as bad as I was hurting I could tell she meant it. "I know how much you loved him, child."

I went through the next few days in a coma. I smoked and drank until I couldn't see shit, let alone feel it. Aunt Ruthie came back to my room two days later and gave me the address to the funeral home. There wasn't gonna be no wake. She was having a viewing and the service all at once, to get it done and over with.

We buried Uncle Swag on a rainy Tuesday morning.

Tollie paid for the services, and his little fat wife came out with him too. Tai showed up for me, and her mother sent a sympathy card with no damn money in it. The funeral parlor was packed. Full of shady niggas who had called themselves down with my uncle, but the minute he got knocked they had turned their backs on his family.

I walked around glaring at them niggas. "Look at little Saucy!" they was saying left and right. Well little Saucy had grown the hell up. I gave all them fake niggas my worst fuckin' attitude. Half of them was frontin' like they was grieving for my uncle, while they were really busy sneaking a look at my hips and ass.

I boiled on high throughout the whole damn funeral. It was a crying shame to me that a G as big, jolly, and powerful as my uncle had come down to this. Cold, silent, and stretched out in a cheap-ass suit in front of a bunch of no-good posers. They kept telling me and Aunt Ruthie they was gonna find out who it was that had Uncle Swag murked and take care of that shit. Why the fuck hadn't they taken care of shit by getting him a high-level lawyer and getting him outta the joint? I didn't believe nothing them niggas said, and I walked around that funeral home ready to curse everybody the fuck out. I was so mad that I blocked out my pain. I couldn't hardly look at Uncle Swag's body looking stressed and stiff in that cheap wooden box. Kaz just sat there looking at the floor, so I guess he couldn't stand to look neither.

"Saucy." A guy named Yan pulled me to the side. "Don't even worry about this shit, ya know? Them motherfuckers that got him? They gone get handled properly."

I shook him off and walked up front to sit with Tai and Aunt Ruthie. Kaz had his head on her shoulder but at least he wasn't sitting in her lap no more. Aunt Ruthie put her hand over mine, and for the first time ever there was love for me in her eyes.

"Saucy, me and Kaz are going back upstate tomorrow," she said quietly. "I'll be staying at my sister's house because I'm leaving this damn city for good."

I had nothing to say. I loved this city, the good and the bad. Shit. Not only didn't I have anywhere else to go, there was no other place I wanted to be.

I kept Uncle Swag deep in my heart, and swore all out I'd never love nobody the way I loved him. His murder didn't slow me down though. If anything I was getting wilder than ever, and having a good-ass time in the process.

I'd been working at the Spot for a few months and I was in high demand. I'd met me a real dumb customer, some old head who was in the navy. He lived in Brooklyn with his wife and kids, but liked to party up in Harlem. He moved me out of that raggedy hotel I'd been staying in and rented me a small apartment so I could be available to him on the weekends or whenever he could lie and tell his wife he was on duty. He wasn't all that in the sheets and his breath stank like hell, but I tolerated him because he was getting ready to go back out to sea.

With nobody but Kimichi left in my family, I was living my life in my own way, and that's about the time I met Sincere.

Me and Tai hadn't hung out much since Uncle Swag's funeral. Her moms was still shitty and didn't want me in her crib too much, and I hadn't answered most of Tai's calls because she usually called when I was doing something she would get on my case about. But even when I did call her every now and then just to get up with her, she acted all mad. I had missed her high school graduation and she was still holding that shit against me.

"You could have shown up for me, Saucy," she complained.

I looked at the phone like it was crazy instead of her. I had been smart in school and got good grades when I wanted to, but I had missed so many classes that I didn't have enough credits to graduate so I was gonna have to do another six months. What in the hell made Tai think I was gone show up at a graduation if I wasn't part of the damn program?

"I had to work, Tai," I lied. "You know I'm killing them down at the G-Spot now. I ain't stripping or fucking or nothing. Just working in the coatroom and sometimes at the bar."

"Uhm, yeah," Tai said, and I could tell she didn't believe me. "I started film school, you know. And I'm working at a production studio. They're letting me intern as an event producer and I get to meet all kinds of high-profile artists. It's really cool and I'm learning a lot."

I got hot. Tai knew damn well that I had always wanted to be in the entertainment industry and in front of the camera! If anybody should have been rubbing asses with the stars it should have been me. I couldn't even imagine an artist taking Tai's big ass seriously. She wasn't no eye candy. She didn't have the body, the hair, or the ass appeal. She damn sure wasn't me.

"That's great, Tai," I said dryly. "But I gotta go."

"Wait! I wanna see you, girl. I'll try to swing by during my lunch break tomorrow. We can grab something to eat. I'll buy. 'Kay?"

The next afternoon we were sitting in a pizza shop on 125th Street and Tai was trying to hook me up with some guy she said was her new friend.

"You know how I do, Tai." I picked at my crust. "I meet new niggas every night. I ain't looking for no relationship or no Big Daddy who wants to fall in love and have a house full of kids and all that shit. I'm cool working at the G-Spot. I do what I do, and that's how I roll."

"But you ain't got your own apartment yet either. What's gonna happen when that navy guy goes back out to sea?"

"He paid the rent up for a minute. I'll figure out something else after that."

"It still won't hurt you to at least holla at this guy. He's got connections, girl. I met him at a party his brother invited me to, and the minute he hit the door I could tell he was the shit. People was almost bowing down to him. He's a big willie, Sauce. Just the type you like. He saw your picture on my key chain and said he wanted to check you out."

As it turned out, Tai had picked me a winner. Sincere swung by the G-Spot the next night and caught my set. He bought a magnum of champagne and paid for two hours of my time, and we went in one of the back rooms and sat up talking, drinking, and hitting lines the whole time.

Sincere told me he was a hustler from L.A. who was hooked up with some Haitians and owned a string of liquor stores in New York. They also had a nice drug game going, and had a crew of dirty riders who moved product from Miami to Virginia to New York. Sincere was in charge of distribution in several cities, and was a shot caller who chilled at the top of the food chain. He worked in G's territory, but G got a nice piece of the action so they were cool.

By the time the sun came up the next morning I knew what my next move was gonna be. I jumped right on the bandwagon when Sincere told me what he wanted me to do.

"Check this out, baby. Go 'head out there and tell that big nigga with the two-way that you ain't working for him no more. I'll square shit up with G. Don't worry. It won't be a problem."

Sincere had an apartment in East Harlem. We moved my shit out of that sailor's crib and into his that same day. I lived large as hell up in that joint. I decorated it to fit my personality and everything I put up in there was quality, for real. Sincere was free with his cheese and believed in keeping his woman looking good. He replenished my wardrobe and it was five times phatter than it had been when Uncle Swag was alive. I was living large. Sitting at the top of the world. I shopped my ass off in some of the same stores I used to boost in. Only difference was, now I had a pocketbook full of cash and could buy just about any damn thing I wanted.

But nothing good lasts forever. Six months after I moved in with Sincere he got caught up in some shit. One of the Haitians he worked with got knocked and started snitching. He had some immigration issues and was trying to keep from getting deported, so he gave up a couple of names to save his own ass.

Sincere got snatched off the streets but he wasn't no herb and he'd covered most of his tracks. The only thing they could hang on his head was some bullshit charge for associating with known felons, and for that, they took back his parole.

He got sent to Woodburne Correctional Facility up in Sullivan County for a year. But even the law couldn't keep a good gangsta down. The only thing that really changed in his game was that instead of calling shots from the crib, he was now calling them from the pen.

Sincere told me he was gonna take care of me, locked down or not, and I believed him. Drugs were flowing in prison almost as easy as they flowed on the streets. The guards were shiesty and greedy, and as long as they got paid off they turned a blind eye to what was happening right under their noses.

I made mad visits upstate to see my boo, carrying his "babies" inside my pussy and passing them to him with the silent permission of the guards. Sincere commanded the same respect in the bing as he did on the block, and his money was never short. When I first met him he had told me he was a businessman and I half-ass believed him. But after seeing how he handled his business behind the walls, I knew what he said to be true.

"Always keep your business associates on a string, Saucy," he told me. "Don't never let no niggas think they can do their dirt without you. Make sure you're a key piece of the puzzle, and that without you they ain't got shit."

I watched Sincere do exactly that for ten whole months of his sentence, and I would have rode with him till the end of it for real. But I ran into Akbar downtown one day. I hadn't seen him since right after Uncle Swag got killed, and he was looking clean as shit. We ended up getting some Henny and going out to eat. He told me he'd gotten tagged with a larceny charge for stealing from an electronics store, and they'd sent him upstate to Woodburne for a good minute.

"Get the fuck outta here!" I told him. "I didn't know you was up there! My man Sincere is doing a bid in Woodburne. I ride up there to see him on the regular."

"Sincere?" Akbar looked at me like I was a real fool. "Light-skinned nigga? Built? Got that real slick hair? Down with them Haitians who own all them liquor stores?"

"Yeah." I nodded all proud. "That's my boo."

"Saucy." He sighed, shaking his head like what I said was incredible. "You mean you fuckin' with that grimy nigga after what he did?"

I looked at him like, what?

"You for real? You 'on't know?"

He glanced around, then leaned in close to me. "That's the fool who got your uncle murked. Your boy ordered it up because them Haitians wanted it done. You know most of them motherfuckers snuck over here on a boat anyway. They ain't got no papers. How you think they was getting licenses for all them liquor stores?" Akbar shook his head and took a few swallows of his Yak. "Your uncle was hooking them up, Saucy. When he got knocked and tried to make that deal, they got nervous. They slumped him. Shut his ass down. That's some hard body truth."

Everything in me went cold. An image of Uncle Swag in the shower naked and with a towel twisted around his neck flashed through my mind and I almost fell over.

"Damn," I finally managed to say. I wiped the tears from my eyes and finished the Yak in my cup and then picked up Akbar's cup and killed that too. Pain was running up and down my arms and legs. Sitting in my bowels and making them loose.

The knowledge that I'd been sucking the dick of my uncle's killer was devastating. Despite all the shit I'd been through in my life, all the grimy predators like King, and the Mr. Warrens and the dirty nasty Jacks-in-the-box, nothing, I mean nothing, had ever hurt me so bad.

"That's some good shit to know, man. Thanks for putting me on."

I stayed there with Akbar for a little while longer, but the whole time he was talking I was zoning. I didn't hear shit he said. My mind was in a dark tunnel and I was steady thinking. Planning. Scheming. My boo Sincere was due for a re-supply visit soon, and I was gonna make damn sure it was his last one.

Chapter 7

I TOOK MY last Prison Gap ride on a hot-ass night in September. My game was so tight that I played it just like I had played every other visit over the last ten months. The bus was nasty as hell and rabbits and chickenheads started swinging on each other while I was waiting in line at a rest-stop store. I laughed inside at these bitches and all their man drama. How they loved these cats so much got right past me. The only man I had ever loved was my Uncle Swag, and that's the reason I was riding next to these funky bitches—so I could get inside that joint and do what I had to do.

I almost laughed as I sat there watching Sincere's grimy ass choking off all that dope like he had a dick down his throat. He knew exactly what time it was when I put my hands around my mouth and whispered, *"Swag Robinson,"* to him right before he clocked out for good. Yeah, he'd murked my fam, but I'd laid this ill na-na on his ass and now he was straight outta the game! Fuck Sincere! I didn't care how much he had done for me. My loyalty was to Uncle Swag! The rent on Sincere's apartment was paid for the next month and a half, but I wasn't crazy enough to go back there. I had done them Haitians a favor so I knew they wasn't mad at me, but still. Ya never know. Besides, I had sold every damn thing I could sell outta there before making that last trip upstate, and I used the money to move back into a shitty little hotel so I could keep right on doing my thing.

But a few months later some more drama jumped off that pushed my life in another direction. Some madness went down at the G-Spot. Juicy got caught fuckin' that fine nigga Gino, and Jimmy went bonkers and G ended up getting popped. The cops shut the club down and everybody who had worked there was suddenly ass-out and unemployed in the middle of an ice-cold winter.

Tai was the first one to tell me about it and she sounded happy as hell when she called me on my cell. "Did you hear what happened at your job?"

Damn! Now I was gonna have to find a way to pay for my hotel room. The place was a real dump, but I wasn't there much. I didn't have no money saved because I had to dress and get my high on too. My whole life revolved around getting high and working the clubs all night, then stumbling back to the room to sleep, shower, and get up and hit the streets all over again. I opened my mouth to answer Tai, but she was on a mission.

"Your boss got shot! By that crazy guy Jimmy who be with Flex and them over in Taft. They closing the G-Spot down, so that means you're gonna need a new job."

Tai was a trip. She didn't like me working at the G-Spot anyway, so I wasn't surprised that she was so happy to see it go down. I didn't give a damn about G. That old nigga was scary. Bitches meant absolutely nothing to him. But I liked the job, and most of all I liked the power that lived in my pussy.

"I don't know why you sound so damn happy about that, Tai. Some of us ain't got no mommy we can live up under. I gotta pay the rent on my room next week, and since don't nobody do nothing for me, I got bucks to earn."

"Well that's why I'm calling your stank ass! I met this guy at my job who's a casting director. They're having an audition near the South Street Seaport. D. Man is shooting a video for his new single and they're looking for some principal models. The audition is closed, but my friend said he can get you in."

My ears perked up.

"Principals? They're the ones in the spotlight the most. More spotlight means more money, right? When's the audition?"

I scribbled down the address and Tai's friend's name, then got my ass up. This was my big chance to shine and I knew I had to blow the spot up. I started looking through my gear, trying to find something bomb. I was gonna throw myself together something lovely. It didn't matter how many other hoes showed up, I was claiming the top spot like it was already mine.

I took a taxi down to the casting spot. It was being held in a small hotel that looked like hell on the outside, but was actually clean and inviting on the inside. It was snowing like crazy and cold as hell too. But the moment I walked in the door my ass was on fire. The hall was packed with girls lined up on either side. I sashayed down the middle in slow motion. All eyes were on me as I stripped out of the floor-length mink coat Sincere had bought me, sliding it off my toned arms then slinging it over my shoulder as my white Chanel shorts and sleeveless belly shirt emphasized the hue of my sexy brown skin.

I was slaying them other bitches. Shining like a star. My heels clicked on the floor and I checked them out from the corner of my eye as I strode past. No. No. No. No. No. No. No. No. *Hell* no. None of them birds were holding it like I was. There wasn't a bit of competition in the house.

It was more of the same thing when I stepped in the auditioning room. They put the cameras on me for a test shot and I started cutting the hell up. Dazzling the producers. Stunning the rappers. They'd never seen nothing as sexy as me. I was hot and exotic. My Asian eyes merged with the lens on the camera and held them captive. I bonded with that videotape. I swirled my hips, then turned around and let them see that black woman's blessing I was holding in the back. I heard breaths being sucked in as I gyrated down low, my fly thong peeking out. I gave them sexy combined with just the right amount of slutty. I let my tongue play slip-slide on my open lips, and could almost see those dicks getting hard. I sucked my stomach in and showed off my tight little waist and my nice thick hump of lady lumps, and I swear to God I heard a moan and at least five niggas in that room shot off in their drawers.

"Whew!" the casting director said when I was finally through. The production manager, who was also Tai's friend, took a handkerchief out of his pocket and mopped his forehead. The guy holding the big camera put that shit down and turned his back on us to do an adjustment, and the brother on the small camera, who was gay but still in the closet, gave me a nasty look 'cause his ass was jealous.

"Thanks for coming in," the casting director said, reaching for my hand. I shook it and my expression never changed when he squeezed my fingers twice before letting go. "We'll, uhm, be calling the finalists shortly, okay? Listen for your call."

When I walked out the room eyes was stabbing me like knives from all directions.

"Jealous hoes," I said with a big cocky smile. After the hurting I'd just put down in there, the rest of those bitches could just pack it up and take it home.

I left the hotel walking on a cloud. I had twelve funky dollars in my purse but I felt confident and lifted. I saw the ice on the ground, but damn if I could feel the cold. I leaned against the building watching the traffic go by and replaying my sexy routine in my head. I had a blunt in my purse and I had just lit it and took two long pulls when my cell phone rang. The number on the caller ID was one I'd never seen before, but I answered it anyway.

"Hello?"

"Saucy?"

"Yeah?"

"This is Mackie P. You blew that audition up, baby. We want you to come back."

"Then why'd y'all let me leave?"

He laughed. "You saucy all right. But my bad. You're right.

You're probably on your way home, huh? I should've asked you to stay while you were here. Can you come back for another shoot?"

My broke ass giggled. "What's the magic word?"

"Please. Can you come back please?"

"I guess. But it's gonna take me a minute."

"I'll wait. We'll all wait. Just come back."

I clipped my roach and stuck it back in my purse, then turned around and walked back into the hotel. Sixty seconds later I had swept past all those still-waiting bitches and was standing in front of Mackie P. with my hand on my hip.

"Damn, girl. That was fast."

"I told you," I said, taking the hand he was holding out to me, "it was gonna take me a minute."

I knocked all them other chicks out the box. I got the lead in D. Man's hot new video, and I made that chick he had with him in his first video, *Lil' Baby*, look like a child for real. Just for future security, I broke Mackie P. off with some neck action that had that nigga stuttering, and he hooked me up with private advance auditions with some of the hottest artists on the come-up scene. In a matter of weeks I went from stripping and hoeing in the G-Spot to getting casting requests out the ass.

They couldn't stop telling me how much magic I produced in front of the cameras. In the music industry sex is what sold, and I was carrying a hot exotic package that got mega attention everywhere I went. I loved being on the set too. The hours were long, but the attention was energizing. Set workers catered to me, bringing me water and snacks and making sure I was straight at all times. The atmosphere was one big party. Piff, X, boat, all that shit was passed around freely and I smoked and popped as much of it as I could.

I watched some of the more aggressive extras trying their best to get my kind of play. If they had asked me I woulda told them they were going about things all wrong. How the hell they thought somebody was gonna notice them standing in the middle of the pack, I don't know. Even when I went to an open call, I got my ass out there and made myself stand out. Eroticism was my middle name and I worked hard to be a big success.

I would hear some of them other girls complaining that they didn't wanna take off their tops. They didn't wanna wear the hot little ho clothes. *Shitttt.* I would walk up there with nothing but a stick-on tattoo covering my nipples and leave absolutely no doubt about what I was selling. I learned real quick that I needed to set myself up in some shot caller's cross-hairs. You couldn't get shit in this business if you wasn't in the middle of the playing field.

Let a producer or director tell me to put my pussy on a rapper's arm. I smiled into the camera and wet that arm up. Somebody needed a beautiful girl for an uncut video? I was there. I was relentless. I made connections and networked from my knees. By early spring I was drinking more than ever, but I'd also landed a lead role in one of the hottest urban videos on the air.

Right about this time I started traveling a lot too. I was hitting casting calls in Atlanta and Miami like crazy, and walking out with top spots each time. Those cities were hot! Dirty, raggedy Saucy was flying on airplanes for the first time in her life! I got a blast out of hopping on chartered jets and traveling to different cities between shoots. I was also drinking and drugging and having as much sex as I could, and my name started getting around. I'd pop a triple stack of X, and within minutes my sex drive was off the damn radar. I was known to give the absolute best head on the urban scene and the name "Brainiac" was being whispered by men on sets, in party clubs, and in country clubs too. I didn't fuck with no testers, though. I left all that for the jump-offs who didn't know what they were doing. Nah, Saucy went straight for the stars, and because I was smart and knew how to keep my mouth closed, I got some damn good referrals.

I was at a gentlemen's club in Atlanta one night when some-body tapped me on the shoulder. I turned around to see one of the most popular music moguls in the country, and it shocked me that he was out partying with the regulars, and even more that he had approached me directly instead of sending a tester over to feel me out.

"I think I know you," he said, smiling. His right eye had a little winking twitch to it that I could tell he was trying to control.

I nodded, star struck. "I think I know you too. You look a lot like Marshall George." Oh, this nigga was extra large! I'd seen him in New York pushing a four-hundred-grand azure-blue Mercedes Maybach 62 with a cream-on-cream leather interior.

He laughed. "Yeah. I get that a lot. I don't see it though. That fella ain't half as smooth as me."

We both laughed at that one. Marshall bought a magnum of champagne and I followed him into a private VIP room. He didn't dance, but he said he would like to watch me dance.

"That's if you're cool with dancing for me, you know?"

Cool with it? I was sippin' Krug with the man who had launched hundreds of successful music careers and produced some of the top black movies and comedy shows of the damn decade. If he wanted me to hop on one leg, suck my big toe, and oink like a pig, that woulda been cool too.

But I played it easy. As big as he was in the industry, he wasn't a ruffneck. He was a gentleman and yeah, I knew he was married. His wife was beautiful too, but she didn't have the right kind of body. Her shape was long and slim, but she had a flat ass and no hips. I had heard they was going through some changes, but Marshall was all about his image and you couldn't tell that shit when you saw them out together in public.

I danced for him and made sure he got a good look at the type of curves he was missing at home. He sat there watching me with a big smile of appreciation on his face, and when he called his driver over and told him to get the car ready, it was already understood that I was leaving with him. I followed him out the club feeling like a princess. All them other bitches he could have gotten with and a willie like him chose me? It was almost unbelievable.

He took me out to Buckhead, to what had to be the most expensive hotel in the whole damn state. The suite was huge and of course it was full of high-priced quality shit, and the service was top-shelf all the way as the whole staff went outta their way to accommodate the great Mr. Marshall George.

We sat in a hot bubbling Jacuzzi for a little while, then got out and drank some more chilled champagne. When it was time to get to the good part I was glad to see that Marshall had a dick that hung halfway down to his damn knees! The problem was, that's all it did was hang. I slobbed it down, working that thing like it was the last dick on earth, and the most I could get that snake to do was stretch out a little and yawn. He tried to stuff it up in me, but it was too soft to go inside, even after I sucked his balls and jerked it at the same time.

"Go lower," Marshall urged, pushing my head down.

"Lower where?" I wanted to fuckin' know! I already had a mouthful of hairy balls, where else did this soft-dick nigga want me to go?

"I've got some toys," Marshall panted. "You into toys, baby?"

I laughed inside and thought about my G-Spot days. "I'm into any damn thing you want, boo. This your ass tonight. Do it like you wanna do it!"

Well what did I say that for! Marshall jumped out the bed and ran in the other room where his bag was, and when he came back he had some toys all right.

"This one is my favorite," he said, all excited over what he was holding in his hand.

Saucy was a professional with her shit. I didn't blink, gasp, quiver, nothing.

When I told him this ass was his to do what he wanted with, I meant it. I'd seen toys like this before, and even though I preferred a real dick when I went down that block, I knew what time it was. So I turned over on my stomach and raised myself up a little on my knees. With a big grin on my face, I spread my booty cheeks real wide for him and told him to get busy.

But Marshall corrected me real quick. He didn't wanna

slide his little green butt plug up in *my* ass. Matter of fact, he didn't wanna share that shit with me at all!

No fuckin' sweat, I thought, as I turned back over again. And ten minutes later I had to give it to the man. Once Marshall got his asshole stuffed the way he liked it, I started slobbing his dick down again and that thing got nice and hard and stood straight up in the air. It was thick too, and pretty, with a real fat head on it.

And Marshall wasn't no joke neither. We both got filled up. With his little toy still rammed up his ass, he flipped me over and fucked the hell outta me, drilling that big dick as deep inside me as I could take it. I was hollering and begging him for more, and trying to push away from all that dick at the same time.

Marshall pulled his pole outta me and got a rubber outta his little toy bag. He slid that shit on, then slowly inched himself back up in me until his nuts was almost in me too.

It felt like his dick was jerking around inside of me. Like he was fucking me from the inside out using the muscle in his pole to hit my spot. Marshall leaned over and caught one of my nipples in his mouth, and tongued it. I moved my body underneath him as I fucked up at him, my ass sweaty and my hair stuck to my face.

"Get it," Marshall hollered, straddling my body with his legs. He had me pinned to the bed as he held my arms over my head and grinded into me until my clit started throbbing triple time and I let go, cumming real hard. Marshall nutted too, filling up the glove before falling on top of me, crashed out.

"Ahh," he slobbered all over me. "Girl you oughta get paid for this shit. I swear you got your sex game on lock."

After that I started getting invitations to key parties like I was a celebrity. Marshall was a shot caller who had mad influence in the industry, and everybody wanted to please him. If Marshall said you was in there, then your ass was really in there, and judging by all the invites I was collecting I learned that real fast. I'd be mingling in Diddy's crib one night, and dancing at a party hosted by Jay-Z the next. I was photographed with all of the hottest people and my pictures were popping up in urban magazines like *Sister 2 Sister* and *Vibe* and *The Source*. "Brainiac" became a label I wore with pride and I was damn proud of myself too.

I guess I was smoking Marshall's blunt and drilling his hole so good that he decided I should be rewarded for it. First he leased me a Sebring convertible, then he presented me with the keys to a phat apartment off Central Park and told me to make myself comfortable for as long as I wanted.

"I know you're young and free, Saucy, and I ain't trying to block you from doing your thing. All I ask is that you reserve one day a week for me only, and that you don't bring no other niggas up in my joint."

I was nodding so fast and reaching for them keys at the same time that I probably looked like a greedy little kid eyeing a bag full of candy. The apartment was his personal little fuck den, and while I knew he'd probably had a lot of other tricks living there before me, in my mind none of them counted. I was chilling in that bad boy now and getting into the kind of life I had craved, and that's all that mattered.

Of course not everything I got myself into was good for me. The next time I hit Atlanta I almost got arrested. I had met the singer Chaperone through his cousin, and got invited to a five-star hotel to party with him. When I got to Chaperone's suite his entourage was thick and there were a few local honeys in there keeping them occupied. Alcohol was everywhere, and the room was filled with the smell of crippi and sour diesel.

Somebody passed me a L as I came through the door, and I was taken into one of the back rooms where Chaperone was waiting.

"Hey sexy," he greeted me with a warm hug. We'd only met once before, at a party for The Game, but we'd talked a lot and promised to hook up the next time we were hanging out in the same city.

I took off my jacket and saw the look in his eyes as he checked out my Apple Bottom jeans and candy-apple corset top. My bright red thong was peeking out from the mounds of my ass, and he couldn't take his eyes off me as I pranced around the room checking shit out.

He was laying back on the bed chilling, and when he puffed up a pillow next to him I took off my shoes and cuddled up by his side. We smoked two blunts and talked and laughed as we got lifted.

"You hungry?" he asked when the blunts were gone. I wasn't hungry. I was high. Music was booming in the next room and I started winding my body on the bed, horizontally dancing to the beat.

"Nah. But I'm thirsty though."

Chaperone got up and went to the bar. He fixed us both an Incredible Hulk and I sucked about five of the green drinks down like they was water.

He took my last glass and set it down on the end table next to his and stood over me. I smiled up at him as his fingers touched the front of my corset. He slipped his index finger between my squeezed-together breasts, then rubbed them both with his whole hand. I moaned as he zipped the corset down and my titties bounced out, free. They were incredibly firm. Big and light brown, with perfect dark brown nipples.

"You got it, baby," he whispered, and clicked off the lamp. I heard his zipper come down and I reached for his dick and held it in my hand. It was warm and smooth. Not too thick, and not too thin. But definitely workable.

He rolled me over on my back, and I felt glass against my lips. He held his drink to my mouth as I gulped it down, little dribbles of it trickling down my chin, which he hungrily licked off.

We were on our sides, facing each other and fucking in a nice slow groove when I felt weight settling on the bed behind me. I tried to turn around, but Chaperone clutched me closer to him and pushed himself into me even harder.

"Got damn!" the guy behind me whispered as he pressed against my naked ass. I got the fuck off on getting served by two men at one time, so I reached behind me and felt for his stiffness, then slowly jerked it in my hand.

The three of us rocked like that for a minute. Chaperone was tonguing me while his boy held my leg up in the air and pressed his dick against my wet pussy that was already filled up with an even bigger dick. That shit felt good too. Chaperone was deep-fucking me while his boy stroked me from the back, rubbing his dick on my outer lips and sliding it up and down my ass crack.

I was moaning and grinding as Chaperone took over holding my leg up. He eased his dick out until just the head was in me, then took it all the way out and rubbed it on my clit as his boy slid into me from behind.

I was in heaven. Chap was jerking his dick on my clit and old boy was squeezing my ass and ramming me like a pro. I came hard, wetting us all up and both of them kept right on going trying to get me there again. We switched positions, throwing the spread off the bed and getting right on the sheets. I sucked one dick while I rode another one. I got a tittie fuck and a pussy fuck at the same time.

I don't know exactly when shit changed, but it did. All of a sudden I wasn't the center of attention no more. Them cats was rubbing their dicks together like they were mini-swords. They pushed me to the outer edge of the bed, and old boy got behind me and slid his dick up in me. I craned my neck back and saw that Chaperone had got behind him, and I guess he slid his dick up in him too!

Kay. I was drunk, yeah. Buzzed and lifted too. But stupid? Hail naw!

I jumped outta that bed like it was on fire.

"What the fuck!?!" I clicked on the light. I started screaming my head off and throwing shit around the room. "What the fuck?!?!"

"W-w-wait! Wait! Wait!" Chaperone jumped up and tried to shush me.

"Y'all niggas gay! Y'all niggas gay! Y'all niggas gay!"

Oh I was loud as hell. Chaperone tried to grab me and I swung on his ass. Our naked bodies felt nasty pressed up on each other now, and I coulda sworn I smelled shit coming off his dick. He held my wrists and I head-butted that nigga and tried to knee his swinging balls.

Old boy was the smart one. He let Chaperone tussle with me while he pulled on his pants. By the time his boys bust in the room he was the only one dressed.

"These niggas is gay!" I screamed, pointing at Chaperone. His boys was trying to shut my naked ass up, but the chicks in the joint was looking at the big star and wrinkling up their faces saying ewww!

One of Chap's crew tried to grab my arm. I backhanded his ass and lunged for my clothes. At first they acted like they wasn't gone let me out the room, but all the girls started beefing and bitching saying get the fuck offa her! and the next thing I knew, I was out.

Out, but not down. I ran down the hall banging on doors as I put on my shit. I bitched and screamed like somebody was trying to kill me. "Chaperone is gay! That motherfuckin' Chaperone is gay!"

Security was waiting for me when I got off the elevator. They took me in a small office and threatened to call the cops and have them charge me with public intoxication and disturbing the peace.

"Y'all go 'head," I slurred. "Call them motherfuckers and tell 'em I'm drunk. 'Cause soon as they get here I'ma tell 'em y'all let that gay-ass singer Chaperone push drugs and rape women up there in your suites. Yeah, call the motherfuckin' cops! I'll call them bitches for ya!"

They escorted my ass off the premises and I caught a taxi back to my hotel and fell in the bed and slept my high off. When I got up the next morning I thought I'd dreamt the whole thing. But hell no. I got a huge delivery of flowers from that asshole and a check for two thousand. Hush money. It was real and it had happened, and I was willing to bet I wasn't the first chick Chaperone had tried to flip in his ménage à trois. I didn't give a damn about him being gay. For all I cared, them patty-cake, fruit-loop niggas coulda drilled each other all night long, just as long as they left me out of it.

Chapter 8

A FEW MONTHS later I was partying in Miami when I got a call from Mackie P. He wanted me to do a feature shoot for *KING* magazine. "You really getting yourself noticed, baby girl! My man at *KING* is getting mad requests for you. We got a print feature worked out for you, and my man's photographer wants to shoot you during the Urban Music Awards show. On the beach. In Antigua!"

"For real? Stop fuckin' lying!"

"It's real baby. Plus, we hooked up a video shoot for you at the same time. All of this is promotion for Hawk and Reem's new jawn, *Birthday Cake*. If you ain't got a passport you need to hurry up and get one."

I'd already done cover spots for *XXL* and *Black Men*, but *KING* was in my crosshairs and I wanted to do that shoot real bad. But not only did I not have a passport, I didn't even have a birth certificate. Aunt Ruthie had never given me a copy of it, and after Uncle Swag got killed I didn't wanna ask her for shit. When I got back to my crib I called Tai and told her about the photo and video shoot.

"You can get a birth certificate real easy, Saucy. You have a Social Security card, right? All you need to do is go down to Worth Street, or apply for one online."

I found out that Tai was right and that it would be a simple enough process, but the day I got it and was actually holding it in my hands, my spirits sank down lower than they'd been in a long time. Here I was commanding crazy attention and hooking rich, powerful men like a mutha, and still it wasn't enough. I was dressing in the sexiest clothes, and getting high and doing more fly shit than I had ever dreamed of doing. I was meeting more hot people than I ever thought possible. But none of that shit mattered as I stood there reading that piece of paper over and over again trying to figure out exactly who the hell I was. "Date: November 5, 1987 Time: 12:49 AM Status: Single Live Birth. Sex: Female. Name: Saucy Sarita Robinson. Mother's Maiden Name: Kimichi Min Ju, age 24. Father's Name: David Maurice Robinson, age 32."

Nothing there meant shit to me. Neither one of the strangers who had gotten together to create me had stuck with me long enough to make a difference in my life, but still. For the first time since my cousin Paris died and I sat in that school nurse's office and told her and Mrs. Gladman that King was licking on my pussy every night, I actually wanted to see my mother.

I had just finished getting my nails done at a salon in Harlem that next Saturday when I walked outside and saw Akbar. He had just gotten out of jail again and he was looking good.

"Man, you gotta stay your ass up outta them cells, boo," I told him, kissing him on the cheek. He just laughed.

"Saucy, you a pretty sight for these sore eyes, baby. I seen you in all them videos too. You doing real good for yourself."

"I'm trying," I said.

We sat in his car and drank a couple of Coronas and Akbar offered me some boat.

"Nah," I said, pushing it away. "The last time I fucked with angel dust something told me to go swimming in the Hudson River. And a bitch can't even swim. I can't fuck with that."

Akbar was rolling in his brother's bonnie, and on an impulse I asked him to take me down on 109th Street.

"Who you know over here?" he asked. I had him creeping slow as I peered in doorways and down alleys.

"Somebody," I said, my eyes searching for a skinny, pale-looking female with long black hair. We drove around for a good fifteen minutes before I spotted her. She was coming out of a liquor store with a brown paper bag in her hand.

"Slow down!" I told Akbar. He followed my gaze to Kim-ichi, but he didn't say nothing. We crept along beside her for a full block before I made a move. I waited until she had crossed the street and was heading for a corner store, then I called her name.

"Kimichi!"

She turned around, and when I saw her from the front I was stunned. She looked diseased. Like something rotten was eating through her body and chewing the flesh off of her.

"Seung Cee?"

She took a few steps toward the car and I swear to God I started to tell Akbar to step on the gas and jet down the block. I should have.

"Seung Cee? My baby? Is this you?"

I remembered hating the way she confused her tenses and messed up her words. I had been so embarrassed by her when I was a kid. I was still embarrassed by her now. She stumbled over to the car and I saw the bottle of cheap wine she was clutching in her hand.

"Seung Cee! Whrere you have been? Whry you not come to me?"

"Hi, Ma," I said, staring at her shoes. They were a pair of men's Stacy Adams. Black. Wingtips.

"Let me see you!" She reached in the car and pulled on my arm. "I wrant to see my baby! I wrant to see my Seung Cee!"

I got out the car and stood there in front of her looking like a million bucks. Her clothes were just a bunch of moldy rags. She tried to hug me and she stank like pee-pee and a rancid pussy. People passed by coming and going, some of them walking a wide path around her.

"You look wrich, Seung Cee. Are you wrich?"

I shook my head, embarrassed to even be seen talking to her. "I ain't rich, Ma. I'm just living."

"Me too," she said. She twisted the cap off her Wild Irish Rose and gulped from the bottle. "I on 130th Street now. I sick, Saucy. I need to see dock-tor. You take me, yes?"

She wanted to go across town and Akbar agreed to take her even though I knew he probably didn't want her stinking up his brother's sweet ride. She made me climb in the back seat with her, and I held my breath as she held my hand.

"Seung Cee," she smiled as the car sped down the streets. Her teeth were brown and looked soft and gooey. I could tell she was back on the needle and that pissed me off. The needle was what had started all this in the first damn place. She was the one who had given me my very first hit of poison, and I felt like I'd been getting high ever since.

"Seung Cee, you father is bewry pwoud of you."

I didn't answer her. I was too busy holding my breath.

"Wrait!" she demanded. We'd gone a few blocks, but we were nowhere near across town. "Tell he stop!"

Akbar pulled over to the curb and both of us looked at her.

"Here," she said, passing me her bottle. "I wrant to pee."

I couldn't believe what the hell I was hearing. She opened the car door and staggered over to the curb. I felt sick when she pulled her raggedy pants down and squatted, her nasty white ass-crack showing.

I reached over and let her bottle hang out the window in my hand. I turned that shit over and let the wine flow into the street. Then I put the bottle between my legs and tapped Akbar on his shoulder and nodded.

"Let's move, baby."

Akbar nodded back, and stepped on the gas. I closed the car door as we pulled off, and we left my mother right there where she was. Squatting in the gutter, her piss running in the street with her wine.

Seeing Kimichi did something to me. I made Akbar drive me to a liquor store a couple of blocks away and proceeded to get lit. I got high for days, cooking yay and smoking Ls until my

throat felt burnt. Drinking and busting up in parties, shut-
ting them shits down. I started mad fights, and one day I
passed out on the set after staying up all night drinking until
I couldn't see. Niggas laughed at me, but somebody was cool
enough to drag me into an office and let me sleep it off. Yeah,
I missed out on the pay, but missing the glory of it bothered
me even more.

A few weeks later I went to Hudson Street and applied for
an expedited passport. The record label was paying to fly me to
Antigua of course, but I had blown a big hunk of cheddar on
clothes and jewelry for the trip.

"And don't be sneaking no weed out the country," Tai said.
She had come over to Marshall's apartment and was baking a
chocolate cake while I packed.

"Shut up," I said. "And come sit on this damn suitcase so I
can close it."

"I'm serious, Saucy. We all like to get our buzz on, but I
hear you been doing triple damage lately."

I moved out the way as she plopped her ass down on top of
my suitcase and I swear to God I heard that poor bag groan.

"Where you hear that from? I'm a grown-ass woman. Who
been all up in my damn business and clocking my shit?"

"Calm your ass down," Tai said. She reached between her
big thighs and zipped my suitcase, her fat fingers looking like
sausages as she tucked in the items that were bulging from the
sides. "Ain't nobody trying to get all up in your business. But
if you worried about it then maybe you need to stop putting it
out in the streets so thick."

"What the hell are you talking about, Tai?"

"People are talking about you, Saucy! All the drinking and
party-crashing. How about all that trouble you started with
Chaperone in Hotlanta? You think grimy news don't travel
from Georgia to New York?"

"Tai that's old! Plus them two niggas was fuckin! I ain't
lying. They was bumping each other off with me right there in
the bed."

I could tell she didn't believe me when she rolled her eyes.

She stood up and waddled her ass back toward the kitchen without another word.

"Your shoes are turned over, you know," I said coldly.

She stopped in the doorway. "What?"

"Your damn shoes. Them shits is bent. One is leaning east and the other is leaning west."

She looked down at her feet. They looked swollen and puffed out the top of her shoes.

"That's some nice shit for you to say, Saucy. But don't try to change the subject from you to me. My feet don't have a damn thing to do with you showing your ass and nutting up on people all the time. You think you can say any damn thing you want to and there won't never be no backlash. That's a lie, though. Real life don't work that way."

I smirked and started pushing my lipstick and eyeliner down in my carry-on bag. "Whatever, Tai. You ain't gotta tell me how real life works. I'm out here working this grind on a daily. If I don't really work for it, fuck for it, or suck for it, I don't get it. And *that* ain't no lie."

We landed on the island of Antigua and hit the runway at top speed. I'd started drinking as soon as we were in the air and the four hours it took us to get to Puerto Rico seemed to go by in thirty minutes. The second flight to Antigua was a whole lot shorter, and we drank the whole time we were on that one too. I was traveling with a group of chicks who were backing me up as extras, but everybody on the plane knew that not only was I the principal video girl, but I was also starring in the companion print feature so I was top shit and I acted like it too.

Our hotel was right on the beach, and all the arrangements had been made by the video production manager. Even though he had put me in the same suite as the extras I didn't care. I had my eye on a rapper named Grillz, who wasn't part of the set, but had come along just for the party and kept asking me if he could massage my butt. He had his own suite in the same hotel. He'd been staring between my legs the entire flight and

I knew I could hook up with him. So, as long as those chicks stayed out of my shit and out of my way, the trip would be hot.

They got the equipment unpacked and set up and we started working right away.

The video was for N.J.S.'s hit single, but it was also promoting a sexy new clothing line called Birthday Cake, and they were counting on me to bring my nice fluffy chocolate cake to the party.

I was slathered down in baby oil and they wanted me to wear a hot-pink belly shirt and had given me some real tight low-rider jeans. The birthday cake logo on the back pocket was a small white cake with a candle in the middle of it and a *bc!* emblem was visible in the flame. The jeans fit so nice and low they didn't even reach the dimpled part of my lower back, and I was styling a slamming hot-pink hi-cut thong with little white birthday cakes all over the waistband.

When the set went live I popped out of a huge birthday cake, and the camera zoomed in on my gyrating ass as Robb Hawk got out there and did his thang on the hook.

That's birthday cake!
Girl gimme a slice and I'll slurp that plate!
Blow the candles out, and let's both get straight!
One day of the year is well worth that wait
Gotta work that bake, girl . . .

You might ruin my appetite . . . uhm
If I get holda that tonite . . .
You might ruin my appetite . . . yea!
If I get holda that tonite . . .

A few extra girls joined me on camera as we popped our asses and danced like everything we had was for sale. I pulled off my jeans real quick so they could film the second scene. The scenario they set for that had me standing in my thong and some pink stiletto heels as one of Robb's boys tied a blindfold around my eyes. He spun me around a few times and five rappers took turns trying to pin a tail on my jiggling butt. That's when Robb Hawk broke in with the first verse of his rap.

Mami bad as the kid at the babysitter's!
You can tell lil mama keep a razor wit her!
She cuttin' the rug,
Yea I see a lot of chickens cuttin' they mug
You gotta wonder why they come to the club?
If it's ya hobby to come out to spots and watch,
Might as well get paid with the paparatzz
Never mind them girlfriend, pop ya lock!
While I creep up behind your box . . .
She can whine to the Sean De Paul
Got her ass hiking up my drawers!

Then he cut right back in with that bomb-ass hook and I snatched the blindfold off and started working my shit again.

Good God! That's birthday cake!
Girl gimme a slice and I'll slurp that plate!
Blow the candles out, and let's both get straight
One day of the year is well worth that wait
Gotta work that bake, girl . . .

You might ruin my appetite . . .
If I get holda that tonite . . . uhm
You might ruin my appetite . . .
If I get holda that tonite! Yea!

I danced around in that thong like I was the reason for the whole damn party. When the filming was over, the video extras sat around hating because I was shooting solo stills for the print feature. Who cared? I got in front of that camera and performed like a motherfucker! Every pose was perfect. I had brought crazy thongs in a million different colors and designs and I used them to my best advantage.

They took still shots of me with my ass to the camera, my bold, round cheeks gaping with a colorful thong stuck down my crack, *Battah!* Ass speaking loud and clear to the camera. I'd brought some false eyelashes and bomb-ass lingerie, and in one shot I was laying on my back wearing a black housemaid's bodice and a white fringed thong with a red feather duster brushing against my clit.

Another shot caught me from the back wearing a leather thong and sitting topless on a horse saddle with my back arched and sexy, my ass one big round hump. I had on a white cowboy hat and wore a sneaky, sexy grin, and a party whip was thrown over my shoulder.

But it was the centerfold shot I liked the best. I was on my knees in the middle of a party table with rappers sitting around me in a semicircle. They was all dressed up like kids at a party, with big bow ties and party hats. One was looking at me with his eyes real wide and his hands covering his mouth. Another one was licking his lips and rubbing his hands together. A guy in a plaid jacket was leaning over with his eyes closed and his cheeks puffed out. Like he was trying to blow out a candle. Another artist had on a bright red dress shirt with white suspenders. He had frosting on his chin and was waving a noisemaker in the air.

And me? I was crawling away from the camera on my hands and knees. String confetti, sparkling streamers, and party favors were all over the table around me. I wore a multicolored polka-dot party thong, and they'd stuck two pasties in the same colors on my nipples. A kids' birthday hat was on my head with the rubber band hooked under my chin, and I was "braining" one of those blow-out party toys that squeak and uncurl when you breathe into them. The caption was right above my tooted-up ass and it said, "Now *that's* Birthday Cake!" and I couldn't have said it no better myself. I was partying my ass off and baking the cake was the name of my game.

We rocked Antigua New York style. Somebody ran out and found a liquor store and brought a crate full of bottles back on the set. There was mad downtime so we got to "dranking" and carrying on and pretty soon the set was looking and feeling more like a club than a production platform.

Our party flowed right into the music awards show that night. I'd changed into a shocking white Fendi dress that barely covered my ass cheeks. The back was out, the waist was low-cut and had a front so sheer you could see my dark nipples. Of course I was playing the hell out of a thong. They didn't call me the thong girl for no reason! This one was high cut, silver studded, and sexy as hell. My jewelry matched it to a tee.

The show was live and I felt like one of the happening people. I had mad dudes pulling on my thong! Everybody was touching me and calling me over and trying to get my attention. I let 'em treat me like a queen too. I actually felt worshiped by them and I accepted it with style because I sure as hell deserved it.

I felt somebody touch my elbow. "Saucy Robinson?"

I turned around and saw some big-ass bodyguard-looking monsta in a dark suit. He had a wireless receiver hooked behind his ear and I could tell he was strapped.

"What? I'm under arrest?"

He cracked a quick smile, then tried to look all serious again. "No, ma'am. You're not under arrest, but you have been invited to watch tonight's show from the VIP section with Miss Jackson and her party."

"Miss Jackson?" I glanced toward the front of the room. I knew goddamn well he wasn't talking about Dymond Jackson. With crazy album sales, a thousand music awards, a Coca-Cola commercial, and a warehouse full of flunkies to choose from, why the hell would she wanna hang out with me? I looked at him with a smart-ass smirk and started to walk away. "Yeah, okay."

"I'm for real," he said, grabbing my arm. He pointed toward the VIP area, which was roped off with big red velvet ropes. Damn if Dymond Jackson wasn't grinning and waving me over!

"Cool," I said, and followed him through the crowd.

I crossed that room like I was walking on a cloud. I can't tell you how many people were greeting me and how many guys were mouthing *What's up, China* and trying to touch my hand. But big Billie Badass was walking behind me with the crazy face on, and niggas fell back real quick when they realized he was my escort.

Dymond Jackson stood up and hugged me like we was homegirls or something. Yeah, I knew my shit was tight and I had made some waves in the hip-hop industry lately, but I still didn't expect all this. Somebody in her crew got up and let me sit down next to her, and she grabbed a bottle of Moët from the table and poured me a glass.

"It's about time I met this Saucy everyone's been talking about! I been hearing your name and seeing your pictures everywhere."

"Thanks," I said, sipping my bubbly. Dymond opened a gold Biallo purse and took out a stick. She lit it and pulled, then passed it to me.

"We gotta get together when we get back to the States, girl. I don't know if your schedule is booked or not, but I need some hot chicks for my next video and you have the right look."

I was raised!

"Oh, yeah," I said real quick. "I can clear my schedule, that's no problem. You just let me know when y'all shooting and I'm there."

I sat there smoking sticky with Dymond like I got high with multi-millionaires every day. She was biracial and she wasn't really hip-hop, but she had been featured on some hit tracks with a few big-name artists who had upped their status by bringing her R & B magic to their projects.

"So what nigga you scheming on tonight? You oughtta come hit a few after-parties with me. I wanna get blasted and get my shit off tonight."

I had to make myself not stare at her. I shoulda known this trick was gutter! She came across as all high-class and upscale on television, but one on one she was just a regular head like me.

"I'm actually free tonight. I'm prolly gonna hit the clubs or hotels, though. I ain't on nobody's schedule but my own."

LL was the MC for the night, and Reem Raw was the opening act. He was a Jersey boy who originally came outta the projects in Brooklyn, and he was cutting up in the industry. His lyrics were some of the best, and everybody was talking about how he was destined to blow up because his first cut had already been certified gold. The beat was a smooth Spanish-guitar melody and Reem Raw came out on stage looking fine and fresh. Three girls in tight silver booty shorts were with him and they were shaking titties and ass for days.

Reem grabbed the mic and opened up with his sexy, thugged-out voice.

Shorty chill with the stereotypes . . .
Come see the crib, you can peep what the scenario like
I know you hearing the hype, under streetlights triggas and
     dice,
I be risking my life, gotta grind till I get it precise
But we can chat about that on a later note,
I'm not tryna be fast, but I'm saying tho' . . .
I wanna take it only if you o.k. it tho'
Lift it up, bring it back, then lay it low . . .

The crowd was feeling that shit! Dymond had a big-ass grin on her face. She threw her hands up and started rocking her ass around in her seat.

After Reem bit them rhymes off, his man, smooth singer Spoons Dinero, broke in with the hook and tore that shit up.

Won't you lay your body down I wanna get between ya knees . . .
The way I stroke it and I grind it put it on you like a G . . .
     baabbbyyy
It's the way that yo body moves,
Ohhh you know I wanna roll out with you . . . get a dutch and
     come smoke with you,
And do it like we do it DO IT!

I jumped to my feet and started clapping just like everybody else!

"Stroke it!" Dymond screamed. "Grind it!" She shocked me when she put her fingers in her mouth and whistled, but what the fuck! That jawn was hot as hell!

Reem was back on the mic for his second verse, and Dymond tapped me on the arm. "Listen! Listen! This boy can spit!"

Look baby lemme put it to you like this . . .
It can be a friendship with a slight twist
We can ball out chips on a nice trip,
Or midnight calls for the right fix
Lemme know what it is,
I know you want it from the vibe you was giving off
And you was blushing from the lines I was dishing off,
Something on ya mind? Baby girl get it off!
Love it how ya hips slow grind to a nigga's songs,

I wanna see how you perform when it's action . . .
Aint no time to prolong when it's passion . . .
Put an end to all the braggin and back it
Mami my name's Raw, I plays with the plastic,
Straight six dash nine over here,
Straight Yak no wine over here,
Got the dutchy and the lime over here,
So ma, fuck them other niggas, slide over here! Yea!

Spoons broke in singing the hook again, but everybody in the house was already hooked.

Won't you lay your body down I wanna get between ya knees . . .
The way I stroke it and I grind it put it on you like a G . . .
    baabbbyyy
It's the way that yo body moves,
Ohhh you know I wanna roll out with you . . . get a dutch and
    come smoke with you,
And do it like we do it DO IT!

"That whole fuckin' album is hot!" Dymond screamed when the crowd started clapping. She whistled again, then jumped up and down, her firm beige titties almost busting outta her dress. She was right, though. The cut was hot, but girlfriend seemed like she was about lifted.

The hip-hop reggae group *Action* was up next and they did their thang too. The next few acts after that were a mixture of rappers from the east and west coasts, and the dirty south, and I dug and appreciated the flavor mix. LL was fine and funny as hell too, and Dymond laughed at almost everything he said.

I noticed something about her, though. This chick was a vet for real, because she had the routine down tight. Whenever a camera so much as inched her way she straightened up her act and smiled real big. She had it down, I'm telling you! I'd seen her interviewed on television a hundred times and she acted like she was some rich chick who had been to college. She came across as pure class and bling.

But as soon as the cameras were outta range she got real again. I was almost disappointed. See, a bitch like me was real all the time, but I could understand Dymond's front. She was just like Whitney used to be. Big-ass smile, perfect hair, dripping jewels, clothes just right. But all that shit was a real front for the media because when that crack grabbed hold of Whitney's ass she dropped all them pretenses and showed the world how hood she really was.

Dymond was performing in the second half of the program, and when they came to take her backstage to get ready she told me to stay my ass right in my chair.

"Don't go nowhere, sexy Saucy," she warned me with a smile. Her teeth were white as hell and I wondered how many of them were fake. "Don't you move that phat ass, Mami! I gotta do this little intro, but after that me and you gonna chill."

She put her hand on my arm and I had the nerve to cross my damn legs and nod, playing it cool like she was one of my homegirls from the projects. "Girl, go 'head. I'ma be right here waiting for you."

I'm certain the whole show was live, but I couldn't tell you for sure 'cause I didn't get to see it all. Dymond got on that stage and brought the whole house down. For a half-white girl she sang like a full-blooded soul sistah. Out of all the R & B singers who had taken the stage, her act was the best, no doubt. It was professionally choreographed and she had mad stage props and extras.

She had changed into a sky-blue mini-dress that crept up her long, sexy legs. She stood wide-legged and bent her knees and flaunted those legs as she sang, and when I thought about it I realized that she showed those toned legs damn near all the time.

When she was finished she changed her gear again and came back to the table in another dope mini-dress. This one was jet black with a split up the back, and I had no doubt that those diamonds she was rocking were real.

"Why don't we cut out?" she leaned over and whispered in my ear. "They got parties going all over this place. Let's hit a few."

We jetted while Busta Rhymes was clowning on the stage with his new cut. Dymond's bodyguards took us out a side door and we ended up in a sweet white limo that was spotless inside and smelled brand-new.

As soon as we started to roll, Dymond raised the window between us and her driver, then broke out a silver tray and produced some 'caine from a nice-sized glass vial. I knew that much hit had to be worth thousands, but she tapped out ten lines like they only cost about a dollar each.

"Where are your bodyguards?" I asked her.

She angled her head. "Driving right behind us. We cool, girl.

"Here," she said, handing me a rolled-up dollar bill. I could see enough of it to know it was at least a fifty or a hundred. My mouth started watering as I bent over that tray. I loved what coke did to me, and my greedy ass tried to sniff up all her shit!

We drove around drinking and hitting lines, with music blaring from the speakers. We was laughing and joking like we'd been chilling together forever, and I was having a real good time. When Dymond offered me a triple stack of X, I popped that shit and chased it back with some champagne from the iced compartment near our feet.

Every time Dymond said something funny she leaned over and slapped me on my leg. One time when she did it, she left her hand there. I acted like I didn't notice, and so did she.

We were riding for a good minute, and I sorta wondered where the hell the party place was, but we were having fun. Dymond kept the coke lined up and that X was running through me making me feel good as hell. We started talking about music and Dymond brought up the video proposition again.

"Yeah, just wait till we get back. I'll have my production manager get with your agent with the dates and the payment, cool? And you know I'll tear you off proper, so that won't be a problem. My goal is to give you more public play than you're already getting. You're really a talented and beautiful girl, Saucy. You sure caught my eye."

I laughed. "Oh, I ain't got no agent, but I love doing videos! I like being on film, period. Ever since I was a little girl I fantasized about being in front of the camera."

"Yeah, I love it too. But sometimes some funny shit gets recorded. Did you see that footage of Destiny's Child when Michelle fell and busted her ass? And her girls kept it moving like she wasn't even there?"

She leaned all over me laughing and slapping my leg, and I was laughing my ass off too. By the time we calmed down both of us was breathing hard. But the funny moment had passed and sistah was still practically in my lap.

Outta nowhere she made a move.

She lifted her head from my shoulder as her hand slid between my legs. Her mouth covered mine and at the same time she rammed her finger into my pussy as hard as she could.

I had never felt no shit like that in my life. Nothing had ever snuck into my pussy so quick and with so much force, and I yelped, then squeezed my legs shut on her hand and nutted, screaming into her mouth.

This bitch was all fingers and tongue.

I was on my back and she was finger-fucking me with long strokes, using her palm to press my mound and my clit. Then she climbed on top of me like a man and started humping, her teeth biting into my lips as she squeezed my ass. She moved up and pressed one of her titties to my lips and I opened my mouth and caught her nipple between my teeth. It was pink and hard and I rolled it between my lips, then sucked it the same way I liked to have my own titties sucked.

"Yeah," she moaned, then slid down to her knees and pulled my thong to the side. She gave my pussy a big deep lick, then started sucking my clit and teasing it with her tongue as I opened my legs wider and tried to push her whole face up in my stuff.

My slit was wet and leaking all over the seat, and she was licking and flicking my clit, pressing it with her tongue, then sucking it real hard, then real soft, then real hard again.

She had me going and I reached up and grabbed the head-rest on the seat and held on as I came again. I was still dizzy when Dymond pulled me down on the floor. We got down there and stripped, rubbing our bodies together. I squeezed her titties and played with her pretty nipples. I had never in my life sucked no titties before, and I couldn't believe what I had been missing. She was on top, fucking the hell out of me. Our pussies were hot and slippery and I felt her body starting to twitch. I reached between us and spread my pussy lips wider, letting her rub her clit in my juices as she humped and moaned. She got crazy when I slipped my finger into her tight wet hole, and she started shaking and biting her lips. "Rub my clit," she begged me as I fucked her. "Rub my clit!"

I rubbed it like she told me to, but then she snatched my hand away and went back to rubbing her pussy on me. She moved her slit all over my pubic hair, then back down into my wetness. Her clit was swollen stiff and I was trying to grab it with my pussy muscles. When she started shaking again we both just broke out in a straight fuck, bumping our pussies together as we went all out to get our nuts.

Minutes later my mouth was dry and I wanted her off me. I raised my head and looked at her, and we both squealed and laughed as the car hit a big pothole.

"Everything I heard about you was true," she said, smiling.

I laughed again. If her pussy wasn't still leaking all over me I wouldn't have believed what had just gone down.

"Nothing I heard about you was true."

We got dressed and drank some more Moët and everything was cool. We had driven for so long that I knew damn well we must have lapped around the island ten times and passed at least a hundred parties. Dymond lowered the window and told her driver to take us to a hotel that I recognized as being right near the awards show. We joined the after-party that was already live, and both of us got swept up by some cute artists and danced our asses off.

From time to time we caught each other's eye and grinned. We were having fun and I felt what we'd done was all good. But it was even better the next day when a delivery boy knocked on my hotel door. That crazy chick had sent me a box of thongs! She had also sent me a box containing the diamond jewelry she'd had on the night before. And oh yeah. There was a little sumpthin' else in that box too. A cashier's check. For ten thousand dollars.

Chapter 9

I HAD BEEN back from Antigua for a couple of months when Tai decided to get brand-new on me. You know a buster gotta come on the scene every now and then and shit on the party, and that's just what Tai did.

"You've been running around so much we don't even get to talk anymore, Saucy. I kinda miss ya ass. So when's your next assignment?" It was a Friday night and Tai always had to have fish on Fridays. We were standing in line at this fish joint on 145th Street and the smell of fish fins and old grease was getting in my clothes and making me sick.

I shrugged. "I don't know. I been getting a lot of calls but I'm taking a break for a minute."

Tai nodded. She had her eyes all in this brother's plate as he walked past with a pile of fried shrimp and whiting. The fish was so fresh out the grease it was still sizzling.

"You can afford to do that? I mean, how you gonna get high *and* party your ass off if you don't keep working?"

"Tai, please. Don't start no shit with me." I moved up in the line. The reason I wasn't doing a lot of videos was because I was making enough money on the side. Dymond was my girl. She liked to send a car for me in the middle of the night when she was lonely and wanting her some pussy. She had sex toys out the ass and we'd get buzzed and take turns inserting fake dicks in all sizes and shapes in each other, laughing and play-ing nasty all night. Dymond liked to eat me out and she liked to fuck on top. She would strap on a ten-inch dick and pound my stuff just as good as any nigga. Half the time I just closed my eyes and pretended she was a man, and got off like that.

I kept Dymond satisfied and she told me I was the best piece of tail she had ever had. She must have been giving out recommendations on my ass because every horny nigga in the industry had started blowing up my spot. Plus, she was real free with her gifts and cash, and through her I had met a lot of other sexually frustrated stars who wanted to get their freak on. Shit, everybody had needs, and sometimes it was hard for celebrities to get theirs met, especially if their needs fell out-side of the normal box.

But Saucy was on it. Male or female, I didn't discriminate. I made 'em feel real comfortable with their sex secrets and I sure didn't have a problem being a part of the fantasy. They wanted this? I gave it to them. They wanted that? Well, they got it.

"I guess you probably need a little break, huh?" Tai said. "All that wildin' you been doing lately. And oh yeah! I heard all about that commotion you caused at that Flushing Meadows tennis match the other week. Fighting that damn white girl! Pulling out all her hair! And what the hell was you doing with that Zinger Jones anyway? Ain't you still fuckin' with Marshall George? You living up in his crib! What? All of a sudden you and Zinger got something in common these days?"

I blew my breath out. Yeah, I was fuckin' Zinger Jones. Hell, he was a top tennis star! "Tai, stop hatin'! Damn! You always talking about shit you don't know nothing about! Yeah, I'm still living at Marshall's, but me and Zinger got a lot in common. Both of us are half-Asian, if you ain't noticed!"

Shit, Tai just didn't know! This Asian thing was finally working for me. Zinger mighta been all on ESPN and shit, but he wasn't nothing but an undercover crackhead who didn't mind tricking up his doe so he could get high and nibble on my fortune cookies. Hell, Tai would freak the hell out if she knew some of the biggest music moguls in the business were into Asians.

Take, for instance, Pretty Boy. He was a top industry shot caller and a willie, for real. He had a beautiful wife, a mega-successful record label, a truckload of artists he had developed, and he was even a hot performer. But he also kept prostitutes from Cambodia. He had a smuggling game going where he would swap out pretty young girls every few weeks and got him some new ones. But this nigga's head was all twisted. He was a freak for Asian pussy, but only when they acted like slaves. That's where I came in with my dominatrix whips and chains. Hell, every good master needed him an evil overseer, right? I whipped up some whelps on those bitches' asses while they sucked the black off his dick!

"Go 'head," Tai told the girl behind us, letting her get in front of us. Then she looked at me and folded her arms. "Saucy, the only damn thing you know about being Asian is the fuckin' duck sauce in the Chinese restaurant. And you don't even care about that. So don't pull that 'we Asian' shit with me. I have never even seen you speak to an Asian person. You don't even know they exist. And now, all of a sudden you sitting out in all that damn sun while that rich, big-teefed nigga slaps a ball back and forth across a net, and then you beat his girlfriend's white ass and take off with him on his boat for a whole week? And what the hell was that shit about at the W Hotel the other week? You bust up in they party drunk as hell and screaming on folks, tearing off your clothes and telling niggas to line up to get brained? Them niggas was laughing at you and bragging about how good you spit on they dicks! Every damn body at my job was talking about that shit and I was embarrassed as hell when I heard it! I don't know what kinda yay you been smoking, or how much X you popping or hit you sniffing, or whatever. But you need to slow your ass down, Saucy."

For a second I just looked at Tai. Then I turned around and squeezed out of that fishy little hole in the wall and headed down the street. I wasn't surprised to hear her huffing behind me, all out of breath.

"Saucy! *Saucy!* Saucy, wait!"

"What, Tai?"

"Hold up," she said, letting her shoulder bag hang to the ground. "Okay, I know I just went off. I probably hurt your feelings, and if I did, I'm sorry. But come on, Saucy! You know what I'm trying to say. You got everybody in the industry talking about you! You showing up late, getting stupid on the set, and every other week you're getting passed off to somebody else. Girl, they're tricking you like you ain't nothing but a high-priced sack chaser, and your stupid ass is just giving them whatever they want."

"I don't *give* nobody shit, Tai," I said coldly. "Ain't nobody ever gave me nothing, so just believe that any damn thing I do, I'm getting *paid* for it."

Tai's eyes looked sad and she shook her head. "Yeah. I pity you though. You getting paid, all right."

"*Bitch!*" I shrieked. "You out there busting your ass on a bullshit nine-to-five and you wanna scream on me for jetting all over the world on somebody *else*'s dime? I shop for jewelry in Tiffany and H. Stern while you picking over shit on 125th Street! I get my gear tailored to fit my banging ass, and you still doing the racks at Lane Bryant! Damn right, I'm getting paid. You just a hater, Tai. You's a motherfuckin' hater! Maybe if you stopped OD'ing on fried fish and pork skins and pepperoni pizza somebody might wanna pay your big ass for some pussy too!"

Tai just looked at me. Oh, she was mad as fuck. But she still pitied me. I could see it just beyond her eyes and it burned me up.

"Aiight, Saucy. I don't even know why I fuck with you 'cause I swear to God you crazy and you got some shit with you. But it's cool."

She slung that big-ass bag over her shoulders and waddled away. Who the fuck did she think she was flossing on? She probably had some Cheetos and Doritos and a couple of chocolate-covered donuts in that damn bag, and I started to run behind her and put my foot in her ass.

But I didn't.

I walked down the street until I saw a cab and flagged him down. I told him my address, then sat back and closed my eyes until I was home.

It was two weeks before I saw Tai again.

I'd taken a taxi to 145th Street and asked the driver to wait while I made a quick run. Twenty minutes later I was standing outside her job, wondering if she was gonna even agree to see me.

"Hi," she said when the receptionist let me in. Tai was planning events at a recording and production studio and the joint looked real professional inside and out. She took me in the break room and I handed her the bag I had in my hand.

"What's this?"

"It's Friday, Tai. I got you some fish. It's your favorite and you know you gotta have it."

She grinned and took the bag. "You think you know me so damn good, huh, Saucy?" She set it on her desk without opening it.

"Not as good as you know me. Shit. Not half as good as you know me."

"Ya think?" She shook her head. "Half the time I have to ask myself if I really know your ass at all, Saucy. Sometimes it's really hard being your best friend. You ain't no walk in the damn park, ya know."

"I know. Believe me, Tai. I know. That's why I came down here. I been thinking about all that bullshit I said to you that day. None of it was true. I was just acting ill 'cause you called me out."

"No." Tai held up her hand. "Uh-uh. I appreciate what you said, Saucy. Sometimes it takes hearing the truth come outta the mouth of somebody you love for it to slap you upside your damn head. You ain't gotta be sorry when you telling it like it is."

I didn't say nothing because I got the feeling that shit was supposed to go both ways. Like, if I was really telling the truth about her being fat, then she was telling the truth about me being a jump-off.

"But forget all that, Saucy. You know how we do it. We been going at it since we was eight years old. Ain't nothing changed."

I laughed. She was right. We'd had our first fight the day I showed up in her third-grade class and told her she looked like a walrus. She had knocked the shit outta me, then cried and tried to hug me when my nose started bleeding.

"So you working this weekend?"

I shook my head.

"Good! That means you can hang out with me tonight, then."

I looked at her suspiciously. "Where, Tai? Hang out where?" I wasn't trying to go to no poetry slam and sit around eating peanuts and stale pretzels outta no community bowl.

"I know you heard about it. My studio is producing that Mothers Against Drunk Driving charity show in lower Manhattan tonight. It's at a concert hall downtown. We landed a contract with Freedom Moore to headline it, and he's donating his whole purse to MADD."

"Free Moore? That 'air bling' nigga from Ruthless Rap?"

Tai nodded. "Yeah. The only brother in the game with no Jacob watches and no platinum chains. This is gonna be his last show before he goes into retirement. I've been working with him on this, and he's so cool everybody is gonna be there to see him off. They've got a hot line-up of artists on the program too. One of the executives at my job had to rush to the hospital because his wife went in labor. I got his tickets and backstage VIP passes before he left."

"But I thought that Free dude was broke? Didn't he lose a whole lotta bank after Thug-A-Licious got killed? I heard his business partner cheated him out of a bankroll, and then a bunch of his artists started complaining that they wasn't getting paid."

"Nah, I think most of that is a rumor, girl. People just be

saying crazy stuff 'cause Free ain't into that all click mess, or that flashy bling, big car, heavy jewelry scene. He's just a regular dude who still takes the train all over New York. He's not out there trying to outdo none of these other label execs just to prove how much doe he holds."

I shrugged. "Cool. Sounds good. Want me to meet you down there?"

"Hell no. Girl we ain't hung out in so long we need to roll together. I'll pick you up at midnight, but first I'll stop and get us some Yak. You can find us some nice blueberry smoke, and we'll get buzzed and go catch us a few ballers."

Now that's the old Tai I was used to! The girl who liked to party and have a good time. I sure missed her ass!

"Oh, it's on!" I said and let her hug me before I left. "I'll meet you at my crib at twelve. Make sure you wear something slutty."

I had smoked some green and was already feeling good when Tai picked me up. We took a cab downtown and I was glad she had VIP passes 'cause the line was down the block and all the way around the corner. I was hurting a pair of white Birthday Cake shorts and a banging sleeveless blouse that had a strap in the front that went up over my shoulders and tied behind my neck. My hair was pulled way up off my neck with a platinum bow, and spiraling down in silky black ringlet curls. Platinum earrings glinted from my ears, and a matching bracelet that Zinger Jones had surprised me with was on my left wrist.

I swayed my hips past the waiting crowd, grinning all the way through the door. Tai had a hard time keeping up with me but there was no slowing me down. We were mingling in the crowd when somebody smacked me on the ass. I turned around and saw one of Young Jeezy's homeys, who hugged me and told me I was looking damn good. I told him to tell Jeezy I was his biggest fan!

"Girl, you got that jelly rolling," he said, admiring my hips and legs. I introduced him to Tai, and a few moments later I was sashaying my ass through the crowd again, heading for the stage area. I was charged up, not only from the coke and the smoke, but from the energy all those powerful rappers and artists were giving off.

"We got some good-ass seats." Tai beamed, proud of herself. The stage was done in two levels, and the lower one was where the VIP seats were.

Thanks to Tai and her boss's wife, who was probably screaming "Push! Push!" at that very moment, I was about to experience this show up front and real personal. Our seats were almost dead-front-and-center on the lower stage. Behind us, the tables and chairs were filling up fast because they'd opened the main doors and started letting people in.

It was hard as hell for me to sit still. I wanted to get back up and walk around and see who I knew and who I might wanna meet, but Tai's feet were already hurting and she didn't want me to leave her sitting there by herself.

That kinda irked me because I was used to moving whenever I felt the urge to move. I had never been one of them sistahs who needed to take somebody with them to the bathroom or the damn water fountain and shit. I was a solo act, and if I did have another chick up in my game you could best believe her sole purpose was to direct all incoming traffic my way.

"Envy Me" by 50 Cent blasted over the speakers as people took their seats and I jumped up and started working my goods right there at the table.

"Ooooh!" I grinned at Tai, who was patting her swollen foot to the beat. "That's my cut, goddamn it! That is *my* mother-fuckin' cut!"

And it truly was. I was styled and paid and noticed and requested, and had niggas *and* bitches desiring me. The dirty little girl from the hood was gone, and now Saucy the underdog was right on top. And I planned on staying my ass there.

The show started late, but that was cool. Some lemon-faced guy from Tai's job had seats next to us, and when I saw her swivel her chair around to talk to him, I jetted while her back was turned.

The joint was jumping and filled up to the max. Rap fans and music lovers was ready to hear their favorite artists turn the mutha out. I walked around talking to industry insiders and being seen. Yeah, you know they had photographers snapping pictures out the ass, and I definitely got up in my share.

The lights went low and everybody started sitting down. It felt great to be able to switch my ass all the way up to the front of the joint, weaving between tables and chairs, being seen the whole time. I climbed the four steps to the lower stage and paraded my way over to the table. There were two couples sitting with Tai and that guy she was talking to, and I figured they probably worked at her job too.

"Saucy!" Tai said, introducing me to the guy she was with. "This is one of the top executives at my job, Jaheim Miller. Jaheim, this is my best friend, Saucy."

He reached out to shake my hand, and I almost laughed out loud as both of the other two men at the table stared at me as I took my seat, then looked away real quick. *Yea*, I was saying as I laughed inside. *Don't get your grill tossed lookin' at me, papi. If your woman is wearing that off-label shit, I know damn well you ain't got enough bricks to get with me!*

Diddy was hosting the show, and he got out there and started dancing and shit like the joint was empty and he was all by himself.

"That is one paid nigga," I sighed, then clapped when he finished his routine.

"Paid don't mean shit," Tai said, "when you trying to get out of paying your child support."

I smirked and gave her a look. "Why the hell would I care about his child support? I'm not having *no* nigga's babies!"

I thought I mighta heard Tai mumble, *Well thank God*, under her breath, but then the VIP hostess was at our table ready to take our drink orders. We had finished Tai's bottle before we left my crib, and we'd smoked some trees in the back of the cab. But right now I was feeling kinda gansta and had a taste for either some Old English or Thug Passion, but instead I ordered some more Yak.

"You can bring me a double shot of Hen dog, no ice. And a Coke on the side."

Tai ordered the same thing.

All of the acts were banging. Candy Montana got up there and ripped up the stage. Her and her man Knowledge Graham was doing some real Arrested Development–type, pull-each-other-up shit with their artists, and they had a real big operation going over at Knowledge Is Power Records. I watched her rocking her ass in some tiny booty shorts all over the stage and smirked. Candy thought she was it with that ugly scar on her face. She had booty and could sing, yeah, but I wasn't really feeling her. That bitch thought all that red hair meant something, and them blue eyes too. She just didn't know. She wasn't flyer than me.

Ciara made a quick appearance and sang her little ass off. She had on a pale pink cling dress that fit her real nice, but somebody shoulda told her to pull them damn panties off and invest in a thong. Shit, I coulda thrown her mine because those bloomer lines were fucking up her whole game.

That fine-ass Common took the stage right after her, and he was so close to us I could see down his throat. I had been feeling him from the very beginning and I sat in my chair and melted as Tai lowered her head and waved her arm back and forth in the air like she was catching holy ghost vapors in church.

"Now that," she said, wiping sweat from her face when she was finished. "Is a real mothafuckin' man!"

About ten minutes later Tai was hyped for real.

"Here he comes!" she said excitedly, stomping her swollen feet. "Freedom Moore is coming out!"

I watched as one of the finest niggas I'd ever seen stepped on the stage. All of them pictures I'd seen of him in music magazines didn't even halfway tell his story. He had mad presence like Jay-Z, but was much darker and harder, like Fiddy.

His boy Extra came out behind him, and Diddy turned toward them and announced, "Bringing it to you on some real street shit tonight is the man you've all been waiting for! My man Free is doing this show strictly for charity, 'cause after tonight—he's hanging up his mic and going into retirement!! That means every damn body in the audience oughtta feel honored as hell to be witnessing this final performance of one of hip hop's most lyrical and successful businessmen and artists! Now put your hands together and show your love for your headliner for the night, the CEO of Ruthless Rap and *my man*, Freedom Moore!"

I was on the edge of my chair as the beat kicked up and Extra cracked the air with his bouncin' beat and sexy hook.

Yo, I need the wifey-type!
That's all I need!
Long hair, brown skin, like to blow in the weed,
I need the wifey-type, that's all I want,
Shawty holla atcha boy, we can ball and stunt . . .

"That's me!" I told Tai as Free's female fans started screaming and amping out. "That's *me*, goddamn it!"

Extra stepped up front and hit a real sweet verse.

Yo, I need the wifey-type!
Good-sense college type!
Independent, do-for-herself, with low mileage type!
Not the chicken type, jump-off trickin type
Every time she see me with a broad wanna pick a fight . . .

"Uh-uh," Tai hollered, dancing in her seat. "*That's* you, Saucy! That shit right there is you all damn day!"

I laughed and gave her my middle finger. "Go to hell, Tai!"

I need the real-type, cook a hot meal type
Boys happen to run down, she stash the grills type!
The love-bound type, hold a nigga down type
Beat pop off, first to let off a round type!

Pretty sound type, light-skin brown type
Chinky eyes, long hair, ass real round type
When you beat it down, moan real loud type!
Not insecure always gone be around type

"Oh yeah!" I screamed, jumping up and rocking my hips in big circles as I spanked my own bouncing booty. "That nigga just said my name! *Chinky eyes, long hair, ass real round type!*" I plopped back in my chair and leaned over and slapped Tai's arm. "Say that ain't me, huh? Say it ain't me, miss thang!"

"Sit down, stupid! Here he comes!"

I looked up and damn if Freedom Moore hadn't jumped down off the upper stage. He was walking toward our table with his eyes dead on me. He stepped up on us and took my hand, and everybody on the lower stage started clapping and screaming as he started grooving to the beat. He addressed the crowd then started spitting his shit right at *me*!

What's good? Uh-huh,
Wifey type!
Belly-ring, icy type,
But she never too cool for the Nikes type
The love me type, break down dutchies type,
Quick to bail a nigga out when they cuff me type,
The classy type, bedroom NASTY type!
Give brain but she never gone scratch me type.

I almost fell out. Tai was screaming and stomping her feet and covering her mouth like a damn groupie, but I played that shit cool like big niggas got up on a stage and called me out every night. I knew I had an audience of a few thousand, so I smiled a little and looked into his eyes giving him my fuck-me gaze. I held on to his hand, danced in my chair, and bopped my head to his beat.

The chocolate type! Walk it and talk it type!
Let a nigga knock it down in the office type!

The sexy type, never tryta press me type,
If I ever fall off gone catch me type,
The jersey type
Hips real curvy type
While I cruise in the whip gone serve me type!

The worthy type, hit me off early type,
Five rounds in the sack wanna work me type!
The kinky type! Carry the blinky type!
Recognize I'ma G, wanna keep me type!

He urged me to stand up and I could feel the hater bitches staring at me, their eyes burning through my clothes. I was commanding mad attention under the spotlight and I knew my goodies was looking luscious and every dude in the joint had his booty-googles aimed on me.

But then the music switched up and he really put my head on swole. I didn't know how to act when ol' boy pulled me up onto the main stage with him and held my arm high in the air, slowly twirling me around so him and everybody else could get a 360-degree view. He looked at my ass, then whistled and started muttering his rap like I was hurtin' him and he appreciated the hell outta what he saw.

Them jeans fittin' some type a' way,
Got ya boy in the spot feelin' some type a' way!

With him still holding my hand above my head, I did a real nasty booty dance, hiking it up and letting it drop down low. Niggas was in the house clapping and whistling, and for a minute I got a G-Spot flashback and I actually caught myself looking down to see how much money was landing on the floor.

Free laughed and danced a little bit himself, then he blew the house up with his sexy gangsta rap.

My click so proper!
Get those dollas,
You feeling it, then lemme see you lift those knockers!

Ma, get ya mind straight, make it gyrate!
See ya man with the dry face looking irate!
I'm peepin ya belly button and ya tongue got a ring in it
Now all you missing is a little bit a' Free in it!

It's not like I'm pressing you miss, I'm just prepping you,
Open off what I'm telling you, scared to let me next to you
Like if we end up sexing I might think anything less of you
Maybe I will,
But—
Maybe I won't!
Go down?
Maybe I do,
But—
Maybe I don't!

Diddy was on the side of the stage jumping up and down
on that one! He was pumped on Free's lyrics and making sure
everybody else felt that shit too. Below us, Tai and damn near
everybody else on the VIP stage level were on their feet dancing. People had pushed their chairs out the way and were dancing around their tables. Y'all know what the hell I was doing. I
was up there enjoying the spotlight and selling my goodies like
they was hot buttered buns. Free grinned, then really started
getting nasty on 'em.

We the ones the haters hatin the most!
We pull up to the club,
Taking they bitches while they taking our coats, like yo!

Shawty com'ere lemme feel how them lips is!
The way them hips shift, I can tell you gifted,
You know who the click is,
You know how we get bizz,
And I can put it down, whateva ya twist is!

He let the beat take over as he led me back down the steps
to the VIP area. He paraded me around to every table, pausing
at each one so I could do a little dance for the brothers and they

could see what I was packing. He rapped behind me, shaking his head and pointing at my ass.

She got a bubble in her birthday cake!
Now that's trouble in the worst way—wait ay!

She got a bubble in her birthday cake!
Now that's trouble in the worst way—wait ay!

I grinned and tossed my curly ponytail around and worked my hips like I was his personal video ho. When I got in front of Tai's friend Jaheim, I acted like I was giving him a lap dance. That skinny red nigga didn't know what to do with all this! He actually held his hand out like, don't rub all that big booty on me! Free laughed and took me back to the middle of the stage, then kissed me and turned me toward the audience.

"She's hot, y'all! Show her how much ya love her!"

They clapped and roared as he turned and bowed to me, then urged me to bow with him to the crowd. He led me back to my table and pulled out my chair, then put the mic behind his back and whispered, "Get with me after the show."

Then the beat picked up again and he jumped back up on the main stage rapping.

Now look at Free!
No watch, no chain, but the kicks mean,
Air bling! No cane, wit' a pimp lean!
No names, can't bang on the big screen,
Six teams, make dames wanna striptease
Can't feel 'em with the stains and the ripped jeans,
Ain't a nigga in the game who can rip Free!

Shawty com'ere lemme feel how them lips is!
The way them hips shift, I can tell you gifted,
You know who the click is,
You know how we get bizz,
And I can put it down, whateva ya twist is!

"Whew!" Tai said, as Free went offstage and Diddy came back up to announce the next act. "You the shit, Saucy. Ain't no way I could've gotten up there and did all that!"

I laughed. Shit, brave wasn't what it was about. I got energized when I was appreciated like that. That high level of attention was like go-go juice. It got me high and made me wanna burn some energy and fuck the hell outta something!

"You got those backstage passes, right?"

Tai nodded, fanning her big titties with a limp napkin.

"Yeah. They right in my purse."

"What about him?" I asked, nodding toward the stuck-up-acting nigga she'd said was an executive at her job.

"Oh, it's just you and me, girl. I wanted Jaheim to come but he's gotta go somewhere else." She winked then elbowed me. "I'ma hook up with his cute behind tomorrow, though."

I nodded. That was all good. Let her worry about Jaheim tomorrow. But whether Tai had the VIP tickets or not, I was gonna get with ol' Free tonight. Any nigga who could mesmerize a crowd like that, controlling them with just his style and the words coming outta his mouth . . . well, I was gonna ride high on that performance for a good minute and I had a feeling Free had a lot more power juice left where that had come from.

Chapter 10

"THIS SEEMS KINDA pointless, but," Tai said, laughing, "Saucy, this is Freedom Moore. Free, this is my best friend, Saucy Robinson."

We were backstage in his dressing room and he was sitting on a stool drinking a bottle of Aquafina.

"How you feelin'?" Free stood up grinning, then we hugged and the mood was real light. "You was real good out there. That's what's real. Thanks for giving my fans a little extra sumthin' tonight."

I smiled. "Yeah. It was your last show, plus it was hot. I bet every girl out there woulda done the same thing."

"Maybe. But they probably couldn'ta put it down as good as you did." He took a swig of water then held up his hand. "Damn. 'Scuse my bad manners." He looked at us and flashed his pretty-ass smile, then turned to a small fridge under the counter and opened it. "Y'all thirsty? Want some water?"

Water? I know this nigga ain't just offer me no water! I looked in the fridge and the damn thing was packed with icy bottles of Aquafina.

"Sorry," he said, noticing my smirk. "I don't usually drink this here shit. It's not real spring water. But I guess it's all they had on the set."

I shook my head like hell no, but Tai took the bottle he was offering, shocking me half to death. I had never seen her drink no damn bottled water before, and when he twisted off the cap and handed it to her, I stood there with my mouth open as she chugged it like it was full of grape Kool-Aid and a whole bag of sugar.

"So," I said, looking around. He was fine as hell and could work a mic and a stage, but his dressing area was weak and it was definitely not what I had been expecting from the CEO of no record label, money problems or not. This nigga might as well have been chillin' in a damn broom closet! He wasn't lying when he said he was all about "air bling." He was Ruthless's CEO and his neck was naked like he didn't know how to adorn himself with shine! Somebody needed to call Jacob the Jeweler! Free shoulda been chained out and chilling in a phat dressing room with flunkies flocking around him bringing him drinks and boosting his head!

"Where's the after-party at? I know you hitting the spots tonight, right?"

He nodded. "Oh, yeah. Most definitely. That's part of my job, baby. We got a car outside just waiting to go. I'm rolling with my boys, but we always got room for a couple of sexy sistahs."

Now that's more like it, I thought when he took me and Tai out the side door and I saw his whip. It was a bone-white stretch Escalade, and some of his boys were already inside drinkin' and wildin' with the music loud as hell.

He opened the car door and put me and Tai inside, then sat between us with his arms around our shoulders.

"Oh, shit!" some light-skinned dude sitting across from us shrieked when he saw me. "That's the bitch in them Birthday Cakes!" He shook his head, looking at me like I was bad for real. "Damn that jawn got it. She got it! Free need him a fuckin' tester, I'm his man."

"Sorry, baby," Free said, looking at me. "Sometimes my dawgs get stupid and they just be barking for no reason."

Then he turned to his boy.

"Nah, man. No testers needed," he said real easy like. "This ain't no jump-off, nigga. But yo' ass is about to get dropped off. Yo, Feety," he said to a thick-necked guy sitting near the door. "Eject this stupid-mouthed nigga for me, man."

I laughed my ass off as the guy Feety, who musta been one of Free's bodyguards, opened the door then picked that yellow nigga up by his shirt and tossed him.

We rode through the city with the windows down and the music crazy loud. Free's boys started sparking tips, and I reached for a honey berry dutchy when it came my way and tried to smoke that shit down to the end.

"Take your hair down," Free whispered in my ear. He was rubbing the back of my neck, his fingers massaging my shoulders and then moving up to my scalp. I reached up to undo my platinum clip, and I felt his tongue on my earlobe when my hair fell. He was nuzzling my neck as I smoked the blunt and shook my ass in the seat to the music. He was nibbling and sucking all over my earlobe and that shit was making me hot.

With his lips still teasing me, he took the smoke from my hand and passed it to Tai. Then he touched my chin with two fingers and turned my face toward him and covered my mouth. My pussy was thumping and leaking as he entered my mouth with his tongue. I slid my fingers across his thigh loving how hard his body felt. I tried to squeeze his dick, but he grabbed my hand and stopped me and put it back on his knee.

Then he ran his hand up my bare arm and slid his fingers past my shoulders and back into my hair. I opened my mouth wider to him, and we kissed deep and hard. Just the way he handled my tongue let me know what kinda rhythm he had going in bed. He was strong and a giver. He liked pushing meat and making a chick feel what he was holding.

Tai busted the mood when she reached across him and pulled on his arm.

"Damn, y'all can cut the act now," she laughed. "The show is over, Free. Saucy don't perform for strangers unless she's on a stage, right Sauce?"

Free kissed my lips again, then wiped his thumb across them before sitting back.

"My bad, Saucy," he said, looking at me with heat in his eyes. "My bad for getting carried away like that. That ain't proper treatment for a lady like you, and I'ma come correct from now on."

I grinned but I coulda kicked Tai's ass. I didn't need her to tell me how to handle my action with no man. I had been enjoying Free's sexy-ass tongue. I gave her a shitty look then started grooving to the beat again.

"I know ya'll got something to drink in this big-ass whip," I said, grinning at Free's boys. They broke out some Hypnotic and I made sure I was first to get some. Yeah, I thought as I laughed and balled with this nigga like I did it every night. Free and his boys was real cool. I was about to become the life of the party and if Tai didn't like it she was gonna have a real short night.

We hit every damn party we could find.

I was really feeling that nigga, Free. I liked the way he moved through the clubs like some kinda strong, sexy black panther. He looked dangerous and confident, like he could handle his with no problem, come what may.

And I was right on his elbow too. Blocking bitches who was trying to run up on him and get in his face like they couldn't see he was with me. But I liked the way he deflected that shit though. As soon as one jumped in his grill and tried to press her titties on his chest, he would step back and take my hand, urging me forward and say to her, "Hey baby! Damn it's good to see you out tonight. This my girl, Saucy. Y'all met yet? You probably seen her doin' the damn thang in that hot *Birthday Cake* video. Aiight, Shawty, be cool. Be safe out here tonight. Don't get in no trouble."

And we'd stroll off together, both of us looking fine as hell and letting everybody know we was together. At least for the night.

We was sitting in a booth at Club Xctasy just drinking and chilling. We had danced for about five songs straight and Free was so cool with his shit that his moves looked smooth and tight. I'd showed him up though, giving the crowd a real good look at what I could do, then I got thirsty and we went back to the booth so I could order another drink.

One of Free's boys asked Tai to dance and I laughed my ass off when she took her shoes off and ran out there on the floor. It was good to see her moving some muscle and working up a little sweat.

"Yo, where you stay at, Soy Saucy?"

"Hottt Saucy," I corrected him, but I thought real quick before I answered. Niggas would try to get all up in your crib if you let 'em. Free was a straight baller, and he didn't strike me as the type who needed to ride on anybody's dime, but Marshall George was footing the bills in my apartment and he was the only nigga who got to slide up in that spot.

"I'm right in the city," I said. "Off Central Park. I ain't there that much, though. You know, I travel a lot on shoots and stuff."

He nodded and killed his Corona.

"I rest in Jersey," he said, and right away I pictured one of those phat-ass estates out there where Whitney and Bobby had stayed. I was betting it was real hot.

"Jersey is cool," I said. I'd met a few older cats in the industry who had cribs in Jersey, and I'd spent a couple of nights with a professional football player who lived out there too. "They got some nice houses out that way."

"Oh, yeah," Free said and nodded again. "They do."

"I ain't been out that way in a minute," I said, throwing him a hint. "Maybe one day I'll come chill with you."

He laughed. "You got a blank check for that, Soy Saucy. You can cash that shit anytime."

We jumped over to another club, and then hit a couple of private parties in some phat hotels. I stuck by Free's side the whole night, and he seemed to like having me there. Every now and then we would get our kiss on a little bit and he would touch my hair and tell me I was fine, but I felt like he was holding back on me. Shit, I woulda gave that nigga the best brain he'd ever had in his life if he had wanted me to, but for some reason Freedom Moore was keeping me at a distance. I mean, usually niggas would be trying to trick up on me before they found out my name, but not this one.

Shit, Free was hard. He was G, he was respected by niggas in the game. He was paid, he was fine, he was sexy as hell and he was a big executive on the music scene. But as much as he seemed to be feeling me, and as hot as he had made me feel up on that stage, did a nigga try to palm my ass once the entire night? Nope. We had the motive and the opportunity. He'd sucked my tongue and licked my ears, but did he try to feel some titties or rub my pussy through my shorts? Hell no. I had practically invited myself to his crib tonight. He had to know what time it would be then. Butt naked, spread legs, big black dick down my throat. But did he jump on it? Nope. Not really.

I was still trying to figure him out when his driver dropped me and Tai at her apartment.

"You sure you don't want me to take you downtown?" he asked, holding my hand when I started to get out the whip.

I shook my head real quick, then let him get a small kiss.

"Nah, baby, but thanks. Tai had a lot to drink tonight, and I gotta make sure my girl gets in and gets straight, ya know?"

He seemed to like that. "I can tell you a real good friend," he said. "Lemme get your digits and I'll get back with you, okay?"

Now I liked that shit!

I gave him my cell number and he programmed it into his phone, then got outta the limo and started walking with us up to my old building. I forced myself to act chill when I saw Frank standing outside in his big blue suit and shiny gold buttons. He had watched us pull up and get out the car, and stood there staring with his face all twisted as we approached the building. He saw me looking and stood in front of the doorway and crossed his arms over his big-ass stomach like I wasn't getting in.

"I had a good time tonight, Saucy. I wouldn't mind chilling with you again," Free said and grabbed my hand. He had stopped so I had to stop too. Tai kept walking and I wanted to tell her to wait up just in case Frank got stupid on me.

"I'ma buzz ya," he said, then kissed me lightly on my lips. He let my hand go and nodded toward the building. "Be cool."

I knew he was probably gonna stand there and watch until I was in the building, so I ran behind Tai trying to catch her before she got through the door, but I was too late. Frank was standing out there looking at me with that same disappointment on his face that was there the morning he caught me fucking Dante in his bed.

"Where do you think you're going young lady? You don't live here anymore."

"Move!" I said, pushing past him and throwing my elbow at his nasty belly as I went through the door. I'd partied all night long and this crazy bastard wasn't gonna ruin the mood for me. "Just move, you fat fuckin' child molester! Get the hell outta my way!"

Chapter 11

I FOUND OUT real quick that Free wasn't like the rest of them niggas on the rap scene. Yeah, he was down with all the action and got mad respect in the music industry, but either he was broke for real, or he wasn't impressed by most of the flash and shine and the other shit that truly impressed the hell outta me. I knew he was feening for a piece of this ass, though, and I couldn't wait to turn him out.

Whenever we hung out he would pick me up in a regular old red Honda. It was clean and all, but that shit was so basic you had to roll down the damn windows by hand. It had a dope stereo system in it though, and he liked to pump that shit up.

There had never been shit I liked about a broke nigga, but I did like Free. We talked about all kinds of stuff. Marshall had laid down the rules about bringing dudes up in his apartment, but for Free I broke them real quick. I took him home with me twice, and the first time we sat up just talking. I told Free that Kimichi was a junkie and still living right in Harlem, even though I never went to see her. Free told me some things about his mother too.

"My moms was just out there," he said, looking down at his hands. "She used to drink all the damn time. I mean *all the time.*

One of them mothers who shows up at your elementary school tore down drunk with a nightgown under her raggedy fur coat and rollers in her hair."

I nodded. I felt that shit real deep. Kimichi had been the same way, but it was worse with her because I was the only one in class who had a drunk Asian momma up at the school showing her ass.

"Mine too," I said. "She couldn't talk for shit and embarrassed the hell outta me. I used to wish she was somebody else's damn mother."

"Yeah." Free laughed a little. "Me too. Them days was just crazy. Crazy."

"My father got popped when I was a kid," I revealed. "My uncle took me in and raised me. His daughter got sick and died, so I kinda took her place. He had a little boy too, but I was his heart." Tears came to my eyes when I thought about Uncle Swag and everything that he had done for me.

"So you grew up with a little brother too?"

"Yeah. Kinda. Kaz was real quiet though."

"Not my baby brother," Free said, shaking his head. "That little cat talked all the damn time. I couldn't even go to sleep at night 'cause he would be all in my ear, talking me to death. I miss that shit, though. I really do."

"Where is he now? Is he into music too?"

Free's whole face changed. He looked down at his hands and rubbed them together, then a hardness came over over him as he gazed into my eyes. "He got murdered. In a car. A drunk driver got him. She was holding a bottle up to her mouth when she crashed into a van."

"Did they catch him?"

"Not him. Her. They didn't have to chase her down or nothing. The cops knew exactly who killed my little brother. It was my moms."

Damn. I could tell by the look on his face what kinda pain that musta caused him.

"I'm sorry to hear that," I said. "It musta been real hard to lose your brother and your moms like that. Damn."

"Nah, I didn't lose my moms, Saucy. She's still out there living and breathing. I just walked away from Liz Moore and never looked back. Ain't nothing in this world that could make me speak to her again neither. Didn't shit happen to her that night. She crawled outta that twisted-up pile of metal with nothing but a broken ankle and a sore back. She was so blasted that when they got to her she was fightin' them, screaming and searching all over the car."

"Searching for what? Your little brother?"

"Nah, baby. For her liquor bottle."

Damn. Now I knew why he didn't really drink that much. I hated to see Free feeling that low, so I tried to bring his mood back up. I kissed all over his neck and he rubbed my titties, but that was as far as we got because his phone rang and he told me he had some business to take care of.

"Next time," he promised me on his way out the door. I was mad as hell! I had wanted it to be this time!

But the sexual tension between us was broiling, and we joked about who was gonna make who nut first when we finally did that thang. But it was more than just the dick I was anticipating. I liked hanging around him. Free paid attention to everything I said and made me feel like a priority. He had a power about him that just screamed, "I'm the shit!" and I guess a lotta other females in New York musta felt the same way, because every time I looked up there were bitches ten-deep trying to jump on his dick and get his juice.

"Damn," I said one night as we sat eating crabs in a soul food restaurant out in Staten Island. Free had family out there and had some people he wanted to see, and some bitch who was sweating all over herself in a played-out cat suit was trying to worm her way into his sights. "She act like she know you like that or something."

Free just shrugged and cracked a crab leg open with his tool.

"She's cool. I used to mess wit' her girl, so now she wanna see can she get some for herself."

I looked at him to see if the nigga was feeling himself, but it didn't look that way. He wasn't being cocky or nothing like that, just saying it the way he saw it. For about the tenth time I wondered what this nigga mighta heard about me. I knew how shit got around in the music world, and I had been with enough artists that the name Brainiac mighta gotten back to Free.

"Yeah," I said, testing him out. "Some people do that type of thing. I mean, they'll hear something about you, good or bad, and judge you based on that. Sometimes what they hear might not even really be true."

He shrugged again. "I ain't with that. I don't even listen to nothing nobody else gotta say. Cats know not to come running they mouth around me like that anyway, 'cause I ain't gonna hear it. I judge everybody for myself, Saucy. 'Cause ain't a nigga out here whose judgment I trust more than my own. Nah'm saying?"

I sure was glad to hear that!

"Me too," I said simply. "I don't listen to all the noise going around in the industry either. Half the niggas be lying and the other half just ain't telling the truth."

We laughed on that one, and when Free pulled a big chunk of crab meat out the shell, he reached over and put it in my mouth and I sucked a little bit on his finger.

"I'm a grown man, Saucy. I ain't about playing no kiddie games. When I'm feeling a lady she ain't gotta worry about nobody else coming up on her block. I got credibility with chicks because I believe in having responsible relationships, dig?"

Oh hell yeah, I dug. I dug the fact that this nigga had never even sampled this ass and already he was mentioning the relationship thing. But in the back of my mind I wondered if his shit was all a front and he was really broke like a lot of people said. He hadn't bought me one damn gift! Yeah, he'd taken me out to some dope clubs and restaurants and paid for everything, but all I could do with fancy food was shit it out. I didn't understand how bitches got geeked off of a man buying them a damn meal. Shit, niggas had to buy me diamonds to get my nose open. Pay my rent, lease me a Hummer. Gimme something I could work with.

Normally, I woulda been turned off by some dude talking about responsible any damn thing if it pertained to me and fucking, but I had never been with a nigga like Free before. He had asked me to come to his house in Jersey, and even though he rolled up in that ugly-ass Honda of his, I jumped my ass in like it was a Porsche.

"You got a nigga writing bars again, girl," Free said as we rolled. He had a dumbbeat thumping through his big-ass speakers, and I grinned as he put his hand on my thigh and spit some real sweet shit while he pushed his little-ass car down the highway.

Now Saucy!
You know how bad your body is calling,
For me to give it to you how you want it,
So what's it gonna take for you to come and rock with me?

Yo, what my bank gotta be like to take you out for a bite?
Breeze out on the pike, and take you out for the night?
Aaight, well, maybe my perception is off,
So let's just conversate and see where this connection evolves,
Brown skin, nice slim frame calling the kid,
On my mind while I'm driving, it be hauntin' the kid . . .
So I guess I gotta check for it, dress up real fresh for it,
That main position in ya life? I'm the best for it!
And I guess I can take the first chances,
No lie, 'cause a nigga was hooked at first glances!
I hope I can advance and get some romance in,
Slide you up outta them tight jeans you cramped in . . .

Baby lemme tell you the truth . . . I really feel you and I'm
    tryna make you mine tonight . . .
Know ya need a nigga like me,
I'll be your homey, I'll protect you hold you down when it's
    time to ride . . .

When we pulled up in Free's driveway my mouth was hanging open.

Yeah, his crib was in the same state as Whitney and Bobby's, but it was nothing like I imagined theirs was.

For one thing, it was small.

Real small. Just a regular little house on one of them blocks that you see folks getting up every morning to go grind for a paycheck. Yeah, it was clean and everybody had a decent car and kept their grass trimmed and shit, but there were mad little kids running up and down the block, and chicks my age had big bellies and were sitting on the porch watching Man and Pookie race to the stop sign on their tricycles. Only they called they kids Michael and Peter out here.

I guess my feelings were all over my face, 'cause he just laughed as he unlocked the door and let me in. The inside was small too. Definitely not Whitney and Bobby's joint.

I walked up ten steps and back ten steps. That was the foyer.

For a single baller living by himself this was not what I had expected at *all*. Free's kitchen was tiny, but it was real clean. There were two plates stacked in the rack, but not a dish was in the sink and the trash can was empty and had a plastic bag in it that was folded down over the rim.

His living room was small and the furniture looked old, but nice. He had a small—no, fuck that—a *tiny* television and a banging Bose stereo system, but other than that it didn't look like a whole lot of doe had gone into the place at all.

"The bathroom is right through that door over there if you gotta go," he said, and locked the front door behind us. He turned on the television to a ball game, then turned the volume all the way down and cut on the stereo. There were two bedrooms, but both of them was real small. I heard a track from Spoon Dinero's mixtape hit the speakers as I walked through a small doorway and into the tiny bathroom.

It was just as neat as the kitchen. The sink was baby blue, and so was the toilet. He had a navy blue shower curtain hanging from a real short bar, and a small clothes hamper sat under the sink. I used the bathroom and flushed the toilet, and that shit was loud as hell. I used the noise to cover up the sound of me opening his vanity cabinet over the sink. I saw two razors, a half-rolled tube of Crest, a bar of Ivory soap still in the wrapper, and some expensive cologne. I also saw a small jewelry box, and when I opened it up the most beautiful white-gold earrings lay on a square of cotton.

Without even thinking about it I turned on the water in the sink, and then shook them bad boys out and held them in my hand. They were phat as hell! I ripped off a few squares of toilet tissue and set the earrings in the middle and wrapped them up good before sticking the whole wadded package in my bra up under my left titty. Closing the box back, I set it exactly where it had been and shut the cabinet door quietly. Then I washed my hands, surprised that the towel on the rack was real soft and smelled like Febreze.

When I went back into the living room Free was standing in the kitchen looking in the refrigerator.

"I put your bags in the room, baby," he said over his shoulder. "Go on in there and make sure everything I got is good enough for you. Don't be shy about nothing either. Look under the bed and in the closet too. I keep all my real personal shit in a box on the top shelf of the closet, so make sure you hit that too."

"Oh, you are funny for real," I said, laughing.

He laughed too. "You know how you females like to do. Got ya eyes everywhere. Did you see your little present in the medicine cabinet?"

Aw shit! I didn't know how to act.

"What present? All I did was use the bathroom. I didn't go snooping all through your medicine cabinet, boy!"

Bet I ran my ass back in that bathroom real quick!

I snatched them earrings outta my bra and stuck the tissue in my pocket. Then I opened the vanity cabinet and grabbed the box and set them back inside.

"Ooooh!" I screamed and ran back into the kitchen. "Free!"

I threw my arms around his neck and kissed him all over his face. "These babies are sweet as hell!"

Forget that I had just tried to jack his ass for his jewelry. I sat the box on the counter and pressed my body up against his. Fuck all that waiting and getting to know each other better shit. I wanted some of what he had and those earrings had just guaranteed that he was worthy of getting some of what I had.

I kissed his face, his ears, his neck. I moved down his chest and kissed his left nipple through his shirt, then dropped to my knees and tugged on his belt buckle as I licked the smooth skin on his belly, sliding my tongue around his navel and wetting up the line of curly hair trailing down into his jeans.

"You know what you doing, Soy Saucy?" Free said, looking down at me. I saw what was in his eyes and I loved it. This nigga was weak for me. He was dying to slide his dick down my throat, and I was dying for it too.

"Hottt Saucy," I reminded him as I watched his thick fingers unhook his plain black belt. By now I knew not to expect no designer shit from him like a BAPE or nothing so I wasn't surprised. I placed my fingers over his and helped slide his zipper down, my eyes on zoom and anticipating what I'd see waiting for me on the other side of his black boxers.

I wasn't disappointed not one damn bit. Free had a bomb dick. It was smooth and hard and dark just like the rest of his body, and perfectly formed. It wasn't twelve inches, but it was definitely more than eight, and my eyes wanted to start tearing up as I gazed at it. It was just phat like that.

I pulled out the best of my skills for this special occasion. I wanted to make this dick-sucking an event he would remember for the rest of his damn life. I grabbed it in both hands and stroked it gently for a second, then a little bit harder.

Free grabbed it at the base and guided it toward my mouth, and I opened up for him and slowly inserted it in my mouth, throating that shit inch by inch until my tonsils hurt. My lips gripped his shaft as I reached back with the tip of my tongue and massaged the head. I heard him moan, and I relaxed my throat and sucked the last inch of him down into my neck, tightening my lips and darting my tongue around to slather his whole dick inside my mouth.

I started going at him with pure rhythm. Bobbing my head as I squeezed the bottom of his dick. My mouth kept his dick nice and wet, and I jacked him off and sucked him at the same time, building up to a beat that had this nigga's knees shaking as he held on to the counter and tried to stay on his feet.

Free was really moaning now, going from some short tight humps to a straight-out mouth fuck. They didn't call this shit neck pussy for nothing either. The more he stroked, the more I relaxed my throat, the wetter my mouth got, the deeper his dick was able to slide down in my neck.

My dick-lick was flawless, and I knew it. I loved sucking dick and the juice in my mouth was like hot lava. I put my game down on Free like never before, and when he cupped his hands over my ears and slammed his hips into my face, I took that shit like the bad bitch I was, because I could have sucked his dick every day without getting enough of it.

I swallowed everything in my mouth and loved that shit. My pussy was just as wet as Free's dick, and when he pulled me up by my arms and covered my mouth with his, I pressed against him and sighed as my nipples tingled on his chest.

"Damn," is all Free could say when he could finally talk again. "Your lips, girl. Your tongue. Goddamn . . ."

My fingers traced the thick head of his dick and I was glad he was still hard because I needed me some of that real bad. Free led me into his bedroom and we stripped outta our clothes. He didn't even have to tell me nothing. I turned around real slow, modeling my pretty brown skin and firm body like I was up on the auctioning block and he had some funds.

"It's all there," he whispered, watching me. "Everything I could want is all in your package, Saucy. Your body's perfect, girl. Just perfect."

I knew that.

Free stretched me out on the queen-sized bed with the

Wal-Mart sheets and comforter. I wasn't really feeling the whole cheap cotton thing because the dudes I rolled with liked satin and other shit that screamed comfort and luxury, but when Free pulled the little plaid sheets back I climbed on in and there was a big smile on my face when he got in next to me and put his arm around my waist, pulling me closer.

My body was boiling and Free's dick was on brick. He took one of my titties into his mouth and sucked my nipple gently, rolling it around on his lips until it stiffened and grew larger. I was gasping for air when he slid his fingers down my flat belly and dipped two of them inside my pussy. He played there for a while, then slid down and started licking my clit. I arched my back, shivering on his tongue. He stroked my stuff until cum ran outta me and I made him stop.

"I want some dick," I whispered urgently. "Gimme that dick, baby. Gimme that dick."

Free kissed me, snaking his tongue around wetly in my mouth, then he rubbed my hips and slid his leg over me, about to get on top.

"Wait!" I said, pushing on his hips to keep him from touching me with his dick. I knew what time it was, and I also knew how to play my cards if I wanted this little game to last for longer than tonight. "You got some plastic, boo? You be wrapping that shit up, right?"

I hated condoms, but I wasn't gonna let Free think I was some irresponsible trick who just let niggas dig her out raw.

Free was grinning. "Yeah, baby. I got a hoodie and hell yeah. I wraps this thing up."

A few moments later I rolled that plastic down over Free's dick and he made sure it was on right.

"They didn't have none bigger than this?" I asked. That shit looked like it was cutting off his circulation.

"I'm good, baby," he said, kissing me again. "Now lemme make sure you get good right with me."

And he did me good too. I shivered when he slid into me, hitting my walls and the back of my pussy too. If I thought I was the rhythm master, I was mistaken. Free could fuck.

He was all about satisfying me and his pace had me sweating to keep up with him. He slammed that dick in me so good I thought we was gonna break the bed down. He hit me real, real fast and hard, then slowed down and put it in neutral, idling in it for a few seconds, and then stroking me real deep again until I was racing toward that good place, cumming over and over as he reached between us and massaged my puffy clit.

I was begging him to stop by the time he finally busted again, filling up that rubber. He'd taken me through some serious circuit training, banging me from all angles and at different thrust speeds and tempos until he got his nut in a big crazy blast. I almost panicked when he pulled outta me and I saw the condom had a little split in it, but Free said it had torn when it was almost all the way out, so not to worry. And now he was cuddling me, stroking my wet skin, touching my hair, moving his head to a familiar beat and whispering his rap from earlier softly in my ear.

Soy Saucy!
You know how bad your body is calling,
For me to give it to you how you want it,
So what's it gonna take for you to come and rock with me?

Look a' here luv, you can just kick back and loosen up,
Luckily you chose to fuck with me, so you moving up . . .
You lovin' when I'm writing these raw rhymes, you got me,
That's fine mami, I need more mind than body . . .
Scratchin' my back, mami lovin it when daddy in it,
And anything, I'll make it happen if you happy wit' it
So what it's hittin' for, let me know what the feeling is,
You done with all the rest, now let me show you what it really is!

Baby lemme tell you the truth . . . I really feel you and I'm
    tryna make you mine tonight . . .
Know ya need a nigga like me,
I'll be your homey, I'll protect you hold you down when it's
    time to ride . . .

I fell asleep with Free's sweet words in my ear.

Our bout had been a real mismatch because he had put his sex game down so tight it sent me running to the corner. I woke up alone, and for a minute I had to figure out exactly where I was because the bed felt strange and I didn't recognize the bare walls and ugly drapes. But then I felt something warm seeping out of me and remembered that Free had just dug me out nice and good, and my juices were still running. I sat up and reached over to his nightstand and grabbed a woven tissue box holder, and when I lifted it up I saw the edge of a dollar bill sticking out the bottom.

At least that's what it looked like at first. It had been stuck up through a slot on the bottom, and when I turned the tissue holder over and pulled the money out, I realized that it was a one-hundred-dollar bill, and that there were a lot more of them stuck up in there.

I was counting them when I heard Free coming through the front door. "Where'd you go?" I asked sleepily when he came in the room. The tissue box was back on his nightstand and I was naked with my long legs stretched out.

He leaned over and kissed one of my brown nipples. "I went to get us some dinner. What I ate earlier, that was just a snack, mami."

"Yumm," I said, remembering how he had swirled that tongue in my coochie so good I'd almost pulled the cheap-ass sheets off his bed. "What did you buy?"

"Shrimp," he said. "I'm gonna make us some garlic shrimp, and you can make us a salad."

I opened one eye real wide.

"You want me to fix something? Why didn't you just stop at a restaurant or something?"

Free stretched out next to me on the bed, but on top of the covers. "I hate eating food fixed by somebody I don't know. I eat out when I have to, but I never bring junk up in here. This is my sanctuary from the rest of the world, Saucy. It's where I rest, where I come to get my head straight and to stay in touch with the real me. So let's get in the kitchen and feed each other right with something we made with our own hands, cool?"

Something about the way he put that explanation down felt good to me. I opened my mouth when he pressed his lips to mine and offered him my tongue to suck. He raked his fingers through my hair, then kissed the tip of my nose.

"Come on, girl. Get your fine ass up out that bed. Daddy's hungry."

I threw those covers back and stood up. I heard him gasp as I showed off my juicy light-brown breasts with the cocoa nipples that stood straight out. With my belly ring glinting, I turned around and walked around the bed, then danced barefoot toward the door as he watched my naked ass move. I stopped at the door and looked over my shoulder, then wound my hips around real sexy-like.

"Damn, girl. You gone ruin my appetite," he grinned, shaking his head. "If I get more of that tonight!"

I used the bathroom and took a quick shower. His shower stall was all fucked up! First of all it was the size of half of a regular shower. The damn spout was connected to a hose that ran from the sink's faucet. He had that shit rigged up hood-tight, like a nigga trying to get free cable.

I had to admit it, the joint was small but Free had tried to think of everything. There was some Salon shampoo on the shower caddy and some Private Spa Collection shower gel. I washed my hair then poured gel all over my body and scrubbed myself until my skin felt fresh and clean. I turned off the water and stood there listening.

Free musta been out there in the kitchen getting the shrimp ready. I could hear the music flooding the air above the sound of water running in the kitchen sink. He was playing a Thug-A-Licious club banger. Thug's stock had gone up sky high after his murder, and the fact that he used to spit for Ruthless Rap,

Free's label, and I had sucked the hell outta both of their dicks, was kinda crazy. Thug was hot though, and I nodded to the beat as Free blasted one of his last jams.

> We get it in, my team pack the club out
> Straight to the bar, no Crys, Yak the cup out
> Niggas talk slick, we pull straps and bug out
> Step on the kicks, we might black the fuck out!
>
> I got the haze, a whole batch to puff out
> Goons in the back, waitin for cats to stunt out
> Ladies in the dugout, big breasts and butt out
> No names needed that take the fun out!
>
> I need to see a tongue out
> If not, then cut out
> Your friend comin in as soon as ya ass run out
> We gonna drink till the last glass run out
> 12 AM getting it in till the sun out
>
> Let's move!
> I'm tryna pop off with Mami,
> Hit the floor, show her how we gone pop off the party! Let's
> move!
> I'm tryna blow sticky in the back,
> Shawty dancing in the front, bouncin' wit me to the track!
> Let's move!
> I'm tryna get tips on the liq, sit and watch baby girl strip to
> my hits!
> Let's move!
> We can blow a whole ounce in this bitch,
> Just make sure my squad gets pronounced in this bitch!

When I pulled the shower curtain back I saw two thick towels folded and waiting on the sink. I used one for my hair, then dried off with the other one and wrapped it around my naked body. I walked out the bathroom with my hair slick and silky, not dry enough yet to start curling up. I went back in

Free's bedroom and sat on the bed and started pulling some clothes from my bag.

"Hey." He poked his head in the door, bopping it to the music. "You gonna be dressed soon?"

I nodded. "Yeah, but your neighbors are gonna call the po-po on you for blasting them Thug sounds like that!"

"No they ain't." He grinned and shook his head. "This jawn is sound-proof, Mami."

Since we were staying in for dinner I went ahead and put on a pair of black linen pants and a black and white Girls Rule T-shirt. I left my hair down to dry, but I did jazz myself up a little by putting on the earrings Free had surprised me with 'cause I wanted to show my appreciation for his first gift.

I wasn't really hungry but I was game to cook with him since that's what he wanted. But when I walked into the kitchen he hadn't even gotten started yet.

"I thought you were doing the shrimp? Where they at?"

His eyes got big and he looked all crazy.

"Oh, shit. I must'a left them in the car. I had put everything in the trunk, but they must'a rolled under something. Can you run out there and get 'em for me?"

I stared at him like he had bad breath. He had on a black tee, some nice Evisu jeans and some brand-new Air Force Aces.

"Oh, what? You done got you some and now you feeling yourself, right? Why can't you run out there and get 'em yourself? What I look like, huh?"

He grinned and pulled me up against him.

"You look like a keeper, girl, that's what. But for real, though. I gotta use the bathroom real bad." He pulled some keys outta his pocket. "Run on out there and get the shrimp, Soy Saucy. I promise I'ma cook 'em up so good you won't regret it."

I had my lip poked out, but I surprised the hell outta myself 'cause my hand was out there too. "Gimme the keys," I mumbled.

He put them in my hand then slapped me on the ass.

"That's a good girl. Thanks, baby. This means a lot to me."

I gave him a look, then walked through the living room and opened the front door. But when I stepped outside my mind got knocked outta balance for a minute because his Honda wasn't parked in the driveway no more. Sitting in its spot was the biggest, spankingest damn stretch Hummer limo that I'd ever seen.

It was money green and an older black man in chauffeur's gear was standing beside it, holding the door open with a smile.

"Looking for some shrimp, ma'am? Step right this way."

I didn't know how the hell to act!

I turned back toward the house and saw Free was closing the door behind us and offering me one of his sweaters.

"Boy!" I shrieked, happy as hell. "What are you doing?"

He pulled me over to the whip and guided me inside. "I'm taking you to get some shrimp scampi and a salad, baby."

"B-b-but I'm not even dressed! I don't even have my wallet or my purse!"

Free slid up next to me on the seat and put his big, strong arm around my shoulder.

"You ain't gotta have no wallet, Soy Saucy. Or nothing else neither. When you rolling with Freedom, you can best believe you've got everything you need."

"Where are we going?" I asked when the driver got off Route 4 and headed toward the George Washington Bridge. The sparkling lights of New York City were ahead in the distance, glowing in the sky.

"Sssh . . ." Free put his fingers to my lips. "Don't ask a whole lotta questions and I won't have to tell you not one single lie."

I sat back and relaxed and we listened to some tracks as we sped toward the city. I wanted to smoke some green, but all my stash was in my purse and Free said he wasn't in the mood to get high anyway. There was champagne in the cooler, though, and Free popped the cork and poured me some in a crystal glass, and by the time we got where we were going I had drained two more glasses.

"Okay," I said when the limo stopped outside of an Italian restaurant in East Harlem's barrio. It was on East 114th Street, and it looked closed. There was a pizza shop down the street, but there were no lights on in the front of this restaurant and nobody was going in or coming out. "Did you bring me all the way here to get a slice of Paul's pizza?"

"Faith," Free said getting out the whip. "Have some faith in me girl. I got you covered real tight."

He held my hand as we walked up to the closed restaurant. I saw the name of it was Rao's, and when we were about five steps from the door the outside lights came on and a young white waiter opened the door wide.

"Good evening, Mister Moore," he said, stepping back as we walked inside.

"Sup' Danilo," Free said, dapping him. "What's poppin', son?"

The whole damn restaurant looked empty. I mean shut the hell down. I opened my mouth to say something but Free gave me the sssh thang again so I fell back and followed behind him. He walked behind a counter and down a hall past some bathrooms, then turned around and said, "We can grab us a little plate to go, or, if you ain't too good to eat in the kitchen we can do this right here."

At this point I couldn't figure out how this nigga flowed or how I should act neither. I shrugged. "Hey, I'm down for whatever. I can eat in the kitchen. I just can't cook in that bitch."

He laughed and put his hand on a door. "That's okay, baby. I got you your own personal cook for the night."

Nothing could have prepared me for what I saw when Free pushed that door open. It was a kitchen, yeah, but it was much more than that. That sucker was laid out. Free's soft cut "In My Lifetime" was playing in the background.

There was a long table with a white cloth covering it and red rose petals sprinkled from one end to the other. Five candle clusters burned in their holders, and two places were set right next to each other. Right in front of the table was a cooking station where two Asian guys were standing at an open flame and a tray of shrimp and vegetables sat waiting to go into a hot wok.

"Soy Saucy," Free said and pulled out a carved chair that looked like it was a queen's throne. It had a thick satin cushion, and when I sat down on it I sank down into perfect softness. The chair next to me was the bomb too, but a bigger version of mine. It was fit for a king and when Free sat down in it he completed the whole picture.

Those cooks stood there just waiting for us to sit down. As soon as we did, they showed they asses for real.

They hacked into those poor vegetables like they'd stolen something. Shrimp and broccoli and carrots and red peppers was being sliced and diced and tossed in the air like crazy. They sautéed the vegetables in the wok, but cooked the shrimp right there on the grill in front of us.

I watched them chop garlic and whip butter and make the scampi sauce, then the guy who had let us in brought our salads from the refrigerator and our food was ready. After all that I was eager to eat, and when one of the cooks came out with a bottle of champagne, I was ready for some more of that too.

I'd been out to nice restaurants with plenty of nice niggas, so it wasn't like Free was schooling me on the finer life or nothing. But I was digging this special dinner because of who had set it up. He'd gone through all this just for me, and I knew that dick-sucking I'd put on him didn't have nothing to do with it.

"This is hot," I said, biting into a garlic shrimp. I coulda said more, but that's about as far as I was willing to go. Shit, no matter what some nigga did to impress me I wasn't gonna act but so damn grateful. I knew how to keep 'em trying. Keep 'em stretching and going in their pockets tryna figure out how to hook you. Show any man too much gratitude and a nigga would expect you to be forever grateful. "Yeah," I repeated, just so he knew that I knew. "Real hot."

Chapter 12

"YOU AIIGHT?"

I nodded and let him pull me into his big strong arms. We had just had our private dinner at the restaurant and I was trying to figure out my next move. I was feeling Free. I mean, I really fuckin' was. He wasn't no game. And he wasn't broke neither! He had chips! He had a big, pretty black dick and could fuck like a bull. And that tongue? Damn. He had slurped the syrup from me, licked the sugar offa me, sucked the honey outta me. He was the shit for real. But still . . . I was playing it cool on the outside, while on the inside I was having a big-ass fight with myself. C'mon, y'all. This cat was a paid CEO! A nigga was recognized and respected on the streets! He had groupies hanging off all his ball hairs, but I bet none of them tricks didn't know he was living in a cramped-up shack like he was grindin' for Wal-Mart! Yeah, I would suck the hell outta his dick in private and he could give me all the cash and gifts he wanted to under the table, but if Free was tryna keep a dime like me on his dick in public like that, he was gonna have to step up his game. I had an image to maintain.

"I'm kinda tired," he said, squeezing my thigh. "All I wanna do is get back to the house and watch a little TV with you, baby."

I didn't wanna go back to that tight-ass house! It was Saturday night and I wanted to get up in somebody's party. I needed me some sticky and a bottle of St. Ides. Or maybe some Patrón Silver. Or some Grey Goose. Whatever. I needed me a buzz.

And he was dead on it about one thing. Watch a "little" TV was right. Good thing it was dark in the whip or Free woulda seen my lip sticking out. Damn straight I was catching a stank attitude. Who the hell looked at little four-inch televisions these days? As large as he was in the game, hadn't he ever heard of a damn plasma TV? Or a real shower? Or a crib that was bigger than a damn storage closet?

I made up my mind that I was gonna straight dip. I'd give Free some more bomb-ass head when we got back to Jersey, and then I was outtie. There were a bunch of parties popping off in the city tonight, and as soon as I put some of that knock-out neck action on Free I was gonna catch me one of them. There wasn't a damn thing happening on Free's little block, in his neighborhood, or in that whole sleepy-ass Jersey town, that turned me on in the least.

Besides, Free's motor mighta been wearing down, but mine was just getting revved up. I was a night hawk. I slept most of the day and ran the streets getting my socialize on all night. In New York that was everybody's flow. A whole culture came alive after midnight in the city. Cars would be swishing up and down the streets rushing to someplace hot, restaurants were open for business, people walked the avenues, laughing and clowning like crazy. I can't tell you about the parties that would be jumping off.

Sheeit. The boring-ass block Free lived on was so quiet that if your neighbor farted in the middle of the night you'd swear somebody was outside poppin' niggas off. Yeah, let this cat sleep, I told myself, formulating my plan. First I'd sneak some doe outta his tissue holder, then I'd have his driver bring me back to the city as fast as he could push this whip. I'd tell Free that Tai called and needed me in the middle of the night, and that's why I bounced.

We was driving for a good minute when I realized we were

headed in the wrong direction. Well, I was looking for a party so it was the right direction for me. The wrong one for Free.

"What's wrong?" I asked him, lifting my head off his shoulder.

"Nah, everything's cool, baby. But I do gotta make a quick stop before we head in. Niggas be playin' sometimes and I gotta set some shit straight."

I sat all the way up then, looking out the window.

"We staying in Manhattan? You gone go bite some nigga and you taking me with you?"

He shrugged. "You said you was down for whatever. I thought you was the type a' chick to ride hard witcha nigga?"

"I am," I said, sitting back again. "But you think you got some wins with just you and me? Where your dawgs at? Don't your real niggas ride with you on missions like this?"

Free laughed. "Oh, you about to learn some shit about me, Soy Saucy. I'm a lone ranger, baby. It don't take a whole tribe of Indians galloping behind me for me to ride my own horse. I'ma Clyde nigga. And he didn't need nobody but Bonnie."

I had to bite my damn lip! I wanted to tell him, "Drop my ass off in Harlem, then go 'head and handle ya damn business!"

But he pulled me closer to him and all I could do was go along on the ride as we sped down the highway alongside the Hudson River. I was surprised when we turned into a phat neighborhood on the Upper West Side, not too far from my old crib, and when the whip stopped outside of a high-rise building that was phatter than the one I'd lived in with Uncle Swag, I just looked at Free.

"You shook?" he asked. His driver opened the door for us, and Free got out first, then turned around and looked at me.

"Check it out, Saucy. You ain't gotta come inside with me if you pressed. You can chill right here until I get back, but this is something I gotta do. Now if you think this might be too big for you, cool. I understand. I'm all man, baby. I can get gorilla all by myself if I have to."

I shook my head, but deep inside I wasn't down for this shit at all! He was going up in this phat-ass building to settle some beef? Didn't he know this was a tax-paying zone? The po-po would rush to a call from here quicker than shit.

I got out the car and he grabbed my hand.

"You trust me?" he asked.

Like a damn fool, I nodded.

"Good," he said and led me toward the building.

The doorman let us in and we took the elevator up to the eighteenth floor. The ride was silent, but Free squeezed my hand and smiled as I reassured myself. I had lived in a building like this for years. They had a security guard who checked on the building all through the night. I knew if shit got too hot to handle, I could always slide into the stairwell and hoof it down the stairs.

When we got off the elevator my feet sank into the plush carpet. We walked down a short hall that had pretty wallpaper, framed paintings, and large mirrors hanging on the wall. Free stopped in front of a door that said 18G. I could hear rap music playing inside. He took a deep breath and squared his shoulders, then rang the bell.

We waited. And waited. He rang the bell again. And again, and again. The music was playing but wasn't nobody coming to the door.

"Punk ass," Free finally said when nobody answered. "C'mon, baby. I'll come back and catch this cat another time. He can't hide forever, yo."

I almost ran back to that damn elevator. I sure as hell know I got there before he did. I pounded the call button about twenty times, and when the elevator came I couldn't get in fast enough.

But Free checked me.

"Hold up, Mami," he said, holding the elevator door open with one hand. "This ain't right. I can't just let no nigga slide on me like that."

"Well what the hell are you gonna do?" I shrieked. I was ready to smash him up in the elevator door or leave his ass standing out there by himself.

"Somebody is up in that joint. That's truth, girl. I can feel it. I'ma try one more time. You coming?"

My feet didn't even wanna move. I practically had to drag myself outta that elevator and back down the hall. But when we got outside the door this time, instead of ringing the bell Free leaned over and kissed me, his tongue parting my lips and caressing the inside of my mouth.

"Thank you," he said as he took some keys from his pocket. "Wit' ya shook self."

I stood there looking crazy as he stuck a key in the door and unlocked it.

With the door standing open I could see straight down a hallway, and what I saw made my eyes stretch wide open.

"Come on in, Soy Saucy," Free said, pulling on my fingers. "This is my other joint, baby. Get comfortable. Make yourself at home."

The joint was phat. My mouth tried to fall open as I followed him inside. Now that's what the fuck I'm talking about! I thought, my eyeballs everywhere at once. The boy did know how to live big! It looked like some shit outta MTV *Cribs*. There was a huge projection screen covering one wall, and sculptures of black people in all different poses on stands. Crazy art was on the wall. Leather furniture, a phat fish tank . . .

I was open like 7-Eleven.

I walked around admiring his bar, the pool table, and even the baby grand piano. There were three bedrooms and each of them had their own bathroom. The biggest one was his, and he had a huge bed in there that was low to the ground. The extra-large comforter had the word FREE embroidered in it, with a picture of two big black shackled hands breaking free of the linked chain that had bound them together.

He had a nice stereo system in there and the best carpet I had ever felt under my feet. There was a pretty big guest room, and the smallest room had been set up like a studio. I saw his mixing board and all that other electronic equipment, and I laughed my head off when I saw that he'd stuck a mic in the bathroom like it was a booth. That shit sat up in a holder that was attached to the wall right by the mirror, and had a cord hanging from the end of it.

"Wanna step outside?" he asked, pushing a button on a remote. His living room curtains slid back and there was a deep view of New York City from an angle I'd never seen before.

We went outside on the terrace and I leaned on the rail while Free stood behind me holding me tight.

"You ain't slick," I told him, kissing his arm.

"I'm not?"

"Nope. I knew what was up the whole time, boy."

He laughed. "Yeah. That's why your eyes was so big. You was scared, girl. Tell the truth. Shook to the bone."

I denied that shit. "No I wasn't. I knew you was testing me. I just didn't wanna blow your little plan up by passing with flying colors. It woulda looked too easy."

"Umm. Yeah. I just wanted to see what you was about on the real. Plenty of jawns try to lock a nigga's coordinates when he's got credentials. I been through shit like that before. I just wanted to make sure you was legit, ya know? That you was digging this action for what it is, not for what you might get outta it."

"Them kinda girls be birds, though," I said, leaning against him and making sure he got a good feel from my ass. "I'm not that type."

"I know that now, Saucy," Free said. His soft lips were on my ear and his dick was rising behind me. "Now I know."

Chapter 13

I HAD BEEN kicking it hard with Free for a good minute and it was starting to get deep between us. Free treated me like no other man ever had. We had the most intense sexual attraction I'd ever experienced, and he beat my pussy to death on a regular basis.

Free was a hardworking man, and him and his manager had put their heads together and decided to come out with a compilation album of the greatest hits of some of hip hop's top artists. They planned to call it *Keep It Gangsta* and they were gonna film some clips to go with each track to make a music video.

Some of the scenes they shot in New York and some in Atlanta. The rest they were gonna shoot in Jamaica, and Free asked me if I wanted to go with him. Did I wanna go wasn't the question! I plugged Marshall's hole and gave him some bomb-ass top on Sunday afternoon, and a few hours later Free came to get me and I was *so* on that damn airplane!

Jamaica was banging. I was used to being on sets, but most of the time I was there to prance around half-naked while a rapper did his thing. This time I sat up on that set in a huge honcho chair next to Free like I was a big willie for real. Every industry chick who was there wanted to be me, and I walked around feeling myself on account of Free's celebrity status in the business, and my wifey status with him.

I wasn't whiny or needy while he was tryna handle his business or nothing, but at the end of each day when the set shut down was when I really came alive. We partied all over Jamaica, and I tried to drink every damn drop of rum they had on the island.

We spent seventeen wild-ass days in Jamaica, and the night before we bounced I got pissy drunk. We were getting lifted at the Half Moon resort in Montego Bay when that strong Jamaican yummy hit me on the sneak tip. Plus, I was high as hell too. One of the cameramen had copped a cigar box full of chronic blunts from a Rasta on the beach and gave me a handful. I took them shits in the women's bathroom and puffed like a dragon. Those was the best trees I had ever smoked in my life. I felt fine as long as I was shaking my ass, rubbing all over Free on the dance floor and yanking on his dick through his clothes, but the minute I sat my ass down it felt like somebody smashed me over the head with ten bottles of rum.

"Damn," I muttered, holding my head. Free had gone out front to talk to somebody a few minutes earlier. He had spent the last two days hanging out with some white boy real estate developer looking at property and doing who knew what else. The guy picked Free up in a fresh Jag and I was impressed. I'd wanted to roll with them when they took off, but Free wouldn't let me, saying he needed to handle some pricey business and that I would love my surprise later on. I didn't sweat it though, I just stayed back and chilled with the artists on the set and got lifted. He'd been gone from our booth for a good minute when that rum bit me. I got up and stumbled outside, trying to find him. Instead of ending up in front of the hotel, I found myself out back on the beach. It was real muggy out and I took off the red, green, and yellow sarong Free had bought me at a market, and tossed it in the sand. I walked out of my sandals and staggered toward the water in just my black thong and my red halter top.

The waves coming in looked real white and foamy, and I giggled as I ran out to meet them. I jumped with two feet and went splashing into the water, and when the first wave smacked me it shocked the hell outta me and I staggered backward, then fell on my ass.

"Oh, shit," I said, trying to turn over. The water was up to my chest. I was struggling up on my hands and knees when the next wave slapped me in the ass and wet up my hair and washed sandy water up my nose.

I spit out salty phlegm and coughed and choked, but as the wave went back out I felt my knees sinking deeper into the sand. I looked up and the hotel lights seemed like they were ten miles away. I started reaching toward them, and when the next wave hit me, I fought it, trying to crawl as the water foamed all around me.

I was panicking and gulping as the salty water burned my throat and blinded me. I tried to breathe through my nose and sniffed pure fire. I choked then swallowed and opened my mouth to scream, and that's when he grabbed me.

"Saucy!" Free had my hands and he was lifting me to my feet. "Stand up! Stop fighting! This shit ain't even that deep. Just stand up!"

He put his arm around me and half carried me out of the water. Both of us was soaking wet and I was sniffing and spitting out salt and sand and squeezing my eyes closed to make them stop burning.

"I—I was tryna find you," I gasped drunkenly, spitting out tiny grains of sand. "Where you was at?"

"I told you I had to talk to my man! When I got back in there you were gone. Some cat said he saw you go out to the beach. You lucky I found your ass!"

Walking up a beach was sure a lot harder than walking down one, even if it was short. I took a few steps then stopped to catch my breath and looked at Free, and when I saw all that damn water running outta his jeans I bust out laughing!! That shit was fuuuunnny! His beef and broccoli Timbs was squishing and his green and white Rocawear shirt was stuck to his body.

"What's so damn funny?"

I grabbed him and pressed my wet body up against him. "You saved my life, Freedom! Baby, you saved my life!"

He pushed me away. "Get the hell off me, Saucy. Your ass is *stupid* drunk."

I lunged for him again. "But you saved my life, baby! You saaaaaved meeee! I owe you big time, boy! I'ma love your ass forever 'cause you *saved* me!"

He gave me a disgusted look. "Yeah? Well you remember that shit the next time your drunk ass is out there drowning, okay?"

Free played me all the way back to New York.

I kept trying to kick up a conversation with him, but he wasn't having it. He gave me a funny look when I was ordering some drinks on the plane, then he closed his eyes and pretended like he was sleeping for the rest of the flight. When we landed at JFK and went through customs, he told his driver to put his bags in the limo, and then he flagged down the next waiting taxi for me.

"I'll check you out, Saucy," he said as he put me in the cab. He gave the driver a bunch of bills, then turned back to me. "It's time for me to get back on my grind and you should probably do whatever you do too."

I couldn't believe this shit. He was fronting me off like I was one of his groupies.

"What's wrong, Freedom? Why you acting like that?"

"Acting like what? I'm being me, Shawty. I don't know who the hell you being."

"So that's it?"

All he said was, "I'll holla," and then slammed the door.

I rode home cursing his ass out in my head. He let one drunk night mess up what we had going. I wouldn't have even been out on that damn beach if I hadn't been looking for him and he needed to know that shit.

I whipped out my cell phone and hit him on speed dial.

Whattup, yo. This ya man Freedom. You got the right nigga at the wrong time. Leave a message. Beep.

I pressed call end and snapped my phone shut. It was gonna

feel funny staying by myself again after kicking it with him for so many weeks, but fuck him. Thanks to Marshall I had my own damn bed to crash in and Freedom wasn't the only nigga on my thong.

I didn't know how much he'd given the cab driver, but it had looked like a little bundle and I held out my hand for change when we got to my house.

The cab driver damn sure didn't wanna hand it over.

"Just take out what's on the meter," I told him. "I'll give you your tip."

Free must've given him sixty dollars 'cause he gave me back a twenty.

"Sorry," I said as I dragged my bags out by myself. "I ain't got no change."

Upstairs my apartment seemed empty and quiet. Other than Sundays, I spent every day of the week with Free, and I was already missing him. I left my bags right by the front door and kicked off my shoes and left them there too. I had meant to check my mail before I came up, but I was busy fighting with my bags.

I stripped out of my clothes on the way to the bathroom and sat on the tub naked. I turned on the water and dropped some bath beads in, then thought about Free and went back in the living room to get my cell phone.

It rang as I was picking it up, and I flipped it open real quick and giggled. "Hey baby," I purred. "I knew you'd come around."

"Oh you did, huh?"

I almost dropped the phone. "Marshall!" I screamed.

"Don't Marshall me, who did you think was coming around?"

"You! Who else? It's just that I ain't heard from you in a minute, boo. I thought maybe your wife had you on lockdown."

He laughed. "Nah, baby, we're getting a divorce. But you the one who been out there doing the damn thang. You was MIA for our last two Sundays, ya know. You got some time for Papa tonight?"

I yawned. "Oooh, Papa. You know I always got time for you. It's just that Mami got cramps and she's tired for real. I don't have a bit of energy."

"Oh yeah? Well tonight is your night then. Papa's gonna come over and take good care of you for a change. I'll bring you some dinner and a movie, cool? See ya in twenty minutes."

Shit! I dropped that damn phone on the couch and raced to the door and dragged my suitcases over to the balcony. I opened the door and kicked them out. Then I ran to my linen closet and grabbed a set of clean sheets. In my bedroom, I stripped the dirty sheets off the bed, and threw the clean ones on any old kinda way. Then I ran back into the bathroom and splashed around in the tub, washing my ass like the house was on fire.

I went to brush my teeth and realized my toothbrush was in my bag outside on the balcony. I jetted back out there and dug around in my suitcase until I found it, then ran back into the bathroom and squeezed some toothpaste on the brush, then started scrubbing my teeth real fast. But when I looked into the mirror, I knew I was fucked up for real. On the left side of my neck, right under my ear, was a big-ass hickey. Free had put it on me the morning before, when he freaked me in the shower.

"Goddamn!" I shrieked and snatched the medicine cabinet open looking for my makeup case. But it was in my suitcase. Seconds later I was back on the balcony digging through my other bag. I found the makeup case and patted foundation all over my neck until the redness disappeared.

By now I was sweating and getting funky. I rubbed some deodorant under my arms and pulled my hair back in a ponytail, then ran in my room to find some clothes to throw on.

Marshall showed up faster than I had expected, and the smell coming from the big bag of Chinese food he was carrying turned my stomach.

"You looking good, Saucy," he told me. He kissed me on the cheek and patted my ass. "I brought some egg foo yung. Why don't you go fix us a couple of plates while I pop this movie in?"

Egg foo yung? This nigga had a lot of nerve. Yeah, I knew it was technically his joint, but mi casa was not su casa! I took the bag of food in the kitchen and slapped some of his Chinese goo on a plate. I'd disappeared to Jamaica without telling him and I knew Marshall was past due on his sex thang, but the only nigga I wanted to fuck was Free.

I carried the plate into the living room and Marshall was already lounging on the plush sofa with his feet up and the remote in his hand.

"Thanks, baby," he said as I passed him the food. "You're not going to eat?"

I shook my head. "I told you I got cramps. I ain't really hungry."

"Yeah, I heard that."

Marshall patted a spot next to him for me to sit down on the soft couch, then dug into his Chinese food.

"What movie did you get?" I asked as we waited for it to come on.

He shrugged. "Some grade B bootleg shit. I heard the actress was hot, though."

The onscreen action started with the camera zooming in on a headboard slamming against a wall, and the first thing I thought was, "That shit looks too familiar." But when I realized exactly what I was looking at, I jumped up and yelled, "What the fuck is this?"

On the screen I was straight naked and bent over Marshall's bed while Free hit it from the back like a maniac. I remembered that night real good. He'd swung by real late and had just caught me coming in from the club. I was buzzed and horny, and we'd tried to tear that damn bed down. My titties was jumping and jiggling and oh, ooh! oh, ooh! was coming out of my mouth as I fucked back at Free, getting crazy with it.

"Marshall! What the fuck is this?!?!"

"Oh, this that kinda shit they call bird business," Marshall said, winking with a mouthful of food. "That's when a chicken fucks her stud in another nigga's bed."

I glanced at the screen and saw myself crawl up on the mattress, then turn around and deep throat Free's thick black dick until it disappeared. He grabbed my hair and waxed me up and down his dick as I squeezed his balls and pulled him further down into my neck.

"Nigga . . ." I gasped, not believing my eyes. "You had a fuckin' *camera* set up in here?"

Marshall laughed. "Oh, hell yeah! I always roll the video-tape when I'm rolling with a video ho. I gotta protect my property, ya know?"

I snatched the remote control and stopped the tape.

"That was a bird-man move for real, Marshall. Don't no real man do no foul shit like that."

He shrugged and bit into a big piece of egg covered in gravy. "Whatever, baby. Why should I pay the rent when that nigga's getting your pussy all gummy? My man Free is cool, though. Son done real good for himself in the game and I'm proud of him. But he got his own label and some hot new artists and ere'thang now. Let him set you up like a real willie do. You've got thirty days, Saucy. Thirty days. Then you gotta be out."

I stood next to Marshall wanting to mush his face down in that nasty plate of brown eggs.

Instead I said, "And what? I'm supposed to cry now? You want me to get on my knees and beg because you putting me out your crib?"

He looked up at me, then started unbuckling his belt. "Nah, Saucy. You ain't gotta cry, and you so fine I don't want you down on your knees begging for nothing neither. But I got thirty days' worth of your services left, so what I *do* want you to do," he said, then stood up and opened his pants, "is find me one of my toys, then get on them little padded Chinese knees of yours and suck my fuckin' dick."

I couldn't have blown my game with Marshall at a worse time.

Free was still playing me and I couldn't even catch him on the phone.

I had gotten comfortable having a sugar daddy, and Marshall had been so sweet with his game that I had basically fallen off with all the other niggas I used to trick for money and luxuries. Now all of a sudden I had to worry about finding a place, paying rent, and buying clothes again. I knew I could kiss my drop-top Sebring goodbye because Marshall had already told me he was gonna confiscate that too. Actually, I wouldn't do much crying over the loss of the whip. That shit was for show only, and Marshall knew what the hell he was doing when he leased it for me. I couldn't drive it, and he had made it clear that he better not hear about no nigga driving it neither. The only play the damn thing got was when Tai got behind the wheel and took it for a spin, and that wasn't all that often.

I thought about Tai and wished she would get her own damn apartment. She was still living with her mother, and at times like these that shit was real inconvenient for me because when I needed someplace to stay, Tai sure couldn't help me.

I had called that crack-headed tennis star Zinger Jones and tried to sweet-talk my way up on him, but his bed was already occupied with his white bitch.

"Sorry, Saucy. My girlfriend just graduated from college, yo. She's back in the city now so my shit is back to being legit."

Miami was still sparking with the videos, and a director named Big Z had put in a good word for me with a producer down there. But that gig wasn't starting for a couple of months, and even so, whatever they paid me wasn't gonna be enough to find a quick apartment in New York City.

There were a few other minor niggas I probably coulda pushed in on, but I wasn't trying to go backward. I was used to rubbing asses with the big willies and being seen with the in crowd. Nah, backward wasn't gonna get it.

I looked around the apartment and frowned. Marshall had set it off real proper up in here. Designer furniture, thick carpet, granite countertops and a marble entryway. Some lucky bitch was gonna enjoy the hell outta this joint, but I could guarantee that Marshall's ass wouldn't be getting the kinda brain I'd been laying on him. That nigga was gonna miss me just as much as I missed him. Maybe more.

My mind was racing on fast-forward as I tried to come up with a move that would keep me on the board. I lit a dutchy and opened a bottle of Corona as I tried to figure out which nigga would serve me the best purpose right now. I tossed a hundred names around in my head, from drug runners on the corner, to A & Rs and CEOs of record labels. Every last one of them would have gladly whipped out some cheese to get some of this top action, but then what? I was looking for a willie who could take me on a longer trip, and no matter how many other dudes I thought of, my mind kept coming back to the only nigga who had ever turned me down in my life. Free.

Chapter 14

BUT THAT NIGGA Freedom was on some serious shit.

I called his cell phone thirty-four times before he finally took the damn call.

"What's good, Free," I said, waiting to hear the tone of his voice to see if I could judge his mood.

"Life," he answered.

I waited for him to say something else, but there was nothing but silence on the line.

"Well I hear that. I just called to see what you was getting into tonight. You know, to see if you felt like having a little company."

"I already got company, Saucy."

I looked at the phone like that nigga was bonkers for real.

"Who's your company, Free? Oh, you got some other bitch there with you?"

I heard him sigh. "I don't do bitches, Saucy. Especially drunk bitches."

I just let everything go.

"I'm sorry, Free! Damn I had a little bit too much to drink! Is that a crime?"

"It could be."

I knew he was talking about his mother and what she had done. "Come on, baby. You drink a little bit too."

"Yeah, but I know my limits, Saucy. I got discipline with my shit. I'm never outta control, and I definitely don't embarrass myself or nobody else in public."

"So one mistake and you gone hold that against me forever? Damn, I'm sorry! I thought we was deeper than that."

He sighed again and I knew I had that ass. "Okay, Saucy. Cool. I accept your apology."

I giggled. "So we good, right?"

"Yeah, baby. We good."

"Then I hope you ready for this tonight," I whispered sexily, licking my lips. "I got something real hot waiting for you."

He fucked me right up.

"Sorry, baby. I'ma have to get with you another time. I told you, I already got company."

It had been two weeks since I'd seen Free. Every time I tried to get up in his crib he was either working or busy or too tired to see me. He would talk to me on the phone for hours, but y'all know I wasn't satisfied with that. I had sixteen days left before Marshall tossed me and my shit out on the curb, and that meant I would have to work fast.

It took me a minute to come up with a plan, but once I had it, I knew it would work. I called Tai and begged her to go along with my scheme, and I couldn't believe it when she tried to tell me no.

"You don't even call me for damn-near forever, and then out of the blue I'm supposed to jump like a frog for some old woman in a nursing home? I don't even cook like that no more, Saucy! I'm spending my time outside doing me now instead of in the kitchen."

"Please, Tai. Just do me this one favor and I'll never ask you for nothing else again. I swear! C'mon, this means a lot to me. This old lady I met is so sweet and you know I don't even like old people. I can't wait for you to meet her, Tai. She's been in that nursing home for so long that she's lonely. She cried so bad about being tired of eating hospital food, so I promised her I'd bring her some home-cooked stuff that's been seasoned real good."

"Well then you should cook her something then."

"Tai! You trying to kill that old lady?!? You know I can't cook!"

She sucked her teeth. "You get on my damn nerves, Saucy. I don't know why I keep letting you talk me into doing all kinds of shit for you. I'm supposed to be your girl, not your damn cook. Besides. Maybe they feed that old lady oatmeal all day for a reason. Collard greens might tear her stomach up. Damn. You get me so sick, bitch. You want the chicken baked or fried?"

It was hard as hell getting that shopping cart in and out of that taxi.

I rolled it up into the lobby of Free's building and waited for the elevator. And when it came I got in with my cart full of soul food goodies and stank that shit up real nice. The smell of baked chicken, collard greens, macaroni and cheese, and candied yams was so strong that my stomach started growling and I licked my lips.

I got off on the eighteenth floor and pulled the cart down to Free's apartment with my heart beating fast. I had on a pair of Seven jeans and a matching blue shirt, and a pair of blue and red Prada sneakers and a red Prada purse. I had pulled my hair back in a French braid, and I had rubbed on just a little bit of lipstick.

That nigga let me ring that bell for a good two minutes before he opened the door, and I was just getting ready to say something nasty when he grinned.

"Sorry."

I was waiting for him to tell me what took so long. Especially since the damn doorman had looked at me pulling a damn shopping cart like a bag lady and called up to tell him I was coming.

"What took you so long?"

He kept grinning. "You want the truth?"

I gave him a fucked-up look.

"Aiight. I was trying to decide whether or not I should let you in."

I turned my ass right around and stomped back out the door.

"Saucy! Saucy!"

I let him follow me down the hall, switching my gangsta booty in them Seven jeans as hard as I could.

"Come on, Saucy," he said, grabbing my arm. "You here now, girl. I was just playing with you, girl. Damn. I thought you liked to laugh?"

"Not when the fuckin' joke is on me!"

"Okay," he said, pulling me back toward the crib. "Look at you, got sweat poppin' all off your nose and shit. And you left that big-ass laundry cart in my joint too. Come on back in."

My lip was poked out but it didn't slow my feet down. I went back inside with him and pulled the shopping cart into the kitchen and started unloading it.

"What did you cook?" Free asked, coming over to help me.

I smiled. "I got a little a this and a little that. Some chicken, macaroni and cheese, candied sweet potatoes, and some collard greens." I reached down for the plastic cake holder that Tai had had sense enough to put into a box.

"And for dessert," I said, setting it up on the counter. "I got my boo a 7Up cake!"

"Ummm," Free said, kissing my neck. "That sounds real good, baby. Let me help you fix the plates."

I touched my neck where his lips had just been. I was riding high and almost nutted off that one damn kiss. We ate in the living room and watched a movie. I don't know what the hell happened, or which star was up in it or nothing. I ate a few bites of chicken and some greens, then spent the rest of the time striking sexy poses trying to turn Free on.

When he finished eating and took our plates into the kitchen, I figured he was ready for dessert. I ran into the bathroom and took a tiny yellow and green sunflower bra and matching thong from my purse and stripped outta my clothes and laid them across the hamper. I took my hair down and spread it around my shoulders the way he liked it, then walked back into the living room looking sexy as fuck.

I busted the look on his face when he saw me. I knew how bad he wanted me, and all he had to do was stop frontin' and he could have me. I did a little stomach-roll move that used to drive niggas wild at the G-Spot. And it worked. His eyes got that fuck look in them and he smiled as I stood between his legs gyrating my hips to a slow sexy beat.

"Damn. You always serve up dessert like this after dinner?"

"Hey, a girl gotta do what she gotta do for her man, right?"

He ran his hands up my thighs and gripped my ass. "Yeah, that's right."

I pressed my crotch toward his face and rubbed the back of his neck.

"So we a couple again?"

"Yeah," he nodded. "For tonight."

Tonight my ass. I let that nonsense comment roll right off my back. After I laid this prime pussy on him he was gonna be mesmerized and begging me to stay.

Free stood up to get undressed, and reached into his wallet and got out a condom. He stuck it between the cushions and kissed me and laid me back on the sofa. I reached out to touch him through his clothes, and the moment I did I felt his dick leap into action. I had missed him and I was holding some rock-hard proof in my hand that he had missed me too. He took off the rest of his gear and joined me naked on the couch.

I put my tongue on the tip of Free's dick and tasted that nice sweet juice coating the head. He grabbed his dick and rolled it around all over my lips. I felt his hand sliding down my back as he entered my mouth. The veins on his dick stood out as I ran my lips and tongue up and down his shaft.

I moved Free's hand outta the way and took control. I slid

my body lower and slipped his dick in between my titties, mashing it in my cleavage and licking the head as it peeped through. He helped pump my titties together and I provided all the lip juice we needed to keep things nice and slick. Free got him a titty fuck for a few minutes, then I pushed him off and rolled over underneath him until I was on my stomach.

I felt him massaging my back as he slid down into spoon position behind me, gripping my hips. He humped on me, rubbing his dick on my ass, and I felt him search for his condom, then find it. I turned my head and watched when he took his hands off me to open it, and I was loving the way that dick looked raw and wished me and him got down like that.

With his condom on, Free raised me up into position and I felt my knees leave the sofa for a second as he slid deeply into my wetness. He rocked into me, pumping hard on some real break-up, make-up sex shit, driving me deeper down into the cushions with each thrust.

Free followed me, tagging my ass without mercy. I arched my back and he grabbed both of my titties and rubbed my nipples until I purred. He pulled me up toward him until my back was against his chest, and then he thrust into me real deep four or five times, then slammed me down extra hard on his dick and slid his hands up under my arms and lifted me straight off his dick. I was still in the air as he spun me around until I was facing him, then he lowered me back down on his pole and hit it even harder, juggling my ass cheeks as he guided me on my ride.

I was shocked and turned on by his strength. No other nigga had ever slapped that kinda in-the-air move on me before, and all I could do was rub all over his muscles as I came, bucking and screaming until he muffled my cries with his mouth.

Free wasn't far behind me so I knew he hadn't been fuckin' nobody else. He came a lot faster than he normally did, and I accepted that nut with a smile on my face.

It was hot in the room and our bodies were sweaty. I wanted to ask him for a beer or something, but I was scared he'd think I was trying to get drunk. Instead I told him I was thinking about accepting a video assignment with an artist in Atlanta, just to see if he would ask me to stay.

He didn't.

We got up and went into his sweet bedroom. Free pulled the sheets back and rubbed my ass as I slid between them. I laid there snuggled up under him with my head on his strong thick chest as he talked about the industry and how most black artists spent their money on stupid shit like hoes, clothes, and cars instead of making it work for them so they could earn even more money. He told me that from the very beginning of his career he had developed a five-year plan that would allow him to retire young and rich if he wanted to.

"I never thought I'd be retiring this soon, but I liked knowing my shit was set up proper, just in case. This business is full of sharks, Saucy. And some of these fools out here ain't nothing but bait."

"Yeah, maybe," I told him. "But some people ain't looking five years into the future, Free. What's wrong with living today and having a good time while you young? You so damn serious all the time you sound like an old-ass man."

"See, that's the kinda thinking that fucks so many people up."

"Oh, what, motherfucker?" I laughed. "You tryna say I'm fucked up or sumpthin'? Nigga please! I been using my head since I was six years old, son! I'ma get mines in this mother-fucker, regardless!"

I was still chuckling when I noticed Free had gone quiet.

"Damn, girl," he said, shaking his head. "You so fine those kinda ugly words don't even sound right coming out of your mouth. Slow ya gangsta roll down some, baby. Have some dignity about yourself. Some class. This is Freedom you talking to. You ain't gotta be one of the sons, you know. A player like me needs a lady on his arm, Saucy. Not a dun dun or a hoodrat. Image is everything in this business and I'm trying to keep mine up."

I shut up after that. I felt kinda bad, like Free was saying I didn't live up to his high-class image or something. I slipped off to sleep thinking about that and it musta been around two in the morning when Free rolled over and kissed me softly on the back of my neck.

"It's getting late, baby," he said. "I got a early day tomorrow. A long one too. You ready?"

"I'm already there," I mumbled, halfway asleep. I snuggled down deeper in his big bed, getting my sprawl on in his cool satin sheets. "Besides, I don't have to be nowhere tomorrow. I can sleep all day."

I felt him sit up.

"Well some of us gotta grind, baby. Get dressed. I'll take you down to get a cab."

I opened one eye. "You got jokes, right? After what I just laid on you, I can barely move."

"Well you gotta make some moves tonight, doll. Right toward the door." He pulled the covers off me and slapped me gently on my ass. "Let's do this, Mami. I gotta be back up and out in couple of hours."

This motherfucker was serious!

"Free," I said, sitting up and reaching for him. "Why can't we just chill together for one night? Damn. We had a real good evening and I know you was feeling me just like I was feeling you. Why you pulling away so hard now?"

He swung his feet around to the floor. "What's real, Saucy? I just wanna sleep by myself. You got a fly crib to rest in but you acting like you don't wanna go home. What's with that?"

"I *don't* wanna go home!" I blurted out. "I'm moving out. I gotta find another place real fast and I was gonna ask you if I could chill here with you!"

He went quiet and got a real cold look in his eyes. "You was gonna ask *me* that?"

I looked down at the floor. I couldn't believe it. In my wildest nightmares I hadn't imagined this fish would be so damn hard to hook. I shook inside at the thought that he might reject me again.

"Yeah," I finally said. "I was."

He shook his head for a long time, like he couldn't find the words to express himself. Then finally he said, "Nah, Saucy. I care about you a whole lot. You deep in my heart, baby, that's truth. But our heads are in two different places. I ain't sure about stepping off into no deep water with you, though. At least not right now."

Chapter 15

I DIDN'T KNOW WHETHER to tear that nigga's crib up or fall on the floor and get stupid and start begging. No nigga had ever pushed me aside in my life and I didn't know how to play it without totally playing myself.

Free was quiet when he walked me downstairs and he didn't say shit the whole time we stood there waiting while the doorman flagged down a cab.

"Aiight," he said when the cab pulled up and I got in. He put the shopping cart and the empty food containers in on the other side. "Be cool, Saucy. I'll get witcha."

He didn't seem like he wanted to kiss me goodbye so I just closed the cab door and waved out the window as I pulled away. Free stood outside watching as we drove off. He had on a wifebeater and some Sean Paul jeans, and his hands was in his pockets so I guess that's why he didn't wave back.

But I hadn't been back in my apartment for more than ten minutes when my cell phone rang. I had been planning to wash out Tai's plastic containers and give them back to her, but hell she had a dishwasher so I just left them sitting in the cart and went in the kitchen to get a drink of water when I felt the vibration on my waist.

I yanked the phone off my waistband so hard the clip broke.

I looked at the caller ID before flipping it open and bust out grinning. Yeah! That nigga knew!

"Saucy," he said after I said hello. "You home?"

"Yeah. I just got here a few minutes ago. Why?"

He hesitated. "I just wanted to make sure you got home okay, ya know? New York is a crazy town."

My heart was touched!

"You was worrying about me, boo?"

"A little bit," he admitted. "I mean, I know you hardcore and gangsta and can take care of yourself and all that. But I still wanted to make sure you was cool, nah' mean?"

"I ain't gangsta, Free!"

"You mean you're not gangsta?"

"Yeah. That's what I just said. Couldn't no gangsta give you what I gave you tonight. I'm all woman, Free. And I know how to act like a lady."

"I ain't looking for you to just act like a lady, Saucy. I want you to be one."

I didn't know *what* this nigga was talking about. All I wanted was another chance to make him feel me the way he was feeling me in the beginning and I told him that.

"Just gimme another chance, Free. I know you feeling this, baby. You gotta be."

"Aiight. I'm taking a little trip. I'll be back next week. I'll be staying at my crib in Jersey. I'll pick you up and we can chill for a couple of days to see how shit goes. How's that?"

My mind got busy calculating. I had to be outta this joint on the thirty-first and Marshall had already told me there wasn't gonna be no extensions given. He'd probably have the next bitch up in here ten minutes after I booked. If Free wasn't coming back until sometime next week, then that meant I had one good week to work on his ass before I had to drop him completely and find me a new herb who was wide open. I knew if I was forced to go that route and moved in with some other nigga, it would be over between me and Free for good.

"I guess it's cool. But a whole week? I'ma miss you boo."

He laughed. "Yeah. I hear that. See ya next week. I'll holla."

I took a shower and went to bed with a smile on my face, but as soon as I opened my eyes the next morning I knew something was wrong. I had a nasty taste in my mouth, and when I stood up to go use the bathroom the room spun and my stomach lurched.

"Oh, shit," I whispered, running toward the bathroom. I felt like I wanted to throw up, but I didn't. Chills broke out on my arms and my body started to sweat.

"That fuckin' Tai!" I muttered as I climbed back in the bed. She musta did something really fucked up with that food we ate last night. I was praying whatever I got hold of, Free had skipped it because I felt horrible. I started to call him and see if he felt sick, but I didn't wanna make a pest outta myself or worse, make him think I was desperate and looking for an excuse to talk to him before next week.

Instead, I called Tai. "Girl, that food was nasty last night."

She thought I was giving her a compliment.

"Thanks, Sauce. I told you I put my toe in it."

"Well, you must got some athlete's foot going on because I feel real sick this morning."

"Well ain't you a bitch!" Tai hollered into the phone. "Why do you being sick have to be related to my food? Free ate it, right? Did he get sick?"

"*Uhn*-huh!" I lied. "He didn't sleep all night. I was up holding him while he threw that shit up all over the bathroom. Maybe it was something in the greens, huh? I told you about eating that pork, Tai. It ain't no good for you and it makes you fat."

"Uh-*ha*!" Tai screeched. "I busted your ass! You said you was feeding some little old lady at a nursing home, Saucy! You are such a big-ass liar. I can't believe *shit* you say!"

"Calm down, Tai! I did feed that old lady! But that was a whole lotta food! How much you think one little shriveled-ass old woman can eat? I took the leftovers to Free last night, that's what happened. Damn!"

"Whatever, Saucy. You don't appreciate shit I do for you. You got issues, girl. And I mean that shit."

"I didn't mean nothing by it, Tai. I was just telling you in case you still had some food left over and was gonna eat it. I'm just trying to look out for you girl!"

"Yeah. Good looking out. But I already told you, I don't eat like that no more. I'm making some healthy choices in my life these days. You know. Cutting out all the bullshit that doesn't benefit me."

The way she said it made me think she might be talking about me.

"I gotta be outta this apartment in two weeks," I said, changing the subject. "I'm looking for someplace to stay, but so far ain't nothing shaking."

"What happened with Marshall?" she asked.

"Long story. But basically I just can't deal with him no more. You know? I see his wife looking happy at all them big-time Black Diamond events, grinning all up in his face, when I know damn well how much he wants to be with me. He said he's gonna divorce her so he can be mine full-time, but even still. I just can't do that no more. It's killing him that I'm breaking things off, but it's what I gotta do."

"Well that's smart. Neither you nor his wife should be making life so convenient for that nigga. I don't care how paid he is. But at least when his wife bounces she has her own cheese to take with her. She's smart and beautiful. That new jewelry line is really working for her and those magazine ads with her cute little boys makes people want to go out and buy her designs, but where is all this gonna leave you?"

Ass out, but I wasn't gonna fess up to that shit.

"Oh, I'm good," I said real quick. "You know Free is still large in this game, no matter what went down at Ruthless. He could one day be as large as Marshall, but the good part is, he don't have no wife and kids clocking him."

Tai seemed surprised. "Oh? Free is gonna let you stay with him? You sure about that?"

"Yeah," I said with some attitude. "I'm sure. Why wouldn't he, Tai? We've been kicking it for a minute."

"Oh, okay. I just thought . . . you know."

"Nah," I said. "I *don't* know." I felt myself getting defensive. I was the one sucking Free's dick. Not Tai. "What are you tryna say? Did you hear something different from Free?"

"Saucy. Whatever you and Free do is between y'all. I work with him a lot, but I'm not in his business like that. I was just surprised to hear you say he was sick and in the bed with you this morning because I know he flew to Vegas before the sun came up."

How in the fuck did *she* know?!? Free hadn't even told *me* where he was going!

"You know Jaheim rolled with him," she went on. "I dropped him off at the airport at five this morning and Free was already there so I know he got on that flight."

Jaheim?!? I couldn't stand his bony ass. I didn't know why Tai was dropping his gay behind off. I'd run into him when I was out partying one night and tried to get with him. That herb acted like I was offering him some poison instead of some pussy!

I rolled my eyes. "Did I say what *time* in the morning Free was with me, Tai? No. I *didn't*. Look," I snapped. I was ready to get off the damn phone now. "Some baller is beeping in on my other line. I gotta go. Later."

I had four days left when Free finally came by to see me. He had been back in New York for a couple of days, but every time I called him he claimed he was taking care of business and would call me back when he could.

Well that didn't do nothing but piss me off. I had gone clubbing while he was in Vegas and met this rapper named Quaison from the Lower East Side. He was onstage spittin' but he was only half decent. He musta spotted me out there dancing because he asked one of his homeys to bring me a drink.

That nigga didn't *even* know how long my throat was! I drank up all his dollas and left him with no cents! I ended up going home with him that night and we hit some lines and did the wild thang until his dick was sore. Quaison lived with his mother in a one-bedroom apartment. For some reason his moms slept on a pull-out bed in the living room, giving Quai the tiny little bedroom right off the kitchen. We was high as hell, hitting lines until my eyes felt like they was bulging outta my head. Quai put on a condom and started banging my pussy so good I began screaming like somebody was slaying my ass.

"Shut the fuck up!" he hissed, fucking me even deeper. "My moms is sleeping in the living room!"

I kept right on yelling. That shit felt damn good, and if his moms hadn't known he was in there hitting skins, she damn sure knew now. What did she think we was gonna do back there when we tiptoed past her bed at four in the damn morning?

"You down for some freaky shit?" Quai had asked me when we first got to his room. Shit, I was lifted and buzzed and feeling like a superhero. I was down for any damn thing.

"Let's make us a fuck tape, baby," he said, and whipped out the camera. "We can see which one of us got the best game going, bet?"

I looked at the lines on the dresser and the half a bottle of Patrón on the floor and said, fuck it. Why not? I liked the way my body looked naked and yeah, I'd done a few backroom productions on a couple of video sets. Plus, this nigga was challenging me. Tryna stunt like he might possibly have a better sex game than me. Later for that!

I worked on Quai like he was my pet project. I put my legendary brain game down on him with my finest skills and he repaid me by sucking my clit until I screamed so loud I knew damn well his mama was woke! Quai sucked my toes, licked my back, and my ass too, and I had to admit he was a contender for real. That boy had me sweating and moaning and sticky with cum when he finally told me to look up and smile.

"Say 'brainiac' baby," he clowned.

I lifted my sweaty face toward the camera and stuck both my middle fingers up in the air, then grabbed the Patrón and quenched my thirst.

Fucking around with Quai had been a whole lotta fun, but now I was trying to get with Free. I could tell the nigga was ducking and dodging me and I was right at the point where I decided I was gonna call him one more damn time, and if he played me, I'd give Quaison a call and see what he had poppin'. His crib near Baruch Houses was straight hood, but inside it was pretty decent. Thanks to Free, I might have to make a move downtown instead of crosstown.

But Free surprised me and came by my apartment real early the next morning.

"Sorry I didn't buzz you first," he said, looking around like I mighta had a nigga stashed in the crib. He just didn't know. Fucking him up in here is what had me scrambling for somewhere to stay now.

Free was driving his ugly Honda but I climbed in that baby like it was a Mercedes. It was barely seven o'clock in the morning and I was still tired. My head hurt and I felt dizzy from all the sticky I had smoked the night before. As soon as he took off driving I closed my eyes and crashed out, and when I woke up again Free was nudging my arm.

"Saucy," he said. "It time to roll out. You aiight?"

I lifted my head and looked around.

"Damn," he said and reached toward me. "You got some spit leaking out ya mouth, Mami. Lemme get that."

I struggled to wake up as he wiped my mouth, then I stretched and sat all the way up. We were sitting in Free's driveway, outside of that horrible little shack in Jersey. I really didn't care where we were, it was too damn early and I was tired. I just wanted to go inside and crawl in the bed and crash.

As soon as we walked in the door I took off my shoes and stretched out on the sofa. Free cut on the miniature TV, but I wasn't tryna strain my eyes looking at that shit. I dozed off again and when I woke up Free was standing in front of me holding out a plate of scrambled eggs and some toast.

"Damn, girl! You musta shut the damn club down last night. What time did you get home, five minutes before I rang your bell?"

I sat up and shook my head, and that's when the whole

damn room got stupid. The smell of the eggs hit my stomach hard, and I threw up all over Free's ancient coffee table.

"Damn," he said, trying to stick the plate under my chin to catch what was coming out my mouth. Just the sight of those damn eggs made my skin crawl, and I pushed the plate away and heaved again.

"You're sick, Saucy," Free said, softly.

Tell me some shit I don't know, is what I woulda said if I could have.

He took me in the bathroom and stayed with me, holding me as I threw up water and yellow sludge and cried at the same time.

When I finally managed to stop Free put me in his bed and covered me up, then went in the bathroom to clean up my mess. The house was so small I could smell the bleach he was disinfecting with, and I stuck my head under the covers real quick so I didn't throw up all in his bed.

Free came back in the room and took off his clothes. He got in the bed with me and just held me and rubbed my back. He was whispering sweet shit like, you gonna be all right baby, and don't worry, Free is here. I drifted back off again and when I woke up I felt a little bit better.

I slept all day, and that night Free woke me up and told me to drink a cup of hot tea. It was nice and sweet and felt good to my stomach while I was drinking it, but minutes later I was bringing it back up again.

"Damn, baby," Free said as he helped me into the bathroom. My legs were trembling and I felt so weak I couldn't stand up by myself. I clung to him as he wrapped his strong arms around me and wiped my face and my mouth.

"I'm taking you to the doctor, Saucy," Free said after my fourth bout of heaving. By now my lips were dry and I was feeling faint. Free had been cleaning up behind me all day and he was acting real concerned. As sick as I was, I liked it that he was focused on me and I was enjoying his attention. "You probably got the flu or something, but you need to let somebody check you out," he insisted.

I didn't wanna go see no doctors, but I was too sick to argue with him so when I woke up the next morning and I was still feeling sick, I let him put me in the car and we bounced. The hospital wasn't that far, and when we got there Free took me straight to the emergency room.

This wasn't New York City and I could damn sure tell. Instead of waiting five hours to see a doctor we waited less than two. They had already taken blood tests and made me pee in a plastic cup, and when the doctor came in to see me I was stretched out on the exam table and Free was standing over me, kissing my forehead and playing with my hair.

"Well, Ms. Robinson," he said, pulling a stool out from under the desk and sitting down. "It looks like we've discovered the reason you're feeling so badly."

"Flu, right?" Free said, looking at me all proud like he had already made some grand diagnosis. "She's got the flu, don't she!"

"Oh," the doctor said. He stood up and patted me on the arm. "There's a flu going around all right, but Ms. Robinson doesn't have it. She's pregnant."

Chapter 16

I don't know who cried harder, Free or me.

I mean, I had the tears coming all out my eyes and running down my face. Free's tears was in his heart, but I could still see them shits.

That nigga wasn't half as shocked as I was. I had never been one of them women who got real heavy periods, but as far as I could remember I hadn't missed a single one. I had told the doctor that and he said that wasn't unusual. He told me and Free that some women continue to get their periods for nine months and end up shocked as shit when they sit on the toilet and a baby falls out.

"Has your appetite increased?" the doctor asked.

Free answered. "She barely eats. I ain't never seen nobody eat as little as she does."

"So you haven't gained any weight?"

I looked at Free, and we both shook our heads. "If anything," I told him, "I've probably lost some of my booty."

"I want you to tell me the truth, Saucy," Free said, squeezing my hands. We were back at his house standing in the kitchen. The doctor had estimated that I was about sixteen weeks pregnant. I had been kicking it with Free for just a little longer than that. "You been with anybody else? Could this be somebody else's baby?"

I broke all the way down.

"*Nooooo!*" I wailed, like my heart had been stomped on. "How could you even ask me some shit like *thattttt*?" Snot and tears were flying off my face as I shook my head back and forth hysterically.

"I been with *you*, Free! Nobody else but you!"

"I 'on't know, girl. You keep a lot of talk flying around—"

"I thought you said you was your own fuckin' judge! You said you didn't even *listen* to none of them stupid-ass rumors that go around!"

"Still—"

"I don't want no fuckin' baby, Free! I made sure you used a wrapper *every single time*!"

He stared at me for a second, then pulled me close to him, holding me tight.

"But one broke, baby," he said quietly. "Don't you remember? The plastic broke the first night we got together, yo."

We stayed pressed together like that, rocking each other. I didn't even think about Marshall or Quaison, or that other nigga I'd fucked the night I passed out drunk.

We spent the night holding each other and fucking slowly and quietly. Free's hands were all over me, touching every part of me. He kissed my lips tenderly and sucked on my tongue. I screamed out loud when he pushed my knees back and slid down and buried his face between my legs and licked my slit deeply, sliding his tongue in and out of me, swirling it around my clit. I rubbed his head and arched my pussy up toward him, pulling his face down to meet my thrusts.

I came in Free's mouth twice, and that seemed to turn him on even more. I wanted to give him some head, but I was scared to put his big dick in my mouth. Just the thought of anything near my throat made me think I was gonna start throwing up again. Free understood, and when he rolled me on top of him and gripped my ass, lowering me down on his throbbing dick, neither one of us bothered worrying about a rubber at that point.

When I say that was some of the best dick I'd ever had, I mean it. I felt it all in my soul.

"Oh, Free . . . I love you . . ." I whispered, sucking his nipple and tracing circles around it with my tongue. And the four words my boo whispered back to me were the best I had ever heard. It wasn't like we was just straight-out fucking. Free was feeding me from the center of his self, and I was lapping that nourishment up like a starving cat. When it was over Free rolled me off him and kissed my stomach tenderly, then put his hand on its flatness and slept.

But I stayed awake for a real long time thinking about how I could play this shit to my advantage. I was in Free's heart and loving it. I wasn't lying when I said I didn't want no baby, but maybe having a kid by Free wouldn't be the worst thing in the world. I couldn't see me as nobody's mother, but I knew Free would be the best damn father in the world.

The sun was coming up by the time I closed my eyes. I had thought real long and hard throughout the night, and I decided this wasn't the worst thing that coulda happened to me. I was actually tired of running from nigga to nigga to get my sticky off. Free was a complete package in the sheets and out. I wasn't lacking nothing in his bed, and now that I had him back on lock I could only see the sex getting even better.

The next afternoon Free drove me back to New York. After that bomb-ass pipe he had laid between my legs the night before and then breaking down and whispering how deep he felt for me, Free was real moody during the day like he wished none of it had happened. I kept quiet in the car because I figured he was mad at himself for saying the L word because it had probably been his dick talking and he didn't really mean it. Well fuck him too! Neither did I! But I still needed his ass. I had two days left to stay in Marshall's apartment and I had been selling his shit off so fast there was hardly any furniture left in the joint.

When Free pulled up outside the apartment I didn't know how to be. He didn't even put the car in park, he just sat there with his foot on the brake so I knew this was a drop-off and nothing else.

"See ya later," I said. I was pissed but I wasn't gonna let

him see it. This motherfucker must not know! I hadn't stayed up busting my brain all damn night for nothing. I was up crunching numbers and what-if-ing scenarios to death. Free mighta lost a whole lot with Ruthless, but it took cash to run an apartment as phat as the one he kept in Manhattan, so I knew he still had a decent amount of bank left. I was the one carrying his motherfuckin' baby, not the other way around. He could act shitty if he wanted to, but eventually brothah was gonna hafta recognize!

Free almost clipped my ass in the door he pulled off so fast. He left me standing there on the curb, sucking down his fumes. I went upstairs and looked around Marshall's half-empty apartment and sat down on a big beanbag. I had sold the living room furniture to a lady who lived on the third floor and the money I'd gotten for it might have to go toward renting yet another damn hotel room.

I got mad at Free just thinking about that shit. Here I coulda been sitting up lovely with Pretty Boy and whipping them Cambodian bitches' asses while he paid my credit card bills, or hanging out with Grillz and getting my butt massaged, or riding around in a Escalade all night with that young, fine ass Quaison. But instead I was tossing my whole roll on Free, when that nigga didn't even wanna act right.

I slept like an old fat man that night. Worried or not, Marshall's bed was soft and plush, and if I had found somebody who wanted to buy it, it woulda already been gone. The next morning I was sick again, but I did what the doctor had recommended and ate a couple of crackers that I'd set out on my night table the night before.

I was sprawled out in bed when my cell phone rang. I looked at the caller ID, then let it ring two more times.

"Hello?"

"I been thinking," Free said. His voice sounded real serious, but still real smooth. "About what you asked me a couple of weeks ago."

We both knew what he was talking about, so there wasn't no need for me to front.

"Okay."

"And I think I'm ready for that now."

"You think so?"

"I know so."

"So what made you change your mind? The baby?"

"Yeah, that has a lot to do with it," he admitted. "But I'm feeling you too, Saucy. Even when I don't wanna be feeling you, you still there."

I took a deep breath and let it out real slow. I was 'bout to have this nigga eating outta my hand now. But I kept myself in pocket.

"I got feelings for you too, Free. I admitted them to you last night. But I don't wanna jump off into nothing with you just because we having a baby. Plenty of people have babies but don't hook up. It don't take no father being around to raise no child, you know."

"It does to raise my damn child! I don't care what them other niggas out there do with their seeds, but I'ma nourish mine! Ere' day. You can believe that. I'ma get real personal with my tyke, Saucy. That's what's real, baby!"

My lips curled up in a smirky smile. Oh, I musta said the wrong damn thing. Shit. By the way he responded it was actually the right thing.

Free came to pick me up at about two that afternoon. He was right on time too because I'd just cursed Marshall out.

"Tomorrow is D-day, baby," he'd hollered when I answered a call from him. "I hope you got your shit packed, sweetie 'cause I got fresh plans for the crib tomorrow night, and you ain't included."

"Fuck you, Marshall. You can take this mothefuckin' roach trap and stick it up your shitty ass, nigga!"

"Ouch!" he said. "As pretty as you are nobody would ever believe the kinda slime that comes out your mouth, girl." He laughed. "Or what kinda slime that goes in it, either. I'ma tell you, Saucy. If you ever fall off and need some quick cash, call me, baby. I know some niggas who would pay good money to get their joint waxed the way you work it. Hell, I could put your skank ass out on the stroll and make a quick fuckin' million! Your top is just that good. You must be laying down some kinda ancient Chinese secret! I'ma miss you girl! I really am! "

I opened up on his ass Harlem style!

"Oh, you gonna miss something you blinky-dink motherfuckah! That's for real. Just wait until you get back to your funky-ass apartment. Ain't gone be shit up in here you and the next bitch can use! Now kiss my black ass you limp-dicked, stuttering, butt-plugged, cheesy-balls, saggy-nuts, crooked-dicked, bad-breathed, crusty-eyed, shitty-drawers, waterbug-looking, can't-eat-no-pussy motherfuckah!"

I snapped my cell phone closed so hard it clacked, and when Free rang the bell downstairs an hour later I was still sweating. I looked around Marshall's apartment for the last time and felt real satisfied. Every dish in the joint was in the middle of the kitchen floor, smashed. I'd torn down all the drapes, unplugged the refrigerator, stopped up the toilet, overflowed the bathtub, and cut a big hole in his mattress. That motherfucker didn't know who he was dealing with, but when he walked up in here with his next bitch he would figure it out real quick. I was feeling myself. Getting my confidence up. Saucy was getting her spice back again, and even a rich nigga like Marshall wasn't no match for this.

"I'm coming down," I pressed the intercom and called out to Free, then grabbed the handles on my two gigantic rolling suitcases that were full of clothes and other gifts Marshall and Pretty Boy and Grillz and Quaison and so many others had bought me. I walked outta that box and didn't look back. Where I was going was definitely bigger, and so much better. Let Marshall try to come up in Free's spot blowing me up. That rabbit-looking nigga would get stripped at the steps, and I was almost sure of that.

My first weeks with Free were the shit. We lived at the top of the world and I just couldn't get enough of his pretty smile, his muscled-up black body, the way he handled me in the bed, and the juice he had in the streets. I loved it when Tone, Cuban, Herc, Bandie, and all the rest of his boys were chilling up in the crib, listening to sounds, laying down tracks, and making beats.

Even though he was retired, Free was still doing a lot of song writing and had some new artists on the label that he was trying to help get some exposure. He took me with him to Phoenix and Las Vegas, and we even flew into Canada to check out some new talent he was scouting up there.

Free was always getting invites to award shows and hot parties, and when Tai faxed him his date sheets my eyes would be all over those pages. I'd look for the events that were gonna have the best crowds, the most important people in the industry, or the most press, and those were the ones I begged Free to take me to.

"I don't even look pregnant," I argued when he acted like I should be staying home. "I know chicks who got more stomach than me, and they ain't having no baby."

Free got invited to the BET Music Awards and I was right there on his arm. Everybody was there, Stevie Wonder, Chaka Khan, Beyoncé, Kanye, Diddy, the Wayans brothers . . . it was all that. Afterward Free was invited to BET's Black Carpet Lounge with Danella and Toure, and I was right up in there with him.

Free treated me so special. As soon as I moved in his joint he started feeding me, trying to make me gain some weight. Every time I looked up he was cooking and washing tomatoes and making salad and cutting up fresh fruit. I hated oranges so he went out and got me some vitamin C tablets. He stood over me and made me take them nasty-ass pregnancy vitamins too, and sometimes they kept my stomach upset for the whole day.

Free stayed on me about drinking plenty of water too, and made me take long walks with him. He took me to all my doctor appointments and was there when we saw the sonogram results too. Free was mad happy that he was having him a son, and he told every damn body who would listen that he was about to have a tyke. He barred his boys from smoking in the crib and said that meant no sticky and no ciggs, so all they could do was get their drink on. Free didn't know it, but sometimes I got mine on, too.

I knew he loved me and was just trying to take care of me, but after a minute I started getting sick of him telling me what to do and I was bored as hell. I missed the night life and the parties. I needed to be out there on the street scene getting noticed, and wasn't none of that happening up in Free's joint.

"C'mon, Free," I begged. There was an award show in Atlanta I wanted to go to, and he was resisting that shit.

Free looked at me for a minute, then said, "I told you people be smoking cigarettes and trees and shit like that at them joints, Saucy. You don't need to be around all that. Exposing my tyke to that kinda poison."

"But they giving you an award, baby! You should be there to accept it. Plus, I'm tired of hanging around this damn apartment! I wanna go out, Free. I wanna dance! I danced my ass off with you up on that stage the night you met me, remember?"

He laughed, but not like it was funny. "Oh, I remember, baby. Believe that. I remember."

I finally convinced him to let me go to Atlanta and the only reason he agreed was because Tai was going too.

"Watch her, Tai," he told her when we got off the plane at Hartsfield International Airport. "I need to grow some eyes in the back of my head to keep up with this girl 'cause she likes to get around."

I just looked at Free and rolled my eyes. Tai couldn't keep up with me if she had a high-powered scooter and a motorized ten-speed. I had heard the show was gonna be hot as hell, and I planned on being there in all my shine and getting my party on like it was nobody's business. Even Free's.

Chapter 17

OH! THE SHOW was live!

It was at a huge posh hotel and Free had rented suites upstairs for his whole crew. I stepped up in that sucker in a baby-blue Dolce & Gabbana dress that made my titties look like they was bulging out and my ass look nice and fluffy. My stomach was barely sticking out at all, probably because I was doing mad sit-ups every morning so I wouldn't get fat.

Tai looked kinda cute tonight too. She had on a white dress that made her look a little less blimpy, although them big-ass elephant feet was sticking outta her patent-leather shoes and her ankles looked fat and swollen.

The auditorium was packed but we had the best seats. Free was getting another damn award tonight and they'd reserved almost a whole row for him and his entourage. I went to the bathroom before the show started and ran into a chick named Nae-Nae I used to know when I was working at the G-Spot. G had fired her for bringing her little son up in his joint, and bitches was hot with him over that! Even though we didn't hang together or nothing back then, I was happy to see her, especially when she whipped some trees out her purse and sparked one up.

"Who you here with?" I asked her.

"Oh. No fuckin' body. Just this crazy nigga from the Lower East Side and his crew. He's part of the show, but his ass is real light 'cause we sitting way the fuck in the back by the waiters and shit."

"I'm rolling with Freedom Moore from Ruthless," I said proudly. I looked in the mirror and admired the banging-ass jewelry Free had bought me and smiled. "He's getting a top award tonight, so we chilling up front. How's your baby doing?"

"He's good. Getting big. My mother keeps him."

I pulled a pen outta my bag and wrote my cell phone number on a paper towel. "Call me girl. I got something for your little man," I said. I still had that baby bangle that I had snatched when I was on my way upstate to murk Sincere. "I meant to give it to you a long time ago," I lied, "but when G tripped out you stopped coming around the Spot."

I smoked two dutches with her and by the time I got back to my seat I was feeling nicer than I'd felt in months. I was ready to let my hair down. To relax and get my socialize on. The music was banging and all the artists were pretty hot, but Reem Raw really tore up the floor with his shit.

They all know who the top spot belong to!
They all know how my block rock, we on you!
They all know what these Glock shots'll cause you,
That's how my men play! We keeping it N.J.!

Ask bout me, the boy Reem raps outrageous!
It's amazing the way I format my phrases!
Say what I feel, can't draw back my statements
Yell at me,
You ain't gotta contact no agent, nigga!

There was never fire, Raw spittin on a level higher,
Niggas this Jerz, them bird niggas is feather flyers!
Mash on the cash chase, cause we in the streets grinding like
    bad brakes

R double E M, shoulda never let em out,
Bring your records out,
I blast the whole session out!

I had only seen Reem spit live once before, but every damn thing people was saying about him was true. The boy knew how to work the stage. He had niggas in the crowd spittin' his bars right back at him 'cause his flow was just that strong. The crowd was feeling both him and the beat, and I raised my arms over my head and clapped and bounced as he kept shit real.

This is trench life!
You get it in, then you get right!
Ship white, hit you with it for the bench price!
N.J. add the letter after the R,
It ain't another squad in the same bracket as ours,

It's a mismatch!
That slick rap get 'em gift wrapped!
Strip cats, big stacks so the click strapped
Aiming for the bigger doe, all black triggas blow,
New Jerz South betta act like niggas know!

No slouch, roll out on the audible,
None of y'all niggas can't take it where I brought it to!
My name ringing like bells on the boulevard,
Heaven or hell, ain't a soul spittin illa bars!

The pushers gone keep pushin
The lookers gone keep looking,
Pop some nigga let the shotguns cook 'em!
D.C. to Brooklyn, who got the game locked?
REEM!

They all know who the top spot belong to!
They all know how my block rock, we on you!
They all know what these Glock shots'll cause you,

That's how my men play!
We keeping it N.J.!

"That little nigga raw for real," Free laughed. "He don't sound like nobody else out there. I'ma try and get him on at Ruthless soon. His original flow can help boost my lineup."

I nodded and agreed. Hell, Reem was getting it in, but I was just happy to see Free happy and enjoying himself for once, even though business was evidently still on his mind. I had danced all over my seat and I was still feeling the trees I'd hit in the bathroom when I got the shit shocked outta me. They introduced the next artist and my whole face fell.

"We got some fresh talent in the house!" the MC yelled. "Give it up for my son Quaison!"

I sat back in my chair and crossed my arms. Quai really had some shit with him. Ever since he found out I was putting it down with Freedom Moore, he started losing his focus and scheming on how he could sneak up on some of them Ruthless Boyz and snatch one of their contracts. I had a feeling he was using me to get closer to Free's artists, but the way he was going about it was just crazy. First this fool had called asking me to come give him some head, and when I told him I was pregnant and wouldn't take a cab to his crib, he threatened to send Free a copy of the sexy videotape we made!

"I know that's your baby daddy, Saucy, and I don't really wanna blow you up like that. It's just that I'm feening for you, ma," he told me. "Can't nobody slurp dat brain like you do it, baby."

"That's just wrong, Quai," I told him when I got down to his moms's crib and was sliding his long fat dick into my mouth. "This was supposed to be about us hanging out having fun. Not about no blackmail. Me and you did that movie for kicks and it wasn't even about Free."

Yeah, I went ahead and did what Quai wanted that first time, but when I looked at the tape again I realized how good

Mami was looking on that baby! The next time he called tryna bribe me for some top, I was ready for him.

"Go right ahead," I told him, laughing into the phone. "Show it to anybody you wanna show it to. I look damn good! Niggas gone love seeing me performing at my best! As a matter of fact, I look so hot on that shit I might try to get me a table on 125th Street and move a few copies myself!"

That shut Quaison down real quick and he got mad as hell and cursed me out! He was all about putting that freaky CD out there when he thought it was gonna embarrass me. But once he realized I might make some money off the sight of him licking all inside my ass crack, that shit changed real quick. Quaison didn't know he wasn't slicker than me, but if I had known this motherfucker was gone be down here for the show tonight I might not have been in such a hurry to come.

He came out on stage with that bad-ass New York swagger, looking like a chocolate fuckin' chip. I couldn't remember what the hell I had seen in his young ass other than his pretty eyes and fine body and gorgeous dick. Other than that, he was just regular.

"What's happenin' Hotlanta!" His voice boomed into the mic and I coulda sworn that nigga looked dead at me. "Thanks for the southern love, y'all. Georgia got some of the finest women in the world with the biggest asses on the planet. Fuck Manhattan! I'm moving down south!"

He performed a half-ass track that didn't even make me pat my foot. Tai clapped for him at the end, but I just sat there wondering how he could get up on stage and embarrass himself like that.

"Thank you, thank you!" he had the nerve to holla into the mic when he was done. "I wanna thank everybody who made tonight possible for a nigga like me. You know, there's some old cats in this rap game who done took a serious loss. *Vets!* Old heads who done fell off and hit the floor with a bang! But I don't feel no pity for them. I mean, a nigga gotta know how to keep his business tight in this industry. He gotta manage his contracts! He gotta pay his fuckin'artists! He gotta keep his bitches off they goddamn knees, braining the competition! 'Cause when he don't, a hungry nigga like me might slide up and take everything he got." He did look right at me this time, no doubt. "Nah'm saying?

"So I'ma close my shit out with this one last jawn. I ain't even know I was gonna spit it until I hit the stage tonight. It's gone be a freestyle joint so y'all be good to me. I'm dedicating it to my girl, Brainiac, 'cause she was worth every dollar I spent."

She might be what the big boys desire,
But homey watch ya head cuz her thong's on fire!
Type of body make a thug wanna wife her,
Just watch your head homey cuz her thong's on fire!

No chick can match her
Saucy got the snapper!
Turn you into a stalker every minute wanna track her!
Ghetto princess, every nigga wanna snatch her
And if ya bank's right Brainiac'll get at'cha!

"Saucy? *Brainiac?*" Free said, sitting up straight. "Yo, Sauce, is that kid talking about *you?*"

I froze. I was gonna kill Quai! No this motherfucker *didn't* blow my name up in his rap line! Niggas is really playing dirty now! Putting my shit on front street in public like that! Right in front of my man and all his homeys. Disrespecting me like I was swine for real. Oh, I'd been wrong. He wasn't goin' after none of Free's boys. He was using me to go after *Free!*

All of Free's sons was looking around like, what the fuck? I glanced at Free out the corner of my eye and I knew it was going down. He was ready to flip out. I could see it all over him. He was still smiling and playing shit off for the cameras, but I felt heat coming off of him. I slid down in my chair, knowing I was busted and shit was about to get popping.

Yeah! Gotta pay just to play
Gotta get to her,
Don't make dollars then it don't make sense to her!
She want the Prada and the bagettes, leave a nigga full of debts
She give less than a fuck about the honor and respect!

Cuz her thighs are thicker than grits, hips wide as ya whip
Face of an angel, every pimp try to convince
She slick wit' her lips, for a hit you'll get ya chain pawned,
One lick, I swear the bitch will have you "brain" washed!

Free spoke without looking at me, furious. "Oh, you must be a mouthpiece for real, huh? Niggas spittin' ill bars with ya name in 'em. You do got a good head game, though. Sounds like a whole lotta fools been bobbling ya neck."

You would ride for it, die for it, steal for it, lie for it,
Make a true gangsta cry and swallow his pride for it!
They all fell! Thought Saucy was a rider,
She just hot in her pants?
Nah! Her thong's on fire!

My mind was trying to come up with something but my mouth couldn't utter a word. The crowd was going bananas for Quaison's rap this time, and Free finally turned in his seat and looked at me. Fuck the cameras, his smile was gone and his voice was colder than a freezer.

"Oh, I get it now. My duns duns musta been tryna spare my feelings or somethin' 'cause ain't nobody told me shit. I must be the only motherfucker in the world who been sleeping on your game."

I clowned. "You believe that nigga? You gone listen to a few stupid bars and take them for truth?"

Free's eyes said it all as the audience gave it up for Quai, who was using my reputation to close out his act.

She might be what the big boys desire,
But homey watch ya head cuz her thong's on fire!

Type of body make a thug wanna wife her,
Just watch your head homey cuz her thong's on fire!

She might be what the big boys desire,
But homey watch ya head cuz her thong's on fire!
Type of body make a thug wanna wife her,
But it's the thong baby, ya thong's on fire!

Oh, my ass was in for it, for real. I sat there with my eyes
front and center for the next couple of acts, then I snuck out
of my seat the minute they called Free up on the stage to get
his award. As the cameras followed him, I made my exit. I knew
nosy motherfuckers were staring at me and talking shit about
that rap, but I didn't look left or right. I ran down the aisle and
slipped out the doors. I couldn't believe that fuckin' Quaison
had put me on blast like that! The look on Free's face was like a
whip cracking. That shit cut me all over my body, stinging me
with the pain of his disgust.

My hands was shaking like I was a fiend. I didn't know what
I *should* do, but I knew what I was *gonna* do. I headed straight to
the hotel bar and proceeded to order and gulp down beer and
double shots of Rémy until I couldn't see straight and was having some real trouble holding my head up.

"Sorry, miss," the bartender told me when I tried to order
another round. "You look like you've had more than enough,
and I'd be violating the law if I sold you any more alcohol."

I cursed that motherfucker out!

"Who da fuck is *you*?" I screamed on him, trying to lift my
head up off the bar. Some older dude who had been sitting next
to me the whole time was nodding like he felt what I was saying. "I'm *grown*, goddammit! I tell me when I had enough! Not
you tell me, you greasy gay fuck!"

They put my ass straight up outta there, but it was cool
'cause the old guy sitting next to me helped me get upstairs
to my room and he was funny as hell! He was telling mad jokes
and then laughing at them shits himself, hugging and squeezing all over me every time he reached the punch line.

He helped me slide the hotel card in the lock outside my suite, and when I got the door open he came in behind me.

"They got plenty to drink in that thing right there," he pointed toward the room bar. I staggered over to it and took out a bunch of little bottles of cognac and he twisted the caps off for me and told me some more stupid jokes while I put those little bottles up to my lips and swigged the liquor down, chasing it with some Coke from an open can that had been sitting on the counter.

I was bending over to get me out another one of those little bottles when a blow from the back knocked me down.

I landed hard on my stomach, my face pushed down in the floor and he jumped on top of me and started rubbing his dick on my ass and moving around. The force of the impact rocked me, shaking me up and making me nauseous. I opened my mouth to blast that nigga out, and instead I threw up, choking on the sharp, nasty smell of cognac and beer pooling beneath my face.

"Motherfu—" I started to say, but he pressed down on the back of my head, killing my noise in my own vomit. He hiked my dress up in the back, and fumbled around with my thong, and when I felt his dick enter me I tried to squeeze my legs closed but he penetrated me deeply anyway. I moaned and gagged in puke as he fucked me with quick deep strokes. It didn't take him but a few seconds to finish, and the next thing I knew he was climbing off of me dripping cum, leaving my ass wet and cold.

I wanted to get up, but all that liquor had me, and soon I passed out. I was dreaming and I didn't like it. I was five years old and I was sitting on Mister Jack's lap while his thang jumped outta its box. It was sweaty and hot and poking around my little booty, stabbing me in my pee pee hole and making my butt get wet.

I pushed against Mister Jack and tried to climb off his lap, rolling over onto my back.

"It a nice game, Seung Cee!" Kimichi scolded me as I cried.

"Uvvah kids play it very much, yes? Be still and let Meester Jack finish."

I heard a door open. Footsteps and loud men's voices were coming toward me. I was scared and my butt was really sore. I didn't want to play anymore and I begged Kimichi to make Mister Jack stop.

"SAUCY!"

"Please, Mama," I moaned out loud. *"Don't make me play no more. Please. Mister Jack, it hurt real bad when you touch me right there. Please. Ow, that hurt me, Mama. Please! No! Ow! Mama! Mama!"*

"SAUCY!"

I tried to open my eyes, but shit was too blurry.

"Saucy! Get the fuck up!"

I looked up and Free was standing over me. And so were Tone, Bandie, Cuban, and all the rest of his homeys.

"Yo, what the fuck is going on?" Free screamed. "Close your fuckin' legs, girl! What you doin'? You got some nigga up in here or what?"

I heard him stomping around the room like he was looking for somebody.

"Who you been fuckin' Saucy, huh? That bitch nigga Quaison? Where that sleazy nigga at? Huh? Where the fuck he at?"

He started wilding, yanking open the closet doors and turning over chairs.

"C'mon, man," Feety said, trying to calm Free down. "Ain't nobody in here homes. Take care of ya woman, man. She look like she needs some help."

Feety rounded up them niggas and made them get out, and when the door slammed I still hadn't moved. Free walked over to me and looked like he wanted to spit down on me.

"What kinda fuckin' woman *are* you?" he asked quietly, like he was amazed. "How you getting tore down drunk when you about to be somebody's *mother*? *My* kid's mother? You worse than my moms," he said and stepped up on me, and for a second I wished he would just go ahead and stomp me out.

"You're an embarrassment, Saucy," he said, looking down

on me, making me feel low. I *was* tore down drunk, but I could hear the deep pain in his voice and see it in his eyes too. "A big fuckin' embarrassment."

"Free . . ." I reached up toward him. "He . . . I got ra . . . "

"Save all that shit for the next nigga," he said coldly as he walked away. "'Cause I ain't trying to hear it."

Chapter 18

F OR EVERYBODY ELSE the weekend had just gotten started, but for me it was straight over. Free woke me up bright and early the next morning and told me it was time for me to fly.

"Your flight leaves at nine. Herc is gonna be at the airport waiting for you, and he'll drive you out to Jersey. And that's where I want you to stay, too. There'll be plenty of food in the house when you get there, so feed my seed. I'll fuck with you when I get back Tuesday. *After* I finish handling my business."

I sat up in the bed with my head swimming and the first thing I saw were my suitcases. He had them shits packed and lined up at the door. I still had on my dress from the night before and there was dried vomit in my hair but he didn't even wanna give me enough time to take a shower.

"You had that same shit in your hair last night, Saucy. You wasn't worrying about it then."

He watched me as I pulled my nasty dress off and dropped it on the floor. Last night's thong was on me all crooked and stiff in the crotch with dried cum, not even in between my ass cheeks like it was supposed to be. I tried to fix it as Free stared at me with a crazy face.

The baby was pressing down on me and I went in the bathroom to pee. Bits and pieces of the night before came back to me, and when I realized why my thong was so nasty I wanted to scream and fight. What the fuck! Warren, Jack, King, Jim, James, Paul *and* Tyrone! It was no-good violating niggas who had taught me to take whatever I wanted in life! Thinking *fuck all them niggas and Free too*, I jumped in the shower and scrubbed last night off me the best I could. When I came out the bathroom Free was looking at his watch and grilling me as I reached for one of my bags.

"What you doing?"

For some reason I touched my stomach, which was feeling a little rounder. I pulled my towel tighter around me.

"I'm getting something to put on, Freedom."

While I was sleeping he had packed every stitch of anything that looked like it might have belonged to me. He had packed so good he forgot to leave me out something to wear home.

I took out a pair of Capri pants and a knit vest, and got dressed real quick. Free acted like he couldn't wait to get rid of me, and I was still buckling my sandals when he started rolling my bags out the door.

He didn't say a word as he put me in a taxi and sent me to the airport. I was hoping he was gonna ride with me, but he killed that fantasy when he gave me a one-hundred-dollar bill then passed the taxi driver some ends too.

"Bye," I said in a real small voice as I slid into the cab, but he didn't even look at me. He flung the door real hard and was already walking away by the time it slammed shut.

Five hours later I was sitting in that little cracker-box house in New Jersey staring at Free's Aunt Mercy Ann. She was a hideous-looking old hag, and we hated each other on sight. She wore a jacked-up wig sitting crooked on her head, and she had a big, nasty black mole hanging off the side of her nose. She sat there twisting that shit all day like it was a permanent booger.

I didn't say much to her and she sure didn't have nothing to say to me. She had her shoes off and her feet stank, and my stomach was feeling too funny for me to try to sit there and socialize with her smelling like that. The flight had been jacked up and I couldn't wait to land. I didn't know whether

I was hungover or airsick, but whatever it was, my son musta been mad at his mama because my stomach heaved the whole time.

Herc had picked me up at the airport and driven me straight to Jersey, and when he said he was taking Aunt Mercy Ann food shopping I just waved both of them off. I kicked off my shoes and slid out of my clothes, then got in the bed and closed my eyes. I heard them come back in about an hour later and then the sound of the cabinets and refrigerator being opened and closed filled the little house.

I stayed in that room going from being mad to feeling stupid and back again. Yeah, I'd walked away from Quai but so what? Look at what he had did to me! Licking my ass out on film then threatening to show it to Free. Damn right I was down to show it around first instead of letting him hold that shit over me! What did he expect?

And Free? Shit. I put my hand over my stomach for a second, then took it off and set it on my thigh. This "let's keep the baby" game was his damn idea. This was what he had wanted. To be somebody's daddy and show off his shorty to the world. Of course I dug all that shit that had happened with his moms, but I wasn't her! I wasn't out there lushing and driving no damn kids around in a car, so it wasn't fair for him to talk to me like that! And he didn't even give me a chance to explain what had happened in the hotel room last night! He just figured Saucy was a ho so she musta been doing some more hoeing. He was mad now, yeah, but I knew how much Free felt for me. He loved me and had told me so a whole bunch of times. Now all I had to do was chill and let all the confusion and drama pass on by, and then soon me and my man would be wilding together, right back in step again.

I was miserable as fuck for the next three months.

When Free came back from Atlanta he not only locked me all the way down, he laid out the rules for me in a way I could understand.

"You put bad light on me," he told me. I had been itching to get the hell outta that house and away from his stank-feet Aunt Mercy Ann, but Free had other plans for me. "You gave me some real bad press. You my girl and things, but from now on we gonna do shit my way, Saucy. And you can believe that."

This cat called himself trying to dignify me up. He was the boss and I was the bitch. He decided what clothes I was gonna wear. How I did my hair. What jewelry went with what, and how I should walk, talk, and act when we was out in public.

"Just check out Beyoncé's flow," he told me. "She's all class and shine, baby. B gets down for the camera, but it don't matter how she grinds it up on that stage, when they stick a mic in her grill she opens her mouth and her game is silky clean. She walks it and talks it like a real lady. She's amazing."

Well I wasn't no damn Beyoncé! First of all, I looked better than her. All that fake-ass blond hair and colored eyes, who needed all that when you had chinky eyes and good hair like mine? And yeah, B was real cute and she could sing, but I had a higher ass than she did, and bigger titties too. Plus, my waist was a lot smaller and you could tell if she stopped dancing she was gone be fat one day. As soon as she stopped shaking her ass around the stage or dropped a couple of brats, she'd be walking around here looking just like Tai.

I wanted to kill Free's ass when he told me I couldn't go back to the apartment and get none of my stuff. I wasn't about being no damn prisoner, and I told his ass that.

"You ain't locking me up," I said, when he came in one day and stated that I would be staying in his shitty little house full-time until I had his baby. "I'm a grown-ass woman, Free. And I ain't ya damn wife."

"You ain't gotta be. You my lady and my personal incubator right now. You harvesting my first seed. And until he gets here, I'ma make sure you stay straight."

He took Aunt Mercy Ann out shopping and they came back with all kinds of old lady maternity shit they wanted me to wear. You shoulda seen them clothes! Horse pants! Walrus shirts! Big, calf-length tent dresses, coffee-colored support stockings, ugly black old lady clunker loafer shoes, and the drawers! Goddamn! Huge, horrible Fruit of the Looms that I coulda pulled all the way up over my titties! WHERE THE FUCK DID THEY STASH MY THONGS!?!

But Free wasn't finished.

"And until you learn how to speak right, baby just keep your mouth closed when a whole lot of people are around. Especially them chicks from *S2S* and those kinda joints. You're real pretty, Saucy. Nah, you're more than that. You're a stunna. Beautiful. They all wanna be up in your flow trying to catch your true flavor. But don't let 'em. You ain't gotta say shit, Saucy. Just stand there and take your cue from me and you'll be straight. Matter of fact, a good friend of mine is gonna swing by next week. She'll give you some inside tips on what you can do to improve the kinda image you trying to present. Back in the day she was the one who taught Mary J. and Queen Latifah how to slow their hood game down and come across looking and sounding correct in public."

It burned me the fuck up that Free was more worried about his public damn image than he was about what I wanted! I hated when he turned that big-ass cheetah grin on whenever a camera was around. Forget all that shit about creating the right perception for his damn business. If he had been on his game and his partner wasn't so shady, he wouldn't be having to rebuild his shit up from scratch in the first place!

Between him and Aunt Mercy Ann I stayed mad for three months. Fair Lawn, New Jersey, was dead, dead, dead! It was like a damn cemetery out there! The only action going on was watching little white kids riding skateboards and scooters up and down the street or shooting baskets in the hoop at the end of the block. That's about all I did every day. When I got tired of leaning over the porch rail I went back inside and read some *Vibe, Source,* and *Don Diva,* to stay up on the industry happenings and bring some excitement to my life.

I lived for those few times Free came and got me and took me out to some show or event with him. Yeah, some other bitch woulda been happy to latch onto his arm and smile for the cameras, but it was that whole "image" thing that kept him drawn to me. The word was out and everybody knew I was having his baby. There was no way in hell Free Moore was gonna have them writing no crazy "baby daddy" shit about him in the *National Enquirer*. He was gonna make this shit look right if it killed him. If it killed me too.

So I sat around his little crib getting fat and feeling miserable, while Tai was out there loving life. She called a lot too, just so she could get in my head. That coat hanger had fucked up her uterus so she pretended like she was all interested in my pregnancy. She was always telling me who was doing what on the streets, which top artists she'd been hanging out with, and what slamming parties she was hitting. Whenever I got off the phone with Tai I felt worse than ever. I mean, she was working with some real shot callers and power players, and the way she made it sound she was real popular and they all liked her, inviting her to their phat mansions in L.A. and Vegas and whatnot. I knew damn well if people like that dug Tai, they would love the hell outta me, and I couldn't wait to drop this load and get back on my game.

"You know your boy been going around talking mad shit about Free," she reported to me one day.

"My boy who?"

"You know who. That dude Quaison. He just signed with that small label Crazy Cuts and now he's going around dissin' Free on all his tracks."

"That boy is just stupid. He's outta his league."

Tai agreed. "Yeah he is, because now everybody out there is getting back at him. Saying his lyrics are wack and the only reason he's tryna bring beef between him and Free is so he can get his name out there."

My lip was poked way out. I didn't like Tai having to tell me everything that was going on. "Free didn't even tell me nothing about that. He got me stuck all the way out here in Jersey when all the real shit is happening in New York."

"Just relax, Saucy," Tai said. "He probably didn't tell you because Quaison is a minor player just trying to come up by starting some shit. And besides, you're right across the bridge in North Jersey, girl. I can spit from there to New York, so don't act like you down in Mexico somewhere."

"So what else is going on?" I said, hating that I had to ask, but dying to hear more.

"Same stuff, girl. We're real busy at work and Jaheim is signing more and more clients. Did I tell you we got your friend Marshall George on our account now?"

"That stupid, stank-breath, winky-dink, ugly mother-fucker?"

Tai laughed. "That rich, stupid, stank-breath, winky-dink, ugly motherfucker! Besides, he wasn't all that when he had you living up in his phat crib and paying your bills. I guess Dymond Jackson don't think his breath is that bad. They got married on the hush tip a few weeks ago."

"What!" I damn near shrieked. "And nobody told me?"

"What was there to tell, Saucy? They didn't have no cer-emony. They just called a preacher over to the crib and did it. Wasn't no big party involved, or nothing like that."

"Who cares," I muttered. "I bet she don't know he got a new bitch he moved into that apartment when I left him. And I know he don't know some shit about her that I know either. The last time I seen that girl she tried to front me off, remem-ber? We was at that release party y'all did for Lil Killa?"

Tai sighed in my ear. "You was drunk, Saucy. And pulling all over that girl's dress. She was embarrassed, shit. I woulda been too if you was hanging all off my clothes trying to get me out on the dance floor!"

"Stop exaggerating!" I yelled. "Every damn body was drinking that night. Even you. So don't even try it. Plus, chicks dance together all the time at clubs and stuff. She didn't have to play me like I was just a regular groupie and we wasn't really tight."

"But a slow song was playing, Saucy, and couples were on the dance floor! Dymond is rich and world famous! Don't tell me you was gonna get her out on the floor and slow-grind her pussy! That shit woulda been worse than Madonna kissing

Britney Spears. White girls can get away with that shit, but Dymond's name woulda been on the floor. Nah. She played it *and* you the right way."

"Yeah. Whatever. So you still kicking it with Jaheim, huh?"

She giggled. "Kicking it ain't even saying it, girl. I'm having so much fun with him. You know he went to Cornell, right? So he's smart as hell. He knows a lot of people in the business too, and everywhere we go people treat him like a VIP. Shit, just being with him makes me feel like one too."

Tai sounded real stupid.

"Girl, he can't be all that," I said, rubbing my chest. I had been having some real bad heartburn lately and Aunt Mercy Ann swore that meant my baby was gonna have a head full of hair. Duh, genius! Damn right he was gonna have a lot of hair! Look at mine!

"Why you say that, Saucy?" Tai demanded. "What's up! Why you don't like Jaheim? Don't hate just because I found somebody. You've got Free, right? I'm glad for you."

"Yeah, I'm glad for you too," I made myself mutter.

"Good. Because I gotta tell you something."

Tai sounded funny. Happy. I didn't like it.

"What?"

"Jaheim gave me a ring. A diamond."

I sucked my teeth real loud.

"And? You didn't try to get no earrings or nothing to go with it? No tennis bracelet? No chain?"

She laughed. "Girl, shut up. It ain't that kinda ring." Her voice got low. "It's an engagement ring, dummy. He wants to marry me."

"Word?" I said, my voice dry as sand.

"Yep. We gonna do the damn thang."

"Uh. That's cool."

"Damn girl! Why you so quiet? I woulda thought you'd be jumping up and down for me."

"Tai, I'm knocked up, remember? I ain't jumping up and down for my damn self."

"Yeah. I remember you're pregnant. That's why I'm not

asking you to plan my bridal shower. My friend Kamillah is doing it for me."

"Kamillah? Who the fuck is a Kamillah and what hole did she crawl outta? I ain't never heard you talk about no Kamillah before. So now she's your best friend giving you a bridal shower?"

"I didn't say she was my best friend, Saucy. But she is a *decent* friend. Besides, you don't need to be worried about nothing else right now but your baby. So just come to the shower and relax and have a good time. The theme is gonna be shoes, so make sure you come stepping in your best pair."

Did this bitch just say shoes? I looked down at my big fat feet puffing out of them black penny loafers with the nickel in the slot, and hung up right in Tai's ear.

Chapter 19

M E AND AUNT MERCY Ann were at war. I was tired of her shit. Free had told her to cook for me every day and make sure I ate, and if she slapped one more bowl of thick, nasty oatmeal or plate of big fat greasy sausages down in front of me I was gonna have to hurt somebody.

I was gonna have to hurt Free's ass too.

Tai had been right. This "diss" thing between him and Quaison musta been escalating because Free told me Quai was going around on radio shows like Hot 97's *Jonesy in the Morning* and *The Wendy Williams Experience* promoting his new CD and calling Free out and challenging him to come outta retirement and defend himself on a track.

"That young boy just don't know no better," Free said. "I can shut him down at any time, but if I gotta call out the goonies he's gonna regret that shit."

I wished I was out there to see and hear all that! Quai was stupid, but he had some real heart going up against a guy like Free on the mic. Just hearing about all the beef and the hype had me feeling bored and lonely and if I knew how to drive I woulda jumped in Free's little Honda and been heading toward the city weeks ago.

Free was still trying his best to keep me occupied by bringing me baby books, novels, magazines, mixtapes, and new CDs, but nothing he did could satisfy me. That damn etiquette coach of his was pissin' me off too. Talkin' 'bout my gutter diction and tryna make me say words in some crazy ways my mouth didn't even wanna go. The only reason I even sat through that shit was because I was so bored, and at least challenging her gave me something to do besides wait.

I couldn't wait to have this damn baby. I dreamed about hitting the clubs again and getting my Henny and my Corona on. I was actually looking forward to Tai's bridal shower because at least that meant I would get outta this funky little house and get to talk to some real people.

The bridal shower was gonna be at the Alhambra Ballroom and Free was taking me out there. I had begged him to swing by the apartment so I could get some decent gear to wear, but he killed those hopes real quick.

"Ain't nothing there you can style anyway," he said. "All them rags you got are for the club, girl. You Ms. Moore now, remember? Besides, you prolly can't fit none of that stuff no more anyway. Your booty is powed out, baby. Puffed up and powed the fuck out. I love it."

I had picked through all the dud-looking clothes him and Aunt Mercy Ann had bought me and I almost cried when the only thing I found that looked halfway decent was a long pink dress with big yellow and black bumblebees on it. I'd be damn if I was gonna be up there with a bunch of butter bitches sporting my penny loafers, but my feet were swollen as hell, and other than my gray slippers and a comfortable pair of Nikes, they were the only dress shoes I had in Jersey.

The morning of the shower I felt miserable. I was back and forth peeing and my feet were puffy. My potbelly stomach made me look like a little teddy bear. I stood in front of the mirror and hated my damn dress, although when I turned around and looked at myself from the back, my ass still looked damn good.

Free came by to pick me up in his damn Honda. I hated that car and wished I could plant a bomb in that bitch. I couldn't believe he was gonna make me roll up in that junky-ass car when everybody else was probably gonna be climbing out of a Lexus or at least an Escalade.

Aunt Mercy Ann was laying on the couch snoring her throat raw when we got ready to go. She had a big pillow under her head and her feet was propped up on the arm of the sofa. Them turtle-looking thangs was so stink I had to hold my breath every time I walked past her.

"You look real nice," Free said, holding my hand as we were walking out the door. He meant that shit too. I looked down at myself, and at that moment I knew exactly what kind of dull, drab life Free had planned for me. He had a box that he was determined to make me fit into. This nigga was gonna make me over no matter who I wanted to be. It didn't even matter to him who I really was. It was all about what I looked like on his arm, and what kinda high-class image I presented to his public. Well fuck him right up his self-conscious ass.

"Yeah," I said. I let him put me in the car, and the minute he got in on the other side I grabbed my stomach. "Hold up, baby. I gotta pee."

"You mean," he corrected as I jumped out the car, "you have to use the ladies' room, right?"

I rolled my eyes. "Yeah. That."

I walked back in the house past Aunt Mercy Ann and tip-toed into her room. I jetted over to her closet, eased the door open, and grabbed her bright pink Manolo Blahnik yard-sale church shoes off the floor. Then I closed it back as quietly as I could and tiptoed back out the door. When I got outside Free was talking to somebody on his cell phone. I dashed around to my side of the car and hopped in, draping my old lady sweater over my feet and setting my Fendi purse in my lap.

"Ready?" Free asked.

I smiled and nodded. "Yeah—I mean, yes. I'm ready."

Free fought the city traffic for almost an hour.

"You smell something?" he asked, sniffing as we sat stuck in traffic approaching the George Washington Bridge. "Something smells like corn chips."

I balled my feet up in Aunt Mercy Ann's shoes and rolled

down the window. "Nah," I lied. "But I need some fresh air, though." By the time we turned off Adam Clayton Powell Jr. Boulevard and got to the Alhambra Ballroom I had to pee for real. I practically jumped outta the car when Free pulled up, then waved him off telling him I had to get to the "ladies' room."

"Yo, call me when you ready to bounce!"

I waved again and ran inside. I bypassed the event room and dashed straight to the bathroom, but peeing is not all I did in there. I kicked off Aunt Mercy Ann's stank-ass shoes and stuck some balled-up toilet tissue in the toes. Then I took that old lady sweater and hung it on a hook in the stall, and pulled my long, busy dress up and tucked it until it was up under my titties. I grabbed the two ends that made the side split, and tied those thangs together above my stomach, then let the rest of the dress kinda blouse down around my thighs, like an almost-mini. As set as I could be, I put her shoes back on, grabbed my purse and stepped outta that bathroom and wobbled my puffy ass into the ballroom to see what I could get into.

I was not feeling Tai's fucking shower, and I was not feeling Tai's fucking friends. Most of these stunts was blinged out in some of the finest and most attractive shine and gear on the market. I mean, I dripped a nice amount of ice, yeah. But these hoes was made up and pressed out and looked just like I would have been looking if Free hadn't been busy blocking my flow.

And the shoes! Oh, them bitches was wearing them some shoes.

There were Giuseppe joints, woven espadrilles, high-heeled slides, open-toed sandals, fuck-me pumps, and designer stilettos. The hall was decorated all the way down, and Tai's head table was piled up high with gifts. I had told Free to get her a gift card from Victoria's Secret, and when Tai stepped into the room I was shocked. Victoria didn't have shit on Tai when it came to keeping secrets. That bitch had been working out! She had on a lavender pantsuit with ice glinting everywhere. Her hair looked thick and bouncy, and her damn waistline was smaller than mine!

While my cheeks were bloated and my neck was black, Tai's face was slim and she actually had some cheekbones showing. Her double chin was gone, and she was walking around flossing her new look like she thought she qualified as eye candy now.

"Saucy!" Tai shrieked and *ran* over to me. Tai ran! Did y'all hear me? Tai *ran*!

She grabbed me and squeezed me, rubbing my stomach then pressing her ear to it and talking baby-talk to my navel. "Hey baby boy! Your auntie loves you! Yes she do! Auntie Tai can't *wait* to meet her little man!"

She looked at me and smiled and hugged me tight again. "Saucy! You look so good pregnant girl! You've got that expectant-mother glow, honey. You and Free must be doing real good."

"Yeah," I said. "We doing all right. But look at you," I admitted. "You lookin' real good too, Tai. You finally put down them damn pancakes, huh?"

She laughed. "Hell yeah. But you should hear how Jaheim be complaining all the time, telling me to keep some meat on my bones. That boy likes 'em hefty!"

Tai sure had a whole lotta friends. I had never been one to hang with females like that, so I couldn't get with that at all. She dragged them all over to my table too, grinning as she introduced me as the best friend she had growing up. Yeah, them bitches was dressed real fly, but some of them looked like beasts in the face, and I felt a little bit better knowing that even pregnant and puffy, I beat all their ass out in the looks department.

By the time they rolled out that red carpet I was tired of sitting around feeling frumpy and was determined to let my shit show. A photographer was standing at the end of the carpet ready to take pictures, and all the chicks were lined up ready to showcase their shoes.

Snoop's "Drop It Like It's Hot" was playing and them jawns was stepping down that red carpet. I saw some of the flyest damn shoes in the world. Every last one of them were designer joints too. French Zanottis. Italian Prevatas. Some had studs, others had buckles, some bitches had on hot espadrilles with straps going up their calves, others had on pumps or toe-outs, or heel-outs with sling-back bows.

I had my lips twisted as I watched them prancing and sashaying down that long red carpet. The cameras was flashing and everybody was screaming and laughing.

When it was my turn on the carpet I showed the fuck out.

All those months of being locked up in a house with Aunt Mercy Ann just came pouring outta me and I heel-toed down that carpet as jealous bitches stunted and Snoop Dogg hollered, *"When the pimp's in the crib ma, drop it like it's hot! And if a nigga get an attitude, pop it like it's hot!"*

Oh, I dropped that shit all right. Popped it too. Cut the shit outta that rug. I went down on my swollen ankles and popped my booty all the way back up. I got down low, too. So low I smelled the corn chips in Aunt Mercy Ann's shoes. But I kept it moving because the photographer was snapping mad photos and I was backing dat ass up and working that red carpet so hard them bitches 'fessed up and gave me my props!

I was feeling myself, clapping my booty cheeks and showing off my shape when it happened. I was coming to the end of the carpet and the end of the limelight too, when I said fuck it and dropped it one more time for the road. I got down so low my ass cheeks hit the back of my heels, and at that moment a big gush of water burst from my pussy and splashed all over my feet, that pretty red carpet, *and* Aunt Mercy Ann's funky church shoes.

"Shit!" I said. I was stuck down there, leaning back on my hands and trying to get up. Everybody was still clapping and screaming, Go Saucy! but then Tai got hip to what was going down and ran over and grabbed me under my arms and pulled me to my feet.

"It's okay, Saucy," Tai said, holding on to me as I stood there wet and in shock. "I got you girl," she said. "I'm right here for you." I looked into Tai's eyes and they confirmed exactly what I was thinking. My ass was about to have a baby! And that's when that first labor pain stabbed me so hard it took my breath away and I knew it was time to call Free.

Chapter 20

OMAR NASIR MOORE was born at 9:14 that night. He weighed five pounds and two ounces.

I pushed him outta my ass, but his father named him. Free's little brother had been named Nasir Omar Moore, so he wanted to pass on that name but with a little twist. I went along with it, figuring it was better than naming the boy François Junior, after Free.

Free and Tai was both by my side the whole time I was in labor, encouraging me, praising my little weak-ass pushes, wiping sweat off my face and holding my hands. Tai had her cheeks puffed out real big trying to show me how to breathe right, and Free just kept saying, "I can't wait. I just can't wait!"

And he didn't have to either. I had only been in the labor room for about twenty minutes when I felt like I was taking a big shit and the baby slid right outta me.

Free cut his cord and wiped him off and whatnot, then gave him to me to hold.

"Here's your mommy, Nasir. Let mommy see what kinda beautiful thing she did today."

I took him. He looked wrinkled and his mouth was wide open and screaming. He had a lot of straight black hair, and his eyes were just like Kimichi's. Asian. But Tai pointed to his ears and said he was probably gonna be dark like Free, and he was definitely gonna be handsome.

I was glad when a nurse took him away to be weighed and measured. I was tired already, but nobody seemed to give a damn about that. About an hour later they brought the baby into my private room all wrapped up in a blanket. The only thing you could see was the top of his head, which they had covered with some kinda baby skully. Free and Tai were going on and on over him, and after a while I thought they were getting kinda carried away.

My room was filled up with so many flowers and balloons and teddy bears it was crazy. Free had bought most of it, and I guess Tai had bought the rest. The nurses tried to get me to give Nasir my breast milk, but just the thought of it turned me off.

"You can do this, Saucy," Free said, his eyes lighting up as Nasir's lips tried to get to my big titty. "You can do it!"

Well I didn't wanna fuckin' do it!

But I did. But only for about ten seconds. That shit hurt so bad I snatched him off me and handed him right back to Free. It was bottles all the way after that, because they were my titties and I refused to cooperate.

My body felt real nasty after giving birth. I didn't even get no stitches but my stuff still felt stank and wide open. Free musta known better than to take me back to Jersey, because as soon as me and the baby was discharged he had a spanking limo waiting outside the hospital ready to take us back to his apartment. He had a car seat in it and all kinds of baby toys, and he put Nasir in himself and even buckled him up.

Unfortunately, Aunt Mercy Ann was waiting when we got to the apartment, and when Free saw the look on my face he started explaining shit in a hurry.

"Aunt Mercy Ann is just gonna help us out for a little while, Saucy. You ain't used to getting up all night with a baby, so it's gonna be hard until we get adjusted."

He had went bananas making the extra bedroom into a nursery for Nasir, and there was a bed in there for Aunt Mercy Ann, next to a crib and a changing table and diaper bags and whatnot. I hadn't bought one thing for the baby while I was pregnant, but Free had thought of everything. Wipes, powder, all that.

"Tai picked out the animal kingdom stuff," Free told me. The wallpaper, rug, and comforters in Nasir's crib had all kinds of animals on them.

I nodded. The room was cool, but I wanted to make sure Aunt Mercy Ann knew to stay her ass in the room with the baby and the hell away from me.

"I'm not pregnant no more, Free. I don't need nobody watching me."

He hugged me and kissed my lips softly. "This is help for you, Saucy. I swear, it's just help. Nothing else."

I had to give it to Aunt Mercy Ann, though. She helped all right. That heffah straight took over. She changed all Nasir's diapers, boiled his bottles and put the milk in them, washed his clothes out in the sink by hand, and fed him and rocked him at night when he cried. I didn't have to do much of nothing except hold him every now and then, but that didn't last long because Free was all over him and Tai was forever coming over holding him and singing to him too.

It didn't take me long to get tired of the whole scene. After spending three months on lockdown in Jersey, I was bored as hell. I was getting outta the shower about three weeks after I had Nasir, and I stood in front of the mirror for about thirty minutes straight, just staring at my body from all angles.

I was still tight. Nice and tight. No nasty wiggles on my ass or stomach. And definitely none on my firm titties. The only real weight I had gained was all that damn water around my ankles, but now they were nice and slim again and so was my face. My titties were even fuller than usual, even though the doctors had given me some medicine to dry up my milk. I turned around and looked at my ass, and I was relieved to see that it was still hot. High and round, plumped up and sassy. Yeah. Saucy still had it, and she was just about ready to flaunt it again.

• • •

Free was signing more and more acts, and staying gone a lot on business too. I started hanging out downtown a lot. Wilding with some guys I met at Club Vance on my first night back out on the town. I ran into that fucker Quaison too, and the first thing I did was jack-slap him right upside his big head.

"I'm sorry, Saucy! For real, girl. It was about publicity, baby. That's all! Don't be taking everything so personal, damn!"

"Don't take it personal? You don't know the kinda drama your stupid ass caused me! Plus you played yourself like a straight sucker," I told him. "That's why your shit failed to launch, nigga!"

That beef Quaison had started was beyond dumb. How he thought he had any wins going up against Freedom and them Ruthless Boyz was a mystery to me and everybody else. He had dissed Free and so many of his Ruthless cats on his tracks until they all ganged up on him and started killing him in their lyrics. DJ Gita G put out an underground mixtape calling Quaison a soft nigga who had gone to private school somewhere in Midtown, and had never lived the gangsta life he rapped about. Them niggas floored him on the radio, on HBO, and on 106th and Park, talking about him like he was a booger that they could flick off their dicks at any time. He was still out there on the music scene, but all the insiders knew he had fallen off. Them Ruthless Boyz had drug his ass so deep through the mud till it was only a matter of time before people stopped buying his records altogether.

"Fuck all that, Saucy," Quaison said, trying to kiss me. "I'm telling you girl, this is business! Ya boy need to come on outta retirement and battle a nigga himself instead of sending his dawgs after me like that. But it's cool. I'm back in the studio, baby. Laying some shit down that's gone make ya man Free look like he hiding real deep behind all them bitch-niggas' balls."

I just shook my head. Quaison didn't get it. All that bullshit he had spit about Free? That nigga had taken it personal. The last thing he wanted or respected was somebody fouling up his name, and Quaison had tried to do that in a major way.

Through music. And that was something Free just wasn't gonna tolerate.

"Why 'ont you come chill at the crib for a minute, though? Lemme make it up to you, cool? Let's hit a couple of parties, ya know? You looking good as ever, baby. I bet you still got them slick moves, too."

Did he say party? I was all on it and as much trouble as he'd gotten me in, he didn't have to beg me neither. Free was outta town so I stayed downtown at his moms's crib for three days straight. Quaison mighta been stupid, but he was a big willie on the Lower East Side and he liked to have fun. We partied nonstop. He copped some chronic that blew my mind. I stayed nice and buzzed day and night, drinking Thug Passion and Patrón tequila, and everything else Quaison and his boys brought up in the crib.

Quai took me down to their laundry room real late that night so he could dry his moms's clothes. She was bitching and looking at me all crazy when he brought me in, and screamed on him about leaving her gear in the damn washing machines for people to steal.

I sat up on the folding table and watched him pull their wet clothes out the washer. He tried to hurry up and throw them in the dryer, but he dropped some and I laughed my ass off when I saw his mama's big old drawers laying on the floor along with a washrag and a dingy sock.

"What's so damn funny?" he laughed over his shoulder, scooping the clothes up and throwing them in with the rest. He slid some quarters in the slot so the dryer could begin.

"Your mama's big-ass Fruit of the Looms, dammit! That's what!"

He laughed right along with me 'cause he knew that shit was funny too. He walked over to the table and his hand shot between my legs, squeezing and demanding.

"Boy I just had a baby. I can't fuck yet," I told him, pushing his hand away from my pussy. My checkup wasn't for another ten days, but Quai had lifted up my shirt and was sucking all over my titties and licking my nipples with his whole tongue.

"Yes you can," he whispered, reaching into his pants.

I couldn't believe this fool was taking his big dick out right there in the laundry room where any old body could walk in and bust us, but the next thing I knew it was throbbing in my hand and I was spitting on it, lubing that baby up so I could squeeze it and rod it.

Quai stood there grinning with both hands on his hips, looking down as I jacked his meat, keeping a dope pace going. He tried to get to my pussy again, but I snapped my legs closed.

"I told you I can't fuck!"

Two minutes later my pants was down and I was bent over that laundry table taking that shit from the back. Quai tried to go easy on me since it was my first time since having Nasir, but I liked it hard and so I started bucking back like a mule giving up that ass to the fullest and forgetting all about them doctor's orders not to fuck.

It felt so good to be wildin' and knowing we might get caught, and to have a nigga who appreciated my body and couldn't stop complimenting it.

"Damn you look good from the back, mami. This some deep juicy pussy, baby. This the hottest piece of ass I ever had. This some wet Jacuzzi pussy, girl! Yeah, do that thang wit' ya ass all vibrating again! Damn that shit looks hot! Do that again!"

A nigga like Quai was just what I needed after being cooped up so long under Aunt Mercy Ann, and I spent the next four months making up for lost time. Sneaking down to Baruch, getting my head lifted, and doing me to the fullest every time Free turned his back.

Free was still knockin' this shit out every now and then, but it wasn't the same as it used to be between us. I gave him head so good that my neck ached and my mouth got sore, and yeah, he still pummeled me down sometimes when his nuts was heavy and he was about to bust, but all the tenderness was gone outta our bed. I knew he still loved me, but Free hadn't spit me no sweet rap, cuddled up with me and watched a movie, or licked my pussy in months. He acted like I had hurt his heart real bad, but he wouldn't tell me what I had done. We didn't even talk a lot no more unless he was giving me some instructions or information about Nasir, but other than that, our shit was falling flat.

And speaking of Nasir, Free and Aunt Mercy Ann acted like they didn't trust me with him or something. Just because I had made one fuckin' mistake! I mean, damn. I ain't never had no baby before. Was I supposed to know everything? Free was out of town one night when Aunt Mercy Ann told me to watch Nas because she was tired and didn't feel good. Nas was sleeping in the bed with me when he started whining and crying, waking me up. I was real tired and I didn't understand why Aunt Mercy Ann didn't come in there and get him. I patted his back for a little while, but he still wouldn't shut up.

I finally got mad and rolled outta bed and staggered into the kitchen. I got one of his bottles from the refrigerator and twisted the cap off and stuck it in the microwave for a minute. But when I got back in the room and tried to feed him, Nas freaked out. He took two long sucks from the bottle and then he *screamed*, for real!

Then *I* freaked out. Aunt Mercy Ann came busting in the room asking me what the hell I'd done to him, and when I tried to tell her I was just feeding him, she grabbed his bottle and sucked from it, then snatched Nas out of my arms.

"You dumb-ass chile!" she shrieked, prying his mouth open so she could look down his throat. "You burned him!" she accused me, turning away from me like she didn't even want me to look at Nasir. "That damn milk is scalding hot!"

"I didn't know . . ." I muttered, not knowing what else to say. Nas was still screaming like crazy. Shit! It was Aunt Mercy Ann's damn fault anyway! She knew I was sleepy. She was probably awake the whole time, listening to Nas cry! Free had brought her here to help me. Why hadn't she gotten her fat ass up out the bed to feed the baby?

Ever since then Free acted funny whenever I was feeding Nas. I didn't know what his damn problem was. Couldn't a person make a mistake?

Tai was still working and planning her wedding to that doofus-ass Jaheim, but she came by the crib three or four times a week and played with Nasir and brought him more shit that he didn't even need.

"Damn, Saucy," she complained one Thursday night. Free was gone, and Aunt Mercy Ann had laid down because she was sick again. I was trying on a dress by Tadashi I had just bought, and making some calls to find out where the party was gonna be tonight.

"You stay running the streets, girl. Every time I come by here you either gone or on the way out. Are you spending any time with Nasir? I don't never even see you holding him or playing with him hardly at all."

"You ain't here all the time, Tai. He's been with me all day. My son is well taken care of."

"I know he is. By everybody except you, though. Look at him!"

Nasir was sitting in his little baby seat grinning and trying to put a toy in his mouth. Everybody said he looked just like me, but the only place I saw it was in his hair and his eyes. I kissed his hand and then his nose and he smelled real good. Free had him dressed in baby Rocawear and tiny Nike sneakers and his Aunt Mercy Ann kept him neat and clean and his hair slicked down at all times.

"See?" I said. "He's fine, Tai. He knows who his mother is."

She stepped in front of him and he started waving his arms and acting all excited. "He knows who his auntie is too!!" Tai said, unbuckling him from the chair. She picked him up, then started yelling.

"Saucy! This boy is soaking wet! When's the last time you changed him?"

I looked at her dumbly. Shit, I had been busy tryna find something to wear and something to get into. I couldn't remember the last time I'd taken him out the chair.

"Girl!" Tai said. She carried Nasir into his room and I could hear her in there putting him on the changing table and opening and closing drawers looking for him some clothes. She was just mad because she couldn't have no babies of her own. Fuckin' abortionist! All that noise she was making woke Aunt Mercy Ann up too, because I heard her in there acting like the boy hadn't been changed in two weeks or something. Talking shit to Tai like I didn't care about my own son.

"Give him to me," I heard her tell Tai. She came stomping out the room carrying Nasir and his little baby tub. He was naked and she gave me an evil look, then went in the kitchen and got him ready for his bath.

I got a call from Quaison just as Aunt Mercy Ann put Nasir in the sudsy water. He was splashing around and cooing out loud.

"Yo," Quaison said when I answered my cell. "I'm outside. Bring ya ass on down. We partying in Philly tonight."

I was dressed and ready to step in less than fifteen minutes, and as I walked past the kitchen on my way to the door Aunt Mercy Ann and Tai were getting Nasir into his pajamas, and both of them looked up and gave me a funky eye.

"I'm telling François," I thought I heard Aunt Mercy Ann say, but I didn't give a fuck. I kept it moving right along, never breaking my stride. She could tell Free any damn thing she wanted to tell him. Freedom wasn't going nowhere. I was his baby's mama, and neither one of them infertile bitches could give him the gift that I had given him. They both needed to stop hatin' and get off my clit.

I partied all week long, coming in and out the crib just to wash my ass and change my clothes. Sometimes Free was there when I came in, and sometimes he wasn't. It didn't really matter because I stayed too high to care. Just as long as I could find some bills in the bottom of his tissue box, I was cool. At one point I had gotten a little worried that the stack was getting low, but when I looked again that shit was tall again, so I relaxed. This was just a little pocket change to Free. He worked all the time and his artists was going platinum every day. He was always out there wheeling deals and doing some kinda business, so what the fuck. He wouldn't miss no small-change doe like this anyway.

I stayed gone for days, and on Friday morning I swung my tired, raggedy ass by the crib to recharge my juice after hanging out for three nights straight. Free wasn't home, but Aunt Mercy Ann was. She was in the room she shared with Nasir and even though the door was closed I could hear her in there moving around and talking to him like he understood what she was saying.

I wanted to see my son, but I didn't wanna have to fuck with Aunt Mercy Ann. I was gonna have to smash that old lady if she didn't pump her brakes, and I got tired of Free taking her side every time there was some static between us.

I walked past their room and into mine and Free's. Fifteen minutes later I had brushed my teeth and washed my hair in the shower, and was crashed out asleep in our big-ass bed.

I woke up hours later and it was almost dark outside. Aunt Mercy Ann had brought Nasir's bassinet into the room while I was sleeping. I could hear the shower running in her bathroom so I figured she wanted me to watch him while she got a few minutes to wash her ass and them stank-behind feet of hers.

I got up real quiet so I wouldn't wake Nas up. I peeked down at him and he was sleeping and looking so cute and kissable with his pretty skin and curly hair that I leaned over and put my lips to his fat little cheek. Aunt Mercy Ann must have just given him a bath because he smelled like Johnson's baby lotion and his neck had powder all over it.

I got dressed real quick then went in my bathroom to comb my hair. When I came out Nasir was still sleeping. I kissed him again, then walked out the room, leaving the door open. The shower was still running in Aunt Mercy Ann's room, so I eased out the front door and took the elevator downstairs.

I met Akbar down on the Lower East Side and was drinking with him and one of his boys who was a bouncer at a club down there. Two chicks walked in and sat at the bar and started talking to each other and Akbar's nose popped wide open.

"Damn," he said to his boy who was standing up there with his arms crossed and eyeing these two made-up heffahs too. "Them jawns is staring like fuck!" He turned to me. "What you think, Sauce? That one in the black shirt. She look like my type?"

I looked down the bar. Me and Akbar had been friends for a while, and although we used to fuck around for a minute, he was really just a homeboy who was there for me, no pussy required. I checked out the chick in red and something about the way she laughed and held her head cocked sideways looked real familiar to me.

It took me a second or two, but when I got it, I *really* got it!

"Tareek!" I yelled, jumping outta my chair and running toward him with my arms out. "Boy what you doin' your ass up in here wearing a fuckin' dress!"

We hugged all over each other, laughing and jumping up and down.

"Tareeka, baby," he corrected me, twirling his dress around and stepping slow so I could check out his shit. "It's Tareeka now, Saucy. I told you I was gonna be a bad bitch with big titties one day!"

I laughed so damn hard it wasn't funny. Tareek had some bodacious titties that was phatter and firmer than mine, and when he twitched his ass round in that dress I almost couldn't believe he had a booty, hips, all that!

"This my friend Stubbs," he said, introducing me. "Saucy was my best damn friend in the world when I was a kid," he explained. He grinned, then grabbed my shoulders and gave me a big fat kiss on my cheek. "Shit, girl. You was my only damn friend."

Tareek was still living in his old apartment but he told me his father had died in a car accident and his brother was living somewhere in the south.

"I don't hear from him girl, but you know Taleb always did have a stick up his ass! I guess I embarrassed him when I showed up at Daddy's funeral wearing a cute black skirt, but fuck him! This is *me*!"

I couldn't stop staring at him and I was damn sure gonna joke the hell outta Akbar and tell him Tareek was definitely his type.

"But," I said, shaking my head, "how you get all them titties, boyfriend? The hips is looking good too, Mami."

He laughed. "It's the hormones, you know. Me and Stubbs is getting ready for our operations. There's a whole lotta shit you gotta go through, but the hormones is part of how they start getting you ready for it."

I grabbed Tareek's hand and took him over to Akbar and his boy and introduced them. I could tell Akbar knew something was up just by the way he was staring at Tareek but I was gonna let him figure it out for himself.

I had just sat my ass back down when Free blew up my cell phone.

"Saucy where are you?"

"I'm right off the FDR Drive. Why?"

"Because I'm at the fuckin' police station."

"What? Why? What'd you do, Free?"

"I trusted your dumb ass! That's what the fuck I did!"

I shook my head trying to understand because he wasn't making no damn sense. I turned my back on Tareek and them, and pressed the phone closer to my ear.

"Just tell me what to do, Free. I didn't do shit to you, but if you locked up, just tell me what you want me to do."

"You left my son in the house by himself," he accused me in a deadly voice. "You was so bent on running the streets that you said fuck your own baby, and left him in there alone with nobody to take care of him!"

"Aunt Mercy Ann was there!" I screamed. "She brought him into our room so she could take a shower, and when I left the crib she was still in there! She was the last one with Nasir, Free. Don't you let her blame that shit on me!"

"She wasn't there, Saucy. She was with me. I came home to take her to pick up a prescription and get something to eat while you was sleep. So was Nas. Before we left I rolled his bassinet in our room so you would hear him if he cried. I can't believe you got your ass up and walked past our son and out that damn door."

My mind was blown. I concentrated on trying to figure this shit out.

"She was in there, Free. I swear to God, I heard her in the shower. She was there."

"No, she *wasn't*. Did you knock on the door and let her know you was leaving? No. Because she wasn't in there. Nas was by himself when he woke up and started crying. When he didn't shut up for over an hour, that old cranky dude next door came over and banged on the door. When nobody answered he called downstairs to the security office. They called the cops, Saucy, and when they showed up, security unlocked the door and let 'em in."

"Oh my God . . . I coulda sworn she was . . ." I didn't know what else to say.

"I got there right when social services was taking my son out the house, Saucy. The cops brought me and Aunt Mercy Ann down to the station so we could give statements, and the only reason I'm about to get Nas back is because the doorman vouched that me and Aunt Mercy Ann left the building two hours before you did."

I was struck dumb. I couldn't believe this shit! I knew I'd heard that damn water running in Aunt Mercy Ann's shower.

"Well how is Nas? Where they got him at?"

Free's voice slapped me through the phone.

"Oh, so you finally thought to ask about your son, huh?"

"I'm sorry, Free. For real, I am."

"Oh, I know you sorry, Saucy. It's sad, but I been knowing that for a good little minute now."

It was about a month later when I found myself walking into the Brown Box Theater on Free's arm. It was his twenty-seventh birthday and Tai and Jaheim had set up a huge-ass party bash for him. The place was swarmed and it looked like everybody in the industry had turned out to celebrate his day.

Actually, it was gonna be a double celebration and Free had a lot to party about because his latest project was being unofficially released tonight too. Free had named the collaboration album *Keep It Gangsta*, and it had some of his wildest tracks on it from his heavy-hitting days on the mic, plus it pumped some hard cuts from Thug-A-Licious, Rhyme Mastah, and Gutta Brown. The video that Free had gone to Jamaica to shoot was ready too, and it was gonna be running all on MTV and BET in a couple of days.

I was kinda surprised when Free invited me to come out with him 'cause shit had been real shaky between us ever since the night he claimed I left Nasir home alone. We'd had a big fight when I got home, throwing down in the crib ghetto-style. Free had slung me down to the floor, and when I got up I tried to burn his ass with a hot iron, but he slapped it outta my hands. I still got him though. When he tussled with me and tried to hold me down, I bit his damn thumb all the way down to the bone!

Yeah. It was ice-cold up in that camp for a good minute. I straight didn't speak to Aunt Mercy Ann at all, and whenever I tried to do something for or with Nasir, she jumped in and took over. And whenever me and Free was both in the apartment at the same time we acted like strangers. Nah, I acted like Free was a stranger. Free acted like I was stinking up his crib or something. The nigga didn't even wanna speak when he saw me! He would just slide right past me like I wasn't even there, and then if I turned around real fast I would bust him looking at me with love and hate at the same time. I didn't know what the fuck his problem was. I begged him to talk to me, to give me another chance. I really missed that closeness we used to have and I knew he still cared just as much as I did, but everything I said went in one of his ears and bounced right back out.

But tonight was going different. Free was being the old nigga he used to be. Talking and laughing and giving me mad attention like the cat who had opened my nose up wide almost two years ago. Free was looking real good too. He had on all white from head to toe. An ice-white suit, white shirt and tie, white shoes, slamming white hat. All his boys were dressed in white suits too, except they was shining in chains and rings, and Free was still holding it down with that air bling.

He had let me pick out my own outfit for the night and I could tell he wasn't disappointed by my choice of a gold Fendi dress that had cost three grand. We hadn't fucked in a long time and I knew he missed it. He had sat on the bed watching me as I got dressed, and I gave his ass a real hot show as I slid into a gold thong and matching push-up bra. He had a funny smile on his face the whole time, and I loved that shit.

When we got in the limo things were even better. Free popped open a magnum of Cristal, and poured me some and watched me drink it.

"This is for you, Saucy," he said, putting his arm around me. "It's really your night tonight, baby. I want you to be comfortable and have a good time, okay? I want you to feel your best and shine your brightest."

Free had some chilled shrimp in the whip with sliced lemons and cocktail sauce to go with them too, and he didn't even look at me funny when I stuck a lemon in my mouth and chewed on the rind. He actually fed me the shrimp by hand, and I giggled as I licked his fingers and tried to suck on his thumb.

"Not now," Free laughed as I reached for his big dick and squeezed that shit. He moved my hand away and slid my fingers through his.

"You ain't even hard," I complained, and Free laughed again.

"Don't worry about this dick tonight, baby. You gonna have time to get plenty dick later on."

Artists from a lot of different labels were scheduled to perform tonight, and as soon as we got out the whip I recognized a lot of rappers and ballers that I used to party with when I was just starting out in videos. Me and Free walked inside holding hands and waving to the crowd, smiling like the beautiful motherfuckers we was!

Inside the auditorium I was pissed to see that that bitch Dymond had showed up. I spotted her and her entourage on the other side of the hall. Marshall was with her too, and she shoulda been leading her little lapdog around on a leash. I *so* wanted to tell that nigga Marshall that outta the two of them, his wife was a better fuck and gave much better head, but I was wrapped in Free's strong arms tonight so both of them could just kiss my ass.

But my eyes got real big when I saw Quaison was there too, sitting a few rows up from Dymond and Marshall. He must've slid in with somebody's posse 'cause I knew damn well Tai hadn't invited him. Free led me down to our seats in front and I held tight to his hand and acted like I didn't see his number one public enemy glaring at us from the other side of the room.

Tai's agency had billed this event as the hottest urban birthday show on the planet, and the press was out to see if it was gonna be true. I saw MTV and BET cameras, one from *The Black Press*, and two or three from cable channels, but there were also a lot of independent cats taking shots for *The Source*, *XXL*, *Don Diva* and other black urban magazines.

Of course there were crazy mics stuck in Free's face. It was his big night and everybody wanted to hear from him. I stood next to him determined to make him damn proud. I knew I looked all class and polish, just the way Free wanted me to look. I had on a floor-length, back-out, shimmering light gold gown, with a simple diamond pendant around my neck. My bag was a small, classy clutch, and my shoes were made of the same shimmering material.

Whenever somebody important spoke to me, I answered just the way Free's little stiff-ass etiquette coach had taught me. I smiled and maintained eye contact and made sure I kept my words in the right tense and with all the *ing*'s intact. I felt real stupid talking like a damn white girl, but I did it because it seemed like me and Free might be starting to vibe again and I wanted to show him that I could make the right impressions and bring positive points to his image.

After talking to a million people and being interviewed by a bunch of press, we finally made it down to our seats just as the show was about to begin. Dougie Fresh was MC'ing on the mic, and the first thing everybody did was stand up and sing "Happy Birthday" to Free.

It was live. I stood next to Free with the overhead lights coning us and sang to him with a big-ass smile on my face. Everybody in the whole damn joint had their eyes on us, and my man stood there grinning at me like he loved the ground I walked on.

I loved seeing that look in Free's eyes. It made me hot, and I decided no matter what he said, I was gonna suck his dick down to the bone when we got back in that limo!

The entertainment lineup was fierce, and Tai and them had picked some of the best artists in the industry to perform for Free's special night. There was also a line of new niggas standing around near the side of the stage, and in between each music act a few of them would go on the stage one by one and say a few words about Free and how he had inspired their music or opened doors for them in the business and whatnot. Then they each got five minutes under the new-jack spotlight to spit a freestyle aimed at showing Free luv. Some of them cats were lyrical masters and plenty of love was in their rhymes.

Free was digging that shit, I could tell. The smile never left his face. Even when they called him up on the stage to say a few words, which everybody knew wasn't his favorite thing to do, he was still grinning. I squeezed his hand as he stood up. I knew he hated having the lights all over him, and he definitely wasn't one to get on the mic unless he was giving up a killer rap.

"Whassup, people," Free said, and the audience exploded with screams and applause, giving him props like he was da man.

"Y'all know I'm a man of few words and I ain't one to go around runnin' off at the mouth, so I'll just say, thanks for showing love for my new jawn, *Keep It Gangsta*, and when the show is over make sure you stick around for the after-party. Peace!"

I was grinning my ass off as Free walked across that stage

looking good as hell. No jewelry, air bling, but his gear was top shelf, his kicks banging, that gorgeous grin, them dimples and that goatee . . . goddamn. But the best part was the fact that every hatin-ass female in the joint could see that big powerful nigga was heading straight back to me.

"Yo hold up!" Dougie Fresh hollered just as Free was about to hit the steps. "We got one more artist who wanna give up some luv for Free!" He turned to his left and my blood ran cold. "Sorry, son! You shoulda stepped ya ass up with everybody else! But here's ya new-jack minute. Gone and show Free ya luv!"

"What it do!" Quaison hollered into the mic like he was enjoying the crowd. "Whewwww! This feels good, man! Very good! Yeah, I got mad love for my son's stepdaddy! What's good my niggaz? I know I wasn't invited but lemme smack ya'll niggaz wit' some fiyah right fast! Let's get into this . . . I see you, Sauce! Let's do it, baby! Yo Freedom, you ain't *hustle*! You *knew* somebody who *knew* somebody, but nah nigga that 'ont make *you* somebody! Nope! Gimme the track lemme lay my heat, I'm up next! Lemme take my seat! It's Qua Dawg! You ain't *hustle*! You *knew* somebody who *knew* somebody but nah, nigga that 'ont make *you* somebody! Nope! Gimme the track lemme lay my heat, I'm up next! Lemme take my seat! I'm at the top of the list, young nigga fresh outta the trench, I smell like pussy? That mean I'm fresh outta ya bitch! I'm on another level fuck it, niggas can hate! Scared to come outta retirement? That's a g-nigga's requirement! Cuz I'm New York's top pick! And my nine spit! Chew your food and treat ya girl like a side dish! So when I hit—I smack it outta the damn park! Money can buy a nigga anything but a damn heart! You lying to the people, you was puss from the damn start! Coward scared to battle so I call you a damn mark! You see how I slay tracks and see how it ain't rap, you slide through my strip, and get ya g-ride banged at!—"

Dougie Fresh had heard e-damn-nuff. He snatched the mic from Quaison and started doing his human-beat-box thang to the same beat that Quai had been freestyling to. The crowd got

so hyped off that shit till everybody was clapping and stomping their feet to Dougie's shit, and ignoring Quai as he stood on
the side of the stage looking stupid as fuck.

Still throwing that lip fire, Dougie ran across the stage and
gave Free a big hug and beat-mouthed "happy birthday to you"
as Free finally walked down the stairs and back to his seat.

"Now let's hear that shit one more time for my man, FREE-
DOM MOORE!"

Free sat down next to me and the cameras onstage panned
over us and he grabbed my hand then held it up in the air and
grinned.

"What's wrong with ya nigga, Saucy?" he leaned over and
asked me as soon as the camera had panned back.

"My nigga?"

"Yeah. That sleazebag motherfucker up there talking shit
like he wanna get murdered. Dude is cranky. When's the last
time you had his dick in your mouth?"

"What?!?!" I had just started clapping for the next act, but
I stopped and turned to face him with my eyes popped out.
"What the hell you talking about, Free? I didn't know he was
gonna get up there and act stupid! I ain't even been with that
nigga!"

"Yeah, so I'm his son's stepdaddy, huh?"

"Free how I'm supposed to know what that motherfucker
talking about? Shit, don't let that nigga get all in your head
and mind-fuck you! Nas look just like you and you know he's
yours!"

Free laughed. "Calm down, Saucy. I'm just playing. It's
all cool. 'Cause guess what?" He put his hand into his jacket
pocket and pulled out a folded piece of paper. I reached for it,
but he snatched it back. "Know what this is?"

All of a sudden instead of sweet words there was ice chips
coming outta Free's mouth. But he was still grinning for them
damn cameras.

"I was planning on giving it to you after the show, but this,"
he said, looking straight ahead, "is my guarantee that tonight
is gonna be the last fuckin' night you ever sit your trifling ass

down next to me anywhere and enjoy a minute's worth of anything that I've put in work for. It's my petition for full custody of Nasir, baby. My lawyers filed it yesterday. So you about to get served with your subpoena, and I'm about to get my tyke, yo. And I ain't got nobody to thank for that but you."

I couldn't believe this shit! Free was buggin' the fuck out!

"What? You talkin' crazy, Free. You or nobody else ain't taking my son from me." I was ready to get loud, but his guard Feety reached over and touched my arm. He looked at me with a killer face and shook his head twice, like don't even fuckin' try it bitch.

I sat there as Free cheesed for the cameras and the crowd while steady calling me all kinds of dirty hos and crabs and nasty rabbits out the side of his mouth. It was like he was full of my shit and couldn't hold it in not one minute longer. Pain was in his voice when he asked me how many times I came up in the crib and kissed on his son after sucking dicks in the streets all night long. He told me that no matter how much love he mighta had for me, I could never step my foot back in his crib no more, not even to get my clothes or any of my papers, and definitely not to see Nasir.

"You unfit, Saucy. A fuckin' pig takes better care of her young. You left my shorty in the house by himself. That ain't cool, baby. It's criminal."

"But Free! It was only for a little while! You came right back home. Plus, how was I supposed to know Aunt Mercy Ann was gone?"

He laughed loud as hell then, and that's when I knew the two of them had set me up.

"See, that's just it. You wasn't supposed to know. But you *was* supposed to check. But don't worry yourself about none of that shit no more! I got a cab waiting outside for you, ma, so you can step right now. Everything you had when you met me is in the back. Take ya nasty gear and roll. Just stay the fuck away from me and my son!"

This nigga was serious. He was done. All night long my mind had been on the wrong track. Here I had been planning to get him home and fuck his brain out backward, and he had been planning to make me feel all cozy and secure, then wait until the show was over and take me outside like trash and toss me the fuck off. Like I hadn't laid up in pain and pushed out his baby! Like I hadn't sucked and slobbed his dick down real good, or licked them big balls the way he liked them licked. Like I hadn't stayed locked down in his New Jersey shack and put up with his stank-ass Aunt Mercy Ann!

Free couldn't say enough nasty shit about me. He went on and on, like a toilet that had gotten stopped up, then overflowed. The shit Free was talking made me sound like I wasn't nothing but a big bird whore, a two-cent backseat trick, and now he was kickin' my ass outta his life like I was a stank piece of rotten fish.

I felt myself get sweating hot. Swelling up like a fuckin' balloon. If I had a gun I woulda shot Free's ass. But a knife woulda been better. I wanted to stab him in his throat and cut that fuckin' smile off his face and make sure every damn body in the house got a good look at me doing it.

"Just calm your ass down and relax," Free said again, clapping as another act finished on stage. " 'Cause this ya last time in my light, baby. So you better enjoy it. Sit back and shine for the rest of the night, because you'll never have another one like it on my dime."

Oh, I was gonna shine tonight. Damn right I was. The MC had just introduced Reem Raw and his man Robb Hawk on the stage. They was looking good in some black Dickies with red tees under them, and I stood up and jetted before Free or Feety realized what was up. I ran over to the middle of the stage and hiked my three-thousand-dollar Fendi dress up, then threw my leg over and climbed up there and joined Reem and Robb in their act.

Holding my dress up to show my legs and grinding my ass like I was on a pole, I looked over my shoulder and told them niggas to work with me.

"C'mon!!" I screamed, grinning and laughing. "Help me flip this hot Jeezy joint!" Then I snatched that fuckin' mic outta

Reem's hand and put Free's shit on blast for the whole damn world to see.

"He ain't the *tyyyype*!" I imitated my nigga Jeezy, singing into the mic at the top of my lungs.

"He ain't the *type* to be runnin' his mouth, so I keep it gansta wit' him, put his *DICK* in my mouth! *Yeaaaaaa*, not a whore, just a real *bitch*! Say what you scared to say! *I* know you feeling this, that's *riiiighhht*, that's *riiiight*!"

Robb and Reem didn't know what the fuck to do. But they was professionals so I guess they figured this was part of the show and the show must go on!

I looked down at Free. That nigga wasn't smiling no *more*! I turned around and bent over at the waist and jiggled my ass at him, then danced all up on Reem, as Robb got busy and hit 'em with a bridge just like I hadn't just got my ass up on the stage and fucked up their flow.

Cute face, tight waist, nice Fendi so,
Yes, I'll holla my nigga, I don't solicit hoes!
I button my lip up, that's why I get to take yo bitch home,
    home, yeaaaa

Reem was doin' his thang, but at the same time he was looking at me like I was bananas and hesitating like he didn't wanna shit on his man Free.

"C'mon!" I told him. "It's just a crazy little surprise!" I jumped back in there, center stage, making up moves and lyrics as I went along. I grabbed Robb by his Dickie shirt and started going down his body trying to undress him and hump his leg at the same time.

"I'll take my *Fendi* off, if you take them *Dickies* off! I ain't tryna love you, I'm just tryna get my *sticky* off! I'll get it nice and wet! Pull it soft, call me a *boss*!"

I turned around and faced the crowd, and did one of my old G-Spot moves. I looked over to where I had seen Marshall and Dymond sitting, and directed my booty flow their way.

"The way I fire *dick*, take your *chick*! Put Dymond's tongue up on my *clit*, got her like I want her lesbian relation*ship*! Her man hatin' it, pleasing me all times of the night! Marshall's mastur*bating* it! Ménage à trois, *cravin'* it! I'm spon*taneous*! Sexually *dangerous*! When you take your Dickies off, best believe you getting licked!"

I looked over my shoulder toward Free, and he was staring right at me, embarrassed as fuck! I gave it all up to him, braining the mic and acting like I was sucking a big long dick.

"And I only take *pipers*, long dicks for all-*nighters*! You gotta lick before you stick! That's a rule for *vaginas*! Fuck attack from the *back*! I'm the queen of my *highness*!"

Half the niggas in the joint was screaming, the other half was probably hoping I would suck their dicks tonight! Robb broke back in with his bridge.

Cute face, tight waist, nice Fendi so,
Yes, I'll holla my nigga, I don't solicit hoes!
I button my lip up, that's why I get to take yo bitch home,
home, yeaaaa

Then the DJ dropped the beat for a second and Reem Raw got his shit in while I arched my back and popped my ass all over that stage.

Ch-ch-ch-chill!!! What's poppin boyz? N.J.S.!
Reem Raw got it locked, what it be like!
Ya nigga got 'em, 'bout to show 'em what a G like
Real homey and I'm hitting the track hard,
Hit her wit a bundle and she gettin' the pack off
Bring the money back, then I go in her back hard
Come roll with a KING
She can hold the kids down, she can keep herself clean,
My chick! My bitch!
My QUEEN!
It's REEM!!
Never runnin my mouth, I wanna hit it from the Lex to the
house,

Good dick, good shit, keep her neck to the south,
Stretchin' it out,
Hood bitch all I need on my side, move out!
So holla at me, I'm wit it,
Let's get it poppin fast!
I'll give it to you so right,
Make the hooptie feel like you in a topless Jag!
Said Reem got that one of a kind rap,
I might hurt somethin' if you get me behind that, that, that,
    that, that . . .

I opened my mouth wide and busted on Free one last time as I was booty clappin' my way off the stage and the crowd was wildin' and going bananas.

"He ain't the *tyyyype* to be runnin' his mouth, so I keep it gansta wit' him, put his DICK in my mouth! *Yeaaaaaa*, not a whore, just a real *bitch*! Say what you scared to say! *I* know you feeling this! That's *riiiighhht*, that's *riiiight*, that's *riiiighhht*, that's *riiiight*!"

I looked across the stage and met Tai's eyes. Her mouth was hanging open and Jaheim was just shaking his head. Fuck 'em! Fuck all of them!

Chapter 21

BUT IF I thought Free was gonna let my little public stunt knock him out the box I was dead wrong. I ran down the stage steps and tried to jet past Feety but that big nigga snatched me up and twisted my arm behind my back. He slammed me down into the seat he had been in, then sat next to Free in my seat as the next act took the stage.

Whoever was coming to the stage was about to get straight ignored because all around us voices was buzzing as people talked cash shit about what they'd just seen and heard. The music public loved them some Free, just as long as he was on top and looking large. But a video chick like me had just made that nigga look soft and weak, and the whole damn industry was gonna be blasting the news about my performance before the night was over.

I guess Free figured that out and decided to do something about it. He stood up and gave me such a look of hate that I tried to ball up in my chair. I twisted away from him and Feety and pulled my knees up to my chest and covered my head with my arms and hands.

But the ass-kicking I was waiting for never came. When I lifted my head and took a peek, Free was already walking up on the stage, right in the middle of the act in progress. He said something to Dougie Fresh, then snatched the mic from some young boy as the beat changed to something slower and funkier.

The next thing I knew, that cone light was shining right on me, and so was everybody's questioning eyes.

"Damn! I guess it's true what they say, huh?" Free spoke into the mic, nodding toward me. "You really *can't* turn ya ho into ya housewife!"

Every damn body laughed. Loud as hell.

"But for real, yo. I think it's time for a lil Q&A session. What y'all know about that?"

Man, oh man. Ol' Mistah Freedom opened his mouth and came straight outta retirement on my ass! He started spittin' some illa shit that fucked all our heads up!

I got a question!
Lady you mad, cuz I don't speak when I breeze past?

I got a question!
Lady you mad cuz you stuck wit' a sleazebag?

Now what's the answer?
You was loose, till you crashed tryna speed fast!
It's gone take a lot more, bitch, to slow up Free's swag!

The crowd went crazy! They loved it!

Then the cone light swept across the room and swung over to where Quaison was sitting. Free got loose and let him have some too.

I got a question!
Homey you hatin' cuz your flow game's gar-bage?

I got a question!
Homey you hatin' cuz my flow game's flaw-less?

What's the answer?
I don't take shots at no-name artists!
I got a hundred styles plus every one of them is bonkers!

"Freedom's back!" the crowd screamed. "Freedom's back!"

Oh, this nigga was back and straight playing "questions and answers" with me and Quaison! The MC musta given the stage people a signal because when Free turned toward me, the cone light swept back over on my side of the room and lit me up again. Free opened up the shooters and blasted me with his big gun.

I got a question!
Miss, you cryin' cuz your boy won't accept you back?

I got a question!
Miss, you cryin' cause you just miss where the comfort at?

What's the answer?
Bottom line, you tried to catch me in a fuckin' trap!
But I ain't slip in a minute, so save it for that other cat!

As the cone light swung back over to Quaison, I saw Tai run down the stage stairs, and seconds later she was sitting beside me, putting her arms around me like she was trying to comfort me. I shrugged her off. Quaison was sitting over there shook, but I'd be damned if I'd let Free make me feel like I was nothing! The light started sweeping faster as Free pointed to Quaison.

Listen homey!
Is it cuz I keep it gansta as I say I do?

And then to me.

Listen baby!
Is it cuz I don't trust you enough to stay with you?

Then back to Quai.

Now listen homey!
Is it cuz I'm too grown to be tryna play with you?

Then to the whole damn crowd.

Cuz y'all don't understand, I'M THE MUHFUCKIN' MAN!

Oh, he was the man all right. He was feelin' his damn self, and hearing the way the crowd was going crazy, they was feeling him too. I sat there with my head up, not letting no motherfuckin' body see that I was ashamed! Free wasn't doing nothing but fuckin' up his own reputation because these same niggas clowning and clapping for him was gonna be talking about him when he was out there on his knees begging me to come back. But he still had a few questions for me.

I got a question!
Could it be baby you honest and you keep your word?

I got a question!
Could it be baby you lying and you just a bird?

Now what's the answer?
Bitch, you still won't get a penny offa what I earn!
And baby if I'm wrong, I'll just take it as a lesson learned!

Free started going back and forth again. But now, not only was the spotlight following him, the crowd was too. It seemed like everybody in the whole goddamn joint except me, Tai, and Quaison was turning side to side with Free, clapping they hands and hollerin', *I GOT A QUESTION!* at the top of their damn lungs! Free was grillin' Quaison again and that shook little herb looked like he was tryna slouch down in his seat.

I got a question!
Is it maybe we get gravy and we goin' hard?

I got a question!
Is it maybe you hatin' cuz you just fallin' off?

So what's the answer?
If you 'bout it, I'm 'bout it, and we can spark it off!
When I sic my goonies on you, you gone wish I called them off!

Tai grabbed my hand and squeezed it hard when Free turned his fury on me full-force again, and anybody who was listening to his sick lyrics knew how bad he was fuckin' me up. Just killing me.

I got a question!
Could it be shawty, you was down for the whole ride?

I got a question!
Could it be shawty you was stuntin' the whole time?

Now here's the answer.
Tho' I give two fucks, cuz I can hold mine,
Little did you know, bitch you was sleepin' on a goldmine!

That nigga lifted his chin and tooted his lips and made a *pattooie* motion at me, like he was spitting down in my face, then cut his eyes and burned the last of his gats firing on Quaison. The crowd was still with him. Going strong and shouting, "*I GOT A QUESTION!*" loud and clear.

I got a question!
Look my nigga, is you ridin' or you hidin' out?

I got a question!
Lemme know if this some shit we gotta iron out!

Here's the answer.
Get this money and the bar, we can buy it out!
Hoes? We can fuck 'em all. Cars? We can drive 'em out!

I got a question!
You hate it how I bounced back when I took a loss?

I got a question!
You hate it how I ride tracks like a fuckin boss?

Now here's the answer.
Violate that, you cats get ya melons tossed!
Play ya hand like a real man, and pay the fuckin' cost!

Listen homey!
Is it cuz I keep it gansta as I say I do?
Listen baby,
Is it cuz I don't trust you enough to stay with you?
Now listen homey!
Is it cuz I'm too grown to be tryna play with you?

Cuz y'all don't understand, I'M THE MUH'FUCKIN' MAN!

Chapter 22

WHAT FREE DID to me was so damn wrong! He wouldn't answer his cell phone and the doormen wouldn't even let me in the lobby of the building. That nigga was a big fat fraud. If he loved Nasir the way he claimed, he woulda never been able to put Nas's mother out in the street.

Tai said I was the one wrong for getting up on that stage with my dress all hiked up and shaking my ass like that. Ask me did I give a damn!

"Y'all ruined the whole damn event," she complained. "All that work we put into making Free's birthday pop-off big, and you and him both get out there and show your asses."

I just shrugged. "He started it. Talking all that shit to me, calling me all them nasty names. He pulled them court papers out on me, so I pulled some shit out on him too."

"Girl you looked wild as hell up on that stage, Saucy. Had that pretty dress rolled all up over your ass cheeks with your thong showing while you was talking all that nasty dick-sucking shit." Tai shuddered. "I was too damn embarrassed. For both of you. I can't tell you how many people are talking about it on the internet. Wendy Williams blasted your ass on the radio. Callers on the Ed Lover show were wildin'. You can catch a film clip of the whole thing over on YouTube and

MySpace.com, and you can still see clips of it playing on BET too. The good thing is, people are blowing the phones up asking where they can get them some more of your tracks!"

I waved my hand. I wasn't no rapper, just a real bitch like I had said. Besides, all that had happened two weeks ago and I wasn't dwelling on it. I was living a free life and back on my game. No man had ever shit on me like Free had, and from now on I was gonna stay on top and get what I could get outta every single nigga I met.

And I needed to hook me a herb real quick, too. Since Free had put me out, Tai was letting me stay at her crib. Her mother had had a stroke a few months back and was recovering in a long-term rehab joint, which is the only reason Tai had let me in. She said her mother would die if she knew I was staying up in her house, and made me promise not to go nowhere near her parents' bedroom. So I slept on the sofa whenever Tai was home, but you better believe when she was gone I got right in her mama's big pretty bed and rolled my ass around in it. But trust me, living up in there with Tai was almost as bad as staying with Free. Tai was my girl and stuff, but she had picked up some of Jaheim's stupid-ass habits that got on my nerves.

She was the one who insisted I had to sleep on her living room sofa, but every morning she got up with the pigeons and got on her loud-ass treadmill that was right next to my head and ran for what seemed like three hours. That made me mad because she could see I had not so long ago got in from hanging out and was trying to get me some damn sleep.

And that flimsy nigga Jaheim. I couldn't stand his square ass. Coming around looking at me like I wasn't shit. We argued all the damn time. I heard him telling Tai that I was probably out there selling pussy, and I told Tai that motherfucker was probably out there selling ass! Just the way he talked around his tongue shoulda been a damn hint. Sounding like a uptight white boy from the Catskills or something. But Tai was slow and Jaheim had her blinded. She was still making all these big-time wedding plans. She had invited all Jaheim's peeps, politicians in his office, corporate executives, and a bunch of religious dudes from his church. I just couldn't see it. Instead of taking her money and splurging on something for herself, she was tricking it out on a wedding with Jah!

I was getting so damn tired of hearing every little detail too, but I tried not to let Tai know that. Ever since that night I had tried to lure Jaheim into my mix, I just couldn't see my girl with a non-fucker like him. Damn right he was gay. He musta been yeasting Tai up to get her money because if he could turn this phat ass down then that meant he wasn't really into women. I didn't know a single straight heterosexual nigga who would take a chick like Tai over the splendor that was me, so what else could it be?

I ended up moving outta Tai's place a few weeks later even though I had drank and smoked up all my doe. They had gotten a new girl to model for the Birthday Cake ads, and didn't even tell me why. She sure as hell didn't look half as good in them jeans as I did. Video jobs was getting real hard to come by too, and I just couldn't understand it. There was mad new artists cutting records left and right, and a lot of them were paying good money for videos. I would hear about an audition and run down there as fast as I could, and then I wouldn't get picked! Yeah, they might offer me a spot as an extra, but I walked away from those real quick. I just couldn't see going from the top spot down to the bottom especially when there was no explaining it. My body was still ten times hotter than all of those chicks put together, and my looks beat them all out too.

"Maybe it's 'cause of that nasty funk you give off," Jaheim said when I came in complaining about an audition one day. I knew I wasn't getting a callback without them even telling me. The minute the assistant called me in the back and they looked at my call sheet, they all of a sudden wanted a real light-skinned chick for the part and told me they'd keep my number on file.

I had stopped over by Baruch and smoked some sticky green with Quaison's homeboy Brickett to bring me down off my mad trip, but I was still kinda pissed, and when I walked in the door and Jaheim opened up his faggot-ass mouth, I went straight off.

"You just hatin' because I wouldn't suck your damn dick," I screamed.

That long-legged yellow freak walked toward me like he was gonna do something and I ran in the kitchen and snatched a butcher knife out the drawer.

"Come on, you scrawny motherfucker! I'll *find* me some dark meat to cut off your bony ass! Just come on!"

Tai jumped up and got between us.

"Saucy! Put that fuckin' knife down! What is wrong with you? Girl, you can't be coming up in my house disrespecting my fuckin' man! We just don't get down like that!"

"Look at her," Jaheim said. "Pulling a knife on me like some hood bitch. And in somebody else's house! Free should have shut you down a long time ago, Saucy. You're lucky to have a friend like Tai, but you don't know the first thing about friendship. All you know is grime, sister. Grit and grime. That's all you know."

That motherfucker had just insulted me for the last time. I dropped the knife in the sink and pushed past Tai. I went in the hall closet and got the two huge striped laundry bags that Free had put my clothes in, and started filling them up with whatever I saw that belonged to me.

"I see how you living, Tai," I said as I was packing. "You gonna let your nigga talk to me like that and stand up for him over your girl. I'm good with it, though. 'Cause when his swishy ass leaves you, you gone come running right back to me."

Tai looked at me real crazy.

"Saucy, I have never come running to you for anything in my whole fuckin' life."

I nodded and dragged my bags toward the door. "You remember them words, bitch. Because one day you gonna eat 'em."

• • •

I moved in with Quaison even though his moms didn't like it. I didn't understand what her big problem was because I didn't spend no real time there anyway, other than to sleep and take a shower. I hung out with Quaison and his boys in the studio, and partied with them in the clubs most of the night.

I had stopped trying to contact Free. He still wouldn't take no calls from me, and I knew better than to knock on the door because he had an order of protection against me. I wanted to see Nasir, but the last time I went over there Free called the cops on me and they locked me up overnight. I had been standing across the street watching the building when him and Aunt Mercy Ann pulled up in that raggedy Honda. I couldn't believe Free had my baby up in that rattle trap, but he did. I ran across the street as soon as he got Nasir out the car seat, but I only got one good peek at him before Free threw a blanket over his head and turned his back on me.

"Get the fuck outta here, Saucy!" Free said, and broke out with Nasir toward the building.

Aunt Mercy Ann was still at the car. She had the nerve to roll them big-ass eyes at me. She rolled them so hard I was surprised one didn't pop out and skid across the ice. But I had had enough of that bitch too. She had lied and told the cops she caught me shaking Nasir one day 'cause he was crying! All I was doing was trying to rock him, and I had told her that. Yeah. I was sick of that old moley-nosed bitch! I couldn't get to Free, but she was a whole lot slower and I ran up on her and swung, punching the shit outta her. She tried to turn away and run toward the building but I caught her upside the head again, then ran behind her and gave her a big flying kick in her wide ass. "That's what you get for making me leave my damn baby in the house, bitch!"

I kicked her in the ass again, this time higher up her back, and don't you know that damn doorman ran out and grabbed me? He threw me on the cold, icy ground and fell on top of me, and we was still down there fighting when the cops pulled up!

"She hit me!" Aunt Mercy Ann screamed, holding the side of her face. "Arrest her, she hit me!"

I spent the whole night in a cell, but I didn't feel a minute's worth of regret. That old bitch had treated me real bad, and she was due that ass-kicking for real.

I had used my one phone call to call Tai, and she still sounded mad at me but she came and got me out. That's what friends were for.

"Saucy, you gonna run yourself right in the ground," she told me as she drove me toward Quaison's crib. "I be worrying about you, girl. For real."

"I just wanted to see my son, Tai. I don't care what that judge said. They don't have no right to keep my baby away from me."

She sighed. "Nas is fine. I kept him the other night because Aunt Mercy Ann was sick again. You could have killed that old woman, you know. Punching her out like that! You know she's got a bad heart."

"Free let you pick Nas up?"

Tai nodded. "Yeah. I been getting him a lot because Free is working so much and Aunt Mercy Ann has been real sick and he doesn't like to burden her. That boy is so big, Saucy. And smart too. He has your hair and pretty eyes, but Free's temperament. He's a cute little mess."

I was jealous! Tai wasn't Nas's goddamn mother! Not only was Free letting her take my baby whenever she wanted, she was standing up here in my face telling me about my own kid like he was really her son!

"So when's the next time you gone have him? Call me so I can come by and see him."

Tai shook her head. "Saucy, you know I can't do that. I promised Free I wouldn't do nothing to violate his court order and he trusts me to keep my word. Besides, I take him straight from Free's crib to my apartment, and Jaheim is always there. You know?"

I thought about it for a minute, then nodded. Hell yeah, I knew. She didn't wanna let me in her crib to see my own damn son because that nigga Jaheim was up in there.

"C'mon, Saucy. I see that crazy look in your eyes. Don't

even think no stupid shit because this ain't about Jaheim. It's about Free having custody of Nasir."

"He's my damn son, Tai!"

"I know he is. So what are you doing to try and get him back? You didn't show up for the court date, then you roll up on Aunt Mercy Ann and beat the shit outta her. You think that's making you look like a mother who really wants to have her child?"

"I still wanna see him," I mumbled. "I should be able to at least see him."

Tai sighed and put her arm around me and drove with one hand. "I think you should be able to see Nasir too. I really do. If it was me I would be going crazy without my baby."

"I am," I sniffed. "I am."

She sighed again, then pulled me close and squeezed me.

"Hand me my purse," she said, stopping at a traffic light. I gave it to her and she reached inside and handed me a colorful piece of paper that had been folded like a booket.

"Check this out. How 'bout this. Our Black History Month celebration is coming up in the next few weeks. We're holding it at Jaheim's father's church, and Free and Nas are gonna be there. Why don't you just swing by and take a peek at him?"

I looked at the program I was holding and my face lit up as my mind worked like a little computer. Tareek was still living in Harlem in the apartment connected to the record shop his father used to own. I ran into him and his friend Stubbs every now and then when I was partying on the Lower East Side, and he was still a hot mess. A couple of weeks ago I had talked this fine-ass cop outta bustin' him and Stubbs for tryna work a corner in their little mini-skirts. "Ms. Tareeka" owed me a big favor and I knew just how he could pay me back.

"Now wait," Tai warned. "That don't mean come up in no house of God starting no shit, Saucy. It means come by, slide in and get a glimpse of your son, and then slide back out, cool?"

"Cool!" I said.

"But you gotta promise me you won't try to talk to Free,

you won't try to take Nasir, and you especially won't swing on Aunt Mercy Ann."

"Jaheim father is a minister, right? It's gonna be at his church?"

Tai nodded. "But you gotta promise you won't start no shit right over your baby's head, Saucy. You deserve the right to see him, but don't nobody need no unnecessary drama. You know?"

I nodded real quick, wondering if Tai knew what she was doing for me.

I smiled. "Thanks, Tai. You always there for me. Always. I love you, girl."

She hugged me again. "I love you too, Saucy. That's why I put up with your crazy-ass shit! And don't worry. You know what kind of friend I am, girl. I'ma be there for you until the day you die."

Chapter 23

THREE WEEKS later I was finally getting a chance to see my son. I was still kicking it with Quaison at his crib, but his friend Brickett had started liking me. He was asshole-ugly, but he sold some good powder and all I had to do was spend some time with him and he let me have as much of it as I wanted for free.

Tai had told me not to come up in the church starting no shit with Free, and I had promised her that I wouldn't. I didn't have no church clothes, so I put on a pair of tight black corduroy pants, a white T-shirt, and a long black shirt over it, and that was about as homely as I was willing to get so it was just gonna have to do.

It was cold as hell outside, and by the time I slipped into the church I was freezing. They say niggas draw heat, and it was sure warm up in there. I peeked in the hall and saw the pews was packed. People was standing around talking and sitting around laughing and carrying on.

I found the stairs and went up to the projection room. An old man was sitting up in there. I pulled my long black shirt over my head and took it off, then pushed the door open and went inside to talk to him. Two minutes later I had found the ladies' room and was sitting inside a locked stall. I stayed there chilling for a little while, waiting until the program got started before going back in the chapel and slipping into a back pew.

I had to scan the room from side to side, looking over and around all them big ugly church hats before I spotted Free and Aunt Mercy Ann. They were sitting way down front with Tai, and when I stood up I could see Nasir sleeping in Aunt Mercy Ann's arms.

My baby was so big! He had a lot of curly black hair and he was light brown like me too. I grinned as Aunt Mercy Ann rocked him on her lap. It didn't matter what they did to keep me away from him, they couldn't take away the fact that I had carried him in my stomach and he was *my damn son*!

I sat back down and looked around. It was a big, pretty church, and those Pentecostals sure knew how to throw a party and get their sang on too. Everybody was swaying and patting their feet and clapping their hands, as I just sat there listening to a whole bunch of holy lyrics that didn't mean nothing to me.

Jaheim's father was easy to spot because he looked just like his son, but older. Like a walking bag of high-yellow bones that somebody had stuck inside of a suit.

When all the praises and testaments were over, Jaheim stepped up to the podium. He had on a pair of dark shades, and if his people didn't know what them glasses was hiding, I sure couldn't wait until they found out! That damn hypocrite! Thought he was better than me? He damn sure wasn't smarter than me. I was about to show and prove that to him and everybody else. I couldn't stand the way he walked around like he was high class and up there above me, Tai, and everybody else. Tareek and his boy Stubbs had only had to knock him around a little bit, and Jaheim's sweet ass had caved in and bent right over. They had given him three chances to pay the cost or play the game and get put on blast, and that arrogant nigga had refused to deal and told them to kiss his black ass.

I was half listening as he talked about how important people like Sojourner Truth and Harriet Tubman were. But when the lights dropped and the overhead projector came on and shone on the big screen they had set up in the pulpit, my heart started beating real fast in my chest.

Yeah, motherfucker! I thought, clenching my teeth. What did he call me? Grimy and gritty? Well Jaheim had fucked with the wrong grimy chick because I was about to get me some payback in a real gritty way. And it had been real easy too. A couple of packs of powder donated by Brickett, and Tareek and Stubbs had been more than happy to do the job.

That toothless old deacon they had upstairs running the film projector had been easy to control too. Hey, a big-titty stunna wearing a white belly shirt in the middle of the winter was something to look at. When I told him Tai wanted to use a different DVD for today's program he had never suspected a thing. And how could he? He couldn't take his eyes off my firm knockers and flat stomach long enough to have any sense!

And now, I sat in that back row and waited as the music came up and Dr. King's face appeared on the screen. Jaheim was narrating from the podium and looking up at the screen at the same time. It took him a minute to realize that somebody had flipped the damn script, but when his tooted-up hairy yellow ass came on camera, he damn near collapsed. Tareek, with his big ol' hormonal titties and snake dick, had on a hot pink teddy and was holding his hard dick and slapping Jaheim all in the crack of his ass with it.

A loud gasp went up in the church, and Jaheim's mother screamed when a shot of Stubbs straddling a black-eyed, busted-lip Jaheim and squeezing his perfect round titties while his dick hung in Jaheim's face came into frame next.

"Turn that off!" Reverend Miller's voice boomed toward the drunk in the projection booth. "You turn that craziness off right now!"

Oh, them sinners in hell was screaming for ice water.

Tai was standing there holding her stomach and covering her mouth. Jaheim's mother needed to cover her damn mouth because all that hollerin' she was doing was just sparking everybody else up. I saw her go down to the ground as a bunch of saints rushed over to help her. I stood up and saw Free. He was standing over Aunt Mercy Ann, fanning her real fast with her big church hat as he held Nasir in his arms.

Jaheim was still up at the podium. His face was twisted in pain and he was reaching out toward Tai.

"I knew I should have told you!" he moaned. Dufus must didn't realize the damn mic was still on, so we all heard him loud and clear. "I'm sorry, baby! I should have told you about this!"

For once Tai did the right damn thing.

She turned around and ran up the aisle, crying as people in the pews reached out and tried to touch and comfort her. I can only imagine the pity and shame she must've seen in their eyes, and I tried to get my face to show that same thing, but unfortunately, when Tai's eyes met mine on her way out the door, she busted me getting my laugh on.

They say death comes in threes, so I was watching my back.

Aunt Mercy Ann had a heart attack at the church. I guess seeing that abomination-looking Tareek with all them titties *and* a dick was too much of a shock to her system. Free had called an ambulance and gotten her to the hospital, but it was too late. She died on the way there and I sure didn't miss her.

A few days after the Black History Month ceremony, Tai opened her eyes one morning to hear Jaheim calling her name. He was hanging on the ledge outside of her bedroom window, but by the time she jumped out of bed and ran over to him, he slipped. Or he let go. Whatever. Any way you put it, nineteen stories is still a long way down.

And how did I know all this? Free told me. Yep. He made it his business to roll up on me on the street and tell me that I had killed two people he loved, and that he would never, ever forgive me.

"You's a twisted bitch, Saucy. Psycho. You need some real help, and I ain't lying."

"But how is any of that stuff my fault?" I wanted to know.

"I didn't make nobody jump out no window! And I wasn't nowhere near Aunt Mercy Ann!"

Free ran shit down to me real quick.

"I sent somebody out to find them two freak niggas, Saucy. Yeah. We got to 'em. They was trying to get they sex changed anyway, right? Well we changed it for 'em real quick. But first we had a little talk with them motherfuckers, and your name just came pouring out they mouths. We know all about the gat they pulled on Jah when they broke in his crib and kicked his ass then made that video. One of them niggas said you set the whole blackmail thing up, and even though Jaheim went ahead and paid them niggas all that money to get the DVD back, you'd already had some copies made and told them you was gonna ruin his whole life with it."

That was a lie! That skinny bastard Tareek! He told me Jaheim had refused to pay up so they beat his ass and left without the money! "Them faggots is lying, Free! I never saw a dime of that money, and I swear on my baby, I didn't have nothing to do with that shit!"

He shook his head.

"On your baby? Damn you's a snake, Saucy. You even lower than I thought. But Tai knows you set her man up, yo. She seen it in your eyes, and she heard it from Tareek and Stubbs's mouth. Your shit is wide open, Saucy. You done hurt a lotta people, shawty. People who really loved you. And now some of them wanna hurt you back."

"Where's Tai now?" I said. "I need to go check on her and see if she's okay."

Free laughed. "You go near that girl and she'll slump you. Stay the fuck away from her, Saucy. She don't wanna see you."

"Where the hell is she, Free! Tai is my best friend and I wanna know where she is! Now where the hell is she?"

Free turned to walk away, then spoke over his shoulder.

"Tai's staying at my crib now. She's with *me*."

Chapter 24

NEWS ABOUT JAHEIM'S death spread through the music community quicker than shit. Everywhere I looked somebody was holding a memorial service for him like he was Tupac or Biggie or Thug or somebody special. They even ran a special program on BET dedicated to him, and Tai was there looking horrible. They showed a shot of her and Free sitting together in the front pew at his funeral. Who the hell did Tai think she was? I wondered. Sitting up there in that big black veil and holding my son on her lap looking like a tore-down Coretta Scott King!

And Free must have gone around telling everybody that Jaheim's big bungee-less jump was my fault, because all of a sudden everybody was blaming me. I didn't push nobody off no window ledge, so that shit wasn't fair. But if I thought video jobs was hard to come by before, them shits were totally dry now. Even sessions I was already scheduled to do was being canceled. Every other day I was getting a call from somebody's flunky assistant telling me my services were no longer needed.

That kinda messed with my head a little because, c'mon. I had rolled with the best of them. I was a dime, a hot-ass mami, and if Tai and Free wasn't so busy dragging my name in the damn mud I would still be getting the top slots that I deserved.

And that funny, half-white bitch Dymond had the nerve to call me!

She left a message on my phone telling me I was a ho and a sick murderer! I called her right back and told her the biggest ho I knew was her new husband, and the only thing I had ever killed was his asshole when I rammed poles up in it.

But what was worse, I went to a release party with Brickett one night that was being given by Mary J. Blige at some big-ass estate in the Hamptons. Everybody was chillin', listening to gully cuts, dancing, and watching movies. Yeah, I was ripped, but so fuckin' what? It *was* a damn party, right?

I loved me some Mary. She was my favorite female singer, and when her old cut "No More Drama" came on, I got up and started dancing and singing that shit like it was my own! Well damn if Mary didn't get jealous! Everybody was clapping for me and telling me to sang that shit, and Mary came over and interrupted my flow wanting to know who had let me in. When I told her Brick, she swelled up and said, "Well you and Brickett both gotta go. Please leave."

Oh! You couldn'ta told me *she* was gone stunt! As blasted as she used to get? Now that she had a good man and wasn't drinking no more she wanted to get brand-new? I flipped that bitch a bird and kept it moving.

Pretty Boy was one of the most connected friends I had in the industry, but one day I called him to ask for a favor and a Chinese-sounding trick answered the phone and told me Pretty Boy no talk to me no more.

"Oh, he gon fuckin' talk to me, you sucky-fucky five-dollar ho straight off the smuggling boat!"

"I sowry," she said slowly. "Pretty Boy he no talk to you no more."

But the worst thing of all was when that nigga Quaison fell off. He started boning some fat Puerto Rican girl from Riis projects and all of a sudden that motherfucker couldn't speak nothing but Spanish. All of this shit was his fault from the gate, and he had the balls to tell me that nobody in the whole industry wanted to deal with me no more?

"Yo, Sauce. They done X'd you out, baby. Your stock is looking real weak. You bad for a nigga's career, ya know?"

Well what about *my* goddamn career! Niggas was pissin' and shittin' all over me like I was a nothing! As much as I had done for all of them, and this is how they treated me? Hell, I had done it all. Every fuckin' thing them niggas wanted. Sucked their dicks, performed in underground movies, stripped in private clubs, fucked ballers in dirty trailers on sets.

And this is how they was gon treat *me*? Man, fuck all them herbs! If them dirty industry ballers wanted to put their feet in my face and hold me down, then they could bring that shit on 'cause it was about to go down!

It was go-to-war time and I was ready to blast the whole damn hip-hop recording industry out. The ammo was in my hands and I knew just the right rocket I needed to launch that shit. With all the dirt I had on the big willies of the music world I was a walking weapon of mass destruction and you can best believe I was about to blow all them motherfuckas up!

I made a quick call to a dude I knew who worked in BET's corporate offices. I had done a few quickie favors for him when his wife was pregnant and couldn't fuck, and when I ran my story down to him he passed me on to his boy at *BET Exposed*. All I had to do was tell this guy a little bit of what I knew, and two minutes later he had me scheduled to report to their studio for filming the next Monday morning.

A few days later I was sitting around freezing in a cheap hotel room listening to WBLS and trying to figure out my next short-term hustle. My girl Wendy Williams was on the air talking about a yacht party she was going to in Cape May that night. People liked to talk trash about Wendy, and yeah, she had talked that same kinda trash about me after I blew up Free's birthday party, but I wasn't mad at her. All she did was speak whatever was on her mind, and most of the time when she was talking bad about somebody she was telling the whole truth so fuck them haters!

"Oh yeah," Wendy was saying. "This is gonna be one live Saturday night! Marshall George is hosting it for his newest business partner, Freedom Moore, and everybody who is anybody is going to be there. I mean, Jay-Z, Jada Kiss," she started rattling off names like she was spittin' a rap, "that cute-ass Busta Rhymes, T.I., Fabulous and that hot Jersey cat Reem Raw who came out of the projects in Brooklyn, Robb Hawk and that dude Papoose, Usher, Beez, Trina, Little Wayne, Missy Elliott, and Janet Jackson, who's looking real good after losing all that weight, that smooth singer Spoons DiNero from N.J.S., and I heard Will and Jada are gonna stop by too! Damn, that is one hot-ass list! This is gonna be a night to remember! Sorry, people, but it's a private affair and not open to the public, so don't come trying to crash. But y'all know me. I'll come back with all the juicy details, so if you ain't there, by the time I finish giving you the 411 you gonna feel like you was there!"

Them mother*fuckers*!

Here I was sitting up in some nasty roach-infested rat trap, and Free and his posse was chillin' on a yacht? I only had two hundred dollars left to my name. Just enough to pay this week and next week's rent on my room, but I wasn't about to let no party I wasn't invited to pass me by. I got my gear together the best I could, and put on every piece of jewelry that I hadn't already pawned. I took my last bit of money and stuck it in my bra, then jetted my ass over to Grand Central Station. I was looking good and smelling fine. I had a fifth of Henny in my bag to keep me warm, and I was steady sipping on that shit as I rode the first Greyhound rolling south to Cape May.

I was lit by the time I got down in south Jersey. I took a cab to the marina and asked some white people where the party yacht was.

"A friend of mine owns it. Marshall George. I know y'all heard of him before. He's the host for MTV's *Who Wants to Be a Rap Star*. Yeah, he's just that big."

"Oh yeah!" a skinny, baldheaded white guy said. "You're talking about that 181-foot floating resort down at the end of the long pier over there." He whistled. "It's a beauty. It'll set you back about eighty thousand a day to rent that lady. They must be having some party." He eyed me swaying in my heels tryna stand up straight. "Have fun. You look like you've already gotten started."

"Hell yeah," I answered, switching my ass as I walked off in my six-inch stiletto heels. "The party mighta already started, but it ain't really gonna get live until I get there."

I sashayed down the long walkway to the end of the pier where the music was just bouncing off all that dark water. I got my strut on, tossing my ass all over the place as I walked through the crowd of people getting on and off the yacht.

When I got to the boarding ramp I saw two toy cops standing there shivering. They was fake security guards with radios instead of guns. I opened my coat and walked up to them.

"Name?" the guy said to me, looking down at the list on his clipboard.

"Hoezetta Woodson."

He ran his finger down the list, and of course he didn't find that name.

"I'm sorry, ma'am. That name's not on this list."

I laughed. "I know it's not, silly, because I made it up!" I touched his arm and leaned into him. "I was just making sure you was on your game, ya know? Making sure you don't let just any old body up on my man's property."

He laughed, trying his best to keep his eyes off my chest. "Name?"

I opened my mouth to answer, but the female guard butted in.

"Hey! I know you!"

She looked at me with a wide, rotten grin. She had a flat yellow pie-face with red freckles, and a jacked-up perm.

"You don't remember me? I met you going up to Woodburne on a visit. Our niggas did they bids at the same time."

I had no clue who this bitch was.

"Oh yeah! I remember you girl! You still ain't got them teefs fixed though! How you been doing, boo? You been okay?"

"Excuse you!" she said like she wanted to be mad, but she was still grinning all over herself.

"You doin' videos and stuff now, right? Me, I went back to school and got my GED. Now I'm in college and working security on the weekends. You know a sistah gotta make ends meet. My man caught another charge while he was in there, and I just couldn't do no more time with him. But you!" She nodded, admiring me. "I see you hooked up with Free Moore! I seen y'all in magazines, on the internet, everywhere. Matter fact, I just saw your little boy a few minutes ago. Is that your sister who's watching him?"

"Hell no," I said, waving my hand and trying not to stagger. "Girl that's my fuckin' nanny! But I better get on in there and get my goodnight kisses before she puts my baby to bed. You be cool, sister okay? I'ma try and get you some backstage passes to a Ruthless show before you leave!"

I ran up the ramp like the cops was behind me. The yacht was big as hell, and that was good because I didn't want to be seen. Not yet. I found a bathroom and took off my coat, then finished off the last bit of Yak in my bag, and when I busted up in that main room and started dancing all over the place you shoulda seen the look on Dymond's face.

"Get this bitch outta here!" she screamed, and I rolled up on her ass like a Harlem trooper. I snatched that bitch by her blond hair and swung her down to the floor. She was on her back with her feet all up in the air as I wiped that damn floor up with her. Yeah, you know all them niggas jumped on me, but before they got *me*, I got *her* ass real good. I banged her head on the floor and kicked her all in her face, denting her grill with the heel of my shoes, and then a bunch of arms was yanking me, twisting my arms behind my back and pulling me off her.

"Fuck all a' y'all!" I screamed. "All of y'all are grimy! Ain't nobody up in here clean!"

The music stopped and suddenly I had everybody's attention. Marshall was looking at me with his eye twitching like he wanted to kill me, and a couple of ig'nant-ass artists were laughing at me from over in the corner.

I saw people moving to the side to let someone through, and I was shocked as hell when Tai appeared carrying my son. He had on some cute blue and white baseball pajamas with the feet in them, and a little blue boxer robe with a hood. "Who let you up in here?" Tai hollered. Her face was all twisted up and ugly, like she hated me or something.

"Oh *fuck you*, Tai! This is my baby daddy's affair, remember? You ain't nothin' but the goddamn nanny. My cheap replacement. If you wanted a fuckin' baby so bad you shouldn'ta sat in that bathtub stabbing yourself in the pussy tryna give yourself no goddamn abortion, NANNY!"

She based right back. "I'll be that nanny, you drunk bitch. 'Cause I'm the first face your son sees every morning and the last one he sees at night. He sleeps with his head on *my* titties all night long! He's calling *me* Mommy, you shitty bitch! So where does that leave *you*?"

I swear to God if they hadn't held me back I woulda killed Tai's ass. She knew damn well she didn't talk to me like that. Ever. The only reason she was even trying me was 'cause niggas was restraining me. Somebody musta ran and got Free, because the next thing I knew he had grabbed me from behind and was dragging me up a short flight of stairs and outside to the deck.

"Get the hell off me!" I screamed, fighting his ass like I was a man.

It was cold out there and white puffs was coming out my mouth as I cursed him out. I scratched the skin off his hands, then reached behind me and tried to scratch up his face too.

He slung me away from him.

"Girl is you crazy? How the hell did you get in here?"

"The same way everybody else got in here, stupid ass! I walked in! You done got even dumber since I left your ass. You was already slow. But damn! Look at you now!"

His breath came out smoky.

"Saucy, get your ass off this boat before I have to hurt you."

"Oh, so you gonna hurt me? You threatening me? What you gonna do? You gonna beat my ass? You gonna have one of your boys fuck me up? You gonna get your dun duns to rape me? Well when I go on BET I'll make damn sure I tell the world about that shit too!"

The look on his face was disgusted, but I knew this nigga could still get shook behind negative attention.

"Yeah, I'm going on *BET Exposed* first thing Monday morning, sucka! All ya'll niggas gonna get aired out. I'ma put y'all out there naked! I'm givin' up names, dates, *and* locations. I'ma let everybody know how that fake bitch Dymond ate my pussy out like it was at the top of the USDA food pyramid! And how her man Marshall likes to get his asshole plugged and how that fucker gave me genital warts too! Just wait until I tell the world that Chaperone is gay for real, and Zinger Jones is a limp-dick crackhead who smokes up ten G's a week. You *know* I'ma tell 'em how Pretty Boy got that whole international dominatrix sex slave thing going on at his mansion and can't shoot his dick off unless somebody's ass is ripped and bleeding! And yeah, I bet you really *was* down with ya partner Linnay for the whole ride. He sittin' up in jail by himself right now, but I got a feeling you was standing knee-deep in the tub when he was washing all that drug money through ya label, and I *know* the feds are gonna be down to hear about that!"

Free's mouth was open. "You crazy, Saucy. Crazy for real, girl. Your fuckin' brain is rotten."

The door opened and Tai stepped out on the deck. Nasir was still sleeping with his head on her shoulder and she pulled his hood up to cover him.

"Fuck you, Free," I said, then, "Gimme my goddamn baby, Tairene."

She put her hand on Nasir's back and looked at Free.

"Don't you look at that fuckin' sperm donor! Nas is *my* damn son. Now give him to me."

Tai fucked around and gave me the same look of disgust

that Jaheim used to give me, and it burned me up from the inside out.

"What's up, Tai?" I said, walking up on her. "You got something in your eye?"

I swung a roundhouse punch on her, capping her real square on the side of her head. That bitch almost threw Nasir at Free as she started swinging on me. She got a lucky one in, banging me in my nose. I fell back on my ass as blood dripped down my lip and slid off my chin then fell between my titties.

Free stood there holding my son as Tai screamed on me in the freezing cold. She had on a real cute red sweater and she was wearing the diamond choker I had bought her right after Uncle Swag got knocked.

"You ain't shit, Saucy! You fucked over your mama, your baby, *and* your man! I don't know how I ever thought you was my friend!"

I was trying to get up when that bitch ran over and spit on me.

Tai spit on me! That scary bitch really spit on me!

I wiped that shit off my face and laughed.

"Yeah," I said, backing up. "You like to spit on people, huh? Well that's why your man Jah was spitting on that he-she's dick when he slobbed it down! Did you see the whole tape? No? Well I did! Jaheim was getting his rocks off the whole time! His dick was hard as a pipe when them nasty wannabe she-men was digging up in his ass and popping his doody-string!"

Tai's eyes got big and she moved closer looking like she was gonna jump on me again.

"Saucy!" Free said, moving toward me. "Shut the fuck up! Tai, she's drunk. Don't pay her no mind. Take Nas and go back inside 'cause this bitch is dru—"

"You shut the fuck up, Freedom!" I screamed. "This is between me and this bitch right here!"

I laughed real loud at the look on Tai's face, backing further away 'cause this ho was bound to start spitting again when she heard what I was about to say next.

"Yeah, Tai. You always been jealous of me! Bitch just admit

that shit. I'm fine, and you just flabby. I'm a stunna and you just a stunt! You been hating hard on me ever since that day your nasty, booger-nosed daddy stood up there and finger-fucked me right in your living roo—"

I saw Tai's face change from disgust to shock and alarm. I took another step backward and a low rail hit the back of my legs, sending me down. Tai reached for me, but she wasn't fast enough to catch me. My stiletto heel slid across the ice. I grabbed at the rail and missed, and before I knew it, I was falling.

Down . . . down!

The last thing I saw was Free and Tai standing together at the rail. They were looking down at me and holding Nasir between them, his head snuggled against his daddy's neck. Free reached out and put his arm around Tai's shoulder and pulled her close, and that's when the ocean opened its mouth and swallowed me whole.

And at the end . . .

THE WHOLE DAMN script had been flipped. I was falling backward and I didn't have nobody to blame but myself. I was bobbing around in an ocean full of my own mistakes, and for a hot second all I could think was damn. God*damn*! See there. This time I'd really fucked up. I'd crossed the last damn line, and the look in their eyes said it all: trifling and greedy. Scandalous and conniving. I held my arms out as I splashed around, gulping amd gasping. I was waving, grabbing at liquid, reaching for them and praying that they would save me. The water was closing around me. Icy, just like my heart had been. Salty, just like my tongue. Grimier than my soul. Burning my eyes and choking me. Stuffing my nasty words back down my throat. Dragging me under as Free's pretty brown eyes watched me go. Damn! I thought again, and for the first time in my life, I surrendered. There was no point in struggling. The way they stared at me, I was already a body. The love in their eyes hurt me so bad . . . it made my death feel good.

New York, New York—

Music mogul François "Freedom" Moore and the lovely Miss Tairene Watkins were married yesterday in a private ceremony at their posh new estate in southern New Jersey. Dozens of celebrities, friends, and family members were on hand to witness the romantic garden event, which one guest tearfully described as "the most beautiful union ever."

The bride is an event organizer for some of the most powerful icons in the urban music industry. Dressed in a simple but elegant lace gown complete with a veil and a three-foot train, a teary-eyed Watkins carried her stepson Nasir Moore in her arms as she walked down a flower-strewn aisle in preparation for the wedding service which was performed by the Reverend James Miller, the father of her ex-fiancé.

Freedom Moore is the CEO of Ruthless Rap Records, a music company that was embroiled in a bitter scandal last year after the violent death of the label's most promising artist, Andre "Thug-A-Licious" Williams, who was knifed by a fan during an NBA finals game. Soon after Williams's death the label was besieged with conflict between Moore and his former business partner, Linnay Woods, who was accused by several artists of illegally diverting royalty earnings into his personal accounts.

Earlier this year, Woods was convicted of tax evasion, fraud, bribery, and embezzlement, and sentenced to ten years in federal prison. Moore, who was awarded all assets of the company, and who some believed to have taken a major financial loss as a result of his partner's criminal activity, is reportedly a shrewd, frugal investor who seized autonomy in the company and quietly set about rebuilding his empire to the multimillion-dollar mega-producing enterprise that it is today.

Recently, Moore and Watkins experienced twin tragedies in the loss of two people who were paramount in their lives. Watkins's fiancé, Jaheim Miller, tragically fell to his death from the window of their nineteenth-floor apartment, while her best friend, Saucy Robinson, who also happened to be Moore's ex-girlfriend and the mother of his young son, Nasir, accidentally fell off a yacht leased by mega mogul Marshall George, and drowned in the frigid waters off of Cape May.

"It was our friendship and loss that brought us closer," Moore says of his short but intense relationship with Watkins. "We both loved and lost the two people closest to our hearts, but through it all our new love was born and I discovered the woman I'd been waiting for my whole life."

His new bride agrees. "We've both experienced a lot of pain and heartache, but look at what we've gained. Each other. And now," she said, playing with the handsome baby boy she bounced in her arms, "not only do I have a new best friend and husband, I also have a beautiful son who I've been loving since the moment he came into this world."

The new couple and their son plan to honeymoon on the island of Jamaica where Moore owns a villa called *Soy Saucy*. The luxury property sits on a private beach lot that Moore says he purchased while visiting the island with Robinson nearly two years ago. Plans for Watkins's adoption of Nasir are already under way, and although the past was traumatic and troubled for this enterprising young family, their future looks bright and promising.

Dear Bookclub Reader:

Thong on Fire and the haunting journey of Saucy Sarita Robinson lingered on my mind long after I typed the last word. This cautionary tale of a young girl tossed into a cruel world stained with urban blight, and whose twisted, self-destructive ideals ultimately led to her downfall, is all too familiar in inner-city neighborhoods. Some of us have witnessed the trials of girls like Saucy firsthand, and the consequences are often tragic and heartbreaking.

Issues of poverty, sexual abuse, addiction, promiscuity, and compromised morals are more relevant than ever in our communities today, and as Saucy's story has shown us, the repercussions can be deadly, both in fiction and in life.

I hope by exposing these issues in *Thong on Fire* dialogue will be sparked and action initiated to help rescue our youth from the grimy, biting traps that are waiting to ensnare them.

Points of discussion your book club might find helpful are:

1) The media-driven images that tell our youth who and what they should aspire to be.

2) The importance of instilling self-reliance in young girls so they learn to search inward for motivation instead of looking for a "baller" to meet their needs.

3) A positive dose of self-respect that is never up for negotiation.

4) Rejecting the media's objectification of young women and building their self-esteem.

5) Methods of fortifying our youth and ourselves against the glittering, powerful lure of street life.

NOIRE